MW00917681

BOOK 1 OF 3

Cover art by A.R. Wise
Photo sourced from istockphoto.com

Maggie,

Thanks for stopping
by to see me at
Comic Con!

<u>314</u>

PART ONE : THE SERPENT'S COIL

CHAPTER 1 - It Begins Again

Widowsfield
March 14th, 1996

"It's going to happen in three minutes."

Mark Tapper sat on the edge of his son's bed and tried to comfort the eight-year-old. He considered calling an ambulance, but didn't know if what Jeremy was suffering from qualified as an emergency. He decided to wait for his wife to get home, since she'd be there in just a few minutes anyhow. She'd left work early when the school called, but Mark was able to get to Widowsfield Elementary to pick Jeremy up first.

"What's going to happen in three minutes?" Mark glanced at the clock on the nightstand that displayed 3:11 on the stomach of a Batman figurine.

"I told you," said Jeremy. The desperation in his voice terrified Mark. "The Skeleton Man's coming."

"I don't know what that means, kiddo. Help me out here." Mark tried to wipe sweat from his boy's brow, but Jeremy jerked away as if frightened by contact. "Who's this Skeleton Man you keep talking about?"

"He's coming, and then everyone's going to go crazy. Dad, I don't want to kill you again."

The statement was more than a little disconcerting. Mark stood up and put his hands on his head in exasperation as he stared down at his quivering child. He'd tried to stay calm through all of his son's outbursts, but he couldn't take it anymore. "That does it. Mom can meet us at the hospital. Do you think you can walk, or do you want me to call an ambulance?" This manic episode had confounded the school nurse, and it was getting worse the longer it went on. When Mark picked his son up from school, Jeremy had simply been crying, but now his mania had gone from concerning to disturbing.

"There's no time. I can already hear his teeth." Jeremy looked at his father and chattered his teeth, as if he was freezing cold. Then he looked at the clock and they both saw the time change.

3:12

Jeremy put his hands under his pillow and bunched it up so the sides covered his ears. He clenched his eyes shut and continued to weep. "You should just kill yourself. Make it easy. Just shoot yourself in the head and get it over with. You can't handle what's coming. No one can."

Mark was frantic now. His hands were shaking and he rushed out of the room to compose himself. The last thing Jeremy needed to see was his father breaking down. Mark felt helpless and terrified. Something was happening to his son, and he had no idea how to fix it. When he'd been called in by the school he expected to hear that his son had thrown up, or got in a fight, or anything other than this. Jeremy had never shown signs of a mental disorder and Mark was utterly unprepared for what was happening. He broke down after he closed his son's door, but there was no time for weeping. He rushed down the stairs to get the phone and call 9-1-1.

The cord on the kitchen phone stretched long enough to accommodate his pacing as he listened to the automated voice tell him that his call would be taken in the order it was received. He glanced at the green numbers displayed on the microwave's clock.

3:13

"Widowsfield County 9-1-1," said a woman's voice on the phone. "What is your emergency?" She sounded elderly, and kind, immediately affable.

Mark didn't know where to start. "Hi, my name's Mark Tapper."

"Howdy, Mark," said the operator. "What's your emergency?"

He'd been struggling to answer that question himself, and had trouble relaying it to her. "It's my son, Jeremy. I got a call from his school because he was having a, like, I guess a mental breakdown or something. I don't really know. I had to pick him up early from school because he was crying and talking about how someone named The Skeleton Man is coming." He chuckled out of nervousness and felt embarrassed for it.

The clock held steady at 3:13, seconds away from the time that Jeremy had warned about.

"It's okay, sir. We can get someone out there if you'd like."

Mark stared at the clock, dreading the coming change.

"Sir?" she asked after he didn't respond. "What's your address?"

It changed.

3:14

Nothing happened and Mark breathed a sigh of relief. He didn't know why he was so scared. "Sorry, what was that?"

The operator didn't respond.

"Hello?" asked Mark.

She gurgled on the other line, a wet, throaty expulsion of sound, as if the woman had started to choke. Then he heard a shrill scream. Someone else in the operator's office had become frightened. The gurgling continued.

"Hello?" Mark asked again and looked at the phone as if expecting to be able to see what was wrong. He pushed in the wire that connected the phone to the base on the wall to make sure it hadn't fallen loose.

He was in the kitchen when he caught sight of the green fog outside. It had been a gorgeous spring day just moments earlier, but there was no sign of sunlight now. The town had been blanketed in fog that glowed as if illuminated deep within by a pulsing green light. Mark took tremulous steps toward the window above the sink. The phone went dead, and he let it drop to the floor where the cord pulled it skittering backward across the tile.

"Holy hell," said Mark as he leaned over the sink.

The fog was thick enough to cloud his view of the houses across the street. Even the Oak tree in the front yard was hazed. Waves of green light flashed within the fog, as if he were watching electricity roll out from some machine within. It crackled and coursed along metallic objects, giving shape to things lost in the mist.

Then he saw a man lean out from behind the tree. The fog was too thick to see any details, but the stranger was very tall and thin, and he retreated back behind the tree as soon as Mark saw him.

"Dad," said Jeremy from upstairs. He didn't sound panicked anymore.

"Yeah, Jeremy," said Mark as he backed away from the window. He wanted to go out and confront the stranger, but was afraid of the mist and still concerned for his son. "Are you okay?"

Jeremy didn't answer.

He heard small, light footsteps running across the floor upstairs, headed down the hall from the bathroom to Jeremy's room.

Mark stopped staring out the window and ran to reach Jeremy. He bounded up the stairs and was confronted by his son at the threshold of the boy's room.

"Jeremy," said Mark as he paused at the top of the stairs. "Do you know what's going on?" He asked as if afraid his son was somehow responsible for what had happened outside.

"I tried to warn you."

5

Jeremy held a straight razor to his own throat.

"Buddy, put that down." Mark took a tentative step, like a cop approaching a suicidal man.

Jeremy looked at the blade and smiled. "This isn't for me, Dad. It's for you."

"What are you talking about?"

"The Skeleton Man's here, and he taught me how to hate."

"Put the razor down, Jeremy." Mark's authoritative tone was beleaguered by fear.

The razor reflected green light from a nearby window. "We're going to try something new this time. The Skeleton Man remembered something that he wants to try on you." Jeremy giggled, as if talking about something cute a puppy had done. "He's so excited. He doesn't want to hurt me, but if you take another step then we won't have a choice. He'll slit my throat just to watch you cry."

"What's going on, Jeremy? Who's The Skeleton Man? How did you know that something was going to happen at 3:14?"

"I think we've done this before," said Jeremy. "I think we've been doing it for years." He seemed confused, but then shrugged off his uncertainty. "We'll keep doing it until we get it right, I guess. Do you want to hear what we're planning for you?"

"I just want you to put the razor down."

Jeremy looked down at his father's feet as the man came closer, and he pressed the razor harder against his own throat. "Don't do it, Daddy."

Mark retreated a step and held his hands out. "Okay, Jeremy. Okay, I'm backing up. Now just put the razor down. Can you do that for me?"

"Dad, I told you, this isn't for me. It's for you. He's only going to hurt me if you don't do what he says. Don't you get it?"

"No!" Mark's terror overwhelmed him. "I don't get it, Jeremy. Please tell me what's going on."

Jeremy nodded, his cherub visage turned wicked by the blade he held to his own throat. "The Skeleton Man wants me to put you in the bathtub, and then we're going to pour boiling water over you until we can peel your skin off."

"What?" Mark's question escaped as a whimpering whisper.

"And if you can stay awake, then we'll pour the chemicals on you." Jeremy grinned. "It's going to be a lot of fun, Dad. And you want to know the best part?" He didn't wait for an answer before continuing. "You're going to let us do it. You know why?"

Mark didn't know what to do other than comply with his son's insanity. "Why?"

"Because if you don't, I'll slit my throat. You can either die like we want you to, or watch me kill myself. Daddy, I don't want to die; I know how much it hurts. So you're going to have to do what we tell you. Okay?"

The front door opened. Mark didn't want to turn and look, fearing that if he took his eyes off Jeremy then his son might hurt himself. He hoped that his wife had come home, or that the 9-1-1 dispatcher had been able to track the location of the call and send police. Instead, he heard several light footsteps running through the house, followed by the happy chatter of children.

"My friends are here," said Jeremy. "They'll start boiling the water. Are you ready for your bath?"

"What the hell is going on?"

"My best guess," said Jeremy as he glanced up. "God gave up."

Mark thought about rushing his son to steal the razor from him, but Jeremy seemed to anticipate this and pressed it harder to his throat. The blade sliced the boy's skin and Jeremy winced as blood coursed down the black handle.

Jeremy's eyes welled with tears. "Please don't kill me, Dad! I told you, I don't want to die. All the Daddies hate their babies!"

"Put the razor down!"

"Don't come any closer," said Jeremy. Blood dripped off his knuckles. "This hurts! I'm scared." It was as if it were someone else holding the knife to Jeremy's throat.

"Okay! Okay!" Mark backed up a step.

Jeremy relaxed the blade, but the small cut continued to bleed as the boy cried. "You need to go get in the bathtub. Please? Don't make this any harder than it has to be."

"This is insane," said Mark. "I don't understand what's going on. Why are you doing this?"

"Because it's what The Skeleton Man wants."

"Who the hell is The Skeleton Man?"

Pots and pans rattled as they were taken out of the cabinets downstairs. Mark could hear the children laugh as they filled the pots with water. He heard them trying to work the microwave as well.

"He's the man in the mist," said Jeremy. "He's the one that keeps the children safe. He's our only friend. Without him, we'd be as lost as you, and none of us want that."

"Safe from what?" Mark was in the bathroom now, edging backward as his son stayed out of arm's reach.

"All the ones that came with him. The ones that will poison you unless we stop it from happening. You'll turn evil, like you did all the other times. We can't let that happen. The Skeleton Man showed us what the Daddies do."

"What other times?" The bathroom was small, with a porcelain tub that took up the opposite side. The toilet and sink sat between the tub and the door where Jeremy stood with the razor still pressed against his neck. Mark backed up against the tub and staggered. He grabbed the plastic shower curtain to steady himself and two of the rings that held it up snapped loose. He fell to a seated position on the edge of the tub.

Jeremy shook his head as if he felt sorry for his father's ignorance. "All the other times we tried to save you. You're one of the dead ones. There's no saving you, but you can still save me."

8

Mark felt helpless. He was a big guy, over 220 pounds, and he worked out in the basement every night. His job kept him fit as well, and he prided himself on his physique. However, none of his strength could help him now. He often said that he loved his son more than life itself, and that he'd do anything to protect him, but now he was being forced to prove it.

"You've lost your mind, Jeremy. Something's wrong with you. Trust me, I'd never hurt you." He started to stand back up and reach out to his son.

Jeremy reacted as if his father was threatening to strike him. His eyes grew wide and he moved back as he yelled. "You're hurting me now! Can't you see that? Look at my blood, Daddy! You're killing me."

"Stop it, Jeremy." Mark cried out, but didn't dare to move forward.

Jeremy dug the blade into his neck and cringed in pain as he shouted for mercy. "Daddy, don't hurt me like this! Please don't hurt me."

"Okay, Jeremy, tell me what I have to do. Tell me what you want."

"Get in the tub, Dad!"

Mark stepped into the bathtub with his arms outstretched as if to assure Jeremy that he was being submissive. "Okay, I'm in. Now put the razor down."

"Take your shirt off," said Jeremy with the razor still pressed to his bleeding throat.

Mark did as he was told and tossed the shirt to the floor. A chill came over him as a waft of green fog trailed across the hallway behind Jeremy.

"You can't expect me to just sit here and let this happen," said Mark.

"If you don't, then The Skeleton Man is going to make you watch me kill myself. Is that what you want?"

"I'm not going to let that happen," said Mark. He got angrier the longer this went on.

Jeremy stepped back and leaned to the side as if listening to someone in the hall. Then he came back into the bathroom. "If you step out of the tub, or try to knock away the pots of water, then I'm going to kill myself. It's important that you know that. You have to do as you're told, Dad. Okay? Do you understand?"

"No, God damn it! No, I don't understand, Jeremy. Why are you doing this? Please just put the razor down."

"We've tried to let you live before, but The Skeleton Man was right about you," said Jeremy. Blood ran down his arm and dripped from his elbow. "This is the only way we can save the children. It has to start with the Daddies dying."

"Then why are you going to boil me? Why did you say that you're going to strip my flesh and pour chemicals on me? Don't you think this Skeleton Man is the evil one? Buddy, I'm your Dad, you've got to trust me."

"No," said Jeremy. "I've made that mistake before. There's only one person that I trust now, and we're going to do this the way he wants."

A pair of cautious footsteps came from the hall. Mark heard water slosh over the side of a container and hit the floor as two children yelped in surprise.

"Be careful," said one of the high pitched voices.

"I am, you be careful," said the other.

Jeremy stepped into the hall so his friends could come in. Mark recognized the two boys that carried the water. They lived in the neighborhood, although he didn't know their names. They were wearing oven mitts and carrying a large Pyrex bowl filled with steaming water between them.

"We got this one from the micowaver," said the younger of the two boys. His childish wording belied his horrific intent as he waddled into the room. Water spilled over the side and the boy swiftly moved his barefoot to keep the water from burning him. Both of the boys had muddy feet that left tracks across the linoleum as they approached.

"Don't you dare," said Mark. He backed into the corner of the tub and knocked over a bottle of shampoo as he did. "You get away from me with that."

The two boys stopped and looked back at Jeremy as if to ask what they should do. Jeremy looked at his father, disappointed. "Don't fight this, Dad. You need to sit down and let them pour the water on you."

"Fuck that," said Mark. He tried his best to avoid cursing in front of his son, but the current situation absolved that concern.

"You want to watch me die?" asked Jeremy.

"No, of course not," said Mark. "But I'm not going to sit here and let your little friends pour boiling water on me either. This is crazy." He stared at the bowl instead of looking at Jeremy. The water wasn't bubbling, but he had no doubt it was searing hot. He was familiar with how water heated in a microwave doesn't bubble, but can still get hotter than water boiled on a stove.

"What happens if you die?" asked one of the boys of Jeremy. Then he looked at Mark and added, "What if he tries to fight back?"

"Then The Skeleton Man will slaughter all of us and start over." Jeremy spoke with utter certainty, as if this was a possibility he'd known for years and had come to accept. "My Daddy will have killed us all."

"No, Jeremy," said Mark. "You've gone insane. This is crazy!"

"Just throw it on him." Jeremy spoke like a callous war criminal instructing his soldiers to execute a prisoner.

"Okay," said one of the boys. They stepped forward and tipped the bowl on its side as they threw it into the tub. The glass bowl slammed into Mark and the water seared his skin. He staggered back as the wave hit him. He fell against the cold tile wall where he slid down as the water stung his skin. He swiped away the wetness as he screamed and writhed.

11

"The water's going down the drain," said Jeremy, disappointed. "Someone plug the drain or else we won't be able to cook him!"

One of the boys stepped forward to do as Jeremy instructed, but Mark slapped the child on the side of the head, sending him smashing into the wall. The child crumpled on the bathroom floor and cried out in pain.

"Hey!" Jeremy screamed at his father. "Do you want me to die?" He swiped the razor across his cheeks and cried out in pain before pressing the blade against his throat again. "Is this what you want? Don't hurt my friends or I'm going to keep cutting myself up."

Mark looked at the skin on his arms where he'd tried to block the wave of scalding water. His arms were brilliant red and the thick black hair seemed to be melting off him. He growled in pain and anger and then slammed his hand down on the tub's plunger. He seethed as he glowered at his son. "Fine. Bring it on. I'm not going to let anyone hurt you, Jeremy, not even yourself. If this is how I have to prove it, then so be it. Do your worst. But just remember what I did for you. I'd do anything to protect you. You're my son. I'd do anything for you."

Two more children appeared at the door with another bowl of water. The steam swirled in the bathroom and mixed with the fog that had started to fill the house. As the torture continued, and Mark suffered wave after wave of boiling water, he thought he saw a man lean in from the hallway, peering through the thickening steam to watch Mark's agony.

The Skeleton Man's teeth chattered as he watched another daddy die.

16 Years Later
March 9th, 2012

"I love these kids," said Alma Harper. "I've had some great groups this year."

"That's wonderful to hear," said Principal White. She walked with Alma through Trenton Elementary. Class was in session, so the halls were empty except for the hum of teachers and children speaking behind closed doors. The walls were papered with drawings of mythical creatures that the third grade class had done for a recent project. Half of the pictures were of smiling unicorns and the other half were demonic monstrosities, probably drawn exclusively by boys. The charter school prided itself on ignoring many of the social norms associated with gender, but that didn't change the fact that most boys liked to draw monsters while the girls preferred flowers and smiling faces.

Alma had her guitar strapped over her shoulder and adjusted it as they walked. She towered over Principal White, who was a short, pudgy woman in her fifties. Alma's tall, lanky figure was accentuated when standing next to her boss, and she often felt embarrassed by it.

"Alma, I'm afraid I have some bad news for you."

Alma was aware of recent budget cuts, but she'd been assured that her music class was safe. Of course, employees on the brink are rarely warned before the axe falls, and education jobs suffer more from callous cuts than just about any other industry.

Alma slowed her pace and her dread must've been revealed by her pallor because Principal White was quick to console her. "It's not that bad," said Mrs. White. "You're not losing your job. We still need a music program."

Alma put her hand over her heart and was surprised by how fast it was beating. "Thank goodness. You scared me."

"We love you around here, Alma. And more importantly, the kids love you."

"Thanks," said Alma as she started to walk at a regular pace again. "But you said you had bad news."

"I do," said Mrs. White. "I know you've been in your room for a couple years now, but we're having a lot of trouble with the budget. We're doing everything we can to

13

deal with it, and I'm afraid we had to give your space to the new remedial math program."

"Okay," said Alma, a mix of concern and sorrow in her tone. "So where am I being moved to? The old room was already too small for us. I can't imagine trying to cram all of the kids and their instruments into a smaller space."

"I know, Alma. Trust me, I've been trying to figure this out for a long time. I had to come to a decision because Mr. Franks wants to start building his new math room over spring break."

Mrs. White guided Alma down one of the school's hallways that led to the lab rooms, auditorium, and cafeteria.

"You're kidding," said Alma. "Spring break starts tomorrow. I thought you were talking about this happening at the beginning of next year. Are you saying I only have a week to get a new room set up?"

"I know this is last minute," said Mrs. White.

"Yeah, you're not kidding." Alma had always been told that she was too nice for her own good, but this situation tried her patience. She ran her hand through her long, dark hair and scratched at the top of her head as she sighed. "I'm glad I didn't have any spring break plans. Looks like I'm going to be busy."

Mrs. White put her hand on Alma's back and smiled up at her. "As soon as I heard about this, I knew we had to come up with a good solution for you. I got together with a few of the other teachers, and some of your students, and we came up with a plan."

"Thanks," said Alma.

"You've got people looking out for you," said Mrs. White.

They came to a stop in front of a lab room door and Mrs. White had an odd grin, as if she was desperately trying to hide something from Alma.

"How long have you known this was going to happen?" Alma was suspicious of the principal's giddy demeanor. "What are you up to?"

Mrs. White shook her head and giggled. Her face was turning red and she refused to look directly at Alma as she swung the door open. She pushed Alma into the room and suddenly the deception was revealed.

"Surprise!"

A chorus of voices greeted Alma as she was pushed into the room. Her knees buckled at the sight of over a hundred kids lined up on stadium style seats along the far wall. Music notes had been painted on the walls, and a piano was situated to the left of the entrance, its black lacquer reflecting the sparkling lights high above. The cherry wood floor vibrated from the applause of the teachers, children, and parents that had gathered for the surprise.

"What's this?" asked Alma as tears sprang to her eyes. She put her fingertips over her mouth as Mrs. White continued to push at her back to force her further in. "What did you guys do?"

Mrs. White took Alma's guitar case and handed it to a teacher's assistant who then placed it against the wall. The crowd was still clapping and saying a myriad of kind things as Alma pressed her hands over her mouth as she cried.

There was a camera crew in the corner with a news reporter who waited with a microphone. They walked into the center of the room as Mrs. White finally backed away. Alma turned to look at the principal and saw that she was overjoyed. Mrs. White's face was beet red and she waved at her eyes in an attempt to stop crying. "Surprise," she squeaked, hardly able to speak.

A tall woman in a black and grey pants suit stepped forward from the bleachers. It was Blair Drexler, the head of the PTA. "The local news station contacted us and set all this in motion. They heard about how the recent budget cuts were going to threaten your music class, and got together with us to try and stop it from happening. Not a single one of us on the PTA were going to let that happen. We knew we had to protect your class."

15

Alma had trouble standing. She stumbled and Blair rushed forward to provide support. "How did you do this?" asked Alma as she gazed around the room.

"We voted and unanimously agreed to use the proceeds from the jog-a-thon to fund the construction of a new music room. And the Channel 7 news team helped out a lot too." She turned to look at the news crew and a thin, strawberry blonde woman stepped forward. The reporter quickly wiped away a tear and composed herself.

"Hello, Miss Harper," said the reporter. She was a gorgeous young woman, with a thin waist that tapered to wide thighs. She wore massive heels that shamed Alma's penny loafers, but even the three inch boost couldn't raise the petite reporter to the music teacher's height.

"Oh my gosh," said Alma as she wiped away tears. "I can't believe this. How did this happen?" She burst into laughter and Blair joined in. They hugged and then Alma continued to try and compose herself for the cameras. "I must look like a wreck."

The kids on the bleachers laughed and spontaneously started cheering again. One of the second graders, a sweet boy named Billy, ran off the stands and past the gathered teachers and parents, several of whom tried to catch him. He collided with Alma and wrapped his arms around her legs.

"Surprise, Miss Harper," he said as he embraced her.

She knelt down and pulled him into a tight embrace. This initiated a rush from the stands as the other children decided to join in. Everyone was laughing as the kids pushed their way to Alma, each wanting to get their chance to hug their favorite teacher. The cameraman and reporter were forced back as the swell of children surrounded Alma.

After a few minutes of chaos, Principal White was forced to try and get things back in order. "Okay everyone, that's enough. Let's get back to our places so Miss Harper can breathe!" She clapped her hands, which was a familiar move of hers that signaled she wanted attention. "Let's go, kids. Back to your places." The crowd dispersed and Alma was left crying in the center of the room.

Blair held Alma's hand as she spoke. "We're lucky to have you, Alma, and we thought this was a good way to show it."

"I still can't believe this," said Alma.

"Miss Harper," said the reporter as she stepped back into the middle of the room. "I'm Rachel Knight, with Channel 7 News." She reached out to shake Alma's hand. "We're honored to be a part of this, and I just have to ask, how does this feel?" She put the microphone in front of Alma.

"Oh my gosh, I can't even think of how to say it. Look at me," she held her hands out in front of her and watched them tremble. "My hands are shaking. I'm stunned, shocked, overwhelmed, absolutely in love with all of you." She raised her hands and shouted out to the students, parents, and fellow teachers. They reciprocated with another round of applause. "Thank you all so much."

Mrs. White stepped beside Alma and rubbed a circle on her back. "I don't think you have to worry about spending your spring break putting together a new music room!"

Alma pulled the principal in for a hug. "You got me, Helen! I can't believe you did this."

"It was my pleasure," said Mrs. White. "You're a good teacher, and we want to keep you around here for a long time."

"Well, this was a pretty good way to do it," said Alma.

"Good," said Mrs. White. "Then my plan worked." They both laughed and embraced again.

The reporter interviewed Alma about how she felt, and what it was like to be surprised this way. They discussed how Alma had always wanted to be a music teacher, and that this was the best day of her life. Then the reporter asked if Alma had any siblings, which seemed like an odd question, and Alma struggled to answer. "No, not exactly. Why?"

"No reason, just curious," said the reporter.

"So what's next?" asked Helen White. "Do you need to interview Alma any more?"

"Oh please say no," said Alma. "I'm a total wreck right now."

Rachel laughed and shook her head. "Don't worry. We don't have to do anything right away. We'd still like to get a follow-up interview with you, but we can do that later. We'll just need you to sign a few release papers, and then we'll spend some time getting exterior shots and maybe speak with a few of the kids. If you want, we'd be happy to buy you dinner tonight for an interview. That way you can have a chance to relax and absorb all of this."

"That'd be great," said Alma.

The man behind the reporter lowered his camera. He set it on the floor and then wiped off his sweaty hand before offering it to Alma. "Hi, I'm Stephen."

"Hi," said Alma as she shook his hand.

"Do you mind if I just ask you one quick question?" He didn't wait for permission before asking. "Are you the same Alma Harper that was involved with the Widowsfield incident in 1996?"

Rachel put her hand on the cameraman's chest and pushed him backward. "Not now, Stephen." She smiled at Alma. "We'll talk to you tonight. Okay?"

Alma nodded.

All of the joy of the moment dissipated at the mere mention of Widowsfield. Alma's hands still shook, but now it was for a new reason.

CHAPTER 2 - Family Reunion

Widowsfield
March 14th, 1996

"How are you feeling?" asked Kyle's mother. She placed her palm on his forehead, and then his cheek to check his temperature.

"Pretty yucky," said Kyle. He pulled the covers close to his chin as he shivered. It was an odd sensation to be cold and sweating at the same time. No matter how many blankets were piled on top of him, he never seemed to get any warmer.

"You feel pretty hot. That's not a bad thing though. I think your best bet is to let the fever try to burn away the sickness. I bet you'll be up and running around again in just a few days." She tucked the covers down around him and then started to collect the used tissues that littered his bed. "In the meantime, I want you to stay in this bed and drink lots of water. Can you do that for me?"

"I guess so," said Kyle as he wiped his nose on his hand. "Can you bring up the VCR?"

His mother rolled her eyes and hesitated before answering. "You know how I feel about you watching television all day."

"Please? I'm so bored."

She finished collecting the tissues and put them in the overflowing Spiderman trashcan in the corner of his room. "What about your comics?"

"I read them all." Kyle looked at the stack of Image comics that his mother had picked up for him at the Jackson Comic Shop where he had a file. They filled the file each week with his various favorite comics, and he'd fallen behind on picking up the newest issues. Wednesdays were the day that new comics were released, and if his file hadn't been cleared the shop's owner would've stopped saving them.

19

"You read all of those?" She looked at the stack of bagged and boarded comics on his nightstand.

"Yes, I told you, I'm bored. Can you please bring me the TV from the den with the VCR in it? I want to watch a movie."

His mother sighed and then capitulated. "Fine, but just one movie. Okay? I don't want you rotting your brain in here. You know how I feel about having TVs in the bedroom."

"I know, but I feel like sh…" he almost cursed, but caught himself before he did, "…shadoobey."

His mother smirked at his nearly foul mouth and muttered as she carried his trashcan out of the room. He coughed, despite not needing to, in hopes his mother would hurry to get the television if she felt bad about how sick he was.

She eventually brought the 19" television with the built in VCR and set it on his dresser. He asked her to let him watch his father's copy of Goldeneye, but she laughed off the request and put in Toy Story instead. He didn't complain.

Somewhere around the point in the movie where the toys go to Pizza Planet, Kyle closed his eyes. He didn't mean to fall asleep, but the next thing he knew he was waking up on a cold pillow that was wet with his sweat and drool. He wiped off his cheek and looked around in confusion. The television displayed snow, the movie long over, and the clock on his nightstand revealed that he'd been asleep for over two hours.

3:14

"Mom," he said and rubbed his eyes.

He glanced out the window and saw that the previously bright afternoon had turned dark. At first he thought a storm had come through, but then he recognized that it was fog he was looking at. The fog flashed with green light and he pulled the covers up over him tighter. The flash of electric

20

green light rippled through the fog as if he were watching monochromatic Northern Lights.

"Mom," he said with more insistence.

Something moved beneath his bed.

He leapt into a sitting position and pulled the covers up closer to him as he yelped. There was something scratching at the floor beneath him, and it seemed to get excited by his voice.

"Mom, help!"

She didn't answer. The green light flashed outside and cast devilish shadows across his room.

"Mommy!"

The scratching became more intense, and then the creature under the bed started to groan. It made a guttural sound, like the gasps of a choking victim shortly before they succumb.

"Mommy, please help. There's something under my bed. Mommy!"

He continued to scream as the scratching got worse. He was terrified of getting off the bed, afraid that whatever was hiding below would grab at his feet and pull him under. Yet, despite how loud he screamed, his mother wouldn't answer.

He turned and pulled one of the wooden swords off the wall above his bed. He held it tight against his chest as he stood on the bed and prayed. Then he gathered his strength before leaping off the bed in the direction of the door. His bare feet slapped against the wood floor and he wasted no time fleeing. He only dared to look back once he was safely in the hall, far from whatever had been hiding under him.

Kyle saw the top half of his mother's head on the floor, with her fingers sprouting from the wood like the tops of carrots. She was scratching at the floor and he could see the top of her head wiggling as she tried to speak. Her body was fused with the floor, and as he reached the stairs he could see the bottom half of her body hanging from the first floor ceiling, beneath where his bed was.

"Mommy," he said in shock.

She gurgled and scratched before her legs went limp, dangling from the ceiling.

Kyle fled the house, desperate to find protection from what had happened within. Fog enveloped the rest of the block, but drew an unnatural circle around his house, as if the home was somehow protected from it.

"Help," Kyle called out at the house across the street, which was shrouded by the fog. A dog barked from within, and a flash of green electricity crackled along the curb. Then Kyle heard teeth chattering, and saw a tall, thin figure appear at the door of the home. The man spread his arms as if welcoming his neighbor in for an embrace. Kyle ran to him, desperate for protection.

16 Years Later
March 9th, 2012

Alma was anxious about meeting with the reporter, not because of the story they were going to run, but because of the offhanded remark by the cameraman about her relation to the mystery of Widowsfield. It had been nearly 16 years since that awful day, and she tried for all that time to forget as much about the investigation that tore her family apart as possible. She would've refused to meet with them, but wanted to make sure her past wasn't going to be part of the story. The last thing she needed was to be contacted by her father about why she had allowed reporters to discuss their family's dark history.

"Alma." Rachel waved at her from across the small dining room. She was seated at a table with the cameraman, Stephen. The meeting was set up at a local Chinese Buffet restaurant, and the smell of sticky sweet chicken and pork sickened Alma. She'd been a vegetarian for years, not for any altruistic or health related reason, but because the thought of eating flesh sickened her. It had bothered her since the day her brother disappeared in Widowsfield, 16 years ago.

"Hi." She stared at Stephen's plate, which was loaded with fried pork covered in a fiery orange glaze and mixed with rice. It was steaming, and the sauce clung to his chin as he smiled up at her. He wiped his lips off on a red napkin that had been in his lap before he got up and pulled out a chair for her.

"Want me to get you some food?" he asked, trying to be nice.

"No, thank you." She sat down with Stephen to her right and Rachel across the square table from her. The reporter had a sparse amount of food on her plate, and no meat.

"Not hungry?" asked Rachel.

Alma shook her head. "Not really."

Rachel tilted her head and sympathetically asked, "Not a fan of buffet food? Me neither. This was his pick." She jabbed her thumb in Stephen's direction.

"I thought you'd have the camera equipment here," said Alma. "Aren't we supposed to be doing an interview?"

Rachel smiled and squinted as she bobbed her head as if about to apologize. "Well, that's not really the case. We've got everything we need for the story. I guess I should just come out and admit the truth. You see, Stephen and I have a side project going on that's been gaining steam lately, and we thought you might be able to help out with it."

Alma was confused and looked back and forth between the two of them. "How?" she asked with suspicion.

"Stephen started a website last year about haunted houses. It was sort of a pet project for us, and we filmed a few videos to put up on Youtube, never really expecting much of anything to happen."

Stephen wiped his mouth again before he interrupted Rachel. "Yeah, it was just for shits and giggles initially, but now we're starting to pull in serious numbers."

"Okay," said Alma, afraid of why they were talking to her about this. She could guess where the conversation was headed, and didn't want to go there.

"A couple months ago, Stephen caught something on camera in a house out near Pittsburgh," said Rachel. She absently stabbed her fork into a piece of fried zucchini on her plate. "We didn't even see it at first, but one of our viewers did. Stephen was calling out the name of a little girl that was supposed to have died in the house and in the corner of the room you could see the shadow of a figure. It's hard to really tell what it is, but the net just went bonkers over it. We split the video up to just show that scene, and it's gotten almost a million hits already."

"Okay," said Alma, hesitant to let the conversation continue, like she was being forced to watch a movie she'd seen before with an ending she hated, but didn't want to spoil it for the others around her.

"We're trying to make sure that we take advantage of the exposure and put up new content on the site that can get people to keep paying attention to what we're doing," said Rachel.

Stephen was quick to continue. "You've probably seen all of those shows on TV these days about ghost hunters and stuff, right?"

Alma nodded.

"That's sort of what we're trying to do, but with a more serious take on it. We want to go to places that have ghost stories, or unsolved crimes with a supernatural feel to them, and do a story about them." Stephen dropped his fork and flung syrupy red sauce in an arc across the wall behind him. His utensil bounced off the edge of the table and fell to the floor. "Shit, sorry," he said as he retrieved it. The glazed pork had collected a wealth of carpet fuzz when he picked it up. "Gross." He put the fork on the plate and covered it with his napkin.

"Smooth," said Rachel in jest.

"So, you two are partners in this website?" asked Alma.

"Yeah." Rachel seemed to recognize why Alma looked confused. "Oh, I'm sorry, I forgot to mention Stephen's not just my camera guy, he's my husband." She held up her left hand and pointed at her naked ring finger. "They don't want me to wear a ring on camera. All part of the illusion, you know?"

Alma shook her head. "Not really."

Stephen got up to get a new plate of food from the buffet and set his hands on his wife's shoulders to massage her for a second. "Rachel's supposed to be the hot, single reporter. They don't want viewers to know she's taken."

Rachel rolled her eyes and sighed. "Yeah, it's a sleazy business."

"Well, at least it pays well," said Alma.

Rachel gave a quick laugh and straightened her posture. "You'd think, right? Truth is, reporters get paid like shit. You think teachers have it bad? Try being a reporter on a local news show."

"Really? I had no idea. I just assumed you guys made a lot."

"Not unless you're an anchor." Rachel looked over her shoulder at her husband. "He makes more than I do, by a lot."

"That's why we're trying to get this site off the ground," said Stephen on his way to the buffet table, out of earshot.

"Look," said Alma sharply. "I have a feeling I know where this is headed, and I should just stop you before we go any further. I can't help you with your site. I've left that part of my life behind me."

Rachel visibly deflated, and she looked nervous as she continued to stab at the zucchini on her plate. "I understand. I really do, but will you just hear us out?"

"Honestly, I probably couldn't help you out anyhow. That happened when I was eight years old. I don't even remember it that well anymore."

"Stephen's been working really hard on this," said Rachel. "He's been interviewing people from the area, and is convinced this will be the best way to start off a web series. I think you should just hear him out. He'd love to ask you some questions about what you saw there."

25

Stephen overheard them as he came back with a new plate of disgusting fried meat. "Did you tell her?" He sounded disappointed.

"She saw it coming," said Rachel. "Probably because of your none-too-subtle introduction at the school."

"Sorry to be a bummer," said Alma. "I really can't help you though. I don't know anything more than what's already been out there. And to tell you the truth, I don't believe all the ghost stories anyhow. The police said that the disappearances were due to a fight between a motorcycle club and the mob. They said that the people in the town are probably all living in Mexico or something, hiding from the mob."

"Yeah, but that's crazy," said Stephen. "An entire town just packs up and moves because of some drug running mob deal? I know it was a small town, but there were still a couple thousand people there. To think they all just packed up and left is crazy."

"What's crazier?" asked Alma. "That, or that they all got abducted by aliens, or sucked up into an alternate dimension, or whatever other crazy conspiracy theory is out there now."

"You told the police that you saw the green light that night," said Stephen, almost as if trying to confront Alma with a lie.

"I was eight," said Alma. "Who knows what I saw? I don't remember any of it." She had a habit of avoiding eye contact when she lied, and tried to stare at him when she spoke, but still averted her gaze when she said that she didn't remember that day. The truth wasn't that she couldn't remember anything, but rather that she couldn't remember pieces of what happened. There was a large chunk of time that had been lost to her.

"Have you heard about the Widowsfield lights?" asked Rachel. Her light tone calmed the conversation. "Not just what the police report said you saw, but the phenomenon that's been going on out in Missouri ever since the day the people in Widowsfield went missing."

Alma shook her head. "I try not to pay attention to the rumors anymore."

"People that live near Widowsfield say that they can see green lights on foggy nights," said Rachel. "They've even started to film it. Stephen talked to someone out there that posted a few videos. You can watch some of them online. It's actually pretty creepy."

"And you don't think that's staged?" asked Alma. "Come on, the people making those videos are setting out green lights on foggy nights and then taking video of it. There's nothing mystical about that."

"And that's what we want to find out," said Stephen. He was excited about the project, and Alma could understand how that could be infectious for people around him. He had an almost childish exuberance about the subject. "We want to approach this type of thing differently than other shows out there. Our goal is to go in with various viewpoints. Some of the people on our show will be skeptics, and others will be believers. I'm going to find a local out there that has seen the lights, maybe even someone that has been to the town a few times. It won't be hard. I had to go through Branson last year for a story, and I met a girl that's been out there. That's what got me thinking about doing the site in the first place."

Alma noticed that Rachel looked away as Stephen spoke. Without even knowing the couple that well, Alma could ascertain that Rachel was perturbed by something Stephen had said. She didn't have time to contemplate it, because Stephen continued excitedly.

"This should've been a huge national, if not international story. I mean, come on, a whole town disappears in modern times and no one pays any attention? The whole thing stinks of conspiracy, big time. And with the supernatural angle to it, this is a goldmine of a story. But we're not going to just go in there and focus on the ghost angle. We're going to try and dispel any of the fake crap out there, and only bring out the truth."

"I doubt there's anything supernatural to it," said Alma.

"I'm on your side, Alma," said Rachel. "I always try to think of the most reasonable solution to things, and I agree that the people of Widowsfield probably just fled the mob. It was a pretty small town, and it's not impossible to think that the majority of them were mixed up in the meth ring." She crossed her arms and sat back in her chair. She looked over at her husband as she continued. "Did you know that right around the time all this went down, the DEA had just changed the laws around pseudoephedrine? They made the sale of large quantities illegal, and they discovered a meth lab in Widowsfield after the disappearances. I don't think that's a coincidence."

Stephen shook his head and frowned as if he thought Rachel's point was ridiculous at best. "They found a tiny little meth dealer's set up. It wasn't Breaking Bad or anything in there. Shit, I bet there's a home meth lab within walking distance of this restaurant. They're not exactly rare." Then he looked at Alma and got excited again. "But you see, that's the kind of thing we want to go over on our show. We want to explore every possibility, no matter how ludicrous they are." He cast a snide look at his wife.

"It sounds great," said Alma. "But I'm not sure what you want from me."

Rachel and Stephen looked uncomfortable. It seemed that they were wary to ask for what they wanted, as if they knew it was asking too much. Stephen eventually explained, "We were hoping to convince you to come with us to Missouri, to go to the place where your brother disappeared."

"We're leaving tomorrow," said Rachel.

Alma laughed uncomfortably. She felt like she was being attacked and had to defend herself. "No way. Sorry, but I've left all of that behind me. Besides, my brother didn't disappear there. The police agreed with my father. My brother was kidnapped from his room."

"Yeah," said Stephen, "but that's not what you told them originally. You told them he was..."

28

"I know what I told them," said Alma, and was immediately embarrassed by her abruptness. "But I was eight years old. Remember? I had a bad dream, and that's all there is to it. You have no clue what this whole ordeal did to my family. It ruined us." She looked back and forth between Stephen and Rachel as if admonishing them for daring to bring this subject up. "I haven't talked to my father for more than a few minutes in almost a decade. My mother…" she faltered and cleared her throat. "My mother killed herself."

"I know," said Rachel. "I'm sorry."

"And the worst part is, every year around this time I get a call from someone that wants to dig up the past. I get letters all the time from people with all sorts of insane theories. They say that the government was involved, or that some corporation with a facility near there was doing tests on some Greek boat they bought," she laughed at the absurdity of the next theory. "For fuck's sake, I even had one guy say that sightings of Bigfoot skyrocketed right before the people in the town disappeared. He accused me of trying to hide the fact that the government kidnapped everyone in the town to turn them into Sasquatch super soldiers."

Rachel chuckled and then gave Stephen an apologetic glance.

"It's nuts," said Alma and couldn't help but smile.

Stephen looked pensive. "I've never heard anything about a Greek boat. What was that one about?"

Alma shook her head and laughed in exasperation. "You don't get it. That's the point, it was bullshit. All of it is just bullshit. Just like the 9-11 conspiracies, and the faked moon landings, and the magic bullet that killed Kennedy. People turn things into conspiracies because they have some deep-seated notion that the world is more mystical than it really is. The people of Widowsfield disappeared because they were involved in a drug ring that went bad. That's it. A small town like that, where everyone knows each other – it's not crazy to think they all knew about the drug ring. And my brother was kidnapped in the middle of the night, from his bedroom, and not by some creatures in the fog." She was frantic now, and had trouble keeping herself from crying. She got up and got ready to leave. "Look, I'm sorry, but I can't help you. I'm sorry. Good luck and everything, but I'm going to go. Okay? I'm sorry."

Stephen got up, but Rachel was faster and motioned for him to sit back down. "It's okay, Alma. Don't be sorry. I understand."

"I just," Alma tried to explain herself. "I just left that part of my life behind me, and I've been trying to move on ever since. I just wish I could. Every damn year it all starts up again."

"I can imagine," said Rachel as she walked to the front of the restaurant with Alma. "I'm so sorry to have dragged you into this. We never meant to hurt you."

"I know," said Alma. "I don't blame you. I'm not mad or anything, I just want to put that part of my life to death." She meant to say, 'to bed,' and was surprised by her violent wording.

Rachel didn't pick up on the Freudian slip. "I get that, but if you ever want to talk about it, or anything, please don't hesitate to call. Here, take my card."

Alma took the business card, if only to be polite.

"The cell phone number on there is my personal phone too." She rolled her eyes and shrugged. "They don't even buy us our own cell phones, if you can believe it. We have to supply our own."

"I hope the whole website thing works out for you," said Alma, looking to end the conversation. "You guys seem like nice people. Sorry I'm being so weird about this."

"No, don't worry about it." Rachel waved off Alma's apology.

"Who knows, maybe one of these days I'll be ready to talk about it. Maybe that'd be good for me, but I'm just not ready for it now." Alma lingered because she felt guilty.

"I understand," said Rachel. "But if you ever do, you know, want to talk, you've got my card. I'm a good listener."

Alma got to the exit and looked back at the two of them. Rachel still stood in the middle of the restaurant, and had a look of concern that reminded Alma of a mother watching her child go away to college. Stephen seemed frustrated, but not angry, and continued to eat his fried pork. They were a good looking couple, and seemed kind. If circumstances were different, Alma might've enjoyed getting to know them. However, the fact that they wanted to dissect Alma's past made them seem parasitic and dangerous. She waved goodbye, feeling a unique mix of regret and disdain at leaving them behind.

She sighed and started to walk through the parking lot, but then jogged, eager to get as far from them as possible. She fumbled with her purse to find the keys to her Subaru Outback. Emotions swirled, sorrow battled with anger, calm fought frenzy, and she wasn't sure if she was about to cry, scream, or laugh. "What the hell," she muttered to herself as she pushed through the things in her purse in search of her keys. She stuck Rachel's business card in a pocket on the inside of her purse as she continued to rifle through the contents.

It was a chilly night, just past dusk, and the moon cast a brilliant blue light over everything. Bats squeaked as they zipped through the night sky, spots of black shooting through blue. Alma found the teddy bear key chain that her ex-boyfriend had bought her and pulled the keys out. She kept meaning to take the teddy bear off the chain and throw it away, but every time she started to, she stopped. Her relationship with Paul had always been tumultuous, and all of her friends consistently pleaded with her to stop going back to him, but there was an undeniable bond between them. She wasn't sure they'd ever get back together again after the way it had ended six months earlier, but she was certain she'd never stop loving him. She thumbed the soft fur of the keychain and wished Paul was here with her now.

31

The ring caught on one of her white plastic wrapped tampons, which fell to the ground beside her car. She cursed and picked it up. When she knelt down she saw the shadow of a man cast by moonlight against the side of her car. For just a moment, her heart fluttered as she thought it might be Paul, as if rubbing the keychain had somehow summoned him like a genie from a lamp.

"Alma," said her father in a frantic, hushed whisper.

She yelped in shock and stood to face him. She pressed her back to the car and held her mouth with the hand that her keys were in.

He was ragged. His clothes were a tattered mess and his hair was greasy, with strands of grey and black sticking up in various directions. His eyes were wide and darted back and forth above dark circles. He hadn't shaved in weeks and his stubble was almost completely white. "Alma, baby. Baby girl. Alma, what did they want?" His words flit past his lips too fast for him to properly say them, causing the syllables to mix together between quick breaths. He had sores on his lips and cheeks, as if he'd been scratching at himself until he'd bled. "Did they want you to go with them? You can't. You know that, right? You can't go there. You've got to let that die. You've got to let it die."

"Let me go!" She pulled her arm away from his grasping hands like a disgusted royal squirming to escape a leper.

"Don't fuck me like this, kid." He scowled.

"I said back off." She palmed her keys so that they poked out between her fingers as she made a fist. She gripped the teddy bear in her palm as if holding a pair of brass knuckles.

"You're never going to save him." He backed away, just as Alma had asked. Then he glowered as if he suddenly remembered a hatred he'd forgotten for years. He surged forward and grabbed the back of her head with one hand as he pressed the other against her mouth. All at once, she was a child again, caught in the grip of a sadistic father, tasting the grime of his palm as he kept her silent. He pressed himself against her tall frame, and still towered over her, just as he did so many years ago. She clenched her eyes shut and a hundred terrible moments were suddenly fresh in her mind. It was impossible to breathe, to scream, to do anything but cry as he growled at her.

"You better keep your mouth shut."

It was easy to retreat into her mind and let the assault end. If she closed her eyes and sang a song to herself, the end would come eventually – it always had before. The little girl she'd been for years was always with her, waiting to help comfort her through moments like this. Just sing a song, Alma, and the pain will stop. Hum and focus on something nice.

No more songs.

She thrust her fist into his abdomen, the keys like knives between her fingers. He gasped and staggered back as he gripped his wound. He checked his hand for blood, but there was none. Her punch hadn't cut him, but seemed to have hurt him enough that he thought it had.

The taste of his oil stained hand was still on her lips.

"You want a fight, old man. Let's do this." Her stilted, terrified tone belied the courage of her words. She was on the brink of tears.

"I didn't kill Ben."

She expected him to attack, but he paced in the parking lot instead. She kept the keys in her fist and was ready to defend herself, but her father wasn't willing to fight anymore. He stared up at the night sky as he walked back and forth.

"I know what you think, and what your mother thought, and what everyone else thinks, but God knows the truth. God and me, we know, I didn't hurt that boy. Some devil did it."

"Why are you here?" asked Alma. Her father lived two states away and she never told him where she'd moved.

"To warn you, you dummy." He spoke as if chiding a friend instead of threatening his child. "I want to keep you safe. That's all I've ever wanted. I want to protect you." He took a step toward her and she stiffened at the approach. "You might not believe it, but I love you, Alma. I always have."

"You had 24 years to prove that to me, and you screwed up each and every one," said Alma. "Now get in your car, or bus, or however the hell you got here, and get out of my life."

He looked sad for a brief second, but then grinned. His meth rotted teeth and sunken cheeks were a wicked sight, accentuated by raw sores on his chapped, cracked lips. "Darling, I'll never be out of your life. We're family."

"Do your family a favor and die, asshole."

He whistled and shook his head. "Look at you, girl. Acting like a tough one now? You're no tough one. You're a pretty little flower. You're my pretty little flower."

"This pretty flower has thorns." She jangled the keys in her hand for emphasis.

Her father chuckled and shook his head. "Listen to you. You're a toughie now, huh? All right, all right." He held up his hands and backed away again. "Nothing but love for you, girl. Swear to Christ, nothing but love. I'm here to protect you."

Alma found that hilarious and couldn't help but guffaw. "You, protecting me? That's rich."

"I'll never stop protecting you," he said, his skittish mannerism helped turn his promises into threats. "I'll always be there for you. I'll always watch out for you."

Alma saw Rachel through the window of the restaurant. The reporter had just noticed the confrontation in the parking lot and was rushing to help. She stopped at the entrance, her hands pressed against the bar that would open it, and looked at Alma. She was uncertain if she should come out and was looking to Alma for approval.

Alma nodded to her and Rachel opened the door a crack. "Call the police," said Alma.

Her father turned and yelled out at Rachel, "Stop! Don't do that."

Rachel closed the door and ran back into the restaurant, screaming for the owner to call the police. Alma saw Stephen standing near the door, and Rachel's panic alerted him to the gravity of what was happening outside. He rushed to action.

"Get away from her." Stephen burst through the door, causing a rapid tintinnabulation as the bells above the entrance bounced. He didn't wait for Alma's father to comply and ran into the parking lot, ready to fight.

"Stay out of this," said her father.

Stephen stopped for just long enough to get into a tackling stance. He bent his knees and lowered his shoulders while keeping an eye on his target. Alma almost expected him to extend his right arm and touch his fingers to the ground like a defensive lineman, but Stephen bounded forward before he got that low.

"Stephen!" Rachel screamed from the restaurant entrance.

He was already crashing into Alma's father. He lifted the thin man into the air and Alma heard her father's breath escape in a sudden huff. She dashed to the side as Stephen rammed the old man into the Subaru. Stephen didn't hesitate after impact and brought his right arm up to Alma's father's throat. He pushed at it as if trying to pop the man's head off.

"Stephen, let him go," said Rachel as she ran forward.

An older Asian woman appeared at the door and gasped when she saw the altercation. "Oh my gosh. You need to go. Get out of here. I'm not going to have this in my parking lot. Get out of here. Now!"

Alma enjoyed watching her father squirm. She couldn't help but smile as Stephen choked him.

"You need to leave," said Stephen. "Take your junky ass back to Pennsylvania and leave your daughter alone." He released the old man, but then grabbed Michael Harper's shirt and pulled him away from Alma.

"Don't go with them," said her father as he rubbed his throat. He staggered away, walking backward as he stared at his daughter. "Let it die, girl. Bury it." He turned and ran into the night.

Stephen panted and looked prideful, his face flushed and eyes wide from the adrenaline rush. He smiled at Alma, expecting her to thank him. Instead, she scowled.

"How did you know he was my father?" Alma looked from Stephen to Rachel. "How did you guys know he was from Pennsylvania? Did you bring him here?"

"No," said Rachel. "Not exactly."

"What do you mean, not exactly?" asked Alma.

"We met him first, when we were doing the story of the haunted house," said Stephen. "We knew he was accused of killing his son, and that he was tied to Widowsfield. We got a hold of him to see if he'd be interested in taking part in the story."

"How did he end up here?"

"He must've gotten here on his own," said Rachel. "We didn't bring him."

Alma tried to grasp the situation, as well as her emotions. She was furious, but knew that the two hadn't meant any harm. Alma's family had kept the discord between them a secret. Stephen and Rachel couldn't have known what their meddling could cause, but that did little to keep Alma from hating them for it. "I can't believe this. It's like a nightmare." She laughed nervously. "And I was having such a good day."

"I'm sorry about this, Alma," said Stephen. "I really am."

The restaurant door opened again and the Asian woman frowned even as she spoke. "I called the police. They'll be here soon. Get out of here, now."

"Can I go in and get our things?" asked Rachel. "I still need to pay for the food."

36

The woman reluctantly moved aside to let Rachel in and then glared out at Stephen. She pointed at him and said, "You get out of here, jackass. Don't come back."

He saluted her and snickered. "That sucks. I liked this place." He inspected the dent in the side of the car as Alma unlocked the door. "I'll pay for the damage."

"That's okay," said Alma. "I don't care. I just want to go home."

"I'm sorry for all of this," said Stephen.

Alma got in as Stephen stood beside the car, holding the door open. She turned the car on and music blared before she had a chance to turn the volume down.

"We can help you bury the past," said Stephen as a last ditch effort to get Alma to agree to the trip.

"You're off to a hell of a start."

She was prepared to leave and reached out for the door's handle.

"I know about Chaos Magick," said Stephen.

Alma halted. She didn't even breathe as she looked at him.

"You said you don't believe in the supernatural, but I know about 314."

She pulled the door away from him and slammed it shut. She turned the music up until the speakers crackled. Her tires squealed as she raced away.

CHAPTER 3 - Rekindled

Widowsfield
March 14th, 1996

"Hey there, Claire," said Nancy as she came into the office. It was only a few minutes until her shift started, and she'd already been reprimanded for being late three times in the past month. The last thing she needed was to lose another job.

Claire was already in her seat with her headset on. She had the cubicle closest to the front door, which she said she liked because it gave her a chance to smile at everyone as they got to work. The sweet old woman tapped on her watch and smiled at Nancy.

"I know, I know, but I'm here, aren't I? I'm not late."

"You'd better hurry up and get to the time clock," said Claire. She was a rotund, cheery old woman whose husband was a train conductor, a fact that Claire talked about endlessly. She was anxious for him to retire so that they could move to their ranch in Wyoming. Nancy had heard all about it, several times, since starting her job at the Widowsfield County Emergency Services Center.

Nancy threw her purse onto the desk in her cubicle across from Claire. The two of them sat with their backs to one another, and had been working the late shift together since the recent merger with Alden County. "Back in a minute," said Nancy as she pat Claire's shoulder.

"Get a move on, sweetie," said Claire as Nancy ran down the hall to the break room where the time clock was located.

Nancy pushed past Darryl, who danced away with his coffee cup held high as he whistled at her. "Cutting it close, princess."

"Shut up, Darryl," said Nancy. She was a fan of coffee, but there was something amiss about the smell at three in the

38

afternoon. Darryl was always drinking it, and the scent threatened to reset Nancy's internal clock, convincing her that they were like everyone else and started their work day in the morning instead of late afternoon.

"Testy, testy," said Darryl. "What was it this time, Nancy? A train? A funeral? An earthquake? You know Mike told us to clock in ten minutes early. Doesn't matter if it's not three yet, you're already late."

"Seriously, Darryl, shut it." She dropped her card into the machine mounted on the wall and heard the robotic crunch as it stamped a hole in it. She breathed a sigh of relief when she pulled the card out and saw 2:58 printed on it. She waved the card in the air as if it were a Poloroid and then dropped it back into the metal sleeve beside the door. "Made it."

"Like I said, you're still going to get bitched out."

"Well, whatever. Mike can go fuck himself. I had to deal with a sitter for my kid because something happened at the school and they shut down the afterschool program for the day at the last minute. My mom can't pick him up until four, so unless Mike wanted me to let the kid wander the street for a half hour then I really didn't have a choice. Now did I?"

"I don't care about your sob story, darling," said Darryl. He was a tall, obese man. He had no chin, and his neck seemed to extend from his chest to just under his lip. He had a beard, and tried to shave it to help make it appear as if he had a chin line, which just accentuated his turkey wattle.

"Then why'd you ask?" She slid past him, out of the break room and back into the hall.

He followed behind and sipped his coffee. "Just being nice. You should try it sometime. Doesn't hurt to be affable, you know."

"Thanks for the advice," said Nancy as she got to her seat.

Darryl grumbled as he walked to his cubicle on the other side of the room.

"Don't let him bug you," said Claire without turning.

"I'm trying. He's just so…"

"I know, I know. Some people get their jollies pushing other people's buttons." Claire finished whatever she was doing on the computer and then swiveled to look at Nancy. "I'll tell you the best advice I ever got. It was from my grandma, way back in the dinosaur years when I was a kid. She sat me down after I got in a fight with a girl that made fun of my dress. We didn't have much money, and I had to wear the same clothes for weeks at a time. My shoes had holes in them that we taped up, and baths were a once a week affair. No kidding, we were poor. Anyhow, this girl was giving me the what for, getting all the other girls to call me names, and I went and popped her. I got in pretty big trouble, cause back in those days us girls were supposed to be dainty little things. Not me, though. I was a firebrand for sure. My granny told me that there're two different types of people in the world." She held up one finger, "You've got the doers," she held up a second finger, "and you've got the doubters."

"Okay," said Nancy as she faced away from Claire to log into her computer. She wasn't trying to ignore the old woman, but she wasn't exactly paying attention either. The station had been befitted with a new login system that utilized a faster modem, but it still seemed to take forever, and Nancy hadn't gotten used to the interface yet.

"The doers are the people that give it a go. You know the type, the ones that get out there and make things happen."

Nancy just nodded as Claire talked. The old woman rarely went five minutes without telling a story. It was a habit that had taken Nancy several months to get used to, but now the incessant chatter was actually something she looked forward to. On nights where the county stayed quiet, and no crimes or accidents were called in, it was nice to have someone like Claire, with a wealth of tales, ready to spin a yarn at a moment's notice.

40

"And the doubters are the ones that get their self worth from pointing out the failure of others. I didn't even really pay attention to her at the time, but when I grew up I saw what she meant." Claire paused and reflected on her childhood. "Want to hear a dirty little secret?"

"Sure," said Nancy, only half listening.

"I used to be a doubter. I'm ashamed to admit it, but it's true. I used to be one of those catty old crows sitting around and picking at anyone that dared stir my ire. Hard to believe, I know, but it's the truth. I loved gossip, and bought all those celebrity rags, spent my time chatting on the phone with other women about who was fat, who was gay, who was cheating on who, and all that nonsense. Waste of time, honey. That's all that is. And you know what turned me around?"

"What's that?"

"Cancer."

Nancy stopped and looked back at Claire. She'd never heard anything about Claire suffering from cancer. "What do you mean?"

"Oh yeah, honey. I don't talk about it much, but I had quite a cancer scare a few years back. Nothing will ever set you right like getting up close and personal with the grim reaper. After something like that, I'll tell you, you just don't have the gumption to be a doubter no more. I pulled myself up by the bootstraps, beat the disease, and started focusing on what's important in life. It took me most of my years to finally pay attention to what my granny said, but I haven't forgotten it since."

Nancy was going to respond to what Claire said, but then she heard the beep of a new email as it showed up in her folder. She looked and saw that it was from her supervisor, Mike.

"Aw fuck," she said as she opened the tersely worded email. "How did he know I was running late? He's not even here."

Claire rolled across the short gap between their cubicles. Her headpiece's wire stretched to its limit as she looked at Nancy's screen. "It's the new system. He can track when you log in even when he's at the headquarters in the other county."

"But I punched in at three on the dot. Two minutes early actually," said Nancy as she pointed down the hall at the break room.

Claire shook her head and pointed at the screen. "I'm talking about the computer. You're supposed to log in ten minutes before your shift starts."

"Are you serious?" asked Nancy.

Claire nodded and then rolled back to her cubicle. "Yep. Sorry, honey."

"I thought computers were supposed to make our lives easier," said Nancy. "This sucks. Next thing you know they're going to be installing cameras in here so they can watch us."

"What's the email say?" asked Claire.

"Nothing new. He's just being a dick, reminding me that I've already been warned about being late and that our quarterly review is coming up."

"That doesn't sound good."

Nancy was about to put on her headset, but then set it on her keyboard and groaned as she rubbed her eyes. "I swear to God, Claire, this place is going to be the death of me."

"Don't be a negative Nancy," said Claire, and then she turned and chuckled. "That's a funny name. Isn't it usually negative Nelly? I'm going to change it to negative Nancy if you don't cheer up."

"Thanks," said Nancy with a groan. "Do you mind if I transfer my calls over to you for a minute. I need a quick smoke. I'm already having a shitty day."

"Go for it, I'm not going anywhere."

Nancy hit the numbers on the phone to facilitate the transfer. All calls that went into the center were routed to a free line first, which would ring for a few seconds before being sent back into the round robin exchange, ensuring that no call was left unanswered for too long. Every day a report was generated that showed how many calls each line answered to make sure no one was avoiding work, but Nancy had discovered that transferred calls counted as a hit on both lines, subverting the system. It caused a slight delay in the answer for the caller, but allowed her to catch much needed smoke breaks from time to time.

She saw Darryl peering over the wall of his cubicle and gave him a snide grin. He shook his head and looked back down at his computer as she went outside.

"Why don't you go and fuck yourself, Darryl," she whispered as she went out the door. She smacked her hard pack against the side of her hand until a cigarette sprung free. She quickly lit it and took a long, satisfying drag.

Winter seemed unwilling to disappear entirely, and there was a chill in the air despite how sunny it was. She crossed her arms and shivered as she paced in front of the building. The ashtray had been pulled far from the entrance in an attempt to keep people from smoking by the door, surely a result of employees like Darryl complaining about having to walk through a cloud of smoke to get to work. Nancy flicked her ashes onto the pavement and flipped off the far away, waist-high ashtray as if it offended her.

She glanced in through the front window, past the patchy bushes, at her empty cubicle. Claire's seat faced the window, but Nancy could only see the side of her coworker from this vantage, the rest was covered by the fabric wall of the cubicle.

The phone rang and the incessant buzzing was loud enough to hear even with the door closed. She watched as Claire shifted to click the button on the computer that would answer the call. Nancy took another long drag and looked away from the building, toward the small downtown area of Widowsfield. It was quiet, with only a few cars pulled up to the Salt and Pepper diner on the corner and a UPS truck parked in front of the Anderson Used Book Store. The Widowsfield Emergency Services building shared a parking lot with a credit union, but there rarely seemed to be anyone at the lonely bank.

She closed her eyes and dwelled in her own thoughts for a moment. It had been a long few weeks, and there was no end in sight. She was stuck in a workaday world, at a job she hated, with a mountain of bills waiting at home and no prospect of relief. She felt like crying.

The cigarette burned to the filter far too quickly. Her excuse for a break, minutes after getting to work, was over. She glanced at the clock on the bank's sign at the entrance of the parking lot.

3:14

She looked for Darryl's Chevy and then flicked her cigarette butt onto the hood before flipping off the car. A swirl of smoke wafted in front of her face and she waved it away only to see more smoke appear, as if her arm's movement had cast a spell bringing with it a grey mist. She looked down and saw thick smoke filling the parking lot, like water moving slowly through the town.

"What the fuck?"

She kicked at it, and the mist wafted up where it sullied the air. A flash of green light erupted near her and an electric zap cascaded up the gutter on the side of the building. Dogs started to bark as the fog swept through the streets. Then a massive black shadow was cast over the ground as something flew by above, blotting out the sun for a second. She tried to look up, but the fog surged skyward to block her view.

The dogs started to growl, and she saw black shadows zip through the fog in the parking lot. The movement caused the mist to ripple before a green wave of light flashed from within.

Nancy quickly opened the door and ran inside as the fog snuck in by her feet. She kicked at it as if it were a corporeal entity. It dissipated around her leg as she pulled the door closed.

Someone was groaning nearby. It was a wet gurgle, as if someone was choking. She saw Claire in her chair, rolled into the center of the space between their cubicles, staring at her. It took a minute for Nancy's brain to register what she was seeing. It seemed impossible, and she blinked several times before accepting that it was real.

Claire's body was partially sunk into the chair and her headset was pressed into her head. The microphone stuck out of her throat and the headset jutted from her ear as if someone had plunged it into her, but there was no blood to be seen. Her arm was trapped in the armrest of the chair, and her left leg was below the seat while her right was above. She was twisted, and when she tried to speak only a gurgle came forth. Spittle dripped down her chin as her eyes darted back and forth, terror seizing her as she struggled to get free.

Nancy screamed and backed away.

That's when she saw the creature outside. It was the size of a child, but with the head of a dog. The monstrosity clawed at the glass door with hands that looked neither human nor canine, but a bloody, pulpy mix of both. The creature snapped its jaws against the glass, spreading its lips wide to bare vicious white teeth. It seemed to be trying to bite her through the glass.

"Somebody help," said Nancy just before the windows broke all around her. Green electricity cracked through the room as the humanoid dogs rushed in from all sides. She tried to fight them off, but they held her down as their maws ripped at her clothes and flesh. They tore at her, shaking their heads back and forth, nipping at one another to secure a spot for the kill. Their nude, childlike bodies writhed over one another as their grotesque heads gnawed at her bones.

Out of the corner of her eye she caught sight of a man standing near the bank's sign in the parking lot. He was tall and thin, but his features were hazed by the fog. Then a flash of electricity illuminated him for just a moment. His lower

45

jaw was shaking, and there was no skin on his cheek, revealing his teeth even from the side as he stared at something across the street. She could hear his teeth chattering and despite the horror she endured at the mercy of the dog-like creatures, she was relieved the man in the mist was focused on something other than her.

She should've been dead, but nothing could end the pain. The fog swirled around her and lifted her head to force her to watch. The green electricity zapped in her ears, stinging and burning, as the creatures ripped her apart. She could see her bones, her intestines, her heart, and her lungs. She watched as the monsters fought over her meat.

The fog wouldn't let her die. The mist was capable of trapping her spirit, and she was conscious even though her body ceased to live. The flashing green fog kept her alive and forced her to witness every agonizing moment until the creatures plucked out her eyes. Then she was forced to listen.

16 Years Later
March 9th, 2012

Alma stared at her apartment complex from the safety of her car. The yellow lights in the parking lot cast a hazy hue over the scene, as if a polluted mist had descended upon her life.

"Are you here?" she asked as she chewed on her thumbnail. "Did you find out where I live, you son of a bitch?"

She could see her apartment door, on the middle floor of the three-story building. Each section of the apartment complex was connected to the next by a concrete, railed landing with stairs that zigzagged down. From her vantage she could see her nondescript door as June bugs and moths fluttered around her porch light.

Was her father hiding in the shadows? Was he waiting for her?

She reached for her purse and got her cell phone. She flipped over to her page of contacts and thought about which of them might be able to help her. Several of her friends were out of town, and others didn't answer her call. She kept trying, even selecting people she hadn't spoken to in years. The few people that answered all had excuses as to why they were unavailable.

Alma led a reclusive life, only venturing out to go to work and the occasional concert. She wasn't socially adept, preferring the comfort of a late night movie alone than a party. She didn't make friends easily, and when she did they usually tired of trying to convince her to come out. Alma always had an excuse why she was staying home for the night, and eventually the new friend would stop calling.

There was always Paul.

She looked at his icon on the phone. He had a wide, beaming smile and a stoner's eyes. "Fuck it." She tapped his icon and waited, half hoping he wouldn't answer.

"Yo," he answered with a lethargic greeting.

"Paul?"

"Alma? Holy shit." She heard covers rustle and assumed he was in bed. "To what do I owe the honor?"

"Paul," she sighed, regretting this already. "I need your help."

"You got it, babe. What's up?"

Alma had a mixed reaction to his voice. His lounging baritone, each syllable drawn out as if he savored them all, caused an equal amount of disgust and adoration in her. While their past convinced her to hate him, she couldn't help but love him a little.

"I need a place to stay."

He didn't answer.

"Paul?"

"Yeah?"

"Did you hear me?"

"Yeah, yeah, sure. I heard you. Just, you know, thinking about it." He sighed and she could hear him scratching at his scalp like he always did when conflicted.

"Never mind." Alma was annoyed and ready to hang up.

"You can stay here, Alma," said Paul. "You're always welcome, you know that. It's just that, well, you need to know that I'm not alone here. You know what I mean?"

"You've got a roommate now?" asked Alma.

He paused for a telling second before saying, "Sort of."

She understood what he meant, and didn't know how to respond. "Maybe I'll just get a hotel."

"You don't have to," said Paul. "You can stay here if you want."

"No," said Alma. "Don't worry, I'll be fine."

Alma and Paul had been together long enough for him to become familiar with the underlying meaning of certain phrases. Every couple develops passive aggressive mannerisms, and Alma was as guilty of it as anyone else. Paul knew that when she said, 'I'll be fine,' it really meant anything but that. And if Alma were being honest with herself she would admit that she deliberately used that tone to stoke Paul's compassion. It wasn't that she wanted to guilt him into helping her, but rather that she needed him to hear how hurt she was that he was sleeping with another girl. Even though they'd broken things off, for the third time, six months ago, Alma still hadn't moved on and the revelation that he had was agonizing. Six months was far too long to dwell on a failed relationship, but Paul and Alma had kept in contact over the break, and she always thought they would end up together again. It was agonizing to find out that Paul felt differently.

She could hear him push the covers off as he got up. "Babe, stop being silly. If you need help, I'm here for you. What's going on?"

"I just need a place to sleep for the night."

He chuckled. "Yeah, sure, and I'm the first person you call? Come on, Alma, don't treat me like I'm an idiot. What's the matter?"

"You weren't the first person I called." She had a spiteful bite to her words. "I literally called everyone else I could before I called you."

He stayed quiet, and Alma felt bad for attacking him.

"Look, I'm sorry," said Alma. "I've had a crappy day."

She heard his beard scratch on the phone and then a beer bottle hiss as it was opened. The cap clinked on the counter and she could imagine the scene, his kitchen littered with bottles, some upright and others overturned, and a seared pan on the stove, probably filled with burned macaroni. He was always a mess when they weren't together.

"Door's open," he said callously. "You know the address." Then his tone softened and Alma could tell that he was sorry for being gruff with her. "If you want my help, I'll always be here for you. I didn't mean to sound nasty, I've just had a long day. A buddy of mine got in some trouble and I've been trying to help him out. It's a long story." He groaned and Alma could hear his beard scratching on the receiver again. "I want you to come here, Alma. I've been meaning to call you, but just haven't worked up the courage. Come to my place and I'll help you with whatever you need."

"You've been working up the courage to call me by banging some girl?" asked Alma.

"It's complicated," said Paul.

"I'm sure it is."

His voice lowered and he spoke quickly, "Look, babe, I want you here. The door'll be open."

He hung up.

She looked down at her phone in shock, as if he'd cursed at her. "You asshole." She tossed the phone onto the passenger seat and then stared up at her apartment as if the conversation might've given her strength to attempt to go home, if for no other reason than to avoid giving Paul the satisfaction of seeking his help.

She grinded her grip on the top of her steering wheel as she looked up at the swirling bugs in front of her apartment door. If her father was going to hide, where would he do it? She looked at the shadows that plagued the space between her car and the apartment door. He could've been in the bushes along the building's façade, or on the other side of a stairwell, faced away from the parking lot and out of her line of sight. Maybe he was already in the apartment. He could've lied to the office, and showed them his license to prove he was her father, convincing them that he was here to surprise his daughter. He could be in there right now, hiding.

Had she left the bedroom light on?

It was on now. She could see her bedroom window from the car. Had she left the light on this morning? She often did, but how could she be sure? What if it was him? What if he was in her room, searching through her drawers, planning his assault? He couldn't have gotten here before her, could he? What if he did?

"Nope." She yelled out as if celebrating her decision not to chance fate. She put the car in reverse and sped out of the complex's lot, a chill running down her spine the whole way as if she'd just barely escaped with her life. Whenever she finally decided to come home, she wouldn't be alone.

Alma intended to go to a hotel, but she passed them all on her way to Paul's. His studio apartment was in the city, in a neighborhood that was in the midst of a planned renewal. It was going to be called 'LoDo', standing for Lower Downtown, and city officials promised that the rejuvenation would attract new business. They hoped to push out what they called the 'unwanted element' and restore a sense of pride to the neighborhood.

Alma wondered what element Paul fell into.

His studio was above a tattoo parlor, and was accessed by a stairwell in the rear. She parked next to a row of Harleys beside the parlor and could hear the raucous music as soon as she turned off the car. Tattoo parlors often stayed open late to host parties, and this one was no exception. When she'd lived with Paul, they attended several of the bashes that the parlor's owner threw, and she had a couple lasting reminders of those nights on hidden parts of her body. It's hard to turn down a free tattoo when you're drunk.

"What the hell are you thinking, Alma?" she asked herself. "Don't do this. Just go to a hotel. Don't get out of the car."

She fiddled with the keys as they dangled from the ignition. The teddy bear keychain that Paul bought her on their first date, back in high school, spun from its chain.

"Fine."

She took the keys out and put them in her purse along with her phone before she got out and headed for Paul's door. She raced up the wooden stairs as if scared she might reconsider. She didn't have a coat, and the chilly night caused her arms to break out in goose bumps.

She stood in front of the simple white door, hesitant to go in. There was a new mat at her feet that read, 'Welcome.' She wondered when he bought that as she wiped her loafers on it.

Why did she wear such plain shoes to work every day? She looked at her drab outfit and thought about how nice Rachel looked at the restaurant. Alma needed to start dressing nicer. She was suddenly embarrassed that she had been filmed for a news program today. And now she was standing in front of Paul's apartment, dressed in clothes she should've thrown out years ago. The once purple top had faded to mauve and her jeans were worn out in all the wrong spots. Then a terrifying thought came to her that she hadn't considered before: What if his new girlfriend was here?

The door opened and Paul greeted her. "Hey beautiful." He glanced up and down, inspecting her. "You look good. Did you start jogging again?"

"Don't patronize me. I look like shit."

He rolled his eyes, sighed, and turned away from her. "Fine, whatever. You look like a washed up hag. Get in. It's cold."

Paul looked good. He was a big guy, both in height and width, but his weight was sexy. He lamented his former football physique, but she often tried to convince him that some girls liked hefty men, and she was one of them. He had a gut, but it wasn't a loose one. It was as if he were just a big, bulging muscle. His beard was trimmed down from its once bushy length, but was still thick, and he'd shaved his long hair down to stubble, revealing a head tattoo of a snake that she'd never known about. He had a tank top on and a pair of torn jeans that he hadn't bothered buttoning or zipping up all the way.

"I like your hair," said Alma as she walked in.

He rubbed his palm over the stubble. "Yeah? Thanks. I lost a bet."

Alma glanced around the impeccably clean apartment. She couldn't believe the sight, and knew that he hadn't been able to simply clean up in anticipation of her possible arrival. "What the hell is this?" she asked as she looked around. "Did you hire a maid or something?"

He rubbed his belly, which was a trait that she'd always loved about him. Every morning when he got out of bed he would stretch and his long arms would nearly touch the ceiling before he'd bring them back down to rub his stomach. It was one of a thousand endearing traits that she recalled.

She knew she was falling back in the same old trap. Alma let this happen far too frequently, but even when she recognized the pattern she was helpless to avoid it. The comfort of familiarity was alluring. She recalled all of the things she loved about Paul, but none of what she hated.

Alma glanced around the studio apartment, relieved to see that Paul had asked his slut to leave.

"No. I've been trying to keep things nice around here. It hasn't been easy. You know how I am."

"Yeah, I do." The cleanliness was a nice change, but she felt oddly uncomfortable in the apartment that had once been her home away from home. It seemed somehow foreign now.

"Want a beer?" he asked, already headed to the corner of the studio where the kitchen was set behind a breakfast counter.

She nodded and walked with him while still surveying the changes in the apartment. A new flat screen television was mounted on the wall and had tall speakers one either side of it. There was a new coffee table, cherry wood with a glass center and metal legs, and the top of it wasn't littered with bottle caps and ashtrays like she would've expected. All of the changes were welcome ones, but she felt a pang of sorrow that she hadn't been around to see them. She would've preferred that Paul stayed exactly as he was the day she walked out, as if it was impossible for him to live without her.

When they got to the kitchen, Alma was almost sad to see that there wasn't a burned pan of macaroni on the stove. She felt like a mother visiting her son's new home for the first time, expecting disaster, only to discover that he didn't need her anymore.

"Here you go," he said after he popped the top off a Milk Stout Nitro and handed it to her.

"Glass?" she asked.

He smirked and winked. "That's my girl." He retrieved an extra tall pint glass from the cabinet and gave it to her.

This was their beer, and she knew how it was supposed to be poured. As opposed to most brands, this one needed to be hard poured. Instead of daintily tipping a glass to keep the head from exploding, this beer had to be overturned and plunged into the glass. It was a technique that they'd taught a hundred guests, and it had a noticeable effect on the flavor of this beer.

She took a long drink and then sighed in satisfaction. "I needed this. Thanks."

53

He put the two bottle caps in the garbage, which wouldn't have surprised anyone but her. In all their time together, she couldn't recall ever seeing him throw a bottle cap away instead of just tossing it onto the nearest surface.

"Are you going to tell me what's wrong?" he asked. "Or am I going to have to get you drunk first?"

She sat on a stool on the opposite side of the breakfast counter from him. "My dad showed up."

He stiffened and raised his eyebrows. "Oh shit. Really?"

She nodded and tilted her glass to watch as the foaming brown color of the beer slowly turned black. "Yep. He found me at a restaurant where I was meeting with a reporter."

"A reporter? What was that for?"

She smiled as she recalled the start of her day. "My school surprised me with a new music room, and the local news sent a reporter to cover it. They wanted to interview me, so I met up with them at the China Buffet on Fairmont."

"That's awesome, about the room and the reporter, not the buffet. That place sucks."

"I know, right? I hate that place." She smiled as she looked down at her beer. It was nice to be with Paul. They understood each other, which was a comfort she direly needed. "All in all, I was having a pretty great day until Dad showed up. Turns out the reporter had interviewed him in Pittsburgh…"

Paul interrupted her, "Why?"

While the two of them had shared a lot, she'd never revealed anything about her history with the Widowsfield incident. "They were, I don't know, doing a story on the king of assfucks or something. Doesn't matter. The point is: He followed them to me."

Paul drank his beer and stared at her over the rim. She could see by his expression that he sensed she wasn't telling him the whole story. When he lowered the glass there was foam on his mustache.

He wiped his mouth on his arm. "Want me to beat his ass?"

"No. I already had a guy do that for me. Now there's a Dad-sized dent in the side of my car."

Paul frowned and his eyebrows sunk as if he were scowling, but his menace was comedic as he asked, "Who do you have beating up guys for you? I'm supposed to be the one protecting you."

"Yeah, well you've been busy porking bar sluts." She thumbed in the direction of the nearby queen bed that Paul had made up in an attempt to hide what had occurred there just hours before.

"Hey," he said as if offended, "don't call my hand a bar slut. She's a fine lady." He wiggled his fingers.

"Gross."

He ignored her condemnation. "I know you and your dad have a bad relationship, but is he dangerous?"

"Uh, yeah," she said as if he should've known.

He shrugged. "I don't know, you never told me the details. You just said he was a dick, and that you never wanted to see him again."

"And I don't."

"Do you have a restraining order or anything like that?"

She shook her head. "No. My mom moved us back here where she grew up. I moved in with my grandparents after my mom…" She was surprised by the grief that swelled from the mention of her mother's passing.

"I gotcha," said Paul to end the conversation and spare Alma the pain of recounting any more. "Maybe you should think about getting one now."

"Could I? I'm not sure I've got enough against him to warrant it. Hell, I hurt him more than he hurt me at the restaurant."

"Still might be worth looking into."

She nodded and took another drink. "Maybe. For now, I just want to stay as far away from him as I can. I'm afraid he's going to show up at my place or something."

"Hey, if you want, I can go round up some of the guys downstairs and we'll take you home. If the fucker shows up, we'll make sure he never does again."

"Yeah, sure," she said sarcastically. "That's the answer. We'll just beat him to death and bury him in a shallow grave. That's a good idea."

He tilted his head to the side as if convinced it was a good idea. Then he laughed and shrugged like he'd meant it as a joke all along. "I didn't say anything about killing him, just hurting him a little."

"I didn't come here to hire a hitman."

"Well, while we're on the subject, why did you come here?"

"I guess I just wanted to be somewhere that I felt comfortable," said Alma. "Although it's kind of weird here now. It's all so different. In a good way, but different." She drank her beer and scanned the apartment.

"You know my offer still stands, right?"

"What offer?" she asked.

His shoulders sunk and he sighed, tired of playing this game. "You know what offer. I'll always take you back. If you want me, I'll drop whatever else I've got going on for you." He looked away as if embarrassed, crossed his arms, and leaned against the counter on the other side of the kitchen. "I wish it weren't true, but it is. No matter how many times you break my heart, you're still my girl, for as long as you want to be."

"Stop it," said Alma. His confession was everything she wanted to hear, and she felt her ears flush as blood rushed to her face.

"I'll always love you like a new favorite song."

She loved it when he said that, and he knew it. He grinned at her, and if it weren't for her conflicted emotions she would've hopped over the counter and torn his clothes off right then. Instead she cleared her throat and said, "I have to go to the bathroom."

"You know where it is."

Alma finished her beer and then headed for the bathroom, a tiny room that was the only private spot in the apartment. It had only a shower, toilet, and sink in it, and all three were jammed as close to one another as possible. She marveled at the cleanliness of the room as she closed the door and stared into the mirror.

"Don't do this, Alma," she whispered to herself. "I can't believe you're going to do this." She set her purse on the counter to search for her lipstick and perfume before doing her best to fix her makeup. "This is stupid." She repeated the phrase over and over as she went through her routine, applying mascara, foundation, and even a pinch of glitter between her breasts. She winked at herself in the mirror and said, "You're such a slut." She was almost giddy, and couldn't help but smile. The on-again-off-again nature of her relationship with Paul was torture most of the time, except for when they were just about to kick things off again. In these moments it felt like she'd just started dating someone, but without the nervous tension that led up to having sex for the first time.

She stopped and stared into the mirror. "Do you really want this, Alma? Are you sure?" She thought about it, and then smiled as she nodded. "Yes I do." She snapped the button closed on her purse, confident in her decision to rekindle her relationship with Paul, if even for just one night.

Alma lifted the toilet cover to pee.

There was a used condom floating in the bowl.

CHAPTER 4 - Doors

Widowsfield
March 14th, 1996

"Well look at you two," said the paunchy waitress at the Salt and Pepper Diner. Her red hair was curled and a pair of sunglasses was stuck in it as if she planned to leave work to enjoy the sunny day any moment now.

"Hi, Grace," said Desmond.

"Hi, Mrs. Love," said Raymond.

"Hi sweetie," Grace rubbed the boy's buzz cut as she walked up to their booth. "Now, isn't it a school day? What are you doing here now? Did school let out early or are you playing hooky?"

Desmond chuckled, slow and uncomfortably. He was a simple man, a mechanic at a garage a few miles out of town, and he lacked social graces. He wore all denim, with only a glimpse of the white t-shirt beneath his buttoned top. It was as if his entire identity revolved around his job, and even when not at work he strived to maintain a semblance of the uniform. "Well, Grace, I got Ray out early today. We're on our way to our cabin in Forsythe for a little fishing over spring break. Ray's been pretty excited about the trip. He didn't even want to stop for food, but I told him I wasn't hitting the road before stopping in to see our favorite waitress."

"Is that right?" she looked down at Raymond.

"Yes ma'am." Raymond was a sweet boy, but she wasn't sure if he was simple-minded like his father or not. They looked similar, with thick midsections and squat heads, noses that were pushed in and jowls that jutted forth, but Raymond's bright blue eyes were a defining attribute that contrasted his father's beady black ones.

Grace tapped her order pad with a pencil and smirked at Desmond. "You two aren't planning on getting into any trouble, are you? You'd better not be cheating on me with some strumpet out there, Desmond." Grace often chided him as if they were an old married couple. Her husband hated how flirtatious she was with patrons, but he was half a state away at a trade show and she needed the tips.

Both Desmond and Raymond chuckled in an identical manner. Grace adored these two, and had known them for years. It was easy for Desmond's mannerisms to make people uneasy when they first met him. His disability wasn't immediately identifiable, which made people nervous around him. However, given time he always proved to be a caring, kind man. Nothing was more important in his life than his son, and he exemplified that with every waking moment. Grace rarely saw the two separated, and they were frequent customers at the Salt and Pepper Diner.

Desmond also had a daughter, who was older and had fallen in with a bad crowd. She was often a source of angst for Desmond, and was well known throughout town for her drug habit. Desmond, who had inherited a large sum when his parents passed, had bought his daughter a cabin in town to try and keep her near him, but their relationship had crumbled over recent years. Grace thought that the way Desmond doted on Raymond was as recompense for his lost daughter.

"Don't worry," said Desmond. "There's no one for me but you, Gracie. Right, Ray?"

"Yes, sir."

"All right," said Grace as she eyed them both suspiciously. "I'll take your word for it. But you'd better keep an eye on him for me." She pointed the eraser side of her pencil at Raymond as she talked about Desmond. "He likes to pretend to be a good boy, but you and I know the truth. Don't we?"

Raymond snickered and nodded. "Yes ma'am."

"What's it going to be today?" asked Grace, ready to write down their order. "Same as always?"

Desmond nodded. "I'll have the Salisbury steak, and Ray will have the BLT."

"Actually," said Raymond, "could I get the grilled chicken sandwich?"

Grace looked over at Desmond, surprised at Raymond's order. "Well, heavens to hogs, the boy's changing things up on us, Dezy."

Desmond looked nervous. "I guess so. His taste buds must be changing or something."

"No," said Raymond. "I just want to try something new."

"Juan's going to have to throw the chicken on the grill, so it might take a few extra minutes," said Grace. "I'm happy to have you around as long as you'll stay, but I know you're in a hurry to get fishing."

"That's okay," said Raymond as he glanced out the window beside their booth. "We're too late already. It's past three. I want to try something different this time."

"You got it, kiddo," said Grace. "Want fries with that? Or are you going to throw me for another loop and order coleslaw?"

Raymond shook his head and chuckled. "No, ma'am. Fries would be fine. Thank you."

"Sodas for both of you?" asked Grace.

They nodded.

"All right, boys. Back in a minute." She sauntered off and stuck her pencil behind her ear. Two plates were already set in the ready window between the counter and the kitchen, under the heat lamps. One was a Salisbury steak and the other a BLT. Grace tapped her palm on the shelf and her rings clattered on the metal, alerting the chef.

"What's up, Gracie?" asked Juan as he scraped the grill.

"The kid wants a chicken sandwich, not a BLT."

Juan set the metal scraper on the edge of the flat grill and walked to the window. "No shit?"

Grace stuck her ticket on the clip wheel above the divide and spun it for him. It was the only ticket on the wheel and he snatched it away to look it over. "What do you know about that?"

"Times they are a changing," said Grace.

Juan looked as if he was about to respond, but then stared at something over Grace's shoulder. "What the heck?"

Grace turned to see what he was looking at. The street outside had been blanketed by a green fog. It was as thick as smoke and wafted over the street as if made of liquid. "Holy hell," said Grace.

"Do you know what that is?" asked Juan. "A fire or something?"

"Not sure, but I saw something like this once. Back when I lived in Gary, Indiana, there was a junkyard that caught fire and all the tires burned up; sent a big cloud of green smoke over the whole damn place. Dollars to donuts the old Sanchez yard caught fire."

A blast of green electricity rippled across the air outside, sticking to light poles and dancing along the edge of a UPS truck down the road. The fog billowed and puffed, encompassing more of the view every second.

Juan cursed and then said, "That's no tire fire."

Dogs barked and small shadows raced through the fog, as if children were running by. "What in the blazes?" asked Grace as she stared out into the thickening mist.

"Call the cops," said Desmond as he walked with his son toward the front of the restaurant.

"Yeah," said Grace. "Juan, get the police."

"I don't have no phone back here. You call from out there."

"God dang it, Juan, the phone's two feet from you." Grace walked behind the counter to the white phone beside the door that led to the kitchen. Juan stayed in his window, staring at the bizarre scene on the street. She dialed 9-1-1 and then waved at Desmond and Raymond to come stand by her. "Get over here you two, behind the counter."

"What do you think's going on?" asked Desmond as he held his son's hand and walked around the counter to join

Grace. There was a black rubber matt on the ground that was perforated to keep the area behind the counter from getting slippery, but Desmond still slipped on its greasy surface as he walked over it. His palm thudded on the counter as he caught his balance.

Grace shrugged as she listened to the pre-recorded message from the Widowsfield Emergency Services. "Hell if I know. Probably just some prank or something."

"Prank?" Juan's skepticism came off as rude and demeaning. "Get real, girl. That's no prank."

"Well, darn it Juan, stop just standing around," said Grace. "Do something to help."

"Help with what?" he asked, still standing uselessly behind the window between the kitchen and front end.

"Lock the dang doors or something."

"Shit," he said as if she were being funny. "I'm not going near that door. Looks like the devil farted pure hell out there."

"I'll get it," said Desmond.

Grace grinned at him and then turned to sneer at Juan. "Thanks, Dezy. At least we've got one man in here."

Desmond let go of his son's hand to head for the door, but heard Raymond begin to rustle the silverware beneath the counter. He saw his son rummaging through the steak knives.

"It's all right, kiddo," said Desmond. "There's nothing to be scared of."

Raymond held two knives, one in each hand, and looked up calmly at his father. "Yes there is."

"Darling," said Grace as she moved beside Raymond. "There's nothing to be worried about." She stood behind the boy and held him up against her waist with her hands crossed over his chest as she kept the phone perched between her shoulder and her ear. "I'm sure it's just a freak storm or something. Nothing to be scared about. Okay? Nothing to be scared about." She was clearly terrified.

"Then why lock the doors?" asked Raymond in a near whisper. They all knew there was something worth fearing in the mist. It was as if there was an innate knowledge bubbling to the surface in all of them.

Desmond spoke over his shoulder as he walked to the door, "Juan, if there's a back door you should go lock it."

"Yeah, Juan," said Grace. "Stop being a useless turd and go lock the back door."

Desmond turned the lock and Raymond pulled out of Grace's arms as he screamed, "Dad, get down!"

"What?" Desmond turned, perplexed.

A brick flew at the front door from out of the fog. The glass shattered and the brick struck Desmond in the back of the head as shards crashed down around him. He staggered as Juan screamed. The cook's voice was higher than a man of his girth should possess. Grace dropped the phone and tried to grab Raymond, but the boy was too fast for her. He bounded around the counter, still holding the steak knives, to save his father.

The brick had broken the upper half of the entrance, and the mist surged in through the hole. Shards of glass broke and fell as the mass moved in, as if the mist carried weight with it. Desmond was on his knees as the crackling green electricity zapped on the metal door behind him. The silhouettes of children in the mist focused on the Salt and Pepper Diner. Dogs barked and growled as the children rushed toward the restaurant.

"Ray!" Grace cried out for the boy, but didn't know how else to react. She was dazed, terrified, and frozen in place. The phone at her feet continued to ask for her patience; her call would be answered in the order it was received.

Desmond crawled toward the counter, and held the back of his bloodied head. Raymond ran past him, into the surging mist. He swiped his knives through the incorporeal mass and the blades sparkled with green electricity.

"Ray," said Desmond. "Get away from there."

63

"Sorry, Daddy. I'm fighting back this time." Raymond stood defiant in the mist, his knives held out at either side as the swirling vapor pooled at his feet.

The children on the street reached the windows, but the fog was too thick to see their faces. It looked as if the diner had been plunged into a tank of cloudy water. Grace saw mangled, bloody hands pressed against the glass. Blood smeared as the broken, twisted fingers scratched at the windows. She saw a dog's snout appear where one of the children's heads should be.

The shadows of children crowded in front of the diner, but one tall man stood among them. He was impossibly thin, and his arms draped longer than seemed natural. His head shuddered, and Grace could hear the chatter of teeth as he approached. He stood in front of the broken door, but Raymond blocked his entrance. Green light burned behind the crowd, and their shadows danced on the walls.

"No," said Raymond.

Grace felt her throat tighten as the mist began to fill the diner. It was cold and dry. When it brushed against her skin it felt like a bed sheet was covering her. She swiped at it, but it thickened and wrapped around her limbs. She glanced back at Juan, but didn't see the cook through the divide.

"I won't do it," said Raymond as if conversing with the thin man in the mist, though Grace didn't hear any response.

The thin man came closer, and his shoulders rose as his arms bent. She couldn't see anything more than his silhouette, but knew he was threatening the boy. Raymond turned, tears in his eyes, and stared at his father.

"The Skeleton Man wants your eyes, Daddy."

Desmond croaked, but Grace couldn't see him. She was trapped behind the counter as the mist thickened around her. She tried to break free, but it constricted her from all angles. When she tried to speak, her voice was lost, just like Desmond's.

Juan's high pitched screams erupted from the back room. He never did lock the back door, and Grace listened to the sound of dogs growling as they tore him apart. She didn't have to see to understand what was happening as the dogs fought over his flesh.

Raymond's knives reflected the green, electric light as he knelt down, out of Grace's view, to slaughter his father. She could see Raymond's face, crying and whimpering, as he dug the knife in. Desmond's legs twitched, but the fog held him down.

"I'm so sorry," said Raymond over and over as the blood squirted from the incisions. He stood up and tried to wipe his brow clean on his arm, but just smeared the blood worse. He set his knives on the counter and walked around as Grace watched, helplessly restrained by the tendrils of mist.

Raymond glanced at her, but then looked away as if ashamed. He took a spoon from the silverware cup under the counter and then returned to his father. Grace didn't understand what he was doing until she heard the grotesque sound of Raymond scooping his father's eyes out of his skull. The wet sound was bad enough, but when the spoon collided with the back of Desmond's eye socket it caused a scraping sound that sent reverberations of fear through Grace. She convulsed, her knees weakened, and she flopped into the mist as if passing out, but was still held aloft.

Raymond tossed two fleshy lumps into the mist and The Skeleton Man greedily bent to search the ground for them. The monster laughed as he retrieved the eyeballs, and his chattering teeth quickened their pace.

"That doesn't make you my Daddy," said Raymond under his breath. His hands were shaking as he set the spoon on the counter, beside the two bloody knives.

Then the boy hung his head as his shoulders slunk. He turned, regretfully, and breathed deep when he looked up at Grace. "He'll let me make it quick."

Grace couldn't respond.

Raymond seemed to be apologizing by the way he looked at her, forlorn and saddened. "It'll only hurt for a minute." He picked up the steak knife and walked around the counter.

16 Years Later
March 9th, 2012

"What did I do?" asked Paul.

"Just, don't," said Alma as she headed for the door. She held her hand up to keep Paul from touching her as she looked away from him. The sight of him sickened her.

"For Christ's sake, Alma, two minutes ago you were all smiles. Now you're treating me like a jerk. What'd I do?"

"More like who'd you do?" she said.

"What's that supposed to mean?"

She glared at him and then flipped him off. "Learn to flush the toilet, asshole."

That helped him understand why she was angry. He pinched the bridge of his nose and shook his head. "Fucking low pressure toilet."

"Have a good life." Alma opened the door.

Paul walked behind her and put his hand on the door to stop it from opening all the way. "Hold up, Alma. You don't have the right to be mad at me for this."

"Excuse me?" She was furious with him for trying to defend himself.

"You're the one that walked out on me."

"Yeah, and I'm about to do it again. Go ahead and call up your bar sluts. Tell them the party's back on." She forced the door open and a gust of cold air stung her eyes, drawing forth tears that had been threatening to come anyhow.

"Alma, what about your dad? Are you going home? Come on, babe, don't be like this." He walked onto the deck with her as she rushed to leave. "God damn it."

She heard him go back inside and then come out again before shutting the door. He was barefoot and wore only a thin t-shirt, jeans, and no coat as he chased her into the gravel parking lot behind the tattoo parlor.

"What are you doing?" asked Alma. "Go back inside. I'm not going to talk to you anymore."

"Fine," he said from several steps behind. "I'm just going to follow you home to make sure your dad isn't there."

She stopped and glared at him in disapproval. "Oh sure, you're going to ride your bike with no shoes on. Go back inside and stop being an idiot."

"I'm not letting you go home alone. If I let something bad happen to you, I'd never forgive myself."

He stood ten feet away from her as they faced off in the lonely lot. The wind gusted again and she saw him shudder, looking pathetic as he stood in the sharp gravel, arms crossed over his thin shirt.

"Stop it, Paul. You're being ridiculous. You can't ride your bike without shoes on, let alone without a coat or helmet. You're going to get pulled over."

He shrugged.

"Stop it."

"I'm not letting you go home alone."

She groaned. "Fine. Go get some shoes on at least."

"You promise to wait for me?"

"Yes, for crying out loud, you giant dork. I'll wait."

"Give me your keys."

"What?" asked Alma.

"Give me your keys so I know you won't take off before I get back."

"Paul, just go get some damn shoes on. There's broken glass all over out here."

"Okay, fine, just give me your keys first." He took a step towards her with his hand outstretched.

She glanced at the shards of glass mixed in with the gravel between them. She walked to Paul so he didn't have to cross it. She slammed her keys into his hand. "Hurry up. It's cold out here."

He lifted the keys and tapped the teddy bear keychain. "Glad to see you kept him."

"Only because I'm too lazy to get rid of him."

67

Paul grinned. "Liar."

"Whatever. Hurry up." She crossed her arms and leaned against the side of her car. She wasn't wearing a coat and shivered in the chilly night air.

Paul ran up the stairs two at a time and Alma took the opportunity to examine the damage on the side of her car. Stephen had slammed her father into the side door with enough force to leave a sizeable dent. She should've called her insurance immediately, but she didn't want to be forced to be around her father any longer than she had to. She feared that if a police report was filed, her father would be given an opportunity to be a part of her life again. As silly as it sounded, even seeing his name on a police report was more contact with him than she wanted. It was better to keep him out of her life entirely.

Unfortunately, the car was leased, and she would have to get it fixed, which would be expensive. Her deductible was $500, and her bank account was already dangerously close to zero.

"Crap," she said in frustration as she passed her palm over the damage. Then she caught sight of a girl standing on the corner, next to the tattoo parlor. She was smoking a cigarette and staring at Alma. She glanced away, pretending not to have been watching.

The girl was young, thin, and pretty. She had dark hair that was bobbed, and bright red lipstick. Her breasts were too large for her blouse, which was probably on purpose, and her jean skirt was short enough to reveal most of her long legs.

Alma didn't need to ask to understand who she was. This was the girl Paul had just kicked out of his bed. Alma knew it by the look of jealousy in the girl's eyes.

All of the hatred Alma felt for Paul was transferred to this innocent stranger. She hated the bitch.

Paul closed his door, drawing Alma's attention away from the pretty stranger. He bounded down the stairs, his leather boots clopping on the wood, and then threw the keys to Alma. She caught them, which was a minor miracle, and got in her car as Paul got on his bike.

Alma's radio was too loud, like always, and she quickly turned it down as she watched the pretty girl approach Paul. He was dismissive, and Alma watched while pretending not to. They spoke for a moment, but Paul started his bike to drown out what the girl was saying. It was an annoying move of his that he had done to Alma several times in the past when he didn't want to argue anymore. The girl scowled and swiped a cigarette out of Paul's mouth before walking away. Alma enjoyed a petty victory and couldn't help but smile as she backed her car out of the lot.

Paul followed close behind as she headed home. Through the entire trip, Alma continued to look at Paul in her rearview. It seemed ridiculous that she'd driven to his apartment, only to return home with him behind her, planning to let him go back home again after. She thought about turning around, and going back to his apartment, but then she recalled the condom in the toilet. She couldn't sleep in a bed that stank of sex, especially not after seeing the slut he'd been with.

The entire night was dizzying. The reporter's interest in her past dragged her back into thoughts she'd been trying to forget. The confrontation with her father played out similar to how so many of their fights had before. And now the argument with Paul was happening just as it had so many times in the past. She felt like she was caught in a spiral, swirling around again and again, revisiting the mistakes of her past over and over. It was impossible to break free.

The last three digits of the license plate on the car ahead of her were 314.

She stared at the number and her heart quickened. That damn number showed up everywhere. It haunted her.

Stephen had mentioned the number before she raced away from the restaurant. He knew about Chaos Magick, and she assumed he understood the significance of the number as a symbol or else he wouldn't have brought it up.

Alma had been introduced to the belief system known as Chaos Magick by her mother. After Alma's brother disappeared, her mother became obsessed with the date. She would hide the number, or the symbol for pi, around the house, claiming it was the only way they'd ever know the truth about what happened to her boy. Alma would wake up to find her mother drawing the number in permanent marker on Alma's body. She would insist that they all focus on the symbol to help bring her son home.

The car ahead turned down a side street, and Alma was relieved that the number was out of her sight again. It brought pain with it, every time she saw it. When she could forget the number she was at peace, but then it would return, forcing her to recall the details of the worst day of her life. Not only did the number's relation to pi represent a circle, but her emotions revolved around it in a cyclical manner as well. No matter how far she thought she could get from that date, it always returned.

Alma got home, with Paul behind her. It had only been a half hour since she left and she stared up at the bugs that gathered around the light outside of her apartment.

"Back again," she said, feeling somewhat helpless.

The bugs swirled around the light, smacking into it and then retreating, sometimes stopping on the wall, but always returning; always smacking into the light and spinning around, like planets in orbit around the sun, over and over. The dance defined their lives. They couldn't get away from it.

Paul tapped on her window with his keys, frightening her. She didn't realize she'd been staring at the door long enough for him to get off his bike and approach.

"You scared the crap out of me," she said as she got out.

"You all right?" he asked. "You've been sitting here staring at the door for awhile."

She nodded and locked her car. "Yeah, sorry, I was just thinking. You didn't need to come, Paul, honestly. I feel bad that you had to leave your friend for this."

"Shush. Like I said, you're my girl, whether you like it or not."

She grimaced as she headed down the concrete walkway to her apartment building. "That sounds kind of creepy."

"Yeah, I guess it does. Maybe you've been right all along, I am a creep."

She paused on the walkway and looked up at her apartment. "I'm too tired to fight anymore. I just want to go to bed. I just want this day to be over."

"Good news," said Paul as he looked at his watch. "It's tomorrow already. Fresh start."

"Is it really that late?" Alma could see between the concrete stairs into the darkness beyond. How easy would it be to hide in the shadows and wait, ready to reach through the slats and grab a victim's ankle? She let Paul go up first.

"I'll help you get to sleep," said Paul.

"You're not coming in."

He was frustrated with her insistence. "Like hell I'm not. At the very least I'm going in to make sure it's safe before you kick me out."

"I didn't ask you to come, Paul." She walked up past him, embarrassed that a moment before she'd allowed herself to rely on him for security. "I just want to go to bed. Go home, Paul."

He shook his head and followed her up.

The bugs swarmed around her face as she forced her key into the cantankerous deadbolt. It stuck frequently, leaving her stranded, trying to force the key in while the bugs swirled around her head. This time the lock opened easily, but the door was stuck in its frame. She had to slam it with her shoulder to get in.

Paul tried to follow, but she pushed him back.

"Seriously, Paul. I appreciate you coming here, but I don't want you in my apartment." It wasn't as clean as his, and she avoided turning on the living room light to keep him from seeing the mess.

He tried to look in over her shoulder, oblivious to the mess and hoping to make sure there wasn't a man lurking in the dark. "Just let me have a look around."

She put her hand on his chest and pushed him back the one step he'd dared to take into the apartment. He looked hurt by the gesture, but relented and moved back. "Go home," she said, and it felt like she was breaking up with him again.

Alma closed the door on Paul.

She couldn't help but cry, and covered her mouth to keep him from hearing through the door. She put her back against the door and slid down until she was sitting on the tile entryway. She pulled her knees up to her chest and cried as she curled up. She started to hum to calm herself, and then looked down the hall at her bedroom.

The bedroom light was on.

The hallway from the apartment's entrance led straight to the master bedroom on the other side. The living room was to the right, with a porch that looked out onto the parking lot, and the kitchen was to her left. The bathroom was down the hall to the left, with a guest room on the right filled with junk she'd never gotten around to unpacking. Straight ahead, down the carpeted hall that led away from the tiled entryway that she sat on, was the closed door of her bedroom, and light shone from beneath it.

Her father could be in there.

She remembered one night, before her brother disappeared, when she came home to find the light on in her bedroom. She was six, and had been playing at a friend's house. There were several bizarre details about that night that stuck in her mind, like how the taste of chocolate raspberries that her friend's mother had made for them was still in her mouth when she came home. She recalled an odd smell that she couldn't identify in her house, similar to what the home smelled like when the oven was set to self clean. There was a spider in the corner, and she walked to the side of the hall away from it, beside her brother's door, on her

72

way to her room. She recalled the feel of the carpet between her toes, and the trail of wetness that went from the bathroom all the way to her room.

Alma didn't suspect anything at the time, and casually strolled to her room, more frightened of the spider than anything else. She ran the last few steps and was relieved when she opened her door and escaped into her room. That's where her father was waiting.

He was nude, wet from the shower, and sprawled out on her twin bed, over the Animaniacs bedspread. He sat bolt upright when she walked in and just stared at her, as if terrified. His eyes were wide, and the whites were nearly awash in red, drowning his black pupils in crimson.

"You," he said and then stared at her.

"Daddy?" she was terrified of him for the first time in her life. He was supposed to be away, on a business trip in Missouri. "What's wrong?"

He stayed in the same position, staring at her, and didn't bother to cover himself. His hair hung in long black, wet strands to his shoulders. He smelled strongly of soap, as if he'd lathered and never rinsed.

"Would you miss me?" he asked finally and then, after a pause, added, "If I were in heaven?"

"What? Of course, I would."

He stared at her, expressionless and silent, for a terrifying moment. Then he said, "Liar," before falling back on the bed.

Alma left to go sleep in her brother's room, but she couldn't recall anything else from that night. In fact, she didn't remember much about her brother at all these days.

She stared down the hallway of her apartment. The door at the end of the hall beckoned her, and she wondered if the floor would be wet between her room and the bathroom.

Alma considered sleeping on the tile entryway. She almost laid down and curled up within the small area, as if it could somehow protect her, but recognized how ridiculous she was being. She stood up, kicked off her loafers, and

73

walked to the kitchen to get a knife from the drawer. Then she took out her cell phone and dialed 9-1, prepared to dial the final digit.

She walked down the hall and didn't breathe the entire way. When she got to the door, she listened against it for any sign of life on the other side.

Finally, she swung the door open to reveal absolutely nothing to be afraid of. She gasped and was nearly relieved, but searched the closet first. Then she walked to the spare bedroom, bathroom, and kitchen pantry to make sure she'd checked everywhere. She was safe. Her father wasn't in the apartment.

She tucked her phone back into her purse in an attempt to keep from losing it, which she often did. Then she closed her eyes and felt an overwhelming exhaustion.

Alma returned to her bedroom and set the kitchen knife on her nightstand, beside the alarm clock. The red numbers displayed the time, 12:14.

She fell back onto her pillows and set her hands over her eyes, exhausted and thankful for a new day. Perhaps this day would go better than the last.

As she tried to relax, she couldn't help but do the math in her head. It was 12:14. One plus two is three. 314.

She turned the clock away from her.

CHAPTER 5 - Recurring Nightmare

Widowsfield
March 14th, 1996

"I don't know what's wrong," said Anna as she looked out of the library window. "Maybe there's a low pressure system coming through or something."

The school's library looked out onto the field that separated Ozark Hills High from its sister school, Widowsfield Elementary. There was a gym class playing soccer and Anna looked for her ex-boyfriend, Clint, who had broken up with her two weeks ago because he wanted to be single for a while. His bachelorhood lasted two days before he started dating the captain of the swim team, Clarissa Belmont.

"Oh yeah, sure thing, Banana," said Jamie. Anna despised that nickname. "You're staring out the window at the football field because you're a budding meteorologist and not because Clint's out there. How stupid do you think I am?"

"I'm serious, I've got a headache and my dad said that weather patterns can cause them."

Jamie gave a sideways glance away from her Social Studies book as she frowned. "Sure."

"Don't be a bitch. I'm not stuck on Clint. He can go fuck himself for all I care."

Jamie folded the book cover's inside flap, made from a brown paper bag from the grocery store, over her page and then closed the book. "Then what's up? For real. You've been in the dumps since the dickhead dumped you. That's not like you, Banana. You're the most fun girl I've ever hung out with, but you've been a total downer lately."

Anna scribbled her black pen in one of the spots on her book cover that had previously been adorned with Clint's initials enshrined in a heart. She'd blackened out the picture,

75

and now the paper bag cover was dangerously thinned. She didn't doubt that her pen marks had managed to cut through the cover to deface the textbook, but she continued to scribble the circles anyhow.

"I'm not going to lie, I mean, I was pretty pissed at him, but it's not like we haven't done this before. You know? We're always, like, breaking up and getting back together again. It's sort of our thing. It's like I have this need to be heartbroken or something."

"Then why do you keep going back to him?"

Anna sighed and shook her head. She knew that Jaime hated Clint, and had since grade school. In fact, most of Anna's friends disapproved of her relationship with the stoner. She was an Honor Roll Student, a member of the Mathletes, and all but guaranteed a scholarship to a major university. Clint, on the other hand, was the epitome of the 'C' student.

"I don't know. Maybe I've got a self-destructive personality or something."

"Yeah, ya' think?"

"Give me a break, Jamie." Anna set her pen down and put her head on her book. She worried that the fresh pen ink would stain her forehead, so she moved the book aside and then set her head down on the cold table.

"I'm just sick of you doing the same thing to yourself over and over. I'm sick of seeing you down like this."

"I told you, I'm not upset about Clint. Honestly. I've just got a really bad headache right now. I don't know why."

"I think I've got some aspirin in my locker. I can get you some after school if you want."

Anna nodded with her head still on the table. "That'd be great, thanks. What time is it?"

Jaime glanced back at the oversized clock above the library's main desk. "Not quite a quarter past."

Anna groaned and then sat up with her arms draped over her head as she arched her back over the edge of the seat. "This day's dragging on forever."

76

Jaime tapped her pencil on her book and looked like she was about to say something, but then decided not to. She set her chin on her hand and stared off at nothing.

"What?" asked Anna. Jaime looked surprised, as if she didn't know what Anna was asking about. "You were about to say something. What was it?"

"It's just that, well, I guess I just want to know why you do it. Why do you keep making the same mistake over and over again? You and Cunt, I mean Clit, I mean Clint," She smirked at her own joke. "You guys are a bad match."

"I guess I just hope he'll change; that the next time it'll be different."

"You know what the definition of insanity is, right? Doing the same thing over and over again and expecting something to change."

"Then call me crazy, I guess," said Anna. "Maybe I'll just take up drinking to calm me down."

Jaime rolled her eyes. "Alcohol's not the solution."

"Chemically speaking, any alcoholic beverage is a solution since the alcohol is mixed up with other stuff."

"Well shit," said Jaime as she started to scribble numbers onto her book's cover. "Break out the Boone's Farm then. Time to get the party started." They both laughed before Jaime mocked her friend. "You're such a nerd, 'Chemically speaking, blah, blah, blah.'"

"It's true," said Anna. "What are you writing?" She leaned over the table to look at Jaime's book.

Jaime looked down at her scrawling.

3.141592653

"Is that pi?"

"Yeah. We were supposed to memorize ten digits of it for Mr. Trager for pi day."

Anna settled back in her chair and snickered. "Sure, for the test this morning. Why are you still writing it?"

Jaime paused for just a moment. "I don't know. There's something calming about it. Is that crazy?"

"A little bit, yeah."

Anna watched Jaime write the sequence over and over, oddly transfixed. Then Jaime wrote the final digit as a 4 instead of a 3 in one line. "You got that one wrong."

Jaime didn't stop writing and didn't look up. "There's no such thing as a perfect circle. There's chaos in all of it." Jaime looked up at the ceiling and then at the window before she asked, "Do you hear that?"

"What?" Anna thought her friend's statement carried an undercurrent of malice. Then she looked down at her own book and saw that she was continuing to draw spirals in the spot where Clint's initials used to be. Her marking had worn well past the paper cover and was digging into the book itself. She dropped the pen and it spun in a circle on the table as if the tip was tied down, with the other end rolling awkwardly around.

Anna heard the chatter of teeth and put her hand over her lower jaw. The noise seemed to be coming from her own head, as if she were shivering but didn't know it. Her jaw wasn't moving, but the chatter continued.

"It's time," said Jaime. "It's starting over again."

"I know." Anna stood up and walked to the window that looked out onto the field. She put her right hand on the glass, her fingers splayed wide, and savored the cold sensation. Dogs howled in the distance and Anna took her hand away, letting her fingertips linger for a moment.

The chatter continued.

"How many times have we done this?" asked Jaime.

Anna knew exactly what she meant, but at the same moment didn't understand at all. It was as if she had wandered into a dream where she was certain everything made sense, but could never have explained it if asked to. She watched Clint on the field and wondered if he would die immediately, or if they would let him live this time.

"Too many to count," said Anna. She looked at the large white clock on the wall above the center desk in the library.

3:14

Her hands were shaking.

The chatter stopped.

"What's going on?" Jaime stood up, and her pencil stayed upright as if a ghost were holding it in place. They both stared at it and the pencil slowly tilted. It finally set down as if time around them was moving at a different pace than they were.

"Anna?" said Jaime as she stared out the window. A thick fog was descending over the field, rolling across their view as if a wave of water had broken free and was about to wash away the students. It sparkled with green light and billowed over the lush grass. It was beautiful to watch as the puffs of fog spread across the horizon. The bright blue sky was eaten away, like vestiges of white paper succumbing to flame. "We're lost."

Anna looked at her friend and nodded. "I know why."

Jaime rushed around the table to stand beside her. Anna felt dizzy and confused. "Why?" asked Jaime. "Tell me what you know."

"I forgot all of it, but now I understand." Anna looked out the window and watched as the gym students were enveloped in the thick fog. "It's like I heard him, or understood him, just for a minute."

"Heard who?"

"The one the kids call The Skeleton Man. He hates the name. He thinks giving something a name is the first attempt to control it."

"What the hell is going on? Why do I feel like I've done this before? What's happening?" asked Jaime.

"He thinks we're too old." She put her hand back on the window and looked across the field at the Middle School that was quickly disappearing amid the haze. "He wants the children. He thinks we already know how to hate, and he only wants the innocent ones."

"Anna, you're scaring me."

Anna watched the shapes in the fog advance. The silhouettes of children ran across the field from their school, and the barking of dogs grew louder. Soon, the soccer players were attacked and chaos erupted in the library. Teachers and students rushed to the window and time returned to normal as everyone panicked.

Jaime moved closer to Anna and ignored the massacre outside. "Why are we doing it again? Why do I know what's going to happen? I've never felt this way before."

"He checked on us this time," said Anna.

"What do you mean?"

The librarian yelled for everyone to get away from the window after an explosion of green light shook the walls. One of the students, a sophomore boy whose name Anna never learned, was stuck inside of the window and couldn't move away. His face had been pressed against the glass when the explosion occurred, and now his head was hanging halfway outside. The glass wasn't broken, but the boy's head was on the other side of it, as if he'd passed through a pane of water instead of glass. Anna saw the boy's eyes search frantically around him before he tried to jerk back. The movement caused his skin, which was fused to the glass, to rip. Blood coursed down the window on both sides as the other students screamed.

Jaime and Anna ignored the bloody scene; they'd seen it countless times before. Jaime pulled Anna between two book shelves, away from the screaming mass, to speak in private. "What do you mean he checked on us?"

"I don't know, I can't explain how I know. I'm not sure what's going on. I just, for a minute, I could hear him in my head. I knew his thoughts. He's looking for a girl he lost. She was an innocent, and he needs her to help him stop this from happening again."

"I don't understand any of that," said Jaime.

"I don't either, but I know he's going to keep doing this over and over until he finds her."

"Then what?" asked Jaime.

"I don't know. For some reason he thinks that if he has her, then he can make this perfect." She drew a circle in the air with the tip of her finger. "He'll complete the circle. Until then we'll keep dying. This will keep happening over and over."

"Why do I know about it this time?" asked Jaime. "I can remember all the other times this happened, and I never felt this way before."

They both stared through the books on the shelves at the chaos in the library. Students were crying as the teachers tried to overturn tables to keep the creatures in the fog from breaking through the glass. Anna knew it was useless. In minutes, the window would shatter and the demonic, twisted children would rush in. They were the children that The Skeleton Man gave up on. They became his soldiers, and their hatred mutated their fragile bodies into demonic, dog-like creatures.

She could hear their paws scratching at the windows.

"He searched us this time," said Anna. "He let us know him because he wants to find the one he lost. He doesn't know how long it's been, or how old she is now. If he can find her, then he can start this all over in a way that he's never done before. He let us know him the way the children do because he wants to find the girl he lost."

"I know her name," said Jaime.

Anna held her friend's hand as they continued to look through the books. "I do too."

Jaime said it, "Alma Harper."

The glass broke.

Jaime and Anna embraced as they waited for their inevitable death. Then it would begin anew, slightly different from the times before, and they would forget the prying mind of The Skeleton Man as he continued to try to complete the circle.

16 Years Later
March 10th, 2012

Alma was in her classroom and an oversized, ornate harp was beside her desk. The instrument's strings were black and thicker than they should've been.

"Miss Harper?" asked one of her students.

"Yes, Dave, what is it?"

Dave had his head on his desk and his arms draped at his sides. He didn't lift his head as he spoke. "Are you pretty?"

"Excuse me?" asked Alma.

Claire Powell, a popular, pretty girl that sat at the front of the class, raised her hand and wiggled her fingers in the air. She didn't wait for Alma to give her permission before she spoke. "He wants to know if you're ugly."

"What sort of question is that?" Alma's heart raced and she felt as if she'd been transported back to high school where social standing was a constant concern. She desperately wanted to be one of the pretty girls, but she wasn't. Llama Harper is what the kids used to call her and she never understood why. They used to cut out pictures of Llamas and tape them to her locker. It was the sort of careless bullying that provided short-lived amusement for the aggressors, and a lifetime of heartache and doubt for the victim.

"Your mouth is bleeding," said Dave, his head still down.

Alma put her hand over her mouth and felt wetness. She inspected her palm and discovered a smear of dark red blood. The children laughed as she searched in her drawer for a handkerchief, but there was nothing but pens inside the desk. She rifled through the hundreds of pens in search of anything that could clean her blood, but there was nothing to be found. The children continued to laugh.

"It's not funny," said Alma as she gave up her search. When she closed the drawer, it rattled as if there had been change inside.

The bell rang and frightened Alma. Her mouth was in pain now and the clanging of the bell seemed to aggravate her mysterious wound. The children sprang from their seats, gathered their things, and rushed for the door. They laughed as they passed Alma, furthering her embarrassment.

Alma went to the counter at the rear of the room where there were paper towels and a sink. There were craft supplies littering the area from the art class that used this room part of the time and Alma shoved the bottles of glue and glitter away. She cupped her hands to collect the cold water and splashed it on her face. The blood and water swirled around the stainless steel drain, but didn't seem to go down. It just kept spinning as the colors blended. Glitter, glue, and paint mixed with the blood and water to create a hypnotic spiral that wouldn't dissipate.

Alma took a few paper towels from beside the sink and put them into her mouth to search for the source of the blood. She felt her shoes sticking to the floor and wondered if the glue had spilled on her feet. Her attention flitted between concerns as the spilled glitter and glue dripped from the edge of the counter.

She felt stinging pain from one of her lower incisors. The tooth wiggled at the slightest provocation. Alma took the paper towel out of her mouth and started to press at the back of the tooth with her tongue. It bent forward until it brushed against the inside of her lip.

The tooth wiggled back and forth as she prodded it. Blood continued to pour out of her mouth as she gripped the tooth between her thumb and index finger. It took no effort to dislodge the incisor and she rinsed it off before inspecting it. The tooth looked normal and healthy, white with lengthy roots.

"Alma?" Blair Drexler, the head of the PTA, was at the door.

Alma swiftly hid the tooth in her front pocket and then rinsed more blood from her face. The water still swirled in the sink, refusing to go down the drain. She didn't turn to greet Blair and focused on the mess.

"Hi Blair," said Alma as she struggled to clean herself.

"Is everything okay?" Blair's high heels clicked on the tile as she walked toward Alma. Blair was an upper class housewife, always adorned with jewelry that was worth more than a month of Alma's pay.

"Fine, fine, I'm fine," said Alma as she tried to hide what had happened. She wiped the counter and tossed the bloody paper towel into the trash. Her blood smeared, as if it were made of oil. The glue and glitter were gone now, as if her blood had soaked it up.

Blair was at Alma's back. "We're all waiting for you."

Alma didn't turn, fearing that blood still stained her chin. "Waiting for me? Why?"

"It's time for your party. We can't do this without you."

Alma shook her head and got more paper towels to clean up with. "No, I'm not going. I can't. Sorry, but I'm just too busy right now."

"It's your party." Blair put her hand on Alma's shoulder.

Someone started to play the harp, which startled Alma. She glanced over to see the principal, Mrs. White, seated beside the massive golden instrument, strumming the black strings. The instrument seemed warped now, as if it had been slowly melting behind her back.

"Don't disappoint us," said Mrs. White. She plucked the strings and the sound they emitted was unnaturally low. Each note seemed to fade in and out as if Alma was moving closer to the source and then away again, over and over.

"Okay," said Alma. "I just need a little time. Maybe, like, ten minutes? Would that be okay?"

Blair looked perturbed, but nodded before walking away. Mrs. White got up from the seat beside the harp and met Blair at the door. Her hands were bloody, and Alma noticed that the instrument's strings were dripping wet now.

"We'll see you in the auditorium," said Blair.

Mrs. White looked at Alma before she left the room. The principal's teeth were chattering as she smiled and left.

Alma breathed a sigh of relief after they were gone and turned back to the sink. She set her hands on the counter and leaned forward. The water had finally disappeared, but the sink's drain catch was missing, leaving only a black hole at the bottom now. Alma leaned further forward to peer into the hole when she felt something fall past her open lips.

Another tooth clinked against the porcelain sink and spun around the basin. She tried to catch it, but the tooth fell into the hole before she could stop it.

Alma clapped her hand over her mouth as she felt another tooth begin to slip out of her gums. She whimpered as she searched her mouth with her tongue. The metallic taste of blood overwhelmed her as more teeth sprang free. The blood gagged her, and she wretched. She had no choice but to open her mouth, but she didn't want her teeth to fall into the drain. Alma stepped back and watched as blood and teeth fell from her mouth and hit the tile floor as if she were vomiting a macabre meal. She staggered to one of the student's desks and fell into the seat. Blood covered her blouse and one of her teeth was stuck between her sock and loafer. There was glitter in the blood on her hands.

Students laughed from the room's entrance. She looked over to see a crowd of children at the door.

"Get out of here!" She screamed at them. Blood and spittle trickled from her toothless gums.

They pointed and laughed.

A tall man stood behind them, shrouded by what appeared to be smoke in the hallway. She couldn't see any details about him except his wide, smiling mouth. His teeth chattered as the children bellowed with laughter.

Alma opened her eyes.

Her pillow was wet from sweat and she pushed it aside as she sat up. It was still dark outside and she put her hand over her mouth to reassure herself that it was just a dream. This was a familiar occurrence. She'd suffered from the recurring dream of her teeth falling out for nearly as long as she could remember. The circumstances of the dream often changed, but the setting was usually the same. It almost always happened in a school, with children laughing at her as the tall man in the shadows watched it all unfold. No one ever helped her.

Alma looked at the red LED display on the alarm clock beside her bed.

3:14

"Fuck you," said Alma as she reached out for the clock. She lifted it and paused a moment to calm herself. Her instinct was to throw it across the room, but that seemed childish. Instead, she decided just to pull the cord hard enough to unplug it, but when she tried the clock slipped from her hands and bounced off the edge of the bed to the floor. It landed with the time face up, blaring the reminder of her mother's insanity in bold, red light.

She groaned in embarrassment, thankful that no one was around to see her pathetic attempt to pull the plug. Alma lay back on her pillow and stared at the ceiling as she recalled the details of yet another of her recurring dreams about her teeth.

Alma stared at the ceiling, which was now illuminated by the red light of the clock on the floor. She was waiting for the color to flash, a sign that the time had changed. It would feel like a minor victory to wait for the minute to pass before putting the clock back on the nightstand. It was a ludicrous thought, and one she wouldn't like to admit to anyone, but it felt sane to her. Perhaps it was a symptom of OCD, but her mother's obsession with the date of Alma's brother's disappearance had turned into a curse.

The red light flickered on the ceiling.

Alma excitedly rolled to the side of the bed and stared down to see if the minute had passed yet. She felt like a child at Christmas, peeking down the stairs at her pile of presents.

3:14

"Mother fucker!" She threw the covers off and got out of bed. This time she would make sure the damn thing came out of the wall.

The number had defeated her, and she was furious. She would later say that her manic behavior was because of her lack of sleep and bad dreams, but in truth her battle with the ever-present number was all-encompassing at times. Alma gripped the clock in one hand while grabbing the cord with the other. She pulled it hard enough that the nightstand fell over as the cord whipped away from the wall. The kitchen knife that she'd placed beside the clock bounced on the carpet.

The clock's number faded away, but that didn't sate her. Alma threw the clock against the wall and it exploded into bits of plastic and pieces of electronics. She yelped as the shards flew back at her.

She started to chuckle at her own insanity as she stared at the remnants of her alarm clock on the white carpet. Her awakening from the dream had left her in a fragile state, and her thoughts didn't make sense to her anymore. As bizarre as it sounded, she'd been afraid that the number 314 would be angry when she broke the clock. She was worried it would try to hurt her.

How ridiculous.

Someone pounded on the front door.

The sound terrified Alma. She cried out in surprise and then clapped her hands over her mouth. The door to her bedroom was open and the hallway led straight out to the front door.

The person outside pounded harder.

Alma looked for her phone, but it was in her purse on the counter beside the front door. She never bothered to get a landline, and instead used her cell phone for everything. Now she regretted that decision as she stared at her purse on the counter, just feet from the front door.

"Alma, open the door," said a stranger. "Or I'll break it down."

She needed her phone, or better yet a weapon. A kitchen knife would do. She looked around for the knife that she'd left on the nightstand, but it had bounced away somewhere in the room and she couldn't find it.

"All right, I'm going to break it down," said the stranger.

"Stay out! Get away from here!" Alma knew she had to act. She ran down the hall and into the kitchen just as the stranger kicked the door. It rattled on its hinges and Alma screamed in shock. She tried to grab her purse, but then decided it was too late to try and call the police. The purse spun on the counter as she abandoned it in search of a knife. Her phone, wallet, keys, and Rachel's business card spread out over the counter as the front door rattled again.

"Alma," said the stranger. "Stay back. I'm coming in!"

"Who the hell?" Her hands were shaking as she pulled a knife from the butcher's block. "Who are you? Stop it! What are you doing?"

The trim around the deadbolt splintered and the door flung open. Alma was on the other side of the breakfast counter with the knife held out in front of her as a tall, thick man clad in a winter coat and stocking cap came bounding haphazardly in. He stumbled forward and lost his balance before cursing as he fell to his knees.

Alma wasn't going to miss an opportunity to get the upper hand. She ran around the counter as the man crouched with his hand on one of the bar stools. He started to ask, "Are you okay?"

Alma was quick to fight, and heard his question after already starting to kick. Her strike faltered when she realized he wasn't threatening her, but her foot still collided with his face. The chubby intruder fell backward onto his butt and clasped his nose with one hand and held out the other to tell her to stop.

"Hey! Hold up, Alma. I'm a friend of Paul's."

"What?" Alma held the knife with both hands, unwilling to believe the stranger and ready to kill him if he dared try anything.

"I'm a friend of Paul's. I'm Jack, well actually Hank, but everyone calls me Jack, it's short for Jacker. Which is a nickname I got in high school because I liked computers, which is probably more than you needed to know. Point is, I'm a friend. Jesus H. Christ, girl, you nearly took my head off." He spoke frantically, as if frightened or nervous.

"What are you doing here?" Alma was suddenly embarrassed, not by the fact that she'd attacked an innocent stranger, but because she was only wearing a long t-shirt and underwear. She pulled the t-shirt down further to cover herself as she backed around the breakfast counter from the stranger.

"Paul needed some sleep." Jacker inspected his hand after holding his nose, seeming to expect blood. He sniffled and then rubbed his nose with the palm of his hand. He was a rotund guy, tall and boyish looking. His whiskers were scant, but he seemed to be trying to grow a beard anyhow. He wore small, round glasses that would've been more suited for a German scientist than a man like him. He was embarrassed by what he'd done to the door and his cheeks were turning red, which gave him a cherub appearance. Curly black hair escaped his stocking cap, pointing out in all directions.

"Sleep?" asked Alma. She shook her head in confusion. "I don't understand."

Jacker pointed in the direction of the parking lot. "He's down in my van, getting some shut eye and I came up here to keep an eye on you. Well, I mean, not actually keep an eye on you; not spying or anything. I'm not a peeping tom, or my nickname would've been Tommy." He chuckled, but Alma didn't reciprocate and he continued to try and explain. "All right, I'm striking out here. You're obviously okay, and I obviously, well, I over-reacted a little." He motioned at the broken door. His mannerisms were frantic, as if he'd taken caffeine pills to stay awake.

Alma nodded and stared at him with wide eyes. "Yeah, ya think?"

"Sorry about that."

"Why are you here? Why is Paul sleeping in a van in the parking lot?"

Jacker was baffled and he scratched at his sparse, scraggly whiskers. "He said we had to keep guard; didn't say why. He just said to keep an eye out for creepy old guys around the complex, and to listen for you to scream for help or something. So that's why, well, yeah," he motioned at the door. "That's why that just happened." He rubbed his nose again.

Alma finally relaxed and put the kitchen knife back into the butcher's block. "For crying out loud, you scared the living crap out of me."

"Well, you paid me back with a swift kick to the nose." Jacker wiggled his nose back and forth and then snickered.

"Sorry, but you kind of deserved it," said Alma, but her harshness softened. "Did I hurt you?"

"No, I'm fine," said Jack. "Although, swear to God, I think you got your pinkie toe like straight up in there." They both laughed and Jacker continued, "Seriously, I think you scratched my brain. When I pay for your door I'll make sure to throw in a couple extra bucks for you to get a pedicure."

Alma laughed, but then pointed at him as if in warning. "Watch it, mister. I don't know you well enough to put up with jokes about my feet."

Jacker put up his hands in defeat and then walked to door to inspect it.

"Everything okay down there?" asked the widow that lived upstairs as she peered down from the stairwell. Alma walked around the breakfast counter and past Jacker so that she could see Mrs. Peterson. The old woman was in her slippers and a pink robe. She was crouched near the top of the stairs and was bent down just far enough to peer into Alma's apartment. "Should I call the cops?"

"No, Mrs. P., everything's okay. I'm fine. Just a silly misunderstanding."

Mrs. Peterson looked at Jacker warily. She was a fragile, spindly old woman, but was fiercely protective of Alma. The two of them often had long conversations in the stairwell, and Mrs. Peterson was always concerned about Alma's love-life. It was as if the old woman was trying to keep Alma from ending up alone in an apartment, just like she was.

"You've got men beating down your door in the middle of the night?"

"He's a friend of Paul's," said Alma.

"Oh, Paul," said Mrs. Peterson with a hopeful inflection. "Are you two back together? I always liked Paul. He'd be handsome if he cut his hair."

"He did," said Jacker as he took off his cap and ran his hand over his own hair. "He shaved it bald."

Mrs. Peterson looked at Jacker and grimaced, unwilling to communicate with the stranger that had just broken down Alma's door. "Alma, you just yell if you need me. Okay? I'll have my phone ready."

"Okay, will do," said Alma as she waved. "Thanks, Mrs. P."

"I've got your back, sweetie," said the old woman as she went back up the stairs.

Alma tried to close the door, but it drifted open now that the trim was broken. "That's not good."

"I'm sorry," said Jacker as he sheepishly shook his head. "I'm an idiot."

"It's okay," said Alma. She'd already started to like the giant oaf. He was sweet, like an awkward little brother, and she felt sorry for him despite having no reason to. "Come on in and have a seat. Want a beer?"

"You just said the magic word."

"What's that? Beer?"

Jack snapped his finger and pointed at her as he nodded. "Bingo. You don't turn into a ton of fun like me by turning down free beer."

"Considering how much it's going to cost you to fix my door, I'd hardly call the beer free." Alma went to the refrigerator to get him a Milk Stout.

Jacker sighed as he looked at the damage he'd caused. "Gosh, I'm real sorry about that."

"Don't worry about it," said Alma. "I'm just joking with you. I'll make Paul pay for it."

"Shoot, he doesn't have any money. Not after getting canned." Jacker plopped onto the center of the sofa with his long arms stretched to either side along the backboard. He looked comfortable, as if the seat was a familiar spot for him despite never having sat there before.

"Paul got fired?"

Jacker's posture stiffened and he grimaced. "I guess I should learn when to keep my mouth shut. I thought you knew that."

"No, I didn't. What happened?"

"It's a long story, and one I've got no business telling."

Alma got a glass out of the cupboard to pour Jack's beer into.

"I don't need a glass," said Jack.

Alma sneered. "Yes you do. This is a good beer, and it tastes better in a glass. How long have you and Paul been friends?" She asked because of Jacker's unfamiliarity with Paul's preferred way of drinking beer.

"About six months. I met him at the shop under his place."

Alma handed the beer to Jacker and suddenly remembered that she was only wearing a t-shirt and panties. "Hold that thought," said Alma. "I'm going to go get some pants on. I want to hear why Paul got fired."

Jacker spoke loud enough for her to hear as she retreated down the hall to her bedroom. "I'm not going to tell you. I don't care how much delicious beer you give me."

"Yes you will," said Alma as she got to her bedroom. "I can be pretty persuasive." She started to walk over to her dresser, but stepped on the kitchen knife that had been on her nightstand. The sharp blade sliced into the arch of her foot. She gripped the edge of the bed and cursed as she lifted her foot to inspect the damage. "Fuck!" She screamed in anger and pain.

"You all right?" asked Jacker from the other room. "Is this for real, or are you screwing with me?"

Alma cursed some more and tried to hop to the hallway as her foot bled. The wound gushed and droplets of blood quickly started to fall to the floor. "Mother fucker."

"Okay, it's for real?" asked Jacker. "I'm coming in there. Okay? Don't be naked or anything."

Alma met him at the door. She propped herself up with one hand on the threshold and the other holding her foot aloft. He stopped dead in his tracks and stared at the blood. His face turned white and his jaw drooped.

"I stepped on something. Can you get me a towel?"

"Oh," he said in a whimper. He was wavering and put his hand on his head.

"Quick," said Alma. "I'm bleeding all over the carpet."

He snapped out of his momentary daze and nodded. "Okay, sure. Towel. Sure thing." He spun in a circle in search of the bathroom, which happened to be right next to him on the left. "In here, right? Yeah, of course it is." He retrieved a towel and then offered it with his arm extended out of the doorway, hiding his face from her.

Alma hopped forward and swiped the white towel away from him. She wrapped her foot and waited for Jacker to come out of the small bathroom so that she could go in. He stayed hidden in there.

"Are you okay?"

"Me?" he asked. "Yeah, fine. Why?"

"I need to go in there."

"Oh, sure. Okay." He hurried out of the bathroom with his hand held against the side of his face, shielding his view of her.

She glanced down at herself, worried that her odd position, with her leg lifted so high, revealed more of herself than she realized. "What's wrong?"

"I got up too fast. I'm woozy. I'm not great with blood."

"Oh, okay," said Alma as she hopped toward the bathroom. "I thought my underwear was ripped or something."

"No, no," said Jacker. His voice was weak, as if he'd grown tired all of the sudden. "I just have a bad habit of…" He stopped talking and started to lean against the wall.

"Jacker?"

He slumped and then collapsed in Alma's direction. She cried out and hopped to the side as the titanic man crashed down, out cold.

"God damn it, Paul," she cursed her ex-boyfriend for his choice of stalwart bodyguards.

CHAPTER 6 - Going Upstairs

Widowsfield
March 14th, 1996

"What are those things?" asked Winnie Anderson, the owner of the used book store on Main Street. She was trembling as she held up a letter opener as if it could protect her from the creatures outside.

"I don't have a clue," said Walter, the UPS driver that had stopped to chat with Winnie after delivering several packages of books that had been sent to the shop owner from a library a few towns over. Walter had pushed his L-Cart, still loaded with boxes, against the inside of the shop's door to block it.

Winnie and Walter had watched the bizarre green fog roll down the street minutes earlier, and saw the shadows of child-like creatures running through it. The howls of dogs, and then the breaking glass, had alerted them to danger. Walter decided to go out onto the street to see what had happened, but Winnie had pulled him back in the shop. She had a long-standing affection for the delivery man, and didn't want to see him hurt.

Walter had laughed off her concern moments before the first creature tried to attack them. It had charged through the fog on all fours, like a dog, but its body was that of a human. The creature was nude, but its skin was ripped as if something had been clawing at it. Its hands were mangled, and looked like they'd been smashed, with bones protruding from the flesh and hunks of meat dangling off the ends. Worst of all, the child-sized creature had the head of a hairless dog. Foam and blood dripped from its maw and the monstrosity was throwing itself against the glass in a desperate attempt to get into the shop.

More of the demonic creatures appeared in the fog and started to circle the building. The Anderson Used Book

Store was situated on the corner of the street, with floor to ceiling windows set in tall arches three feet apart lining the wall. Within moments, the creatures crowded every window and the fog thickened around the building, eclipsing the light and leaving them in darkness.

Winnie's business was suffering hard times, and she'd been trying to save money by turning off the lights during the day, which she now regretted.

"Where's the light switch?" asked Walter as he moved behind the counter to join Winnie.

"Near the front door."

"Forget that." Walter put his arm around Winnie's shoulder as the daylight dissipated. The darkening room revealed light coming in from up the stairs near the rear of the shop. "There's a light on up there. Let's go."

Winnie's modest apartment was situated above the shop. She was certain that she hadn't left a light on up there, but the wooden stairs were indeed illuminated. She followed Walter as he held her hand and guided her to the stairs.

The wooden stairs flashed with green light and Winnie pulled her hand out of Walter's. She took a step back in fear. He turned, but she could only see his silhouette framed by the light from upstairs.

"What's wrong?" he asked and held out his hand for her.

"What's up there?"

Walter looked up the stairs and then back at Winnie. Green light flashed again and was reflected in the oil on Walter's shaved head. "I don't know, but we can't stay down here."

Glass cracked from one of the nearby arches and Winnie cowered from the noise. She still gripped the letter opener in one hand while steadying herself against the counter with the other. "I don't want to go up there."

"Don't be ridiculous, Winnie." Walter took a step toward her.

She swiped her letter opener at his hand and he recoiled from the strike. Winnie wasn't sure if she'd hit him, but apologized anyhow. "I'm sorry, Walter. I can't go. I won't go up there."

"Why not? What do you think is up there?"

She shook her head, uncertain how to explain how she knew that something bad was waiting for them upstairs. "I don't know. I think it's worse up there. I don't know why. I just know it."

"You're not making any sense."

"Don't go up there," she said as one of the windows of the shop shattered. The creatures poured in and their mangled claws scrambled against the bookshelves as they crawled through the darkness.

"Winnie!" Walter screamed at her as he rushed to the stairs.

Winnie curled up on the floor and wrapped her arms around her legs to pull them to her chest. She was in a fetal position, staring at Walter as he ascended the stairs into the light.

"Come on!" He continued to yell at her as he left her behind.

Winnie closed her eyes to avoid seeing the light. She was warm and comfortable in the darkness, and didn't want to know what Walter was about to see. She would rather let the demons devour her than witness the truth. She would rather die than go up those stairs again.

16 Years Later
March 10th, 2012

"He's out cold." Alma stood in the frigid night air in a pair of sweats and a flimsy jacket. She had her arms wrapped around herself as she stood beside the van where Paul had been sleeping. "I tried to call you."

Paul rubbed his eyes as he climbed out of Jacker's van. "Sorry, my phone died. Stupid thing can't hold a charge for more than a few hours. Now, tell me again, what happened?"

97

"Your friend bashed in my door and then I cut my foot on a knife. He saw the blood and freaked out. He fainted right in the middle of the hallway."

Paul smiled. "Seriously?"

"Yes, seriously. Stop smiling, this isn't funny." She tried to look stern, but couldn't help but grin along with him. She slapped Paul's chest to get him to stop chuckling. "I can't believe you made the poor guy stand guard outside my door."

"Jacker didn't mind. He needs something to keep his mind off some shit that's been going on in his life lately."

"I didn't want you to post guard at my door."

Paul stretched and yawned comically loud. "I wasn't going to leave you here without protection."

"So you made your friend guard me?"

"I sat down there for a couple hours before I decided to call to see if he would come help me out."

"You're crazy." Alma started to limp back to her apartment as Paul closed the side door of the white van parked beside his motorcycle. It was the only van in the parking lot, which helped make it easy for her to find.

"Is your foot okay?" asked Paul as he walked behind her.

She looked down at her right foot, which she'd wrapped with gauze before putting on her shoes to head down to the van. "No, it hurts like hell. I cut the hell out of it."

"Come here." Paul quickened his pace to catch up with her. He knelt beside Alma and scooped her into his arms before she could stop him.

"No," she said playfully as he picked her up. "Don't do this; you're going to kill us both." She yelped and pressed her face into his neck as he started up the stairs to her apartment.

"Stop wiggling or you're going to knock us both down the stairs."

"I hate you sometimes," said Alma although it was clear she didn't mean it, at least not at that moment. She wrapped her arms tighter around his neck and enjoyed his smell. His aroma was fused with the scent of his leather coat, a mixture she adored. There was no denying how much she loved Paul and she couldn't stop smiling as he carried her up the stairs.

"There's a thin line between love and hate. Isn't that what they say?"

"Shut up and take me home."

"I'll carry you in my arms through the threshold like we just got married; and then over the big guy passed out in your hallway." Paul and Alma laughed at the absurdity of the moment.

"How did we end up like this?" Alma asked as Paul rounded the corner to head up the final flight of stairs to her apartment.

Paul shrugged and then kissed the side of her head. His whiskers tickled her cheek. "Like what?"

"Apart, and then together again, and then apart again. How did we get so screwed up?"

Paul stopped at the top of the stairs in front of Alma's broken door. "I don't know. I guess I'm a sucker for messed up chicks, and you're a sucker for idiots who don't know a good thing when he's got her in his arms." He tightened his grip around her.

Alma leered at him. "Messed up chicks, huh?"

He grinned as if gloating. "Oh yeah, like really messed up. A borderline mental case."

"Shut up and kiss me."

He complied.

"Alma?" said a man from inside the apartment.

Alma recognized her father's voice and fear overtook her. She tightened her grip around Paul as a chill of terror ran through her body.

"Who the fuck?" asked Paul as he took the last two steps past the stairs that would allow him to see inside the apartment.

The door was still open and Alma was hesitant to look. She couldn't explain the emotions that welled within her as Paul carried her to the open door. For some reason, she was terrified of what lay in wait past the door at the top of the stairs. She couldn't breathe and stared at the door as Paul approached it. Alma knew that her father was inside, and whatever he was doing would traumatize her.

This had happened before.

Paul set Alma down gently and then pushed the front door open further so that they could see what was happening inside the apartment. The moths continued to spin around the porch light, incensed by Paul's approach.

Alma's father was in the hallway of her apartment, perched over Jacker's body. He had one hand on the big man's throat and the other on his chest, as if he was worried that Jacker was dead.

"I heard someone break down your door and I came to make sure you were okay," said her father. "What happened?"

Paul glanced at Alma quizzically. "Is he one of your neighbors?"

She shook her head as the color drained from her cheeks. When she spoke, it was hardly more than a whisper. "That's my father."

Paul's expression instantly changed. His brow furrowed and he clenched his fists as he turned back to face Alma's estranged father. "Oh, mother fucker! You'd better get your ass out of here right now." He didn't pause before charging into the apartment.

Alma was too frightened to intercede, or to warn Paul that her father was dangerous. Instead, she cowered against the wall across the landing from her apartment's door and watched Paul confront the old addict. The terror that seized her was unlike anything she'd felt since her brother disappeared.

A memory was trying to return, and she glanced at the stairs as if they somehow played a part. The act of ascending the stairs to find her father seemed horrifyingly familiar, yet she couldn't explain why. Her throat was clenched, her hands shook, and it was a struggle just to breathe. She had no choice but to watch as Paul protected her.

"Back off," said her father.

Paul lifted the thin man off the floor and threw him down the hall toward the front door. Paul weighed significantly more than Alma's father, and stood a couple inches taller. It was like watching an adult manhandle a child. "Get out of here, you piece of shit."

"I'm her father! I just came here to help. You can't do this to me. I'll fucking kill you, asshole. I'll fucking kill you!"

Paul paused and leered down at the man. He cracked his knuckles and advanced, savoring the old man's terror. "I'm real hard to kill."

"You don't know who you're fucking with. You're dead. You hear me?" Alma's father staggered away from Paul and leaned against one of the bar stools as he stood back up. "I'm not kidding, man. You really fucked up. I'll kill you for this." He still had on the dirty, ragged clothes he'd been wearing when he confronted Alma at the restaurant. His voice still sounded fueled by methamphetamine, and the drug was giving him the courage to face Paul. He held up his fists, and then lunged with a haphazard right hook.

Paul knew how to fight. He'd been a bouncer for years in a college town and had learned how to subdue enraged drunks and drug addicts. He caught Alma's father's strike with a counterstrike of his own. He swatted her father's arm away and then waited for another attempt. He was toying with the old man.

Her father tried to punch again, and Paul deflected the strike with another quick shot to the wrist. The old man gripped his arm in frustration and started to scream at Paul. "You think you're tough? You think you're a big guy?"

Paul sneered. "Yep."

"Well, big guy, let me tell you what I'm going to do," said Alma's father.

"No," Paul interrupted the old man with authority. His voice boomed loud enough that Alma's father flinched. "I'm going to tell you what happens next. You're going to pack your shit and get out of town. Now let me tell you why."

Her father stuttered when he asked, "Why?"

"Because if I ever see you again, I'm going to bury you. This isn't an idle threat, pal. I've never been more serious about anything in my life." Paul stared down at the spindly old addict. "I will bury you."

"You can't threaten me, you piece of shit. I'm her father. I'll always be there for her."

Paul took a step forward, which forced Alma's father to back up. "So will I."

"You're insane."

"Maybe," said Paul. "Now get the fuck out of town. Or do you want to try and hit me again?"

The old man rubbed his wrist and Alma could see that it was already turning purple where Paul had hit him. He turned to her and pleaded, "Alma, baby, don't go back. Let him die. Okay?"

She couldn't answer if she wanted to. In fact, she only then realized that she'd been humming a tune as tears streamed down her cheeks.

"Alma, you've got to promise me. Don't go to Widowsfield. Let him die!" He advanced threateningly, but Paul caught the old man by the shoulder. Her father winced as Paul forced him to the stairs.

"Get out of here."

Paul shoved her father down the stairs and the old man fell to the concrete. His head smashed against the railing and he gasped in pain and shock, but then crawled to his feet and darted away.

"Get your stuff," said Paul to Alma as he still stared down at the fleeing old man.

She couldn't respond and continued to cower against the wall, humming a tune as she wept. Paul turned to her, concerned. "Babe? You okay?"

Alma shook her head and finally stopped humming. She buried her head in her hands.

"Oh shit, honey. Don't worry. I'm here, okay? I'll always be here." Paul rushed to cradle her as Alma sobbed. "I'm not going to let him hurt you." He put her head against his chest and held her. "I'd do anything to keep you safe, babe."

"He's never going to stop," said Alma. "He's just going to keep coming back, over and over."

Paul tried to hush her. "It's okay. I'm here for you now. Alma, I'd never let anyone hurt you. I'd do anything to protect you. I swear."

"I have to go back."

"Go back where?" asked Paul.

Alma didn't want to say, but knew that it was time to confront what had haunted her all these years. Saying the word felt like a curse and she hardly had the strength to utter the name of the town, "Widowsfield."

CHAPTER 7 - Amid Chaos

Widowsfield
March 14th, 1996

Walter saw the creatures attack Winnie, but there was nothing he could do. He was too frightened to protect her, and retreated up the stairs to the apartment above the book store. He slammed the door shut behind him and then locked it. He wasn't content relying on only the deadbolt and started to pile up whatever he could find against the door.

Winnie cried out in agony as the monsters tore her apart. Walter apologized over and over as he barricaded the door, but she'd done this to herself. Winnie had chosen to stay down there. She had time to get up the stairs if she wanted to, but she insisted on staying where the creatures could get her. Walter didn't have time to save her. He would've died too if he tried.

He continued to apologize to her as he piled whatever he could find against the door to keep the creatures from devouring him. Then he heard someone gagging in the room with him.

Walter spun in terror to see who'd made the sound, but there was no one in the room with him. Winnie's apartment was sparsely furnished, with only a rocking chair and couch in front of the television stand. A TV tray was situated beside the couch with a Reader's Digest opened and face down on top of it. There was a bland rug between the couch and the television, and there was a small pile of white foam on it.

He took a cautious step toward the bubbling mass.

A woman's body appeared on the rug, followed by a zinging crack of green electricity that coursed along the metal legs of the TV tray. The electricity popped in the air and was then gone, leaving behind the body of a choking ghost. Her mouth was open, purple lips rimmed with foam,

104

and she stared at Walter before reaching out to him. Her eyes were bloodshot and her wet hair clung to her cheeks.

She was trying to ask for help, but Walter was too terrified to do anything but gape at her. The woman finally succumbed and her head fell back hard against the floor, but instead of thumping down, her head sank through the floorboards. The rest of her body followed, as if it had suddenly dissipated into vapor, and all that was left of her was the white foam on the rug.

"Oh Lord," said Walter. He made the sign of the cross and kissed his knuckle. "Lord have mercy on my soul."

He dared to step closer to the rug, uncertain if he really had seen the woman, or if she'd been a figment of his imagination. "What the hell's going on here?"

Walter got on his knees on the hardwood floor and edged his way closer to the rug. He didn't dare get on the damned thing, and kept his distance, but he needed to see if the foam was real. He started to reach out to it, but then retracted and chided himself. "What are you doing, Walter? Don't touch that." He started to stand up when the woman's arms reach out from the rug. Her face was exposed for a moment, and her expression of helplessness had changed to hatred. She grasped Walter's arm and dragged him forward until he witnessed his own limb disappear into the floor along with the ethereal woman. He cried out in terror, and tried to break free of her grip, but the ghost was inhumanly strong. She dragged his arm into the floor and then reached up to grab more of him. He tried to pull free, but every inch of his flesh that had been pulled through the floor was now stuck within it, and the woman continued to drag him down.

She gripped his hair and pulled his head down. Within seconds he was staring at the darkened first floor of the Anderson Used Book Store. He could see Winnie's corpse, ringed by the demonic creatures that were devouring her. The ghost was below him. She smiled and finally released him before drifting away, down to the first floor and sinking below it as well.

Walter was left dangling from the ceiling, his body fused to the wood above. He clawed at the ceiling and tried to move, but every twist of his waist ignited agony throughout him, as if he were trying to pull himself apart every time he moved. He started to scream for help before he felt his spine crack from his movement.

He was left there to dangle, like a living stalactite; an adornment of chaos; a witness of the horror below. Blood started to flow from his open mouth and his vision faded. He started to vomit, but it wasn't food that slid past his lips. Strips of flesh began to push through his throat and he yanked them out to avoid choking. He pulled forth the fleshy pulp until the strands were too long, and the pain too great, to continue. A few minutes later, Walter finally died, but every second was spent enduring agony that only hell could conceive.

Something was hiding in the shadows of the store, and the creature's teeth chattered as it watched the chaos unfold.

16 Years Later
March 10th, 2012

"I have to go back to Widowsfield," said Alma as Paul held her.

"Why?"

Alma pushed out of his arms and stood up. She squealed in pain when she put pressure on her foot, and then limped through the door of her apartment with Paul following behind. "I don't know."

Paul jokingly responded, "That makes sense."

"No, you don't understand." Alma went to the breakfast counter and started to rifle through the contents of her purse that had spilled out. She found Rachel's card and showed it to Paul as if it should mean something to him. "I don't know what happened there."

"Okay, neither do I," said Paul. "You never told me anything about it. You just said that you wanted to leave that part of your life behind you."

"I know, and I did, but there's more to it than that." She sat on the stool and started to tap the business card against the countertop. She debated calling Rachel now, but it was too early in the morning to wake her. Alma felt frantic and got up to make a pot of coffee.

"Are you going to explain, or what?" asked Paul.

"I can't, that's the problem."

"Alma, you're not making any sense."

"What's going on?" asked Jacker from the hallway. He was still on the floor and was just now waking up. "What happened?"

"Just stay there, Jacker," said Paul.

The big man groaned, but did as he was told. He folded his arms over his barrel chest and sighed.

Alma's hands were shaking as she tried to pour water into the back of the coffee maker. She spilled liquid over the side and had to use her other hand to steady the container. "I don't remember what happened there. I get flashes of things from time to time, but nothing ever seems to make sense. There's a whole chunk of time missing from what I can remember."

"Okay then, what can you remember?" Paul went around the counter and took over making the coffee. He pointed at the stool, commanding Alma to settle down and take a seat without having to tell her to.

"Well, I guess before I go into that, I should ask you what you know about Widowsfield. Have you ever heard the legends and all that stuff?"

Paul nodded as he wavered his hand. "Some of it. I know you get pissed off and stop taking calls on March 14th because there're a lot of people that think you know what happened. I looked up some of the websites about the place, but it all seems like conspiracy bullshit."

107

"Do you know why people think I know something?" she asked.

He looked hesitant to answer. "Every time I brought it up you told me you didn't want to talk about it."

"I know, but did any of the sites you looked at talk about my brother's disappearance?"

Paul poured the ground coffee into the filter and turned the coffee maker on. "Yeah, but every site had a different version of the story. I'd rather hear the truth, if you're ready to tell it."

She wasn't sure she knew the truth anyhow, and started to draw circles on the counter with the corner of Rachel's business card. Each circle started large, and then shrunk with each revolution, like a serpent's coil. "Like I said, I don't remember much of what happened, but what I can has screwed with me ever since…" she was overwhelmed by a sense of sadness that she hadn't expected. Her eyes welled with tears and she dropped the business card to wipe them away.

"You don't have to talk about it if you don't want to."

"Should I leave?" asked Jacker from the floor in the hallway as he lay patiently with his arms draped over his belly. "Or just stay here?"

Alma laughed. Jacker's unintentionally comedic timing was a welcome relief. "No, Jacker," said Alma. "Come here and sit down with us. Are you okay?"

The big man grumbled as he stood up. His frame encompassed the width of the hall, and he looked embarrassed by what happened. "I'm fine. Sorry, I have a problem with blood. It's pretty pathetic. I feel like such a dork."

"Want something to drink?" asked Paul.

"No, I've got a beer around here somewhere. Ah, there it is." Jacker retrieved his beer from the end table beside the couch. "Honestly guys, I'll take off if you want me to. I've already done enough damage here."

108

Paul looked at Alma for an answer. She shook her head. "No, you can stay. I don't think you should be driving right after passing out anyhow."

Paul reached across the counter and set his hand over Alma's. "We can talk about Widowsfield later if you want."

"No," she said. "We can talk about it now. I don't mind if Jack's here." She looked over at the giant as he downed the rest of his beer. "Do you know about Widowsfield?"

"I heard you guys talking about it," said Jacker. "I think I've heard something about it before. The people there disappeared, right?"

Alma led them into the living room and the three sat down around the coffee table. There were stacks of old magazines littering the table, along with several half full glasses situated atop plates that should've been washed days ago. That, of course, reminded her of Paul's spotless apartment, and she felt suddenly shamed.

"Sorry," she said as Paul and Jacker sat down. "Let me clean this stuff up real quick." Alma gathered the dirty dishes and carried them to the kitchen where she checked on the coffee machine. It had hardly started brewing, but the smell was already filling the apartment. She was about to get creamer from the refrigerator when she realized that she was stalling. Alma was trying to avoid confronting her past, even by only the time it would take to make coffee. She forced herself to go back into the living room.

"Okay," said Alma before she took a deep, exaggerated breath. "It's about time I talked about this."

Paul moved to the side of the love seat for Alma to sit with him. Jacker was lounging on the center seat of the sofa, and managed to usurp most of the space there. Alma sat beside Paul and he pulled her to his side with his arm around her shoulder.

"My father used to take my brother and me on fishing trips to Missouri every spring, during our break." Alma started to absently rub her thumb over a ring on her right hand. It was a simple silver ring with holes bored through it in random spots. The ring was the only thing of her mother's that Alma still owned. "It was supposed to be a vacation for us, or at least that's what he used to tell my mother." Her voice cracked and she took a deep breath to steady herself.

Paul squeezed her shoulder and Alma smiled up at him before continuing. "We didn't do a lot of fishing. I was pretty young at the time, I was eight and my brother was ten. We'd been going there for a few years, and my mother would stay home. It was supposed to be a chance for my father to connect with us." Alma twirled the loose fitting ring around her bony finger. "That's not what it was really about. I didn't know it at the time, because I was so young, but my father was using the vacation as an excuse to meet up with one of his girlfriends. God, just talking about it makes my stomach turn."

"You don't have to, Alma," said Paul.

Alma was quick to respond. "No, I do. I know this sounds nuts, and maybe it is, but it's time for me to deal with this; to get it all out in the open." She took off the ring and started the slip it onto other fingers and then back again, as if her hands were desperate to be active. "My father's girlfriend owned a cabin, more of a house really, but everyone called them cabins. They'd rent movies for my brother and I to watch while they did their thing. They would go upstairs, and my brother and I would sit in the living room, watching those stupid movies while they…"

She pointed up and had trouble continuing, but forced herself to say it, "While they went upstairs and had sex. We could hear them, but I didn't understand what was going on. They would spend all day up there sometimes, and my brother and I were left to fend for ourselves. We'd make our own food, and put ourselves to bed every day while at that cabin. If we ever dared go upstairs we would get screamed at. I made the mistake of going up there a few times, and I'll never forget the acrid stench of the drugs they were smoking. My father's been a meth addict for as long as I can

110

remember. That smell, that chemical, ozone-like stink that came out of the room is something I'll never forget."

"Damn," said Jacker. "That sucks. Sorry to hear your dad was such a prick."

Alma laughed inappropriately and shook her head. "You don't know the half of it. We used to get beatings for seemingly random stuff. One day it was no big deal for us to wear our shoes in the house, and the next we were getting whipped for not taking them off at the door. He used to have this belt that he cut holes in, and he only used it for whipping us. He would carry it around with him, and said that the holes made it easier to swing, and made it hurt more. I remember him standing in the kitchen, in his dirty white t-shirt, making breakfast with that belt over his shoulder, like he was just waiting for an excuse to use it."

Paul kissed the top of Alma's head and continued to try and be supportive, although nothing he could do would help her forget.

"I know lots of people had shitty fathers," she said and slipped her mother's ring back onto her right ring finger. "And at least my mother was good to us before she went crazy. A lot of kids don't even have that. But, you get the point: My dad was a Class A piece of garbage. He was out on business a lot, thankfully. I think that's how he met his girlfriend."

"And was his girlfriend's cabin in Widowsfield?" asked Paul.

Alma nodded. "Yeah. I remember that our spring break came one week before the kid's in the town. My brother and I used to watch them all walking home after school, and we would ask if we could go play with them, but my father would always say no. The last time we went there was the week before the town disappeared. I can remember everything about that week up until just after the fog rolled in."

"The green fog?" asked Jacker. "I remember hearing about that part."

111

"Yeah, although it wasn't so much green as it was lit up with green light, if that makes sense. It was thick, and rolled through the street almost like it was more liquid than cloud. And somewhere inside of it there was an electric energy that kept bursting into green light, almost like there was a thunderstorm going on inside of the mist. My brother and I were watching a movie, Toy Story to be exact, and were waiting for the kids to get out of school. We always liked to watch them walk down the street. It was kind of pathetic, really, but we even started giving them all fictional names and pretending like they were our friends. We were waiting for school to get out when the fog rolled in."

Alma heard the coffee maker start to chug through the last drops of water. She wanted to get up and go to the kitchen, but realized that she was just trying to find an excuse to stop telling her story. She spun the ring on her finger and forced herself to continue. "My brother and I were terrified. We didn't know what to do, and my brother…" She paused and stopped spinning the ring. "Jesus Christ, it's even hard for me to remember his name. His name was Ben. I don't know why I have so much trouble remembering it. Sometimes I can't even remember what he looked like."

"I have trouble remembering what my dad looked like," said Jacker. "He died in a car accident when I was twelve. My mom says he looked like me, but I have trouble remembering much about him."

Alma recognized that Jacker was sharing his own pain as a way of trying to help. The big guy was genuinely sweet, and Alma liked him almost immediately. He was the epitome of the teddy bear personality.

"Ben wanted to tell my dad about the fog, but I told him not to go up the stairs. I begged him not to go."

Alma paused for too long, and Paul asked her, "What happened?"

"I don't know." She laughed uncomfortably and looked at them both as she shook her head. "That's just it. I can remember everything leading up to Ben going up those stairs. I was standing at the bottom as Ben went up, and then the fog surrounded the cabin. It blocked out the sun and I can remember the shadows closing in over us. The green electricity flashed and the television died, but there was still light coming from up the stairs as Ben went up. I yelled out for him to stop, and that's the last thing I can remember about what happened."

"The next thing I recall is driving in the car with my father. We were in the fog, and there were shadows all around us, almost like there were creatures running through the mist beside us. They were huge, like dragons or monsters or something, but I couldn't see what they were. The electricity kept flashing and my father was screaming at me to shut up, but I wasn't saying anything. He was driving fast, and was leaning forward as if he was trying to see through the fog. I was curled up in my seat, and my brother was gone. The worst part of all it was that I didn't know Ben was supposed to be there. It was almost like I'd forgotten he ever existed."

"We got out of the fog, and didn't stop driving the whole way home except to get gas. I remember crying, a lot, and my father kept telling me to shut up. He told me that we were never in Widowsfield, and that nothing happened. He said that we were in a different town, called Forsythe, and that we never went through Widowsfield. And he kept checking his watch, over and over, for no apparent reason."

Paul held Alma's hand and she thanked him by the way she looked at him. His massive hand was so warm, and her thin fingers seemed to disappear in his grip. "Neither of us mentioned Ben until we got home, and then my mother went insane. I can remember her screaming and crying and shaking me, begging me to tell her what happened. It felt like she knew that my father had done something to Ben, and just needed me to confirm it, but I didn't remember. Honestly, I didn't even remember who Ben was anymore."

"The police came, and my father was accused of all sorts of things, but no one could prove anything. I told them that we were in Widowsfield, but my father denied it. He said that we passed through the town on our way home, but that we'd been staying at a cabin in Forsythe. He even had the keys to prove it. The police eventually assumed I was making everything up, and that I had heard the rumors about what happened in Widowsfield. They couldn't find any evidence that my father had done anything, so he was eventually cleared of all charges."

"My mother never gave up, though. She was determined to find out what happened. She would take me back to Widowsfield, and try to get me to show her where the cabin was at, but I lied and said I didn't know. I just didn't want to go back there. My mother tried all sorts of tricks to get me to remember, including hypnosis, and even herbal concoctions that were supposed to help me remember past trauma. That's how she got introduced to Chaos Magick."

"What's that?" asked Paul.

"You've actually probably heard of it, but didn't know what it was," said Alma. "Have you ever heard of The Secret? That book that Oprah used to talk about all the time?"

"Yeah, sure," said Jacker.

"That's basically the same thing as Chaos Magick. It's the idea that if you focus on one thing, you can make it a reality. I never studied up on it, but my mother was obsessed with it. She said that we had to come up with a symbol that we could focus on that was tied to the day Ben disappeared. She started with his name, and would write it on slips of paper that she would hide all over the house, but when that didn't work she decided to try the date."

"March 14th?" asked Paul.

Alma nodded and took her ring off. "To be more specific, 314." She held the ring up to show to them. "3.14 is also the number for pi, the ratio of a circle's circumference to its diameter."

114

"Uh oh," said Paul as he made a goofy grin. "We're not getting into math, are we? Because I suck at that."

Alma shook her head and offered a grin. "No, not exactly. The reason it was important is because the date that my brother disappeared was also a symbol; the symbol for pi. In Chaos Magick, you're supposed to choose a symbol that you can focus on to help force everything else out of your mind. My mother started writing 314 on everything, and then switched to the symbol for pi. She would force me to stare at it for what felt like hours at a time."

"Wow," said Jacker. "You had some nutball parents."

"Well, the crazy thing is that it kind of worked."

Both Jacker and Paul sat forward in anticipation of what Alma was going to say next.

"Somehow my mom found out the address of the cabin. She took me back there, and forced me to stare at the symbol. She kept asking about what happened, but I couldn't remember anything. And you know how I was saying that I'd forgotten about Ben?"

Paul and Jacker nodded.

"That was still the case. I couldn't remember anything about him except for what I saw in pictures. It was as if he'd never existed except for how my mother could prove that he did. It was in Widowsfield, when my mother was forcing me to look at the symbol for pi, that I suddenly remembered who Ben was. I remember it so clearly. I was standing in the kitchen, and my mother had drawn the symbol on the kitchen floor and circled it with candles. She made me sit there and stare at it while I hummed a tune. Then, suddenly, everything came flooding back. It was the most intense and terrifying moment of my life. I can't even explain what it was like. One minute I had no brother, and the next I was feeling such terror and grief over his loss. It was overwhelming. Easily the worst thing I've ever experienced, which is why I never did it again."

"That's so creepy." Jacker had moved forward to the edge of his seat and was listening to Alma intently.

115

"It was like my brother was born and died all at the same time. I experienced the emotions of having a sibling all at once. After that, I told my mother everything I could remember about our trips to Widowsfield." Alma sadly shook her head and stared at her mother's ring. "It wasn't long after that," Alma closed her eyes and forced herself to finish the sentence, "she killed herself."

"Oh crap, Alma," said Jacker. "I'm so sorry." The big man seemed uncomfortable and uncertain how to respond. "I know we just met, but can I give you a hug? I feel like you need a big bear hug."

Alma laughed as her eyes filled with tears. Then she nodded and stood up to accept Jacker's kindness. He wrapped his arms around her and she tried to do the same to him, although he was too big for her hands to touch behind his back. He started with a soft hug, but then lifted her off the ground and squeezed her in a tight embrace. "You've got Paul to take care of you, kid. And I know how much you mean to him, so I'll be there for you too if you need me. Okay?"

"Sure, thanks," said Alma as Jacker set her back down.

Paul took her hand as she sat back down. "Thanks for telling us."

"Thanks for listening," she said. "It feels good to talk about it. I need to figure out what happened. It's been too long. I need to know what happened to Ben."

"How do you plan on doing that?" asked Paul.

Alma got up and went to the counter to get Rachel's business card. She brought it back to the living room and handed it to Paul. "The reporter that interviewed me is going to Widowsfield today. She wanted me to go with her, which is why my father showed back up again."

"How did he know?" asked Paul.

"They contacted him first, to see if he'd be willing to go on camera and talk about what happened. He followed them here, which is how he found me. He's desperate to keep me from going back to Widowsfield, which is exactly why I have to go."

"Why do they want you to go?" asked Paul as he looked at the card.

"They're doing a story on the disappearances in Widowsfield for their website. They wanted me to go back there with them and talk about what happened."

"Are you sure that's a good idea?" asked Paul.

Alma responded as if he were joking. "No, not at all, but I've been trying to avoid this for years. I can't keep hiding from it, and maybe this is the best way to force myself to confront it."

"Yeah, but on camera?" asked Paul. "Why don't you let me take you there? We can do whatever you need to do by ourselves instead of with some strangers."

Alma considered the offer, but was already set on her course. "I know it sounds insane, but I've been hiding this for so long; I think the best solution is just to fling the doors open on it as wide as I can. Does that make sense?"

Paul shook his head. "Nope."

"I get it," said Jacker. "You want to force yourself to be honest. I can respect that."

"I think you should be careful," said Paul as he offered the card back to Alma. "I wouldn't trust these people at all."

"Then come with me," said Alma as she took the card.

"All you've got to do is ask," said Paul.

"I'm asking," said Alma. "Come with me to Widowsfield. We can go with these guys, and tell them that we've got final say on what footage they use. You can help me try and figure all of this out. You can be my big, burly security guard."

"Nothing would make me happier," said Paul as he held Alma's hand.

"Are you scared?" asked Jacker. Alma didn't answer immediately and Jacker elaborated what he meant. "I'd be scared out of my mind. I admire what you're doing, but if I were you I'd be terrified of going back there."

"Why?" asked Alma.

"I don't know, I guess I'm just scared of skeletons that want to be left alone in their closets."

PART TWO : RESPITE

CHAPTER 8 - Preparations

March 10th, 2012

Rachel snorted loudly when she awoke. There was hardly a morning that passed where she didn't wake up confused and frantic, and she looked back and forth in an attempt to get her bearings. She wiped the drool off her lips and then looked at Stephen to see if he was still asleep.

Her phone was ringing and the shrill pitch hurt her head.

"Crap," she said as she slid out of bed. The new, silk sheets were slick and she fell to the floor where she cursed again.

"You all right?" asked Stephen without moving.

Rachel bounded up, wearing only a pair of underwear, and pulled the cover off the bed to wrap around herself. "Where's my phone?" Rachel was useless in the morning, and always had trouble figuring anything out before having her first cup of coffee. It took Stephen several months to get used to her manic morning routine, but now he mostly ignored her.

Stephen was laying nude, face down on the bed, and pointed lazily toward the kitchen. "In there somewhere."

Rachel ran off and nearly tripped over Stephen's discarded clothes. "Phone, phone, phone," she said as she searched. "Aha!" It was on the kitchen counter beside an empty bottle of wine. The bottle was one of two that they'd finished the night before.

"Hello," she answered. The blanket fell off her shoulder when she tried to hold the phone against it. "God damn it."

"Did I catch you at a bad time?" asked the woman on the line.

"Depends," said Rachel. "Who is this?"

"Alma, from the school and the restaurant yesterday."

"Oh, Alma!" Rachel tried to sound more cordial. "I'm sorry, I just woke up. I am, without a doubt, the worst morning person you've ever met. And to make matters worse, I'm pretty hungover at the moment. Sorry."

Alma laughed. "I understand completely."

"What can I do for you?"

"Have you and Stephen left for Widowsfield yet?"

"No," said Rachel as she started to make coffee. "We're heading out today. Why?"

"Got room for two more?"

Rachel dropped the scoop of coffee grounds. She needed to give her full attention to the phone call. "You want to come?"

"My friend and I wanted to go, if that's okay."

"Oh my God, yes. Yes, yes, a thousand times yes. We'd be happy to have you. Stephen is going to be ecstatic to hear that you're coming. We've been planning this for such a long time."

"Do you have room for both of us?"

"I think so," said Rachel. "Stephen just bought a shit load of equipment to take with us, but I think he's planning on renting a van. I'm absolutely positive we can make room for you and… Who was it you were bringing?"

"My boyfriend, ex-boyfriend, kind of boyfriend," Alma struggled to encapsulate the relationship. She finally just said, "Paul."

"Sounds good. We'll take you any way we can get you."

"I want to discuss some stipulations about me coming though," said Alma. "I'm still a little nervous about the idea of airing all of this for the world to know. I'd prefer to have

120

final say on whatever you say about me or my past, and whatever footage I'm in."

"I'm sure Stephen will agree to that. You'll have to talk to him about it, but I'm sure he'll be okay with it."

"Okay then," said Alma. "What time do we leave? Oh, and what sort of clothes should I bring?"

"Tell you what," said Rachel. "As a thank you, why don't you let me take you out to buy some new clothes? We'll make a date of it."

"You don't have to do that," said Alma.

"No, I want to," said Rachel. "We'll get you something nice to make you feel good being on camera. Trust me, the right clothes make all the difference."

"Okay, you're the expert."

"Do you still have my card?" asked Rachel. "Of course you do, otherwise you wouldn't have this number. You see the address on the card?"

"Yes."

"Meet me there at ten, if that works for you."

"Sounds good to me," said Alma.

"Great! I'll see you in an hour then."

Rachel squealed in delight and spun in a circle with the phone held above her head. The blanket fell to her feet, but she was too excited to mind. She bounded into the bedroom and leapt on the back of Stephen's legs.

"Guess what!"

"Oh Christ!" Stephen put his head under a pillow and covered his ears, clearly a victim of their celebration the night before.

Rachel put her phone on the bed and started to spank both of Stephen's butt cheeks independently. "Get up, sleepyhead. Butt bongos, butt bongos," she gleefully continued to slap him like an instrument.

Stephen swung the pillow back at her haphazardly and laughed when he asked, "What's gotten into you? How are you not hungover?"

121

"I am, actually, I think I might still be a little drunk. I don't know, but that's not the point. I've got great news. Huge news!"

Stephen started to turn and pushed her off the back of his legs. She bounced on the bed beside him and he slid partway over her, as if trying to pin her down with a sleepy wrestling move. However, when he realized she was partially nude he perked up.

"Are you running around the house naked?" he asked, though he didn't seem to mind.

He groped her, misinterpreting her morning surprise, and she pushed his hand away. "Stop it."

"What?" He tried again.

"Oh my God, stop it. We don't have time. Someone's meeting me here in an hour and I've got to get ready."

"An hour?" asked Stephen. His eyes were barely more than slits and he had a goofy drunken grin as he lecherously stared at Rachel's breasts. "That's way more time than I need."

"Aren't you even a little curious who's coming over?" asked Rachel as she relented and let Stephen play with her breasts.

"Sure," said Stephen for her benefit as he started to lick around her nipple.

"You're horrible," said Rachel, although his attention had started to arouse her.

"Yeah," said Stephen as he kissed his way up her neck.

She closed her eyes and enjoyed his foreplay. She'd learned to enjoy it whenever he took the time, which wasn't as often as she would've liked. He climbed over her, already erect, and opened her legs. Rachel pushed his shoulders up as he had his lips suctioned to her nipple, and forced him to look at her. "Alma's coming with us to Widowsfield."

Stephen's eyes grew wide and a boyish excitement overtook him. "Seriously?" He sat up straight, seeming to lose all interest in intercourse.

122

"Yes, that's what I was trying to tell you. That's who's coming over. I'm going to take her out to buy some clothes before we head out."

Stephen put his hands on his head and looked like a child on Christmas. "This is great! Rachel, this is huge!"

"I know. That's what I was trying to tell you before you started trying to do me."

"What made her change her mind?"

"I don't know," said Rachel. "She just called and said that she's willing to come as long as we let her boyfriend come too."

"She can bring the philharmonic for all I care."

Rachel chuckled. She liked seeing Stephen this excited. "She wants to have final say on what footage airs, and what we talk to her about, but we were going to give her that anyhow."

"Sure, that's fine by me." Stephen got off the bed and started to gather his clothes.

"Hey," said Rachel as she lay on the bed, watching him get dressed. "What are you doing? You're just going to get me all ready to go and then leave me cold?"

He looked at the alarm clock to check the time. "Don't you have to get ready?"

She gave him a derisive grin. "I'm pretty sure we can fit in the few minutes you need to finish up here."

"Few minutes?" He crawled back onto the bed and over her. "Baby, you'd better get ready for at least, like, five minutes of heaven."

Rachel laughed and then squealed as he dove over her and started to bite playfully at her neck.

* * *

"Come in," said Stephen when he answered the door.

Alma was nervous as she looked in at Rachel and Stephen's gorgeous apartment. It was on the north side of the city, on the first floor of a converted duplex. The old, stone edifice was gated with delicately crafted wrought iron and the façade was replete with lush ivy. The wood floor looked old, but beautifully so, with dents and scratches that gave it character. All of the furniture inside was white, with black legs, and looked as if it had been set in place with the purpose of being used for a magazine photo shoot. Even the haphazardly tossed magazines on the glass coffee table looked as if they'd been purposefully disheveled.

"Your apartment is stunning," said Alma.

Paul walked in behind her, and even the sound of his boots clopping on the floor was out of place. Alma knew he was uncomfortable without even looking back at him.

"Thanks," said Stephen. "That's all Rachel's doing. When she moved in, she made me chuck out all my stuff. She likes to pretend she's the one that picked out everything, but don't let her fool you. Her father is an interior decorator. He's responsible for all this."

"Well he can come over to my place anytime," said Alma.

"Hi, I'm Stephen." He reached out his hand to shake Paul's

"Paul." The gruff, one word answer would have to do.

"Come on in, sit down. Can I get you some coffee or something?" Stephen was wearing a pair of tight fitting jeans and a Northwestern t-shirt. He was barefoot, and his steps didn't seem to make a sound as he padded through the room. However, every step that Alma and Paul took seemed to echo like hammer strikes on the wood.

"I'm fine," said Alma.

"Same here." Paul stayed behind Alma, as if more nervous than she was. He slipped his index fingers through belt loops on either side of her waist and stayed pressed against her back.

"Rachel's just finishing getting ready." Stephen picked up a wine bottle and smiled as he held it aloft. "We might've been a little too liberal with the wine last night during our celebration."

"What was the celebration for?" asked Alma as she stood with Paul just past the foyer.

"Besides the fact that it was Friday?" asked Stephen with a smile. "Yesterday was Rachel's last day at the station. Yours was her last story."

"Oh wow," said Alma. "She didn't mention that before."

Stephen tossed the empty wine bottle into a trashcan that had been set aside for recyclables. "That's because she didn't know it at the time. She didn't decide to take the plunge until we got home from the restaurant. We got our first deposit from the online ads from our video yesterday. It was more than twice what Rachel makes per month."

"Nice," said Paul.

"You can say that again. And I'm an independent contractor for the station, so I can keep pulling in an income while we focus on the site. I don't have to work full time for them if I don't want to," said Stephen as he walked to the living room. "Come on in, sit down." He waved them over to join him.

"Should I take off my shoes?" asked Paul. He looked hilariously out of place amid the designer decorations that surrounded them.

"No," said Stephen as he waved off Paul's concern. "Don't be silly. Come on in, have a seat."

"I feel bad that you're going to have to rent a van to haul us," said Alma as she walked to the loveseat and sat down.

"I can ride my motorcycle if you want," said Paul as he sat beside Alma.

"It's no big deal," said Stephen. "I went out and bought a ton of equipment to take with us, so it's my fault."

"Camera stuff?" asked Paul.

Stephen leaned forward and had a glint of excitement in his eyes. He was a handsome guy, and when he was happy his smile was endearing. "Even better. Rachel would kill me if she knew how much I spent on it, so don't say anything."

He glanced over his shoulder to make sure the bedroom door was still closed. "I found a Paranormal Investigation company in Kentucky that was closing up shop, and I bought all of their old equipment."

"What sort of stuff?" asked Paul.

"All sorts of cool things," said Stephen. Alma was reminded of two men at Christmas comparing gadgets they'd been given. "An EMF meter, a thermometer, motion sensors, stationary cameras, night vision goggles…"

"Awesome," said Paul.

Stephen smiled wide and nodded, encouraged by Paul's appreciation. "They're bad ass. I'll let you check them out when we get to…"

The door to the bedroom opened and Stephen sat back in his seat, abruptly ending his excited recounting of his list of new toys.

"Hi," said Rachel as she came out of the room. "Sorry I'm running late."

"No problem," said Alma.

Rachel looked exquisite, even in a simple pair of jeans and a sweater. Alma was suddenly ashamed of herself and looked down at her drab outfit. Rachel and Stephen were a different class of people from herself and Paul, and she felt incredibly out of place when with them.

"You must be Paul," said Rachel as she came around the love seat to shake Paul's hand.

"Hi." Paul looked uncertain if he should stand up to greet her. He shook her hand and smiled, clearly as uncomfortable as Alma.

Rachel turned her attention to Alma and looked like she was greeting an old friend as she reached out to take her hands. "Alma! I can't tell you how excited I am that you decided to come." She took Alma's hands and pulled her off the seat. "I am going to get you whatever you want today. Okay? We're going to go bananas. Shoes, skirts, jewelry, mannies, peddies, anything you want."

"You don't need to do that, honestly," said Alma.

"Yeah, babe," said Stephen. "Let's not spend everything we made the day after we made it."

Rachel gave her husband a wry, knowing smirk. "This coming from the guy trying to hide four crates of stuff he bought off eBay in our storage locker."

Stephen blushed and chuckled uncomfortably.

"Yeah," said Rachel. "I know all about it, bucko. So zip it." She turned back to Alma. "You and I are going to make a day of it. I'll take you to my hair place, and they'll set you up. By the end of the day you'll feel like a new person."

"When are we going to leave for Missouri?" asked Alma.

"We can leave tomorrow," said Rachel. "He's still got to get the van and I'm sure he's going to want to play around with all of his new gadgets. We've got plenty of time. Right, babe?"

Stephen shrugged, aware that he wasn't being given much of a choice in the matter. "Whatever you say, beautiful."

"Paul, do you want to come with us?" asked Rachel, although her tone implied that she assumed he would hate to go along for the girly extravaganza.

"Shopping, hair styling, manicures," said Paul. "That sounds absolutely," he paused, "like the worst day ever."

Rachel and Alma laughed.

"You're welcome to chill here with me," said Stephen. "We can test out all the new toys. We'll fire up the grill and get some beer."

Paul pointed at Stephen with a gracious grin. "That sounds like a plan."

Stephen got off the couch and slapped Paul's knee as he walked past. "Come on, I'll show you the gear I got."

Paul got up and Alma looked at him as Rachel was whisking her out the door. They smiled at each other and Paul blew her a kiss. Rachel had already pulled her out of the door before Alma could reciprocate.

* * *

127

Jacker had parked at the corner drugstore and walked down the block that his house was on. He couldn't risk parking on the street because the police might be patrolling the area in search of him. He knew it was a mistake to come here, but that didn't stop him. He wanted to see Debbie.

It had been a few days since the incident that forced him to pack his things and run away, and he hadn't dared come home since. His girlfriend certainly wouldn't want to have anything to do with him after what he did, and he wasn't sure he wanted anything to do with her either. Yet still he was drawn to her, if only for familiarity's sake. He'd give anything to sleep in his own bed for a night instead of in the back of the van again.

He stopped a few houses down and scanned the simple suburban street for any sign of police. His education of police procedure was sourced exclusively from television, so he made sure to look for unmarked vans that a surveillance team might be hiding in. His crime didn't warrant that sort of attention, but he was paranoid at this point, and had reason to be.

Everything appeared normal, so he dared to approach. He shared a house with Debbie, his girlfriend of five years, and had planned on proposing to her soon. The events of the past week had destroyed that, but Jacker still hoped they could have an amicable split. He wanted a chance to speak with her, but there was no guarantee she wouldn't call the police the minute she saw him.

It wasn't a wealthy neighborhood, and several homes had the requisite car in the lawn that seemed to be a disclaimer of low property value. He always dreamed of buying a condo in the city, but his career had stalled and was now permanently over. After what he'd done, his future job opportunities were probably limited to aspirations of drive-thru manager status.

As he walked down the cracked sidewalk, where the weeds had started to sprout, he wished yet again that he could go back one week and never ask Debbie about her relationship with the stock-boy at the supermarket where she worked. If only Jacker hadn't known the truth, he could've stayed happy.

He wasn't far from home when he spotted a car approaching from far down the street. It was white, and he stared at it for several seconds as he tried to decide if the black bar on top was a luggage rack or a police light bar.

"Oh crap," he said under his breath as he stopped in his tracks. It was a squad car, and it was approaching fast. He didn't want to run, just in case it wasn't him they were looking for, but he was only one house away from his. He turned up his neighbor's driveway and sauntered up as if he lived there. He did his best to act as if nothing was wrong as the squad car rolled up to park in front of his house, less than fifty feet away.

Jacker got to the side of his neighbor's house and pressed his back to it. He closed his eyes and said a quick prayer as he heard the police car doors open. He looked to his left, further up the driveway, but the tall wire fence was locked shut. He knew his neighbors had two German shepherds, and didn't want to risk alerting them by trying to climb the fence. He stayed put, and hoped the police hadn't recognized him.

He heard them knock on his door, and he dared to peer around the corner of his neighbor's house. There were two officers on his stoop, beside the flower bed where Jacker had pulled out a fern that Debbie despised. She had asked him to plant flowers instead, and he'd started the laborious task of tearing out the old plants a couple weeks earlier.

The officers knocked again, and Jacker heard a muffled reply come from inside. Debbie opened the door and greeted the officers. She was in a pair of sweat pants and a Slayer t-shirt, and her loud voice carried easily through the neighborhood. Debbie was far from a timid personality, quick to anger and rooted in her opinions, and she savored arguments. She was a difficult and domineering personality, but that was one of the things Jacker liked most about her. He wasn't afraid to admit that she ran the household, and he actually preferred it that way.

The officer spoke too quietly for Jacker to eavesdrop on, but he had no problem hearing every word his girlfriend said. Most of the conversation that he could hear was just a series of one word replies from Debbie.

"Nope."

"Yes."

"Okay."

And then her volume grew and he could hear the anger in her voice. "If I do, I'll call you. And, to be blunt, I'm surprised that you haven't caught him yet. It's not like he's some master criminal or something. He's not even that smart."

The officer responded, calm and quiet.

"No. No I don't," said Debbie. "I wouldn't let him back in if he came here. I want him in jail more than anyone. More than even that kid's family, I bet. You need to catch him." She annunciated every word of what she said next, "I don't feel safe anymore."

Jacker slid his back down the siding of his neighbor's house until he was sitting on the driveway. He took his glasses off and put his hands over his eyes and rubbed them as he sighed.

Debbie continued to chastise the officers. "You need to find him. Okay? Put him in jail and throw away the key. He's no good to anyone anymore. Not after what he did."

Jacker took a white pill out of the inside pocket of his jacket and let it sit in his palm. He stared down at the non-descript, circular pill and then popped it in his mouth. He hated swallowing pills without something to drink, but he forced this bitter one down anyhow. The past week had already been as bad as it could get. At least these little opiates helped stave off the bigger demons lurking within.

He waited for the officers to leave, and then snuck away. He went back to his van, content with the knowledge that

Debbie wanted nothing to do with him. He was on his own now.

CHAPTER 9 - New Friends

March 10th, 2012

"I don't know," said Alma.

The stylist was a tall, thin, gay man that Alma was fairly certain was wearing more foundation than she was. He had impossibly blue eyes, surely the result of designer contacts, and surgically plumped lips. His stereotypical lisp seemed exaggerated, but he knew how to make a girl feel good about herself, and he used his talents expertly.

"Listen, Miss Harper," he said her name as if he adored the way it sounded coming off his tongue, "I'm here to make you happy. I'll snip and clip whatever you want me too, but I promise that I know what I'm doing." He held her long hair in one hand behind her as if putting it into a ponytail and leaned forward so that their cheeks were nearly touching. He looked at her in the mirror of his station. "I don't charge two hundred a pop for a Super Cuts."

Alma's eyes widened. "Two hundred? Are you serious? Rachel," she turned to look back at the reporter who was sitting across the room from the stylist's station.

"Don't say it," said Rachel with her arms out to her side, fingers splayed as the polish dried. "This is my treat. Too late to back out now."

"Oh my God," said Alma. "I've never spent more than fifty dollars on a hair cut in my whole life. This is crazy." She was more amused than exasperated and settled back in her chair, content to let Rachel pamper her if she wanted.

"No, darling," said the stylist. "This is Laurelies," he said the studio's name with flourish. "And you know what they say about Laurelies, don't you?"

"What's that?" Alma was starting to appreciate the peek into a lifestyle she'd never enjoyed before.

"Laurelies gets the men between your thighs."

"Julian." Rachel chastised the stylist with her tone.

He pointed his silver comb at her. "You know it's true, you slut."

"I honestly don't know why I put up with you," said Rachel.

Julian snickered and turned Alma's chair so that she was facing Rachel. "Please, honey, you know you've always wanted to be my fag hag. Here, look at your friend and help me convince her that I'm right." He held Alma's hair to display the short look that he was hoping to achieve. "Wouldn't she look amazing with short hair?"

Rachel nodded and said, somewhat unenthusiastically, "Sure, I guess so."

"You guess so?" asked Julian, frustrated by Rachel's passionless response. He spun Alma back around and looked at her through the mirror. "Trust me, honey. You've got sharp features and a long face. We want to puff you up a little, you skinny thing. We'll cut the hair here," he acted as if his fingers were scissors as he demonstrated, "just below the chin line. Then taper it up in back a little, to give you a sort of pixie, badass thing. The front will be longer, and I'll show you how to thicken it up to give your face a little more oomph." He thrust his hips along with the onomatopoeia.

Alma looked at herself in the mirror; her tired, same old self. The same face she'd stared at unenthusiastically her whole life. While others often said she was pretty, they nearly as frequently added the aphorism, 'You should pay more attention to yourself.' That was, of course, code for, 'You'd be pretty if you took the time to try and look nice.'

She sighed, closed her eyes, and said, "Okay, do it."

Julian squealed in delight. "Nurse, get my scalpel before she changes her mind." He got the scissors from his drawer and wasted no time before making the first cut. He stopped, a foot long section of hair dangling from his hand, and asked, "Are you sure you don't want to change your mind?"

With the huge chunk already gone, there was clearly no turning back now. Alma shook her head and gave a gleeful yelp. "I can't believe I'm letting you do this."

"Miss Harper, my dear, you're going to be thanking me when this is done. I promise, you're going to get so much dick you won't know what to do with it. And if you need a few pointers, I'll give you my card." He stopped and looked at her through the mirror. "You are straight, right? You two aren't dykes, are you?" He motioned back and forth between Rachel and Alma with his scissors.

"Julian, I'm married," said Rachel as she eavesdropped. "You know that."

Julian shrugged and then got back to cutting Alma's hair. "So what? Rocko was married."

"Shut up, Julian," said Rocko, the effeminate greeter that was casually flipping through a magazine at the front desk.

"I'm not saying, I'm just saying," whispered Julian as if telling Alma a naughty secret.

The stylist spent the next half hour trying to convince Alma to let him dye her hair as he finished her cut. He wanted to dye the tips of her longest strands pink, but she kept telling him that her school wouldn't allow any unusual hairstyles on teachers. This led to a lengthy discussion about Julian's experience as a gay teen in Kentucky before he moved north. Alma wasn't homophobic, but she was also ashamed to admit that she didn't have any close gay friends. It was somewhat intriguing, perhaps even intoxicating, to get a glimpse into the life of someone like Julian. By the time he was done, she would've gladly called him a friend. Suddenly, the two hundred dollar cost of the session seemed more than reasonable.

"What do you think?" asked Julian as he handed Alma the hand mirror so she could inspect the cut. He spun her around and then stepped back in wait, as if hoping for an Oscar nomination.

Her hair hadn't been that short since she was a child. She put her fingers through it, and then smiled as she said, "I like it."

Julian applauded and then raised his arms with jubilance. "She likes it. Hallelujah, she likes it! I told you that you would."

"You were right." She handed him the mirror and then pushed at either side of the bob which caused her hair to balloon up. "I don't know how you got it to puff up so much. I'm just worried that I'm going to wake up tomorrow and it'll just lie there, all flat."

"Easy, easy secrets," said Julian. "It's the magic of science and chemicals and stuff. I'll get you some shampoo and conditioner to increase volume, and then you'll use a spritz. You'll have to get a big round brush like the one I used and then just curl and spritz, curl and spritz. You've got nice hair, even if you don't believe it. You just have to give it a little attention. No more rub, rub," he put his fingers on his own short hair and mimed a bored hair washing in the shower, "rinse, rinse, off to work. From now on you're going to give yourself ten extra minutes to look gorgeous. Okay?"

"Okay."

He put his hand on his hip and cast a wary look at her. "Promise me, Miss Harper. You're too damn pretty not to know it, and too damn sexy not to show it."

"I bet you say that to all the girls."

He gave her a wry, devilish grin. Then he set his hand beside his lips and leaned forward. "It's true, I do, but this time I mean it. You're a stunner, my little music teacher. I want you to give those boys in class something to jerk off to."

"Are you done poisoning my friend?" asked Rachel as she came to stand on the other side of the chair.

"I'm nothing if not the cure." Julian dropped his scissors into a tall glass cylinder filled with blue liquid. "Where are you two sluts off to next?"

"I'm going to force her to let me do her makeup," said Rachel. "And then off to buy shoes."

"Well, aren't you just the sweet sugar mama?" Julian walked with them to the front counter. "Wake up, Rocko.

135

It's time to earn your eight dollars an hour." He pointed at the register and made several jabs at it with his index fingers. "Clickety clack, Rocko."

Rocko didn't look amused as he set his magazine down and started to punch in the numbers. Julian led Alma over to a section on the wall that was lined with bottles of hair care products. Alma didn't recognize any of the labels.

"We're going to get you this, and this, oh, and this one." He handed her three bottles.

Alma looked for a price tag, but didn't see one. "How much are these?"

He shook his head and waved off her question. "On the house, sweetie."

"Really?"

He wavered his head and then pointed at Rachel. "Well, as long as we call her the 'House.'"

"I can't," said Alma. "She's already spent too much on me. This is ridiculous."

Julian stopped her before Alma could put any of the bottles back on the shelf. "You'll have to take it up with her, darling. It's already paid for. Besides, don't let her fool you, Rachel gets the celebrity discount, what with her being a reporter and all."

"Got your stuff?" asked Rachel as she finished with Rocko and met them at the shelves.

Alma grimaced and looked down bashfully at her armful of products. "Rachel, this is too much. I feel like you're spending way too much on me."

"Oh stop it," said Rachel. "Learn how to let yourself be pampered. It's my pleasure. Julian, did you know that Alma is going to be on the news soon because she's such a good teacher?"

"Oh yeah?" asked Julian.

Rachel quickly replied. "Yep. She'd never tell anyone, because she's too modest, but her school put together a big deal for her; paid to get a new music room and everything, just because they like her so much."

136

"Well, well," said Julian. "I would've given anything for just one good teacher growing up. Keep up the good fight, Miss Harper. The world needs a lot of things, but good teachers are at the tippy-top of the list."

"Thanks," she said bashfully.

He reached into his shirt pocket and took out a business card that he then slipped into Alma's back pocket. "And when you want to get freshened up again, give me a ring so I can be sure to give you the celebrity discount."

*   *   *

"I can't believe all this shit," said Paul as he inspected an EMF meter that had been stored in one of several steel boxes in Stephen's storage locker.

"I know. It's like Christmas." Stephen climbed over a stack of boxes similar to the one that Paul had opened. The storage room was located in the alley of Stephen's building, and had been converted from the building's garage to accommodate four similar areas. "Check this out." He hauled up a monitor and another small black box that had a series of red switches on the front of it. "This is for the motion sensors. You can set it up to watch up to fifteen feeds, and the monitor will automatically switch to any that detect something. You can set it to search for heat or movement."

"Nice," said Paul.

Stephen was smiling so wide that it would've been hard for him to stop. "Damn straight it's nice."

"So, you must be pretty big into this ghost stuff," said Paul. "How did that happen? Have you always been into it?"

"Yes and no," said Stephen. "When I was a kid I believed in all of it, but then I turned into a cynical adult, like most of us do. Then, when I was in college, I went for a trip with some friends out to a cabin in Michigan. That night I saw something that totally changed my mind. Ever since then I've been a believer."

Paul set the EMF detector back in its case. "All right then, what did you see? You can't leave me hanging."

Stephen avoided the question for a second, and Paul wondered if he'd overstepped his bounds. Finally, he started to explain, "It was a little boy playing with a toy train in the kitchen." Stephen didn't look at Paul as he recounted the story. "It was in the middle of the night and I was high, and drunk, so at first I thought I was seeing things. I got out of bed and walked through the living room, over a bunch of my friends that were sleeping on the floor, and went in the fridge to get a left-over burrito. I closed the door of the fridge and there he was, this little kid in a pair of pajamas, on the kitchen floor playing with a train." Stephen glanced at Paul, but then looked down as he acted out the ghost's movements. "Just sitting there, not paying any attention to me; just playing with that train. Then, he dematerialized in front of me."

Paul wasn't certain how to respond, and turned to humor to lighten the mood. "Dude, you were eating left-over burritos. That's, like, begging for evil."

Stephen chuckled, but it was clearly for Paul's benefit. "I wrote it off as a side effect of too much weed, and maybe bad Mexican food. Then, a few weeks later I found out something about that cabin that made me lose my shit. Turns out, the guy that owned the place had a little brother who died there from carbon monoxide poisoning. His dad wanted to sell the cabin, but his mother refused to let him. She said that her son was still there in spirit, and that she sometimes heard him playing with his toys on the kitchen floor at night." Stephen shivered abruptly. "Gives me the willies thinking about it."

"That's all sorts of creepy," said Paul.

"What about you?" asked Stephen. "Do you believe in it, or do you think it's all bullshit?"

Paul thumbed his beard just under his lip as he debated how to handle the discussion. "I'd love to believe it, but I'm more of the hardcore skeptic type. I'm not religious or anything either. I'm not trying to discount what you saw or anything, but I have a tough time believing in that sort of thing."

"I get it," said Stephen as he climbed back out of the storage unit. "My wife's the same way, and it works out for us. Helps keep things in perspective. Can I ask you a question, though?"

"Sure, go for it."

"What do you think about what Alma saw?"

"I don't know," said Paul. "Depends on what it is you heard that she saw." He didn't fall for the ploy to get information out of him.

"Well, I got all of the police reports," said Stephen. "It pays to have a reporter for a wife. They said that Alma saw a green fog, and men, or some type of creatures, running through the fog. She said they'd been staying in Widowsfield when the rest of the town disappeared, but her father had proof that he'd been staying at a cabin in Forsythe. The police couldn't find evidence of anything at either locations, and they held her father for as long as they could, but couldn't come up with a case to pin on him for the disappearance of Alma's brother."

"You know just about as much as I do," said Paul. He didn't think it would be appropriate for him to elaborate on any of the other details Alma had shared with him. "Alma doesn't like to talk about it much."

"So what do you think happened? Not with Alma's brother, but with the town in general. Why did everyone just, poof, disappear?"

Paul shrugged. "Who knows? I've heard it was government controlled, and that there was a massive drug cartel operating out of the town. Everyone got taken away and put into witness protection."

Stephen guffawed as if the theory was ludicrous. "Yeah, sure, an entire town gets taken away by the government? That's crazy."

"Maybe, but it's the least crazy of all the theories I've heard," said Paul. "It's easier for me to believe that than some of the other stuff people have said. Why? What do you think happened?"

"That, my friend, is what I'm hoping to find out. I'm not leaving anything off the table. There was some weird shit going on in Widowsfield before everyone disappeared."

"Like what?"

"Well, there's the whole drug cartel thing that you were talking about. There was a meth ring that used Widowsfield as a staging area, but then the government banned the sale of amphetamine except in small doses. That meant the drug dealers had to figure out a new way to make the meth in massive quantity. There's a theory that one of the concoctions they mixed up caused a fire, and a toxic cloud was released in the town that caused everyone to go nuts."

"Huh, never heard that one before."

"It's a lot more plausible than it sounds at first. The race to create new, stronger drugs has led to a lot of insane side effects. People aren't content just smoking a little weed these days. They're screwing around with some seriously messed up chemicals, and the theory is that the dealers in Widowsfield were trying to mix together meth and ecstasy, but ended up causing an explosion that sent a noxious gas through the town. And then there's the military experiment theory."

"What's that?"

"There's a base just outside of Widowsfield that's owned by a company called Cada E.I.B."

"What is it?" asked Paul, unsure he heard the name correctly.

"Cada E.I.B. No one knows much about them, but they seem to be pretending to be a European Investment Bank. Or at least they were. Right after the event in Widowsfield, the entire facility shut down. No explanation, they just closed up shop and got the hell out of the area. Turns out, this same company was involved in brokering weapon deals

140

between countries. They were setting up deals between the United States and places like Scotland, Greece, Romania, and all sorts of other places. It's shady stuff. The theory is that they were testing out some biochemical weapon and accidentally released it."

Paul glanced at the abundance of equipment in the storage unit. "That sounds interesting and all, but I thought you were in this for the paranormal side of it."

"I am, but I also want to make sure to explore all options. I want to treat our viewers like they're smart. If we can find real evidence of paranormal activity, then that's awesome, but I'm also going to look for real world explanations for stuff too. I want the show to be smarter than the rest of them out there."

"So, this show is on the internet, right?" asked Paul. The amount of equipment in the storage locker seemed excessive for a small internet venture.

Stephen looked coy, like a boy whose mischief had been uncovered. "Well, you want to know the truth? You've got to keep it on the down low, because no one's supposed to know."

"Okay, sure." Paul was an intensely private person, and thought it odd that Stephen was willing to trust him with any secret, let alone an important one. Stephen spoke as if Paul had been his friend for years.

"We got optioned." He beamed with pride and excitement.

"What's that mean?"

"Rachel and I were approached by a cable channel. I can't tell you which one – they were real strict about that. They paid us to have first rights on any show we put together. That's why I got all this stuff."

"Wow, that's awesome. Congratulations," said Paul.

"It's been a bit overwhelming, but we're trying to make sure we do everything we can to make this pilot professional."

"And it's just the two of you?" asked Paul. "I would think you'd have a whole crew going along. You know, for lighting and sound and cameras. You're just going to try and do this by yourselves?"

"No," said Stephen and he pat Paul's shoulder. "I've got you along for the ride."

"Oh, I see how it is," said Paul. "You're trying to bribe me with beer and barbeque. You're a tricky one."

Stephen laughed as he closed the accordion, aluminum door of the storage room. "Honestly though, it's not as hard as you might think. These days, with reality shows and everything, viewers have a really low expectation of quality. A lot of the shows on the air don't bother hiring even half the staff that they used to. I've been in the news business for a while, and even the quality of our remote reports is better than most primetime shows. We actually take the time to set up lights and use proper mics. Most of the reality shows out there are a clusterfuck of amateur mistakes."

"I hate reality shows," said Paul.

"You're in good company," said Stephen. "They're the bane of the industry at the moment. A hell of a lot of good people have lost jobs because the American public doesn't seem to give a shit about quality anymore." He scratched at his temple and shrugged. "I say that, but I'm just about to go out and try to film a show without a crew. I'm not usually that big of a hypocrite, I swear."

"And you're planning on shoving all that stuff into a single car?" Paul pointed at the storage locker as Stephen was locking it.

"I was going to rent a van. Speaking of which, I should probably call up the rental place."

"I've got a buddy with a van," said Paul. "He's not doing anything these days. I bet he'd be willing to drive us if you paid him whatever the cost of a rental would be. Then you could use him as an extra pair of hands for filming your show."

"You think he'd come along on such short notice?"

Paul nodded sullenly. "Yeah, he'll be happy to get out of town. He caught his old lady cheating on him and moved out. He was going to get a new place, but then he lost his job after he blew up at work." Paul felt like he needed to assure Stephen that he wasn't trying to invite a mental case on the trip. "He's the most passive guy you've ever met, but the dude got pushed too far. He got sick of getting shit on at work, and combined with what he was going through at home, he just reached his wit's end. Anyhow, I'm sure he'd be happy to come along."

Stephen seemed apprehensive at first, but then nodded. "Sure, man. If you vouch for the guy, I'd love to have someone else that could help with the show."

"I'll give him a ring." Paul got his cell phone out to call Jacker.

CHAPTER 10 - Broken Codes

March 10th, 2012

Alma followed Rachel down the street in the affluent neighborhood. The sun was already setting and she was shocked at how long they'd managed to spend shopping. Alma wasn't the type of girl that normally spent more time at a store than it took to run in, get what she needed, and get out. It was something that Paul always said he loved about her, but Alma would be lying if she said she hadn't enjoyed the day's decadence.

Rachel had taken her to various shops in the city that Alma had never heard of before, and they had lunch at an outdoor café that overlooked the shopping district. During their trip, three different people had approached Rachel, recognizing her from television, and told her that they loved her work. One even asked for an autograph, and Rachel complied although she looked embarrassed while doing it.

"Did you have a good time?" Rachel was headed up to the steps to her apartment when she turned and smiled at Alma.

"Are you kidding?" Alma held up two arms filled with bags. "This was amazing. I still feel guilty that you bought all of this for me."

"Don't mention it. I was happy to do it. I felt like a complete bitch after what happened with your dad. I swear, I never in a million years thought he'd follow us back here to find you."

"Oh don't worry about it," said Alma. "He's a nutjob."

"Still though, buying you a few nice things is the least I can do to apologize." She paused at the door with her keys near the lock. "What do you think Paul's going to say? Do you think he'll like your new look?"

"I don't know. He's never seen me looking like this. Heck, I've never seen myself looking like this."

"Well, you look great, Alma. Absolutely gorgeous." Rachel saw the bashful way Alma turned her head, unwilling to accept the compliment. "I'm serious. You're a gorgeous girl, and Paul will be lucky if you decide to take him back."

Alma and Rachel had spent a good part of the day chatting about Paul, and Alma's history with him. Alma revealed a lot of things that she'd never told anyone, and she attributed her admissions to the fact that Rachel was a good listener. She was always quick with an opinion, but seemed genuinely interested to hear what was going on in Alma's life. Rachel was a talented interviewer, and Alma enjoyed talking to her.

When Rachel asked Alma to explain what attracted her to Paul, she'd struggled to encapsulate it. Their relationship, which had been going on and on since high school, was tumultuous, but Alma couldn't imagine a life without him. He was as important to her as anyone in her life ever had been, and she depended on him more than he knew. Even when they were broken up, she would call him just to hear his voice. Many of those random calls ended with them arguing, but Alma never stayed mad at him for too long. As she tried to explain to Rachel what it was about Paul that attracted her so much, Alma stated that she felt safe with him. That was a luxury Alma didn't often feel, but she knew Paul would do anything to protect her.

Rachel continued her query, "Which begs the question, are you going to take him back?"

Alma shrugged, and then sighed before saying, "I don't know. I haven't made up my mind yet."

Rachel coyly smirked. "Yes you have. Don't try to lie to me."

Alma blushed.

"You've been talking about him all day. He's a lucky guy, and I think you two make a cute couple," said Rachel as she turned the key and opened the door.

"There they are." Alma heard Stephen's voice from inside. "Do we have any money left?"

"That depends on how much you spent on your ghost detecting crap," said Rachel as she went in. "Where's Paul?"

"He's out back with his friend," said Stephen. "They're loading up his friend's van with the equipment. He was able to get us someone else to come along for the trip and help out."

"Oh," said Rachel. "That's helpful." She set her bags down in the foyer and turned to present Alma. "So, what do you think?"

Stephen whistled. "Hot damn, girl! Look at you."

Rachel spun her finger to instruct Alma to model her new look. Alma held her arms out to the side with the bags still looped around them and turned for Stephen to inspect her new black dress.

"You look beautiful, Alma. Honestly."

"Thanks," said Alma. "But you guys spent too much on me."

Stephen waved away her concern. "Think of it as a down payment on what I owe you for denting your car."

"Oh my God," said Rachel. "I totally forgot about that. We're paying for that," she said as if scolding Stephen.

"I will, I will," said Stephen in defense. "Come on in and chill out. I've got burgers and brats on the grill, and Paul warned me that you were a vegetarian, so we got some of those veggie burgers too. And we picked up some beer that Paul said was your favorite," he said and looked at Alma.

"You guys are being too nice to us," said Alma. "I feel like you're buttering us up for something."

Stephen smiled and laughed, but Alma detected a slight bit of reservation in his response. "Well, I still have to get you to sign the wavers and stuff. Once you do that, I promise I'll start being mean to you."

"Okay." Alma put her bags down beside Rachel's. "That sounds more like it. I'm not used to people being so nice all the time."

"Get Rachel to play Scrabble with you and you'll see her mean side," said Stephen.

Alma raised her eyebrows and looked at Rachel. "Be careful, I'm a Scrabble freak."

Rachel stopped, straightened her posture, and glared at Alma as if about to yell at her for something. "Don't screw with my emotions, Alma. Are you serious? Because I'm the biggest Scrabble nerd, like, ever. For real."

"Me too," said Alma pleadingly, as if trying to convince Rachel that it was true.

"What's your favorite word that pisses other people off when you use it?" Rachel seemed to be testing Alma.

She thought about it for a minute. "Xi. It's a letter in the Greek alphabet that's in the Scrabble dictionary."

Rachel's eyes widened and she squeaked in pleasure. "I love you so much right now, Alma. I studied the Scrabble dictionary and came up with all sorts of little words that no one else knows. It pisses people off so much, but I'm always just like, 'Go ahead and challenge me.' They learn not to real quick."

"True," said Stephen. "I won't play with her anymore."

Rachel stepped toward Alma and took her hands. She had an oddly serious look on her face as she spoke. "Alma Harper, would you do me the honor of playing Scrabble with me tonight?"

Alma laughed. "I'd love to, as long as you promise not to take back all the stuff you bought me after I beat you."

"Oh, those are big words, little girl," said Rachel. "I haven't lost a game of Scrabble in over a decade at least."

"Lord have mercy," said Stephen. "It's like the dork circle is finally complete. My wife found her soul mate. I guess me and the guys will just have to break out the Xbox or something."

"Oh yeah," said Alma. "Which friend of Paul's did you say is coming along?"

"A big guy," said Stephen as he held his hand well above his head, "named Jacker."

147

"Oh, okay," said Alma. She looked at Rachel and added, "You'll like him. I only met him last night, but he's a really nice guy."

"Jacker is a weird name," said Rachel.

"He's into computers," said Alma.

"He's a cool guy," said Stephen. "I feel bad about what happened with his girlfriend."

"Why?" asked Alma. "What happened?"

Stephen looked like a deer caught in the headlights as he stared at Alma and Rachel. "I've said too much." He made a zipper motion over his lips and tried to walk away.

"No, no, no," said Rachel. "You have to tell us now. What happened?"

"Sorry, babe, I'm not one of your gossipy friends," said Stephen. "If you want to know, you'll have to ask him. It's not my place to say."

"Oh fine, be like that," said Rachel. "How long until food's ready?"

"It's good to go. I was just waiting on you two."

There was a knock at the back of the apartment and then a door opened down the hall. Jacker leaned his head inside, uncertain if it was appropriate for him to just walk in. "Hello?"

"Come on in," said Stephen.

Jacker and Paul came in through the door on the opposite side of the apartment. Jacker saw Alma first, and put his hand over his heart as he stumbled backward, emphasizing his surprise. "Holy cow, Alma. You clean up well."

Paul walked around his friend and was astonished by what he saw. He blinked his eyes and shook his head. "God damn, babe."

Alma felt her ears burn as she blushed. She ran her hands through her hair and asked, "Do you like it? It's not too short, is it?"

"Do I like it?" asked Paul. "Are you kidding? You look like a super model."

148

"Stop it."

"No, he's right," added Jacker. "You look," he stopped in search of an appropriate descriptor, "stunning." He was stumbling down the hall, and looked disheveled. Alma attributed his odd mannerism to a lack of sleep.

Paul walked past his friend and came to stand before Alma. He put his hand on the side of her face and then gazed up and down at her. He was at a loss for words and could only smile. Alma never felt prettier in her entire life.

"You must be Jacker. I'm Rachel." The strawberry blonde reporter was quick to introduce herself.

"Hello," said Jacker as he shook her hand.

"Tell me what happened with your girlfriend," said Rachel, unfettered by common restraint.

"Rachel, Jesus," said Stephen, embarrassed.

"Sorry," said Rachel. "I don't like to beat around the bush with people. Stephen said you had something bad happen with your girlfriend, and I want to know what happened."

"Normal people try to get to know someone before grilling them with questions like that," said Stephen as he headed for the refrigerator to get a beer.

Rachel shrugged and walked hand in hand with Jacker toward the kitchen table. "Well, I'm not a normal girl. Here, sit down and talk to me."

Jacker obeyed, although he looked uncomfortable.

"Now tell me what happened. I know a lot of pretty girls who are suckers for a guy with a broken heart. Trust me."

Alma and Paul went to sit at the table with them as Stephen got everyone something to drink. The dining room, living room, and kitchen were all connected, but there was a thin, paper partition adorned with Japanese symbols that broke up the area. Paul tried, and nearly failed, not to knock over the decorative wall as he edged his way around the table.

149

Jacker splayed his hands out over the dark wood and tapped his fingers as he sighed. "It's my fault, really. I'm as much to blame as she was."

Paul grimaced and shook his head. "Bullshit." He accepted a glass of beer from Stephen and Alma assumed that Paul had already taught the host how to properly pour their favorite beer because it had the perfect amount of head on it. "Don't blame yourself for it. She cheated on you, plain and simple."

"Is that true?" asked Rachel.

Jacker nodded and then crossed his arms. "Yeah." He was fidgeting, obviously uncomfortable with the conversation, but Rachel either didn't notice or didn't care. She was a consummate journalist, more interested in the details of the story than the ramifications of discussing it.

"Why do you think it's your fault then?" asked Rachel.

"Because, I don't know, I should've paid more attention to her, taken her out more; that kind of stuff."

"But, she cheated on you, right?" asked Rachel.

"Yep, with the stock-boy at her work," said Jacker. "She's a cashier down at the grocery store on Thirtieth and Boston."

"If she's the one that cheated, then she's the one to blame," said Alma.

She hadn't meant it as a barb for Paul, but realized that it would be after she said it. Still though, she didn't feel bad. He deserved to feel guilty for some of his past mistakes.

Jacker stared uncomfortably at his hands as he writhed his fingers in and out of one another.

"All right," said Stephen loud enough to end the conversation. "Let's give the guy a break and focus on the next few days." He set a glass of beer in front of Jacker.

Jacker tipped the glass in Stephen's direction and said, "Thanks." It was obvious that he was thankful for more than the beer.

Stephen sat down and leaned back until the top of his chair rested against the wall. "Let's talk about Widowsfield."

"No, no, no," said Rachel. "Let's save it for the show."

Stephen let his chair drop back down and then crossed his arms. He nodded his head as if coming to the conclusion that his wife was right. "Okay, fine. But let's at least go over the agenda."

"Okay," said Rachel.

"If we leave tomorrow morning we can get there before dark," said Stephen. "I figure we should stay the night in Branson, which is about forty miles from Widowsfield. I stayed at a nice hotel out there the last time I was out, and I'll get us some rooms. I'll try and find a local that knows about the town."

"Like who?" asked Rachel, interrupting her husband.

"I'll find someone. Don't worry. If nothing else, I'll track down the girl I talked to last time. She'd been to Widowsfield a bunch of times and I'd bet…"

Rachel pressed her finger on the table as if pushing an imaginary button. She made a loud buzzing noise and then said, "Wrong, try again."

Stephen grimaced and gave his wife a tired look.

Rachel shook her head and said, "No. We're not bringing along some slut you…"

"Don't be ridiculous," said Stephen. He looked over at the others, smiled, and rolled his eyes. "She's got it in her head that I go out on business trips and meet all sorts of exotic women. You'd think a girl as pretty as Rachel wouldn't be so jealous and self-conscious all the time."

"Tell me about it," said Paul, inviting a sneer from Alma.

Stephen laughed and then slapped the table a few times. "Back on the subject. We'll sleep at the hotel, and I'll try to find someone to take us to Widowsfield. If I can't, no big deal, we'll just go by ourselves. Then, on Monday morning, we'll head out to the old Main Street. It's a ghost town now. We can do some filming there, and get a bunch of b-roll, that's just exterior shots that we'll use to fill in places for the actual show. It'll give us a chance to explore some of the more famous spots around town."

"What spots are those?" asked Alma.

"Well, like I said, there're a lot of theories about what happened," said Stephen. "There was a UPS truck in the area at the time, and the driver disappeared just like everyone else. The guy wasn't from Widowsfield, so it's unlikely he was tied to the meth ring. His truck was found on Main Street, outside of a used book store. We can go there, and check out the store."

"And then there's the hill," said Rachel.

"Right," Stephen pointed at her as he nodded. "Some of the teenagers from the area go to a hill that overlooks a farm near Widowsfield. It's kind of a make-out spot for the kids, but a lot of them have reported seeing a cloud appear over the field, filled with green light, and then suddenly disappear."

"I've seen some videos of that shit online," said Jacker. He was getting infected with Stephen's enthusiasm about the project.

"Right," said Stephen. "It's creepy, isn't it?"

"Heck yeah it is," said Jacker.

"I want to go spend the night on the hill," said Stephen.

"Surrounded by teenagers making out in their cars?" asked Rachel with a grimace, as if this was the first she'd heard of this plan. "Are you serious?"

"I don't think they're out there every night," said Stephen.

"I think you just want to catch a glimpse of some teen girl's boobs." Rachel crossed her arms as she chided her husband.

"That'd be cool too," said Stephen.

"Could I make a suggestion?" Alma was still timid around their hosts, and she had to force herself to speak up to be heard over them as they playfully argued.

Rachel and Stephen turned their attention to Alma. "Sure," said Stephen, surprised that Alma felt like she had to ask permission.

Alma's hands were shaking and she hid them under the table. "I'd like to go to the cabin first."

"Which cabin?" asked Stephen.

"The one that my father used to take us to. It's near the elementary school, on the edge of town, over by the reservoir." Alma looked down at her trembling hands and stilled them between her bony knees. "The last time I was there was with my mother, and I had a…" She stopped and struggled to continue. The others stayed silent as she battled with herself to recount any details of what happened. She felt like tears were about to spring from her eyes. She shook her head, trying to break the odd, sudden emotion, and took a long, deep breath. "That's when I remembered my brother again."

Rachel was quick to ask a question, uninhibited by Alma's obvious emotion. "What do you mean? You didn't remember him before that?"

Alma shook her head and continued to look down. "No. Something happened that day, in Widowsfield, when the cloud came through. I just forgot him. Not just what happened with him that day, but everything about him. It was like he didn't exist. When my father and I got home, I saw pictures of him in our house, but I didn't know who he was. My mother was furious and kept showing us pictures of my brother to prove he existed, and eventually called the police on my father. It was the worst day of my life. The cops interviewed me for hours and kept showing pictures of Ben and me together, but I didn't remember any of it. They eventually just attributed it to post traumatic stress, although they couldn't identify what had caused it."

"Wow," said Stephen as he leaned forward, his elbows perched on the table, to listen intently to what Alma was saying. "How did you end up remembering?"

"At first, I thought I started to remember him, but it was really just a trick of the brain." Alma felt Paul's hands on her shoulders and leaned her head back into his stomach as he stood behind her. She was thankful he was there to comfort

153

her, and she suddenly realized that she couldn't do this without him. "Have you ever heard about the study they did on childhood memories where they Photoshopped pictures of people together in a hot air balloon?"

None of them had, so Alma explained. "They would take a picture of a father and son, and put them in a hot air balloon even though they'd never gone in one before. Then they'd show the people a bunch of pictures of their childhood, most of them real, and the hot air balloon picture would be mixed in with the real ones. Afterward, they asked about the events in the pictures, and almost every time the patients talked about their trip in a hot air balloon with their father. They made up their own experience, and thought of it as real."

"Hold on." Rachel got up and rushed into the kitchen. She came back moments later with a pad and pencil and was furiously scribbling. Then she sat back down with the pencil, ready to write more. "Okay, go on."

"Do you always have to take notes?" asked Stephen with a laugh.

"Yeah," said Rachel matter-of-factly. "I'm a reporter; it's what I do. Go on, Alma."

"Anyhow, I think that's what happened with me. I saw those photos of me with Ben, and I started to believe in them. I made up a relationship with my brother, even though I couldn't remember that he ever existed. Then I went to Widowsfield with my mother, and it all changed."

"What happened?" asked Rachel. She was quick to respond and was ever vigilant with her pencil, ready to take down every bit of information that Alma was willing to divulge.

"Chaos Magick," said Stephen, and his response surprised everyone at the table. "Am I right?"

Alma nodded. "Yes. You mentioned it at the restaurant too. How did you know about that?"

"I've been researching you for a long time, Alma," said Stephen. Then he smiled and sat back. "Not to sound too

154

creepy or anything. I've been looking into supernatural stories all around the country, trying to figure out which one would make a good first feature for our site. During a shoot in Branson, I met someone that told me the local legends about the Widowsfield lights, and that's what got me to start researching it. That's when I discovered that you lived near us. Once we figured that out, we knew it was Widowsfield that we wanted to focus on first."

Alma was confused as she thought about what Stephen was saying. "Then why didn't you come to me first? Why did you go try to find my father first?"

Rachel and Stephen appeared uncomfortable. Rachel was the first to try and explain. "Well, we wanted to test out our format first, so we went to Philadelphia and did that story on the haunted house. That's what got everyone buzzing about our site in the first place. Since we were there, we decided to interview your father."

Alma thought about it, but still shook her head. "Still though, why wouldn't you come talk to me first?"

Neither of them was willing to answer, and it became apparent that they were hiding something. They couldn't hide their guilt.

"What's going on?" asked Alma. "What aren't you telling me?"

"Okay." Stephen put his hands down on the table as if laying out his hand in a card game. "I'm going to be totally honest with you, because you deserve to know everything."

Alma's heart started to beat faster and her hands clenched into fists. She was getting angry, and she could feel Paul's grip tighten on her shoulders. He knew how to recognize when she was getting mad.

"We're the ones that pushed for you to get the new classroom at your school."

Alma's anger subsided, and she felt the tension release from her muscles. "What? I don't get it. Why would you do that?"

155

"Well, we knew that we wanted to get to know you better, and we needed a good way to do it. Rachel proposed the story to her network, and they agreed to go along with it. We got the school to sign off on everything, and we set it all up."

"I thought it was a PTA thing," said Alma.

"It was," said Rachel. "Blair was great, and she did most of the work. She and the others really adore you, Alma. They loved the idea of setting you up with a new music room."

"Then why the subterfuge?" asked Alma. "Why didn't you just come out and tell me this right away? Why go to all the trouble of setting something like that up? Don't get me wrong, I'm happy you did! I just don't understand."

"I think I do." Paul spoke with a tinge of anger in his tone. "You said the school signed off on the footage, right?"

Stephen nodded and looked at Rachel as if silently communicating with her. Alma could see that he was nervous, and knew that Paul had figured something out that she hadn't as of yet.

"And I'm willing to bet that means you own the footage now.

Again, Stephen nodded.

"What does that mean?" asked Alma. "I still don't get it."

"He owns his own company," said Paul. "The station hires him as an independent contractor. When the school signed off on the footage, they were giving him full ownership of it. He can use it for anything he wants, including a story on Widowsfield."

"But what good would that footage be?" asked Alma. "It was just of me at the school."

"The piece would look better if we had shots of you," said Stephen. "We didn't want to go that route, but we thought it'd be good to have some footage of you, just in case. We knew you'd been reluctant to talk about Widowsfield in the past, but everything worked out for the best. Honestly, when we approached the station about the

156

story it was a real shot in the dark. We were shocked they agreed to it. But it couldn't have turned out better. We were able to help pay for a new music room, and we got a chance to meet you."

Paul was quick to intercede. "And you dragged her father into this. And you nearly got her killed last night when her father showed up at her apartment."

"Oh my God," said Rachel. "You didn't tell me about that. What happened?"

"It's a long story." Alma was anxious to avoid the subject. She'd lied to Rachel about what happened to her foot as she limped around all day, and didn't feel like admitting to that now.

"She's too nice to be mad," said Paul. "But I'm not. You two put her through hell for this. Her dad is a nutcase, and he's going to do anything he can to keep your story from getting out there."

"Paul, it's okay," said Alma.

"No, Alma, it's not okay," said Paul. "These two pulled some shady shit here. They put you in danger. They…"

"Paul," said Alma as she pulled her shoulders out of his grip. "I can defend myself. I don't need you fighting my battles for me."

He looked like she'd struck him, pained and ashamed.

"This is getting out of hand." Stephen stood up and walked over to Alma. He set his hand on Paul's shoulder, which was an oddly intimate action and Alma saw that it made Paul uncomfortable. "Paul, honestly, I never meant any harm. I swear, man. You guys have been great, and if I did anything to upset you, I'm sorry for it. I'll help out with your insane dad any way I can."

"It's okay, Stephen," said Alma and she reached out to take Paul's hand. She guided it back to her shoulder, and then around her neck as she kissed it. "Paul, sorry I snapped at you."

"It's okay, babe," said Paul. "This has been a hell of a day."

157

"So, where were we?" asked Alma.

Rachel looked at her pad of paper and said, "Chaos Magick."

"Oh, right," said Alma. "How did you know about that?"

"Your father told us about it," said Stephen as he returned to his seat. "He said that your mother approached him about it."

"Really?" asked Alma. "I didn't know about that." Stephen's knowledge of her past made her uncomfortable.

"They were already separated at the time," said Stephen. "But your mother was obsessed with your brother's disappearance, and the number 314. She wanted the address of the cabin, and she begged your father to spend some time with her, meditating on the symbol for pi in an attempt to remember something about your brother. He refused, and asked her not to force the Chaos Magick on you."

"He doesn't want me to remember what happened," said Alma. "That's why I'm going with you. Whatever it was that happened, I need to know. My mother lost her mind, no doubt about that, but she was right about that damn number."

"Wait, wait, wait," said Rachel. "Are you saying that this Chaos Magick stuff really worked?"

"It did for me," said Alma.

"See." Stephen gloated.

Rachel was unconvinced. "I'm the skeptic of the relationship. It's hard for me to believe in that sort of stuff."

"Same here," said Alma. "And it very well could've been just some mental block for me that I got past when we went to Widowsfield. I'm not saying the Chaos Magick was the reason I remembered everything, but it's true that I was looking at the symbol for pi when, all of the sudden, all of my memories of Ben came rushing back."

"I guess that makes sense," said Rachel. "It probably had more to do with being in that spot, and actively trying to remember."

Stephen chuckled and shook his head. "Or it could be that there's something to this whole Chaos Magick thing." He rolled his eyes and pointed at Rachel with his thumb. "She's never willing to believe anything; a consummate atheist about everything."

"I'm a skeptic," said Rachel. "Isn't that why you married me?"

Stephen shook his head. "I married you because you're super hot."

Jacker set his empty beer glass down hard, which rattled the table. He looked embarrassed and apologized.

"More beer!" Stephen exclaimed as he stood. "That's what this party needs. Who needs another?"

"Everyone," said Paul before quickly pounding the rest of his beer.

"Okay, enough shop talk." Rachel set her pencil down and stared across the table at Alma. "Time for war, my little Scrabble victim."

"Oh crap," said Stephen with a dejected sigh. "Once she starts, she'll never stop. Might as well wave goodbye to the girls for the night."

Rachel was quick to produce an expensive looking Scrabble board that was made of wood and perched on a swiveling base. She told Alma it was a wedding gift, which Stephen said was the worst gift they received, even worse than the bread maker that they'd never used. Rachel flipped over the page that she'd been taking notes on and drew two columns to tabulate points. Within minutes, they were deep into their first game.

Paul, Jacker, and Stephen spent some time in the kitchen, drinking and talking about motorcycles while Alma focused on the game. By the fifth turn, she was already losing by a good amount, which forced her to concentrate. Paul tried to ask her something, but she angrily waved him away and hushed him as she stared at her letters.

"Geeze, babe," said Paul. "Don't be grumpy." He leered over Alma's shoulder, and she clenched her jaw as she tried to will him away.

Then he reached out and took one of the letters off the wooden stand where they were perched.

"Hey," said Rachel. "No helping."

Alma turned, frustrated with Paul for interfering. He'd taken a letter 'C' off her stand, and then he reached down and took an 'A'.

"What are you doing?" Alma asked, annoyed.

Paul pointed at the pad of paper that Rachel was keeping score on. "Give me that real quick."

Rachel slid the pad over and then Paul asked for the pencil as well. She shrugged and frowned at Alma before rolling the pencil across the table. "What's up?" she asked.

Paul set the letter 'C' down first, and then the 'A'. He pointed at the numbers on the corner of the tiles, a 3 and a 1. "The third letter in the alphabet is 'C', and the first is 'A', the fourth is 'D'. What's the number for pi?"

"314," said Jacker.

"I know that, dumbass," said Paul. "I mean after that. Keep going." He started to write the alphabet down on the pad of paper, and then wrote numbers in sequence below the letters.

"Hold on," said Stephen as he picked up his cell phone from a table in the living room. He used the smart phone to go online and look up a longer sequence for pi. "3.141592."

Paul interrupted Stephen as he scribbled letters on the pad. "That's all I need. Look at this shit." He dropped his pencil down and stepped back from the table with his hand over his mouth. He had an expression of satisfaction and surprise, as if he was startled by the simple, nonsensical word he'd written on the pad above the sequence of pi.

Cada E.I.B.

Stephen looked at the word and gasped. "Holy fucking shit."

160

"That's a company based out of Widowsfield," Paul explained to Alma, who was still confused. "Its name is code for pi."

CHAPTER 11 - Together Again

March 10th, 2012

"What does that mean?" asked Alma.

"Cada E.I.B. is a company that brokered deals between the US military and other countries. They helped sell outdated weapons and vehicles to friendly countries."

"Why would their name be code for pi?" asked Rachel. "And it's not even that good of a code. It's not like they were trying hard to hide it."

"But there it is," said Stephen as he pointed at the pad of paper that Paul had written the key to the puzzle on. "Plain as day. That can't be a coincidence."

"It's weird," said Rachel. "I'll give you that."

"Damn straight it's weird," said Stephen. "We're going to have to check their place out. It's abandoned now, so we should be able to get in."

"I don't know," said Rachel. "I'm sure it's a no trespassing area."

"So?" asked Stephen, undaunted by the law.

"So, I'm not going to jail for you, babe."

"This is too big to ignore," said Stephen. "This is the whole story. 314 is the heart of our whole show. With Alma's story, and now this, fucking hell, we're going to blow this thing wide open. I can feel it."

Alma could see how Stephen's excitement could be infectious, but for her it was unsettling. The thought of charging into a sealed facility in search of a link to the number that she'd come to dread over the years was frightening.

"Calm down, babe," said Rachel. "You're getting that wild look in your eyes again. That, I'm-about-to-blow-your-mind look that always means trouble for me."

"Come on, guys," said Stephen as he held the pad up and pointed at the extended version of pi that Paul had written. Alma turned away to avoid seeing the number. "This means something. There's no denying that. We're right at the cusp of it."

"Of what?" asked Rachel. Her nonchalant challenge made it sound as if Stephen's excitement was unwarranted and even a little ridiculous.

"Of everything! Guys, I'm serious, I know we're going to figure this out. This is going to change our lives, man. I fucking know it."

"Or we're just going to get ourselves killed," said Rachel, and the table went silent.

Jacker shivered for effect and shook his head. "That's screwed up, man. You guys are starting to seriously scare me with this shit."

"Too late to back out now," said Stephen, joking with the big guy. "We already packed up your van!"

"You did?" asked Alma as she glanced at Jacker. "Where are you going to stay tonight?"

"Everyone's staying here." Stephen glanced at Paul, who nodded.

"I figured you wouldn't want to go back to your place," said Paul. "Stephen said he'd be cool with all of us crashing here."

"Then we can head out first thing in the morning," said Stephen.

"I need to get my stuff first," said Alma.

"What stuff?" asked Paul. "You got bags full of shit over there." He pointed to the shopping bags from her trip with Rachel.

"Yeah, but I need my other stuff," said Alma. "Can we just take a quick ride back to my place?"

"I can take you if you want," said Jacker. "Might as well load your stuff into the van instead of trying to haul it on a Harley."

"No," said Alma, a little quicker than she meant to. "Paul and I can just take the bike there. It won't take us long."

"You sure?" asked Paul.

She took his hand and guided him to the door. "Yes. Come on."

"All right," said Paul. "I guess I'll see you guys in a few minutes. Jacker, be good."

Jacker gave him a thumbs-up as Alma pulled Paul out the front door.

"What's the big rush?" asked Paul after they were out of the apartment.

"I needed to get out of there." She didn't even realize why she said that. "I think I just needed some fresh air."

Paul bristled in the breeze and shoved his hands into his pockets. His leather coat made a cracking noise as he stretched it, and Alma loved the sound. It was one of the million different nuances of being with Paul that she never realized she missed. She looked up at him, smiled, and a tear fell down her cheek.

"What's wrong?" He was sympathetic as he reached out to comfort her.

"I don't know," she said, honestly. "I really don't."

"Come here, kid." He wrapped his arms around her and pulled her in close. "I've got your back. If you want to hop on the bike, take off, and forget all this shit, I'll be right there with you. Okay?"

"No," she nestled into his embrace. "I need this. I never knew it, but I really need to do this. I've got to erase that part of my life."

"I've got your back, babe. Whatever you decide to do, I've got your back."

She stepped out of his embrace, folded her arms, and looked at him. He stood on the sidewalk, watching her, as the moonlight reflected off his bald head. The snake tattoo that was now revealed on the right side of his head, partially shaded by emerging hair, was facing her. She'd never known the tattoo was there, until yesterday when she saw him with a shaved head for the first time.

"Why?" she asked.

"Why what?"

"Why do you have my back?"

He looked as if the question was an affront. "Because I love you."

For some reason, she didn't believe him. "I don't understand why we keep doing this."

"Oh come on, Alma." He sighed and started to pat the various pockets on his jacket in search of his cigarettes. "We're not breaking up already, are we? We just patched things up."

"We did?" She laughed, although not out of humor. "I don't remember that. Matter of fact, I seem to recall being pretty pissed at you when I found a rubber in your toilet."

He looked tired as he lit his cigarette. He didn't bother responding and let the smoke drift lazily out of his open mouth.

"You've got nothing to say about that?" She took another step away from him and crossed her arms.

"What do you want me to say? I didn't do anything wrong."

He was right, but that didn't make her any less angry.

"We're meant for each other." He took a drag and squinted at her as he did, then he let the smoke come out of his nose as he continued. "You know it as well as I do. We're good together, and not worth a shit apart. Our problem is that we haven't figured out how to fight yet. When we do," he smiled as he mimicked an explosion, "it gets real bad real quick. We just need to figure out how to have civil disagreements instead of all-out battles."

"I don't want to go through it all again," said Alma. "You really hurt me last time." She tightened her grip around herself and took another step away from him.

"I know it." He looked down at the ash at the end of his cigarette, avoiding her gaze. "Want to know a secret about the last time we broke up?"

"What?" Her tone implied that she was already skeptical of what he was going to say.

He took another drag, as if trying to stall his admission. "I started being nasty to get you to break up with me. I was trying to protect you." He flicked ash onto the sidewalk.

"Protect me from what?"

"From me."

Alma shook her head in mild exasperation. "What does that even mean?"

"You were falling back in with my crowd. Just like it always happens." Paul looked up at the moon and seemed to study it for a moment while Alma stayed silent, waiting for him to continue. He changed the subject abruptly. "You know when I fell in love with you?"

"The first time I let you get to second base?"

They shared a chuckle, but then Paul turned serious again. "It was on our third date, back in high school."

"What?" She shook her head and laughed as if what he was saying couldn't be true. "No one in high school is ever really in love. That's just kid stuff."

"No, you're wrong. I fell in love with you on our third date, and haven't stopped loving you since."

"We broke up not long after that." She didn't know what to make of his admission. It didn't make sense to her. "We didn't start dating again until the next summer, when I was back from college."

He continued his story, unabated by her disbelief. He closed his eyes as he recounted the scene. "You were in a light purple dress, with a darker purple string tied up here." He pointed to his clavicle as he went on. "Some of the strings in the dress sparkled, like they were made of tinsel or something."

"I remember that dress," said Alma. "My grandmother bought it for me."

166

"I picked you up in my truck. Remember that shitty old thing?"

She smiled as she took a step closer to him. "Do I? I had to steer as you pushed it after running out of gas on the highway."

He laughed at the memory. "Not my smoothest moment."

"To say the least."

"I remember seeing you come out of your grandma's place, wearing that dress, and I almost couldn't talk. I was just stunned. You had your hair up, and you never wore your hair up. You looked awesome."

"No more wearing my hair up now," said Alma as she tousled her newly shorn locks.

"You got into the truck and just, all of the sudden, leaned across the seat and pecked me on the cheek. It was a real quick kiss."

"I remember it," said Alma. "I was so nervous. That was our first kiss, if you can call it that. I guess I was a bit of a prude back then."

He finally looked at her, and then bashfully back to his cigarette as he flicked it. "That's when I fell in love with you."

"What?" Alma accidentally snorted as she laughed and then put her hands over her mouth in embarrassment. "Because I kissed you? Come on. You were a ladies man back then. You had all sorts of girls clamoring for you."

"It wasn't because you kissed me," he said. "It was because you were scared to. You got into the truck and slid across the seat to kiss me out of nowhere, and then went right back to your side and waited for me to drive off. It was obvious that you'd been planning the kiss for a long time." He locked eyes with her and held his gaze. "I bet you were thinking about it for hours before I picked you up. Weren't you?"

She looked down as he stepped forward, closing the gap between them. "Yes. I was so nervous, you have no idea. I

167

wasn't the sort of girl that got asked out a lot, and you were such a popular guy. I couldn't believe you were going to take me out again for a third time. I knew it was silly not to kiss after going on a couple dates, so I had to get it out of the way. It was such a lame kiss."

He took her hand and rubbed his thumb over her knuckles. "It was the best kiss of my whole life. I've loved you ever since."

"Even when we kept breaking up?"

"Yep. Every time my phone rings, I hope it's you."

"Then why did you turn into such an asshole last time?" she asked. "Why were you saying that you were trying to protect me?"

"Honestly, I was ashamed of myself."

"For what?" she asked.

"For being a nobody. And worse than that, I was dragging you down with me."

"That's silly," she said.

"No it's not. It's the truth. I've got a lot of bad habits, and when we're together I drag you down with me." Alma was going to rebut him, but he spoke before she could. "When was the last time you did coke?"

It was a brash question, and she was taken aback by it. "What?"

"When was the last time? I bet I know," he said. "I bet it was at my birthday party, right before we broke up last time. Am I right?"

"Yes, but what does that have to do with…"

"It has everything to do with it," said Paul. "That's my point. You're a fucking good person, and not just like a normal good person either. You're an honest-to-God, really good person, and every time we get together again I'm forced to watch you sink down to my level. Look, I'm not trying to be a melodramatic emo kid here. I'm being honest when I say that I drag you down, Alma. I always have."

"Come on, Paul. Stop it."

168

"No wait, I'm trying to explain what I've been up to for the past few months." He walked away from her and started to fidget with his lighter as he spoke. It was almost as if he had a speech prepared, and was trying to recall all of the details that he wanted to go over as they talked. She wondered how long he'd been planning this conversation. "You got your dream job, and I was putting it at risk. If your school drug tested you - Fuck, Alma. Your life would've been over, and all because of me."

"I'm an adult. The mistakes I made were my choice."

"And I decided to stop putting you in a situation where you were forced to make that kind of choice." Paul put his lighter back in his pocket and then pulled out what looked like a plastic coin. He flipped the object around in his palm a few times before handing it to Alma.

It was purple and depicted a triangle in the center of an engraved circle. Within the triangle was written '2 months'.

"Is this what I think it is?" asked Alma.

"I joined a few days after we broke up, but fell off a few times. I've been straight for two months now."

"AA?"

"Sort of," said Paul. "It's a different program, but same idea. That's how I met Jacker."

Alma glanced back at the door to Rachel and Stephen's apartment where Jacker was waiting for them.

"He's not just a buddy," said Paul. "He's my sponsor."

"Paul, I don't know what to say." She stared at the coin and flipped it around in her hand several times. It felt like metal, but was lighter than she expected it to be.

"I've been working real hard for this, Alma. I just want another chance with you. And all this shit, with Widowsfield and your dad," he shrugged and nervously scratched at his beard. "The way this all happened now; it just feels like it was meant to be. You know? It feels like I'm being given one last shot to prove that I'm the right guy for you."

"I didn't need you to do this," said Alma as she held up the coin. "I didn't know you had an addiction problem."

"Neither did I." He took the coin, kissed it, and slipped it back in his pocket. "It wasn't until my birthday, when I saw you snorting a line off my bathroom sink, that it hit me. That was my worst moment. I saw myself for what I was, and it wrecked me. I knew that if it weren't for me, you'd never do drugs. Your job was too important to you, but you were risking it because of me. I thought about quitting, but then I thought..." he didn't want to continue.

"What?" asked Alma.

"This hurts to admit, but I wanted the drugs more than I wanted you. That's why I turned into such a prick, and that's how I knew I had a problem, because nothing ever meant more to me than you – or at least that's what I thought until that night. That's when I knew I had to do something if I was ever going to earn you back."

"Paul," said Alma as she took his hands in hers. "You never had to earn me back, all you had to do was ask."

"Well, then this is me asking." He smiled down at her. "Alma Harper, will you take me back?"

She grinned and closed her eyes, then let go of his hands and abruptly turned. "No, I don't think so." She took a long, exaggerated step away as she toyed with him. Then she turned and leapt back into his arms. "Of course I will, you big dummy." She got on the tips of her new, expensive pumps and was about to kiss him, but then put her finger over his lips and pushed his head to the side. She pecked him on the cheek like she had on their third date, when he fell in love with her.

He chuckled, and wrapped his arms around her. "Oh no, that doesn't cut it anymore." He kissed her and then started to spin, lifting her feet off the ground. He stopped, set her down, and then caught her before she tumbled over in her heels.

Alma laughed as she clung to his arm. It had been a long time since she'd worn high heels and she was struggling to get used to them again. The cut on her right foot didn't help

170

either. "Now hurry up and get me home so I can get my stuff and then screw your brains out."

He scooped her up in his arms and walked toward his bike. "Hold on little lady. With a promise like that, you'd better believe I'm going to drive like a bat out of hell!"

Alma let her head fall back as she laughed. She stared up at the stars as they twinkled in a cloudless night sky. She felt happy, and savored the moment.

* * *

Rachel had retreated to the bedroom to change into a pair of flannel pajamas. Alma and Paul had been gone longer than they expected, and Rachel was getting tired. She came back to find Stephen and Jacker playing a videogame.

"Oh crap." Rachel sounded disheartened as she plopped down next to her husband. "Looks like I lost you two for the night."

"Nah," said Stephen, although he didn't look away from the screen. "I just wanted to prove a point to our new friend here."

"And what point is that?" asked Rachel.

"That I could kick his ass at Call of Duty."

"And how's that turning out for you?" asked Jacker.

"Don't get cocky. There's still plenty of time left."

Rachel put her hand on Stephen's thigh, but he writhed away from her and moved up to sit on the edge of his seat. "I hate this damn game," she said and crossed her arms.

"Don't worry," said Jacker. "It's about to be over."

Rachel heard dogs start to bark and Stephen leapt up and yelled, "Fuck off! Are you serious?"

"What's going on?" asked Rachel before she saw Stephen's avatar get mauled by a dog.

"Who let the dogs out?" asked Jacker as he set his controller down on the coffee table.

"Oh wow," said Rachel. "I didn't even know this game had dogs in it. I've never seen you do anything like that." She coyly leered up at her husband.

He grimaced, but tried not to let Rachel's goading annoy him. He pointed at Jacker and said, "That's bullshit. You were camping."

"Call it what you will, my friend," said Jacker. "I call it winning."

"I want a rematch." Stephen pointed at Jacker's controller on the table.

"No!" Rachel swiped the game controller off the table and snatched the battery pack off the back of it. "Game over. I don't want to sit here all night watching you two play video games."

"Then what do you want to do?" asked Stephen. His tone started off like a petulant teen, but then changed as he decided not to pick a fight with her.

"I don't know." She pulled her feet up onto the couch, under her butt, as if nestling in for a long chat with a girlfriend. "Let's just talk."

Jacker and Stephen both groaned simultaneously.

"What?" asked Rachel, amused by their dour faces. "What's wrong with talking? I'd like to get to know the guy that's going to be driving us around for the next few days."

"I'm getting a beer," said Stephen with a defeated groan. "Who else needs one?"

Jacker raised his hand and then Rachel asked for one as well.

"So, Jacker, how'd you get that name?"

The big guy snickered and ran his hands through his shaggy, curly head of hair. "That's a complicated story. The short version is that I'm a computer nerd. Have been ever since I was a kid."

"Did you grow up with Paul and Alma?"

"No. I met Paul just this year, at the tattoo place near his apartment."

172

"What was it that made you two start hanging out?" Rachel's questions came quicker than Jacker was prepared for.

"I don't know. He's a nice guy. We just sort of started hanging out a lot."

"Okay," said Rachel. "Do you ride a motorcycle like he does?"

"No."

"Do you get a lot of tattoos?"

"Jesus," said Stephen from the kitchen. "Give the guy a break, Rachel."

"What?" she asked as if defending herself. "I'm just trying to get to know him."

"No you're not," said Stephen as he brought Jacker a beer. "You're going into reporter mode. Stop it."

"It's okay," said Jacker. "I'm sure it's weird to have some stranger staying at your place right before hauling you through a couple states. I don't mind answering a few questions."

"See." Rachel was quick to stick her tongue out at her husband. "So, do you have a bunch of tattoos hidden under that shirt?"

Jacker was wearing a long sleeve, black shirt with a band name that Rachel didn't recognize. He pulled the sleeves up to reveal bare arms. "Nope. I never got a tattoo."

Rachel was surprised and furrowed her brow. "Then how did you meet Paul at a tattoo place?"

"My friends hang out there," said Jacker quickly.

Rachel adjusted her position as Stephen sat down beside her. He handed her a bottle of beer and then the glass that she'd left on the kitchen table from earlier. She started to pour the beer, but then Stephen took it away from her claiming that she wasn't doing it right. She ignored his tutorial on properly pouring the beer and continued talking with Jacker.

"So what about Paul and Alma?"

"What about them?" asked Jacker.

"Alma told me how they've been an on-again-off-again couple ever since high school. What do you think of their relationship? Is it healthy?"

"Good Lord," said Stephen. "Did you really make us stop playing Call of Duty to talk about relationship crap?"

"Yes." Rachel slapped Stephen's knee. "Now shut up and let us talk."

"Today was the first time I met Alma," said Jacker.

"Oh really?" asked Rachel.

"Paul talks about her a lot, but they've been broken up ever since I've known him. He's been working up the courage to ask her out again."

"No kidding? So he's been pining for her all this time? That's sweet."

"Sweet or super creepy," said Stephen, which earned another slap on the knee from his wife.

"It's romantic, not that you'd know anything about that, asshole."

Stephen groaned and shook his head. "Please. I'm a fucking Casanova. All my girlfriends say so."

"Ha, ha," said Rachel blandly. "Very funny, jerk."

"Honestly, I don't think I've ever met someone more in love with another person in my whole life," said Jacker. "Paul was a mess when I met him. I kept trying to convince him to forget about her and move on, but he was determined to win Alma back. I figured he'd get over it after a few weeks, but he didn't. I'm happy that everything worked out like it did. He deserves a chance to show her how much he loves her." Jacker spoke as if lamenting an old, lost friend. There was a distant sadness in his words.

Rachel scooted over to the side of the couch to be closer to the loveseat that Jacker was sitting on. She put her left hand on his arm and then clasped his hand with her right. "Hey, you okay?"

"Yeah, sure," said Jacker unconvincingly.

"Thinking of your girlfriend?"

Jacker shrugged and didn't look at her. "I guess."

174

"Then don't," said Stephen as if that was the simple answer. "All you need is a super hot girl to give you the right sort of attention and you'll forget all about her."

"Ignore him," said Rachel. "It's okay to be sad. I can't imagine how tough this week has been for you."

"It's been shitty." Jacker continued to avoid eye contact and he tightened his grip on her hand.

"Here, honey," said Rachel as she got a box of tissues off the coffee table and handed it to the big guy.

"Oh crap," said Stephen. "Hey, Barbara Walters, stop making our guests cry."

"Shut up, Stephen." She gave him a dismissive wave.

Jacker chuckled as he took the tissues and wiped his eyes. "He's right. You're pulling some sort of chick-flick voodoo on me. The last thing I wanted to do tonight was start thinking about Debbie." He laughed uncomfortably as he wiped his eyes.

"Give the guy a break, Rachel," said Stephen.

"Okay," said Rachel. She moved back down the couch, away from Jacker, and back into Stephen's arms.

"I need a shot," said Jacker. "Do you guys have any hard liquor in here?"

* * *

Stephen told Rachel that he'd forgotten to pack the Holdsten Quad Meter in the van. He made up the name, aware that Rachel wouldn't know that it was fictitious. Jacker gave him the keys to the van, and Stephen grabbed his cell phone before heading out behind the house.

It was chilly out, and he could see his breath as he quickly searched his phone's list of contacts for the name of the girl he'd met in Branson that was familiar with Widowsfield. He called her, and anxiously waited for the young girl to answer while keeping an eye on the back door of his condo in case Rachel followed him.

"Come on, answer," he said impatiently.

"Hello?"

"Hey, it's me, Stephen."

"Oh hey," said the girl before yawning.

"Listen, there's been a change of plans." He spoke quietly, just in case one of the windows of his condo was open. Then he walked briskly over to Jacker's van and got in, deciding it would be better to talk there than out in the open.

"What's up?" asked the girl.

"Are you still working at the bar?" asked Stephen.

"Yep," said the girl.

"And are you still in the escort business?"

She didn't answer immediately. He heard her rustling, as if getting out of bed. "Hold on," she said quietly. Stephen heard a door close on her end, and then she said, "Not anymore, but if the offer's good enough I might reconsider."

"Okay, good," said Stephen. "I think I've got a plan."

CHAPTER 12 - Manipulations

March 11th, 2012

It was past midnight when Paul and Alma got back to Rachel's apartment. Jacker was smoking a cigarette on the front steps when they pulled up. He waved at them and Paul stopped Alma from approaching once he turned off the bike.

"Do me a favor, babe," said Paul. "Just head on inside. Let me talk to him."

"Why?" asked Alma. "What's the matter?"

Paul didn't want to say. "Just trust me on this one."

Alma set her helmet on the back of Paul's bike and then walked towards the apartment. She waved at Jacker as she passed before Paul sat down beside his friend.

"They went to bed," said Jacker. "Door's unlocked."

"Okay," said Alma. "See you guys inside in a bit." She was hesitant to close the door, as if afraid to leave Paul alone with the big man.

Once the door closed, Paul got out a cigarette and lit it. The two of them sat on the steps in the chilly night air and smoked in silence as a cricket chirped from the nearby bushes.

Jacker finished his cigarette first and flicked it out into the street. "I almost lost it, man."

"I know," said Paul. He hadn't been certain Jacker would say anything, and he would've been okay with that as well. He was here to support his friend in whatever way Jacker needed, even if that meant just sitting in silence. "I could see it on your face when I got here. What happened?"

Jacker looked back at the apartment to make sure the window wasn't open. "Rachel was asking about Debbie, and it just brought it all back, man. Rachel didn't mean anything by it. She's just one of those people that asks too many questions."

"That's her job," said Paul.

"I know. I'm not mad at her or anything. I just had a tough time dealing with it."

"You stink like bourbon."

Jacker cupped his hand over his mouth so that his breath went back into his nose. "Do I?"

"Yeah, man. Bad."

"I hit the bottle pretty hard. I'm not sure I'm like you, Paul. I don't know if I can drink and still be sober – from the hard stuff, you know what I mean. I pounded shots, but man, I'd give anything for a hit." He looked at the crook of his arm. "I think drinking just makes it worse for me."

"Well then don't drink."

Jacker snickered at the suggestion. "Easier said than done, brother."

"No truer words have ever been said, but we've just got to deal with it." Paul nearly finished his cigarette as they sat silent for another long moment. "Tell you what, I'll quit drinking too. We'll quit everything together."

"No, man," said Jacker. "You don't need to do that. You've got your shit straight. Don't go switching it up for me."

"Hey, Jacker." Paul punched his friend on the shoulder and smiled. "How about you shut the fuck up and let me do something nice for you for a change?"

"Honestly, Paul, you don't have to do that."

Paul grumbled and then changed his tone, "Remember a couple months ago, when I called you in the middle of the night, high as a kite?"

"How could I forget?"

"I was crying like an asshole, and you came right over to pick me up. You bought me dinner over at the Mexican place on Taft."

"Uncle Julio's," said Jacker, recalling the name of the restaurant. "Fucking amazing burritos."

"There's something I never told you about that night."

"What's that?" asked Jacker.

178

"I was going to hang myself."

Jacker sat up straight and grimaced. "What the fuck? Are you serious?"

Paul nodded and glanced back at the front door to make sure Alma wasn't eavesdropping. "Yeah. I've still got the noose back at my place. It's hanging in my closet as a reminder of how low I got."

"Fuck, man," said Jacker. "I wish you would've said something. I could've…"

"You did everything you needed to," said Paul. "If it weren't for you, I'd be dead. But I had a person I could rely on, and I owe you for that."

"You don't owe me anything," said Jacker.

"Yes I do." Paul put his hand on the back of Jacker's neck and squeezed as he shook the man back a forth a little. "I need you, big guy. So if turning down a few beers here and there will help you out, you'd better believe I'm going to do it. Understood?"

"Okay, but you've got to do something else for me," said Jacker.

"If you ask me to give you a blowjob, our friendship is going to get mighty awkward all of the sudden."

"Oh," said Jacker. "Then never mind, I guess." They laughed and then Jacker said, "Throw out that noose. Or better yet, burn it."

Paul stamped out his cigarette on the step and then put out his hand for Jacker to shake. "Deal."

Jacker shook his friend's hand and then added, "By the way, Alma is fucking gorgeous, man."

Paul looked back at the door to the apartment. "Yeah, thanks. She knocked my socks off when she got back from shopping with Rachel. Don't get me wrong, I always thought she was beautiful, but holy shit. A hair cut and some make-up go a long way."

"It's more than that," said Jacker. "She loves you. Any idiot can see that. When she's with you, she looks happy.

Bear with me here, cause I'm about to sound like a chick, but seeing you two together has made me believe in love again."

"Holy shit, bro," said Paul. "You are sounding like a chick. What the hell did they do to you in there?" He pointed back at Stephen and Rachel's apartment.

Jacker laughed and then threatened to punch Paul, who feigned a flinch. "I'm serious, man. The past six months that I've known you, I've been trying to convince you to give up on her. I wanted you to move on because I was worried that your whole 'true love' thing was bullshit. I just wanted to tell you that I was wrong. Seeing you two together..." he shrugged and tried to come to terms with what he was feeling. "I don't know, it just makes me feel good. I never felt that way about Debbie. I think I stayed with her because she didn't bitch too much when I touched her boobs."

"Forget her, man," said Paul. "We'll find someone for you. You're too good a guy to be wasted on a tramp like that."

"Two years clean," said Jacker, "right down the drain because of that bitch."

"Every day's a struggle, man," said Paul. "And every day sober is a win. Doesn't matter if it's been two years or two days. You're the one that taught me that."

"Does that make you my sponsor now?"

"Shit," said Paul as he pretended to be deep in thought. "I guess you're right. Oh man, you're fucked." They laughed and Paul reached into his pocket to pull out his sobriety coin. He offered it to Jacker.

"What's this for?"

"I wouldn't have it if it weren't for you. Figure I owe it to you."

Jacker took the coin and clasped it tightly.

*   *   *

Alma Harper touched the walls of her new music room. She was still beaming from the memory of the reveal, when she'd been surprised by her students and fellow teachers at her school. She didn't feel worthy of the work that went into this new room, but she had to remind herself that it was okay to let good things happen. Alma had become accustomed to expecting the worst out of life, and she was trying to have a more positive outlook.

The walls of the new music room glimmered in the dim light. At first, she thought it was textured wallpaper that gave the room such a distinct appearance, but instead she discovered that it was tightly compacted wire. All four walls were composed of thin, black wire that had been pulled taut between the floor and ceiling. She pushed the tip of her finger between two of the wires and found more behind.

"What in the world?" She was smiling as she inspected the bizarre and unique building material. She'd never seen anything like it, and was curious how deep it went. Alma pushed her hand further through the strands until her fingers disappeared within. The metal wires were cold on the outside, but warmer inside, as if she were reaching through someone's clothes in search of flesh.

The tip of her finger touched something hard, and then she felt a hot wetness that caused her to panic. She withdrew her hand, but something came out with her. The liquid that she'd touched within was hot and stung her flesh, and something white was stuck to her as she shook the acidic fluid away. A tooth hit the floor.

"Ben?" asked Alma. She was terrified that her brother was trapped behind the wire wall, although she couldn't explain what caused that fear. She wiped her hands off on her jeans, and then tried to pull apart the wire to look for her brother.

Then another tooth fell from the wall. It made a distinctive ticking sound as it bounced on the wood floor. She stared down at it, and another tooth came loose. Alma released her hold on the wires and stepped back. As she stared at the black wall, more teeth began to push forth from between the wires. They bounced on the floor in rapid

181

succession as more and more sprang out. There were so many teeth falling free and ticking on the wood that the noise became cacophonous. Then, as the volume muddied the distinction of the individual teeth, the noise changed. It no longer sounded like a mass of bones tapping on wood, but rather a single person's teeth chattering in his mouth right beside Alma's ear.

"Pour it in," said a man's voice that Alma recognized as belonging to her father.

Scalding water spewed forth from the wall. It stank of chemicals, and the flood moved too fast for Alma to avoid it. When the first wave struck her, she woke up.

Alma was laying in Paul's arms, on Rachel and Stephen's couch. He was asleep, oblivious to her nightmare. Jacker was in the loveseat caddy corner to the couch where Paul and Alma slept. The big man's limbs were haphazardly hung from various places on the small seat, but he was asleep and snoring despite his uncomfortable position.

Alma glanced at her phone, which was on the coffee table a couple feet away. She debated looking at it to see what time it was, but she didn't need to look to know. There was no doubt in her mind what she would've discovered had she picked up that phone.

It was 3:14.

* * *

"Wake up, freeloaders!" Stephen was chipper and loud as he came into the living room where his guests were sleeping.

Alma threw a pillow at him. "It's too early to be so happy," she said and pressed her face back into Paul's side as they lay on the couch

"Today's the big day," said Stephen as he went into the kitchen. "The van's all packed, and we're ready to go. I'll buy

182

some breakfast on the way." No one responded, so he spoke louder. "Come on, guys! Let's go!"

"Holy shit, dude," said Jacker. "Is the sun even up?"

"It's almost seven," said Stephen. "Come on, we're already running late."

"In my world it's impossible to be running late for anything at seven in the morning," said Jacker, but he sat up anyhow. His hair was standing straight out on either side of his head, making him look like a clown as he sniffled and yawned.

"That's some serious bed head, brother," said Paul.

"You try sleeping on a love seat, see how good you look in the morning." Jacker stood up and stumbled forward, unbalanced. "I feel like the fattest anchovy in the smallest can."

"Alma," said Stephen as he came into the living room with a stack of papers. "Can you do me a favor and look over this real quick? It's the waiver for our show. If everything looks good, just sign and date the bottom of each page. Cool?"

Paul took the papers because Alma didn't want to get up yet. She kept her head pressed into her boyfriend's side.

Alma groaned and finally sat up. "Can't we take showers before we go? I don't want to be in a van with a bunch of stinky guys all day."

"I already took one and Rachel should be getting done soon. I'll kick her out of the bathroom and make her do her hair in the bedroom. She takes for freaking ever to get ready."

"It takes me a while to wash and dry my hair too." Alma instinctually reached for her long hair to drape it over her shoulder, but discovered it was gone. "But I guess not anymore. I forgot it was gone. God, that's weird." She ran her hand through her newly short hair. "It's like having a phantom limb or something."

Stephen heard a hair dryer turn on in the bedroom. "Sounds like Rachel's out of the bathroom."

"I'll jump in the shower next," said Jacker. "Give you three a chance to go over the papers."

"It's pretty basic," said Stephen. "I added in a clause about giving you final say on any portion of the show that features you, or anything about your history with Widowsfield. I even included the footage from the school in there. I want to make sure you know that I'm not trying to be deceptive or anything. It's all there. Look it over and let me know if you have any questions."

Stephen went to the kitchen to make coffee, but watched Paul and Alma as they read the contract. Alma looked it over first, and pointed out a few things to Paul who then took the papers and started reading. The entire show depended on Alma signing the contract, and Stephen was nervous as he waited to see if she would sign. His heart was racing, a side effect of the pills he took every morning to help him get going. When he first started taking the diet pills, he was just trying to lose a few vanity pounds, but they'd become an essential part of his routine now. Coffee hardly had an effect on him, and a few weeks ago he had to go up to four pills each morning instead of the recommended two, but he craved the energy they gave him. He'd never been so productive in his life.

He drummed on the counter as he waited for the water to boil. "Come on, you fucker," said Stephen as he stared at the water in the pot. "Boil, already."

"Stephen," said Alma.

He was startled by her voice. He'd fallen into a bit of a trance as he stared into the pot of water, and jogged back into the living room to see what Alma needed. "Yep?"

"I didn't expect to get paid," said Alma. "Rachel already bought me so much stuff. I feel bad taking more money for doing an internet video."

Stephen and Paul looked at one another. Paul hadn't told Alma about the network deal, which surprised Stephen. Even though he'd asked him to keep it a secret, he expected him to tell his girlfriend.

"It's okay," said Stephen, and he wondered if Paul was testing him. Was the biker waiting to see if Stephen would be honest? He decided not to risk it. "You should know the truth. We're hoping that the show goes beyond just being an internet thing. Do me a favor and keep this part quiet, but we got approached by a cable network about possibly turning this into an actual television show."

Alma looked concerned, which was exactly what Stephen was afraid of.

"Oh," she said and looked back down at the contract. "Wow."

She was reconsidering; Stephen could see it in the way she started to study the contract again.

"It's the same show," said Stephen. "Everything's exactly the same, and we might just use this as a test show. It might not even make it on the air."

Alma set the contract on the coffee table.

Stephen could feel his show slipping away. Alma was going to refuse to sign. She was going to back out. "I'll do whatever you need, Alma. Just tell me what you want and I'll do what I can to accommodate you. This story depends on you being a part of it. I need you, Alma."

"Can you get me a pen?"

"You're going to sign?" asked Paul.

"Yes," said Alma. "I don't care if it's on television. My father wants to close the door on what happened, so the wider I can open it the better."

Stephen thought he'd given her a pen before, and searched through his pockets until he found one. "Here, here," he said as he handed it to her.

He watched in anticipation as she signed and dated the bottom of each page. When she was finished, she gathered the pages and straightened them by tapping the stack on the coffee table. Then she offered them up to Stephen, and he tried not to swipe them greedily away.

"Thank you, Alma," said Stephen.

"Don't thank me yet," she said. "Don't forget, you gave me final approval on everything."

He paused, deflated by the overconfident way she spoke. "I guess that's true," he said and forced a grin.

Jacker got out of the shower and Alma went in next. Stephen used his French press to make coffee for everyone, and they discussed some of the details of the trip. Jacker had a few favorite restaurants that he wanted to stop at on the way, and Paul said that he'd made a trip out to the Ozarks on his motorcycle a few times.

"Once you get out of Illinois, it gets a lot prettier," said Paul. "The Ozarks are beautiful to drive through, especially this time of year. I kind of wish I was taking the bike."

"Why don't you?" asked Stephen.

Paul sat back and crossed his legs. "Maybe I will. I'll have to see about planning a trip sometime soon."

"No," said Stephen, "I mean now. Why not ride the bike behind us?"

Paul raised his eyebrows and seemed intrigued. "I guess I didn't think about it. I'd love to do that. It'd be a good way to get Alma to ride with me on a long trip too. She's okay with short trips, but always says that long road trips are too much for her. This would be a good chance to get the best of both worlds."

"All right then," said Stephen. "It's settled. You can ride your bike while Jacker, Alma, Rachel, and I take the van. That'll be perfect."

"Why do you seem so happy about it?" asked Paul. "Were you worried I'd be farting the whole trip or something?"

"I was," said Jacker.

"No," said Stephen. "Honestly, I had no clue how much shit my wife was planning on bringing." He looked toward the bedroom where Rachel was still getting ready. "She's got three bags full of shit. And I mean, big bags. I don't know how in the hell that girl can fill up so much luggage for just a quick trip like this. I was worried we'd all be sitting on each other's laps."

"All you had to do was say something, man," said Paul. "No need to try and manipulate the situation to get what you want." Paul tapped his finger on the contract on the coffee table and winked at Stephen. "Know what I mean?"

CHAPTER 13 - On the Road

March 11th, 2012

They left the apartment shortly after ten, far later than Stephen had planned. Two hours after, when Jacker was complaining about wanting lunch, Stephen insisted that they make up for lost time and stay on the road. He paid for fast food, but Paul couldn't eat while driving his motorcycle, so they had to stop for a few minutes. Afterward, Alma decided to brave a ride with Paul for a few hours. She loved being on the back of his motorcycle, but she couldn't put up with long trips. Paul always said it was because of her bony butt.

Illinois seemed endlessly flat, only adorned with the occasional rise and fall of small hills. It was a beautiful, sunny day and the bright green glow of spring stretched across the horizon as far as the eye could see. The road was smooth, newly paved, and it was an easy ride as opposed to some of the city streets they usually traversed.

She wrapped her arms around Paul's waist and wished she wasn't wearing a helmet so she could place her cheek against his back. If it weren't for him, she wouldn't have had the courage to go on this trip. Having him along gave her the strength to face...

Widowsfield.

She'd avoided thinking of it the entire trip so far. Alma felt the familiar pang of fear sting her heart. They were headed to Widowsfield, and the horrors that she'd been trying to hide from all these years would suddenly be in front of her again.

314.

She closed her eyes and shivered, not from the spring air, but from the fear that welled within her. Alma thought of her mother, and her obsession with the number that she believed could lead them back to Ben.

314.

Alma recalled one night when she woke up to find her mother writing the number on her arm. She tried to pull away, but her mother held fast and screamed that they had to find Ben.

"Try to remember," said her mother as she dug her nails into her daughter's arm. "You have to look at the number. Okay, baby?"

"Stop it." Alma had been crying as she tried to get away from the woman.

"No, Alma! Look at the number." She was desperate and manic as she forced her daughter to look at the scrawling.

314 was written on Alma's forearm in thick black marker. "I can't remember anything, Mommy. Please stop."

"You're not trying hard enough. Alma, sweetie, I'm telling you this is going to work. All you have to do is try."

"I have tried."

Her mother slapped her hard across the cheek. "No you haven't. You haven't tried hard enough. You let your brother die. You and your father did something to him, and now you won't tell me. You little bitch. You fucking little bitch."

Alma writhed free and cowered against the wall. Her bed was pressed against the corner of the room, and she was trapped as her mother lurched over the other side of the mattress. "Mommy, please stop. I didn't do anything."

"Yes you did! I know you did. Don't lie to me. I know what sort of things your father was doing. I'm not an idiot. I knew he had a whore up at the cabin, and I know you lied to me about it. Don't look at me like that. Stop crying. I know what sort of things you all did."

"I didn't do anything, Mommy."

"You lying little bitch. Your father turned you against me. I don't know how he did it, but he turned you against me. I loved you and your brother so much. Stop humming! Why are you humming? Open your eyes and talk to me. Tell me what you did! I know you're hiding something from me!"

Alma kept her eyes closed and hummed, like she always did when the world was too scary to face.

Her arms wrapped a little tighter around Paul's waist as she recalled her mother's insanity. She was humming as they drove, and hadn't realized it.

They pulled into Branson a little after eight, and went straight to the hotel that Stephen had booked. It was a Holiday Inn on the outskirts of town, but was still surprisingly busy. Alma had never been to Branson, and was shocked by how bustling the town was. Rachel was anxious to go shopping, but no one else wanted to join her. Undeterred, she set off on her own, saying that she'd meet up with the rest of them in the morning.

Stephen wanted to get dinner, but Alma and Paul decided to get room service. Stephen coaxed Jacker into joining him, and the group broke up as everyone went their separate ways.

When they got to their room, Paul sat down on the edge of the queen bed and pulled Alma down beside him. "What's up, babe?"

"What do you mean?"

"You've been quiet – even quieter than normal. You okay?"

"Yeah, just tired, and a little sore from the ride."

"You're lying," said Paul.

Alma thought of her mother, and she took her hand out of Paul's. "What do you mean?"

"I've known you long enough to know when something's bugging you. What is it?"

"I guess I'm nervous. That's all. I haven't been back to Widowsfield since my mother killed herself. I swore I'd never come back."

"You don't have to. It's not too late to turn around and go home." He almost sounded insistent, as if he thought this trip was a bad idea.

"Why? Do you think I should?"

190

He put his hand on her knee and squeezed. "I think you should do whatever you want to do. Doesn't matter what anyone else wants. I think it's brave to go back there, but I wouldn't think you were a coward if you just wanted to go home."

"What do you think about Stephen and Rachel?" she asked.

"I like them," said Paul confidently. He was a good judge of character, much better than Alma. "Stephen's a bit of a snake, but not in a bad way. I think he's just spent his life working in a shitty industry that's filled with backstabbers. He picked up some bad habits, but I think he's a good guy. Although I'd wager good money that tape of his was faked. You know, the one that they made so much money off of online."

"You really think so?" asked Alma.

Paul nodded. "Definitely. Stephen's not a bad guy, but he's the type that'll manipulate others to get what he wants. I bet he doctored that tape and didn't tell Rachel."

"What do you think of her?" asked Alma.

"Rachel's super nice, but she's got to learn when to turn off the reporter thing. I like how she's a straight to the point, no nonsense kind of girl, but she's pretty brash too."

"I agree," said Alma. "I didn't like them much at first, but now I'm coming around. I'm not like you. I don't make friends easily. It takes me a while to get to know someone. Speaking of which, I like Jacker a lot. He's just a big teddy bear."

Paul smiled and nodded, but then bit his upper lip and sighed before saying, "There's something you should know about him."

Alma stiffened, familiar with Paul's tone. He was about to reveal something that he was worried Alma would be mad about. "What?"

"He's a heroin addict."

"Oh, wow. Okay." She wasn't upset, but hadn't expected that.

"That's how we met. He's been clean for awhile. At least until Debbie fucked him over. He relapsed, and I've been helping him back on the wagon."

Alma rubbed Paul's leg. "You're a good friend, Paul."

"I've just got you fooled, little Miss Harper." He walked his fingers up her leg, and then up her stomach until they were between her breasts. He pushed her back onto the bed and lay down beside her. "Because I'm a bad boy. Remember? That's why you fell for me."

"The tattooed bad boy my Mommy used to warn me about?" Alma pushed his hand away and then grabbed his belt buckle.

"Wait," said Paul. He took her hand off his buckle, preventing her from undoing it. "There's one other thing I have to tell you."

"Oh crap," said Alma, again recognizing Paul's tentative tone. "What is it?"

"Jacker's in trouble with the law."

"What? Why?"

"Well, you're right about him being a big teddy bear. He's one of the nicest guys I've ever met, but I saw a different side of him come out this week. After he found out what Debbie was doing, he flipped. He started using, and then just went to shit. I've never seen someone fall apart like that before."

"What did he do?" asked Alma. "Why's he in trouble with the police?"

"You remember how I told you that he lost his job?"

"Yeah."

"Well, he lost it because he put his boss through a plate glass window."

Alma gasped. "You're kidding."

"No, unfortunately not. And it gets worse."

"Of course it does," said Alma as she started to become frustrated.

Paul stood up and started to empty his pockets. He tossed his keys, wallet, and spare change onto the dresser.

"After that, he knew he was going to get in trouble, so he went to Debbie's work. He found the guy that she'd been cheating on him with."

"Oh no, what did he do?"

"What do you think he did?"

Alma sat up and shrugged. "I don't know. He seemed like such a passive, nice guy to me. I can't imagine him hurting anyone. For crying out loud, he passed out from just seeing me cut my foot open."

"I doubt that's the whole story with that."

"What do you mean?" asked Alma.

"I think he's been using," said Paul. "He told me he just used once, right after he found out about Debbie, but I don't know if I believe him. I think he's still taking something. I'm not sure what, but he's been acting weird all week. He's been living out of that fucking van ever since he…" Paul stopped and rubbed his eyes as he sighed.

"He what?"

"He put Debbie's fuck-buddy in the hospital. The kid's in serious condition. Jacker found him in the alley, on a smoke break, and beat his head against the wall until he stopped moving."

"Oh my gosh," said Alma. "I would've never guessed. He seems like such a nice guy."

"That's just it, babe. He is a nice guy. Seriously one of the nicest guys I've ever met. He just got pushed too far and he snapped, and the drugs didn't help."

"Should we turn him in?" asked Alma.

"No!" Paul was angry and spoke louder than he meant to. "Fuck no."

"But he put a guy in the hospital, Paul. I'm sure the cops are looking for him."

"Yeah, and he's got priors. If he gets pinched for this, he's going away for a long time."

"What sort of priors? Who is he? Are we driving around with a career criminal or something?"

"No," said Paul. "It's not like that. He had a rough life, just like a lot of us. He got into some shit that he shouldn't have, and he's been working hard to pick himself up out of that. He fucked up, that's all. And now it's going to cost him his life."

"Paul, Jesus, I don't know what to say. I don't know how to react to this."

"I figured you had the right to know."

"And so do Rachel and Stephen," said Alma.

"No they don't. It's better for them to stay in the dark."

"Then why did you tell me?"

Paul looked at her and reached out to hold her hand. "Because I don't want to keep secrets from you. I want to do it right this time around. You deserve to know the truth."

Alma walked away from him and went to the window that overlooked Branson. "Maybe not. Maybe sometimes it's better not to know."

* * *

"Come on," said Stephen. "Do a shot with me."

"No," said Jacker as he sat beside Stephen at the bar. "Honestly man, I'm good."

"What?" asked Stephen as if Jacker had to be lying. "You've been driving all damn day. You've got to at least let me buy you a drink."

"I'll have a Coke."

Stephen looked offended and ignored Jacker. "Excuse me, beautiful," said Stephen as he waved down the lithe, pretty bartender. The girl held up her finger to let Stephen know he had to be patient.

"I should probably head up and get some sleep," said Jacker.

Stephen grabbed his arm. "No way, pal. You're with me tonight. Rachel went shopping, and I got the go ahead to have some beers at the bar. No chance in hell I'm going to let you take off on me. Sit your ass down, big guy."

194

"Hello, gentlemen," said the blonde haired, blue eyed bartender as she came over. She had studs in either cheek that accentuated her dimples, and vibrant tattoos curled up from under her tight shirt, over her shoulders. "What can I get for you tonight?"

"Now, how in the hell am I supposed to sit here and not ask to see your tattoo?" asked Stephen as he peered at her cleavage. "Does that go all the way down?" He elbowed Jacker as if they were sharing a joke.

"Oh boy," said the bartender with a smile. "Are you that type of guy?" She chided him and then winked at Jacker. "Are you going to sit here asking to see my tits all night?"

Stephen held up his left hand and showed his wedding ring. "A few years ago, yes. But I'm a married man now. My friend here, however, is all sorts of single." He patted Jacker on the back. "Maybe if we get a few drinks into him he'll loosen up a little and start flirting with you so I don't have to."

"Well," said the bartender as she smiled at Jacker. "I'll certainly look forward to that. What am I getting you two started with?"

"How about some whiskey? I'm in a bourbon mood," said Stephen.

"Just a Coke for me," said Jacker.

"Goddamn it," said Stephen. "Stop fighting me on this! Tell you what, darling." He reached out and took the bartender's arm. "Bring me two shot glasses, same size, and fill one with whiskey and the other with water."

"Uh oh," said the bartender. "Looks like we're about to witness a bar trick."

"Zip it, beautiful," said Stephen before he turned back to Jacker. "Here's the deal. She's going to get us two shot glasses, one with whiskey and one with water. The whiskey is mine, and the water is yours."

"Okay," said Jacker. "What's the trick?"

"We both have to drink our own glass one minute after she serves them."

"What's the trick? Are you going to try to get me to turn around or something? Switch the glasses?"

"Nope," said Stephen. "And neither of us can drink our shots before the one minute is up, and I can't use a straw, and I can't leave my seat. If I can get my whiskey into your shot glass before the minute is up, then you have to drink it."

The bartender had the two shot glasses ready and waiting on her shelf on the other side of the bar. She had her lips pursed, restraining a smile, and her eyes twinkled as she looked back and forth between the two of them.

"Okay, you're on," said Jacker.

Stephen shouted and pumped his fist as the bartender slid the glasses over. A few other patrons gathered around them, eager to watch the trick. Stephen loved the attention, and yelled out for more people to come and watch as he took out his wallet. He showed everyone his license and then set it down on top of Jacker's shot glass. Then he flipped the glass over, careful not to spill any of the water.

"What the heck are you up to?" asked Jacker.

"Just wait a minute," said Stephen as he concentrated on the glasses. He set the water glass upside down over the whiskey so that his license separated the two. The crowd around them started to react to every movement as the trick proceeded, and Stephen yelled at them to trust him. Some people were saying that he was going to spill the water, but he hushed them as he pinched the edges of his license. He slid the card back just enough that the water started to slide down into the glass below. The whiskey surged up, the brown alcohol swirling into the water as the two liquids exchanged places.

"Mother fucker," said Jacker. He was too intrigued to be upset as he watched the two liquids switch glasses.

"You know," said the bartender. "Usually when people do this trick it's to get a free drink, not the other way around."

"What can I say, I'm a martyr," said Stephen.

"So you knew this trick and you didn't warn me?" Jacker asked the bartender.

"Hey," she said with an innocent smile. "I was promised that if you started drinking that you'd flirt with me. What's a girl to do?"

Stephen took off the shot glass on the top of the stack, which was now filled with whiskey, and flipped it over as the crowd applauded. He flicked his card dry and slid the shot glass over to Jacker. "Drink up, buddy." Then he pushed the shot glass of water over to the bartender. "How about you do me a favor and fill this up with some whiskey too."

The bartender did as asked and then Stephen held the shot glass up to Jacker. "Cheers, buddy."

Jacker clinked his glass against Stephen's and shook his head. "To the most manipulative bastard I've met in years."

"I'll take that as a compliment," said Stephen before he downed the whiskey. He slammed the glass down and slid it forward. "Doctor, can I get another dose please?"

Jacker slid his empty glass forward too. "Same here."

"That's my boy!" Stephen slapped Jacker's back.

The bartender was quick to fill their glasses, and started to chat with Jacker about the band on his shirt. Apparently she was familiar with them, although Stephen had never heard of the group before. He prided himself on being a great wingman, and knew when to shut up and let his friends pick up the conversation.

Jacker's initial reservation about drinking faded fast. Within a half hour, Stephen was struggling to stay on his seat while Jacker only seemed to get a boost of energy from every newly filled glass.

"Just a Coke for me," said Stephen when Jacker pushed him for another round.

"What? Are you kidding me?"

"Dude, I'm wasted. I'm not even sure I'm going to make it upstairs."

"Hey man," said Jacker. "You started this engine. If you pass out, who the fuck's going to steer."

"I don't even know what that means." Stephen laughed and let his forehead fall to the bar.

"Looks like he's done," said the bartender. The only other patrons still around were all focused on a basketball game, which the bartender seemed disinterested in. Throughout the night she had spent most of her time at their end of the bar.

"I know," said Jacker. "He's a lightweight."

"It's true," said Stephen as he sat back up. "I talk a big game, but when it comes down to it I'm a pussy. Seriously, though, we've got a big day tomorrow. We should get some sleep."

"You never told me why you guys are out here," said the bartender.

"And you still haven't told me your name," said Jacker.

"Aubrey," she extended her hand across the bar. "Pleased to meet you."

"Pleasure's on mine," said Jacker.

"Pleasure's on mine?" asked Stephen. "Smooth, dude."

"Sorry," said Jacker. "All mine. I guess I've had a few more drinks than I thought."

Aubrey was wiping the counter with a white towel as she talked to them. "So, what are you guys out here for? You don't strike me as the country music type."

"Good God no," said Stephen.

"We're headed to Widowsfield," said Jacker.

Stephen thrust his elbow into the big guy's side.

"Oh really?" asked Aubrey with interest. "Why are you headed there?"

Stephen groaned and set his head back down on the bar. "Well, you might as well tell her now, Casanova."

"Sorry, man. I didn't know it was a secret."

"This sounds good." Aubrey tossed the rag over her shoulder. She reached across the bar and rubbed the back of Stephen's head. "Don't worry, Stevie, I won't tell anyone your secrets. What are you two up to?"

Stephen worried that his name hadn't come up in conversation yet, and that Aubrey had revealed their deception by knowing his name. He glanced at Jacker in concern, but the big man hadn't picked up on Aubrey's mistake.

"We're doing an internet show on haunted places," said Jacker, oblivious to the fact that Aubrey and Stephen already knew each other. It had been Aubrey that had told Stephen about Widowsfield back when he had stayed in Branson for work. She'd been an escort at the time, and Stephen had spent the night with her. After hearing her story about Widowsfield, he'd planned on using her as a guide for this trip, and setting her up with Jacker was a convenient way to explain the 'chance' encounter to Rachel.

Jacker continued his explanation, "We're headed out there to investigate the town. Do you know the story about that place?"

She nodded and snorted. "Do I? Of course I do. Everyone around here knows about it. I've been down there a bunch of times. I even saw that creepy green fog once."

Stephen feigned intrigue. "Really?"

"Yep. I grew up near there. A bunch of us used to go up on a hill near the town. It was a make out area, and you could see the downtown area of Widowsfield from there."

"Do you think you could find that place again?" asked Stephen.

"Sure, but it's all closed off now."

"Since when?" asked Stephen. She'd failed to mention that the last time he talked to her.

Aubrey glanced up, trying to recall the date. "I don't know, at least five years now. A company bought the land and closed it all off. The town's still there, but everything is fenced off now. My friends and I still broke into the town from time to time. If you know how to get past the guards you can hang out there without any trouble. So don't worry, I can still get you in."

"Was the company that bought the land named Cada E.I.B.?" asked Stephen.

"Yeah, that's it," said Aubrey.

Stephen smacked Jacker's arm. "How about that?"

"That's creepy," said Jacker.

"What? What's creepy?" asked Aubrey.

"Nothing." Stephen quickly answered.

"Are you two keeping secrets from me?" asked Aubrey. "Do I need to pour a few more of these to loosen those lips?"

"No," said Stephen. "I'm about four past done already. Hey, Aubrey, are you busy for the next few days?" He knew it was integral that he sell Jacker on the notion that this had been a chance meeting with Aubrey. His marriage had weathered a couple past transgressions, and if Rachel knew the truth about Aubrey then there could be divorce papers in Stephen's near future.

Aubrey smirked, and then squinted as she tried to figure out why Stephen would ask something like that. "Yes, I have a job and a life. Why?"

"I'd pay you to come with me," said Stephen.

"Wow," said Aubrey as she took a step back and held out her hands. She smiled and was joking when she said, "This conversation has taken a turn for the worse. I'm not that kind of girl, Stevie."

"No, not cum with me," said Stephen.

Jacker just then realized why Aubrey was startled by what Stephen had said. "Oh! That's fucking funny. He doesn't mean it that way."

"I mean, come with me in a van," said Stephen.

"Yeah, not getting any better," said Aubrey.

"What he means to ask is if you'd want to go with us to Widowsfield," said Jacker. "Show us how you used to break in."

"Yeah, that," said Stephen as he pointed at his nose and then at Jacker.

"I know what he meant," said Aubrey. "I was just screwing with him. Like I said before, I've got a job. I can't just up and leave."

"Then call off," said Stephen. "I'll make you internet famous."

"Who says I'm not already?" asked Aubrey, but then her smile faded to a grimace. "Ew, that makes it sound like I'm a porn star or something."

"Look," said Stephen as he sat up and tried to pretend like he wasn't drunk. "I'll pay you two hundred bucks a day for three days. All you have to do is take us to Widowsfield and do an interview on camera about what you saw there."

Aubrey studied them and crossed her arms. "Two fifty, and no funny stuff."

"Deal," said Stephen before he shook her hand. "We're leaving in the morning, around eight. Give Jacker your number. I'll have a contract for you to review in the morning, but right now I need to go pass out."

He leaned on Jacker's shoulder and then whispered to him, "You owe me, big guy." He waved back at them as he headed out of the hotel bar and tried to remember his room number.

As he reached the exit of the bar, he looked back at Aubrey and smiled. She winked back, and then started talking to Jacker again.

Stephen took out his wallet and his driver's license. He hadn't placed the card back in the wallet because he wanted it to dry off first. Now he looked at his smiling face on the card and said, "Mr. Knight, you conniving bastard." Then he kissed the card and slipped it into his wallet.

201

CHAPTER 14 - The End Begins

March 12th, 2012

"Everyone," said Stephen as he stood beside the van to greet the group. "This is Aubrey."

The petite, young girl smiled at waved. She was even shorter than Rachel, and had dyed blonde hair that was tied up in ponytails on either side of her head. She had studs in both cheeks that sat perfectly within her dimples when she smiled. There were colorful tattoos that adorned her chest and arms, and she was wearing a frilled, black skirt that revealed nearly the full length of her pale legs.

"Aubrey's from this area, and she's going to tell us about some of the things she's seen out in Widowsfield."

"Are you coming with us?" asked Paul.

She held up a green bag that Alma assumed was packed with clothes. "Yep."

"Do we have the room?" asked Paul.

"Well, I thought Alma could ride with you," said Stephen. "And if she wants to be in the van, Aubrey said she'd be willing to ride on the bike with you."

"No, that's okay," said Alma. "I'm fine riding with Paul." There was no way she was going to let a cute little thing like Aubrey ride on Paul's bike.

Paul must've sensed Alma's thoughts because he snickered as he put his arm around her shoulder. "We'll be fine on the bike. Good to meet you, Aubrey."

"One other thing," said Stephen before Alma and Paul walked off to where Paul's motorcycle was parked. "Aubrey says the town is fenced up. It got bought by Cada E.I.B., so we might run into some security out there. We've got a plan if we do."

Rachel came out of the hotel and walked past everyone. She went straight to Jacker's van, which was parked in the roundabout outside of the hotel's entrance, and got in. Her anger was apparent to everyone, but only Stephen seemed to know what was wrong. Alma thought about trying to talk to her new friend, but decided to wait until later to speak with her.

"Everyone ready?" asked Stephen. He seemed apologetic for his wife's behavior, if not a little embarrassed.

"We'll be right behind you," said Paul as he headed for his motorcycle.

Once they were far enough away to avoid being heard, Alma turned to Paul and asked, "What was that about?"

He shrugged and then spit off to the side. "Hell if I know. Rachel looked pissed. They must've gotten in a fight or something."

"I'll have to try and talk to her later."

"Or you could leave it be and let them sort out their own problems," said Paul as he took Alma's helmet off the handle of the bike and offered it to her.

She sneered as she took the helmet from him. "Don't be an asshole."

"Sorry," he said as he put on his own helmet. "I just don't think we know them well enough to get mixed up in their marriage."

"Yeah, you're probably right."

"Like always," said Paul and he moved away as Alma tried to punch him on the arm. "So, are you ready for this? No turning back after today. You sure you want to go through with it?"

"For the hundredth time, yes."

"All right, I just wanted to make sure."

Alma looked back at the van as Paul got on the bike. "What do you think of the new girl?"

"I don't know. Haven't said more than a few words to her. Why?"

"Do you think she's cute?" asked Alma.

Paul paused and hung his head low, fully aware of the trap Alma was setting for him. "I don't know what you want me to say. I only have eyes for you, sweetie." He looked at her and gave a goofy, toothy grin.

"I bet she has something to do with why Rachel's so pissed off."

"Oh yeah?" asked Paul, disinterested. "Well, I bet neither of us know the facts and shouldn't speculate. That's what I bet."

Alma rolled her eyes and sighed as she got on the bike behind him. "Wow, did you have a special cup of dickhead-coffee this morning or something?"

"It did taste a little funny. Did you backwash into it?" asked Paul before he started the bike, muffling any response from Alma. She just slapped him on the back as he chuckled.

Widowsfield wasn't far from Branson, but the trip felt like it took longer than it should have. The winding roads that cut through the Ozarks slowed their progress, but provided scenery that kept Alma's mind off what they were headed out to do. Every time she thought about the cabin, her heartbeat quickened and her palms started to sweat.

"I'm coming for you, Ben." Her whisper was lost in the noise of the road.

They passed a sign that had once read, 'Widowsfield 10 Miles' but had been riddled with buckshot. Each hole was rimmed with rust and the sign's post had been bent backward, as if someone had run into it, perhaps in an attempt to further erase the town from history.

After the sign, the road descended. It was a precipitous decline, and one she remembered from her childhood. This hill always caused her stomach to lurch, which had become a sensation that she learned to despise. She even avoided carnival rides in fear of causing the same sensation and that it would remind her of Widowsfield.

The woods lay beyond, and Alma recalled the fog that had enveloped them sixteen years ago. She thought about her father as he screamed at her to be quiet. And she thought of the creatures in the woods, whose shapes were but shadows in the mist, running along side their car as they tried to escape.

Fear choked her and she felt her body start to shake. She struggled for breath and had to close her eyes as Paul drove down the hill and into the woods that preceded the border of Widowsfield. She tried to concentrate on the hum of the motor and the whistling wind, but her mind seemed determined to think of the creatures in the woods. Those hulking ghosts haunted her, crawling through the trees and reaching out toward the car as if trying to pull her out and into the mist with them.

Then she focused on the only thing that could quiet her fearful mind.

314.

She thought only of the number, and imagined it written in black ink on her arm. Her fear subsided as the number drew her in. Chaos Magick taught that symbols could be used as a focal point to assist in a person's ability to shut out the world around them. For Alma, it was a journey along a razor's edge. There was something wicked hidden in that number, and she wasn't certain she wanted to know what it was.

She tried to come up with a different symbol that she could focus on, and the first thing that came to mind was the teddy bear keychain that Paul had bought for her. She could feel it in her coat pocket, pressed into her abdomen as she held onto Paul. For some reason, the thought of losing him occurred to her, and she held onto him tighter.

Paul slowed the motorcycle and Alma dared to open her eyes.

Jacker pulled off the road ahead and parked on the gravel shoulder. They were out of the woods, and Widowsfield was ahead of them. There was a tall, wire fence that stretched up over the hills to the right, and down into the cover of woods off to the left. It appeared like there was a guard shack and a gate further up the road, but they were too far away for Alma to be certain. The road went on for

205

another couple hundred yards before being cut off by the fence, and there was a second road that turned off the one they were on. It went off to the right, up over the hills and around Widowsfield.

Stephen got out of the van's side door and came over to speak with Paul and Alma. Aubrey followed behind him and Jacker got out as well. Rachel stayed in the van.

"Aubrey was right," said Stephen. "There's a guard shack up there."

Paul and Alma got off the bike and tried to look at the fence that blocked their way.

"You okay, Alma?" asked Stephen. "You're as white as a ghost."

Paul looked back at her and took off his sunglasses. "He's right. Are you okay?"

"I'm fine," said Alma. "I guess I was just a little cold or something."

"Want to ride in the van for a bit?" asked Stephen.

"No, I'll be fine."

"So what's the plan?" asked Paul. "How are we going to get in if they've got it all fenced up?"

"That's where Aubrey comes in," said Stephen.

"My friends and I used to sneak in all the time," said Aubrey. "There's a small dirt road on the north side of town that used to belong to a farmer. It goes through his field, and into the town. They've got a gate up there, but I've never seen a guard."

"And we can get the van in through there?" asked Paul.

"No, not yet," said Stephen. "We're going to have to leave the van and your bike in the field for now. We'll head into town on foot, and find the cabin that you used to stay at," he said as he looked at Alma. "Then tonight, after dark, we'll come back out and use a bolt cutter on the gate's lock. We can probably get away with driving the van with the headlights off, but we might have to push your bike in. We can't risk the noise."

"I don't know," said Paul. "This seems kind of risky. Are you even going to be able to use any of the footage you get in there? If it's private property, can't they sue you for airing anything you record?"

"You sound like my wife," said Stephen. His tone revealed at least part of why Rachel was acting angry. They must've been arguing this same issue last night. "It'll be fine. Anything that we film in the cabin could've been filmed anywhere. No way they can prove we went in the town, as long as we don't get caught."

"I don't know, man," said Paul. "This seems like a bad idea."

"I never thought of you as the law-abiding type," said Stephen. "Aren't you up for a little adventure?"

"I'm not in this for adventure," said Paul. "I'm in it to help Alma." He looked down at her and asked, "What do you want to do?"

Alma looked down the road at the fence, and then back at the woods that they'd passed through. It felt like she'd already taken her first step into this nightmare, and if she soldiered on then she could put an end to this part of her life. "We're already here," she said. "Might as well get it over with. I say we go in."

It was clear that Paul didn't agree, but he stood beside her and nodded. "Then it's settled, we're going in."

Stephen clapped his hands once and looked delighted. "Let's go!" He didn't bother prolonging the conversation, fully aware that once the customer was sold it was time to shut up and take the money. He ushered Jacker and Aubrey back to the van and within a minute they were back on the road.

They headed north and Alma looked out at the fence that had been erected around the town. It looked like a prison, with razor wire looped around the top of the outer fence, and a second barrier behind it. The road curved closer to the fence and Alma saw movement from within the town. There was a white truck with a yellow light bar on top driving through Widowsfield. She assumed it was a security patrol, which didn't help ease her tension about their plan.

Soon they passed where the fence turned, and entered another wooded area. Aubrey was leading Jacker as the van turned off onto a dirt road that went up a slight incline. Once they crested the hill there was a wide field beyond. It was once a farm, but had been overgrown with tall weeds, though no trees had made their way into the acreage.

Jacker drove along what had once been a road, but was now barely a dimple in the weeds, and the van struggled through the overgrowth. Paul stayed back near the hill and watched the van push through the field. Alma heard him curse, but couldn't discern what he was saying over the hum of his engine. He motioned for her to get off the bike, and when she did he turned it, drove off the path, and then parked in the wooded area. He turned off the engine and got off.

"What's wrong?" asked Alma.

"This isn't a dirt bike," he said as he took off his helmet. "I'm not risking riding through this shit."

"So we're walking then?" asked Alma.

"I guess so." He hung his helmet by its strap over his handlebar. Alma did the same with hers and then took his hand as they started down the hill.

"Thanks for doing this," said Alma.

"Like I told you, you're my girl. I'm not about to let you come out here with these yahoos by yourself."

They held hands as they walked through the field. Alma enjoyed her time alone with Paul, and they talked about their plans after this was all over. Alma was excited to return to school, and set up her new music room. Paul was going to try to get a job at a motorcycle shop on the south side where a friend of his worked. They discussed their relationship, and laughed about how things had gone wrong for them in the past. Alma chided Paul on the way his apartment used to be so messy, and he promised that he didn't live like a sloppy college kid anymore.

Geese flew above them, away from Widowsfield and to the north. Alma watched them go, somewhat envious. Despite how happy she was to be with Paul, there was a creeping dread that heightened with each step. No matter how much she tried to ignore it, she knew she was walking back into the worst moment of her life. Despite her desire to leave this behind, here she was, walking right back into hell.

Like summer fades to fall, and winter gives way to spring, this was inevitable. Alma Harper was willingly walking back into Widowsfield.

Her respite had ended.

PART THREE : THE COIL'S END

CHAPTER 15 - Beyond the Shroud

March 12th, 2012

Alma and Paul caught up with the others at the locked gate at the edge of the farm. Only a single bar was set over the road, hinged on one side and padlocked on the other, but the fence connected on either side of it. They would have to break the lock to get the vehicles in, but they could worry about that at night.

"This is it," said Aubrey. She stood near the gate, alone. Alma wanted to hate her, which was a catty response to the stranger's sudden interloping, but she felt sorry for her at that moment. Aubrey looked uncomfortable, and aware that coming on this trip had caused tension between Rachel and Stephen for some reason.

Rachel was still in the passenger seat of the van, which had been pulled off to the side in an attempt to hide in the weeds. Stephen and Jacker had plucked out some of the lighter equipment and were trying to figure out what they should bring, and what should be left behind for now.

"God, this is creepy," said Alma as she walked up to the gate. The dirt road led past a decrepit farmhouse and down a hill, past the barn, to a paved road.

"You can say that again." Aubrey crossed her arms and shivered though it wasn't cold. "I didn't wear the right outfit for this."

Alma looked at the girl's short skirt and designer boots. "Yeah, I'd have to agree with you on that one."

"I was trying to look cute for him," she nodded back in the direction of the guys as they unloaded the van.

"Who?" asked Alma. "Stephen? He's married."

"No, not him. Jacker."

"Oh, really?" asked Alma, surprised and excited. Her initial reaction was dulled when she recalled what Paul had told her about Jacker. She liked him, and loved the idea of him hooking up with a cute girl like Aubrey, but the darker side of Jacker was still a mystery to Alma.

"Do you know him well?" asked Aubrey. "He seems like a nice guy."

"I just met him. He's a friend of my boyfriend."

"Paul, right?" asked Aubrey. "He's a hunk."

"Eyes off the prize, sweetheart," said Alma.

Aubrey smiled and laughed, her dimples in full effect. "Don't worry, I'm no home wrecker. No matter what some people seem to think." She glanced at Rachel who was still sitting in the passenger seat.

"Did she say something?" asked Alma, worried that Rachel had ripped into the new recruit.

"No, that's the problem. She hasn't said two words to me this whole trip. It's super uncomfortable in there."

"I'll talk to her, and try to see what's up. Trust me, she's a sweetie once you get to know her. I'm sure she's just pissed off about something else. I wouldn't worry about it."

Stephen opened the passenger door of the van. "Time to go." He walked away from Rachel, uncaring and cold.

Alma looked at Aubrey and grimaced comically.

"Told ya," said Aubrey. "They were quite the delight to drive with, let me tell you."

Alma patted Aubrey on the back and then walked over to the van. Rachel was still in her seat with the door open when Alma approached. "Hey there."

"Hi, Alma," said Rachel.

"So, what's the deal?"

"With what?"

"With the bitchy-wife routine?"

Rachel glared down at Alma from her seat in the van. "Don't you start on me too."

Alma stepped on the footrest and rose up so that she was closer to Rachel. "I'm on your side here. I don't even know what's wrong and I'm still on your side. Now tell me what happened"

"I don't really want to talk about it," said Rachel.

"You two coming?" asked Stephen. He was standing with the others near the gate. They were ready to go, with bags of equipment slung over their shoulders.

"Tell him he can go fuck himself," said Rachel so that only Alma could hear.

"We'll meet up with you in a minute," Alma yelled over to Stephen.

The others begrudgingly left them behind.

"Are you coming? Or are you just going to sit in the van all day?"

Rachel eventually got out and slammed the car door shut. They started to follow the others down the hill and past the farmhouse.

"Now," said Alma, "tell me what's bugging you."

"I don't really want to talk about it."

"Oh no," said Alma. "I'm not letting you get away with that after you made me tell you everything about Paul and me. I can't afford to take you out and buy you new clothes, a manicure, a haircut, and all that stuff to butter you up until you talk, but I can pester you until you tell me what's wrong."

"It's a long story," said Rachel.

"Then you might as well start talking."

Rachel grinned at Alma. "You would've made a good reporter. You know that?"

"Come on, out with it. What's up?"

"Okay, but you have to keep this between us. Deal?"

"Deal."

Rachel sighed and ruffled her curly hair as she scratched her scalp. "Stephen and I haven't had the greatest marriage

212

in history. We've had some tough times, and I mean really tough times."

"I can relate," said Alma.

"He's a good looking guy, and could've gotten pretty much any girl he wanted."

"And you're a gorgeous girl who could get any man she wanted," said Alma. "What's your point?"

"Well, he had a history, back in college, of getting with a lot of girls. I don't mind about that or anything. Well, that's a lie, of course. I obsess over that type of stuff. But that's all in the past. There's nothing we can do about it."

"Better to just leave that stuff buried," said Alma. "I do my best to just pretend Paul's never seen another naked woman besides me." Alma and Rachel shared a laugh.

"Stephen had a definite type back in the day. I've seen pictures of his old girlfriends and they all look the same: Petite, thin, with blonde hair and tattoos. It's fucking ridiculous. Every damn girl looks like a carbon copy of the one before until you get to me." She motioned at her body. "A red haired, tattoo-less, chubby girl."

"Chubby?" asked Alma, perturbed. "Are you crazy?"

"Look at these hips," said Rachel. "I look like I'm hiding watermelons down here." She slapped her thighs.

"Oh my God, Rachel," said Alma. "You seriously need to shut up right now. You are the cutest damn girl I've ever seen. I'd give anything to have your curves instead of my Olive Oyl, broomstick body. If I ever hear you call yourself chubby again, I'm going to slap you."

"Well, thanks, I think," said Rachel. "Anyhow, last night Stephen texted me that he was headed to the bar with Jacker. I told him to have a good time and that I'd meet him up in our room. I got back to the hotel early and thought I'd go have a drink with them at the bar. Then I get there and find the two of them whooping it up with…" she motioned out at Aubrey and stumbled on her description. "With that little pixie-tart."

"Blonde hair," said Alma. "Tattoos. I get it."

"Right," said Rachel. "Exactly the kind of slut that Stephen used to hang all over."

"Stop it," said Alma, chastising Rachel for continuing to focus her issues with Stephen's past on Aubrey. "Besides, you've got him all locked up now. That's the whole point of a wedding ring."

Rachel laughed at Alma's naiveté. "Sorry, honey. Hate to break it to you, but this," she held up her left hand and used her thumb to wiggle her ring back and forth, "doesn't do shit to stop them from fucking around on you."

"Oh," said Alma. "Did Stephen cheat on you before?"

"No, and yes. Kind of, but not really," said Rachel. "I'm sure that makes a lot of sense. He never really cheated on me since we've been married, that I know of anyway. He just came close once, and it was with a girl that looked a lot like his new little princess up there. And then we get here and he just magically meets this girl at a bar that knows all about Widowsfield and is willing to take us there? Come on. I think he set this all up, and that she's the girl he met out here last time he was here. He just doesn't want to admit it to me, because he knows I'll be pissed."

"Well, she's not interested in your husband," said Alma. "Believe it or not, she's going after Jacker."

"Really?" asked Rachel.

"I know, it's weird. Not that I don't think Jacker's a good looking guy or anything, it's just that he's so big."

"And she's so small," said Rachel. "That would be an odd couple for the ages. God, I almost want to see them hook up just so I can laugh about it. Can you imagine the two of them in bed?"

"Stop it," said Alma as she laughed. "Don't be mean. I admit, it's hard to accept that meeting her at the bar is a coincidence, but I don't think Aubrey's trying to hook up with Stephen. From what I can tell, she's a pretty nice girl."

"Oh, now I feel like a bitch," said Rachel. "I didn't talk to her the whole way here."

"That's what I heard," said Alma.

"I saw you talking to her. Is she mad at me? Does she think I'm a huge bitch?"

They got to the road and turned in the direction of the town. The others were ahead of them, on the side of the road.

"Let's see," said Alma. "Hey Aubrey!" She yelled out to the girl.

Stephen turned and angrily hushed Alma. Then Paul looked back and waved at them to hurry up across the street.

"Oh shit," said Rachel. "There must be someone out there."

Alma and Rachel ran across the street and down into the ditch on the other side. Rachel lost her balance and grabbed onto Alma's wrist. They both fell and slid the last few feet to the bottom of the muddy decline.

"That figures," said Rachel, but Alma quickly hushed her.

The others were hiding low as well and Alma heard the rumble of a vehicle's tires on the road. The wind swished as a truck passed, headed north toward the farm.

"Do you think they found the van?" asked Rachel.

Alma hadn't thought of the possibility of getting caught. She was so focused on going to the cabin to discover what her father had been trying to hide that she hadn't considered the risk involved in getting there. If security found Jacker's van, and called the police, then they could all be in serious trouble. It wouldn't take long for the police to discover that Jacker was a wanted man.

Widowsfield
March 14th, 1996

"She's here," said Jeremy Tapper.

He stopped the two boys that were carrying the bowl of steaming water into the bathroom. They had oven mitts on,

215

and had accidentally spilled some of the hot liquid in the hallway.

"Who's here?" asked Mark as he stood in the tub, his shirt off, waiting for the children to pour the searing liquid on him.

"The Skeleton Man is going to leave us." Jeremy's hand faltered. He had the razor pressed to his neck, prepared to kill himself if his father didn't do what The Skeleton Man asked, but now he felt alone again. The chattering teeth quieted and Jeremy felt lost without the noise.

"What's going on?" asked one of the younger boys holding the water. "Where did he go?"

Jeremy set his hand on the sink to steady himself. "He needs two of them, but only one came back. She forgot, but he can make her remember."

"Jeremy," said Mark. "Put the razor down. Okay?"

Jeremy glanced at the other two boys, both of whom had started to cry. "We're lost now."

"Who's going to protect us?" asked one of the boys.

"I'll protect you," said Mark. He nearly stepped out of the tub, but stopped, fearful that Jeremy would hurt himself. "I'll stop whatever it is that you think is after you."

"No you won't," said Jeremy. "The Skeleton Man protected us. This time he's leaving. He's going to try and find the one he lost."

"He loves her more than us," said one of the boys.

"No," said Jeremy in anger. "That's not true. Don't say that."

"Yes it is true." The boys set the bowl of water on the floor and took off their oven mitts. "He's going to abandon us now that she's here. He's going to let the woman have us."

"What woman?" asked Mark. "I'm coming out of the tub, Jeremy. Put the razor down and tell me what's going on."

"No!" Jeremy pressed the blade against his throat. "You stay there. If he comes back, we have to pretend like

216

everything's the same. Daddy, you're going to get us killed again. If the woman comes, she'll try to grab us."

"What woman?" asked Mark.

"The melting one. She hates the children. She wants to carry us away."

"Jeremy, nothing you're saying makes any sense. I don't know what's going on, but something is messing with your head. There's no Skeleton Man, there's no woman that wants to kidnap you. You've got to believe me, son. Please."

"Dad, you don't know what's out there," said Jeremy. "We do." He was crying as he held the razor to his throat. "It's better not to see."

Jeremy pressed the razor into his skin. Mark cried out in horror as his son sawed at his own throat. The boy fell to the floor and the other children scrambled to get the weapon, anxious to die next rather than face the town without The Skeleton Man to protect them.

March 12th, 2012

Stephen led them through Widowsfield, down side streets and alleys, through yards and a park. It was a small town, quaint but with everything a family would need to live happy. There was a grocery store, now blackened within as if it had suffered a fire; a plumber's shop, with windows still intact but a sign that dangled from a single rusted loop; a flower store, with weeds around the foundation and vines creeping up the façade; and they saw a fire station, with a fire truck still parked in the garage as if no one was interested in salvaging any equipment at all from the town. If all humans were to disappear from the planet, Widowsfield is what the world would look like a decade later.

"This makes no sense," said Paul as he held Alma's hand. "Why would they just leave everything here? You can't tell me there isn't a fire station around here somewhere that could've used that truck."

"No, this isn't how it was when I came back the first time," said Alma. "The buildings were boarded up then. It wasn't like this." They spoke in hushed tones, afraid to alert anyone to their presence.

"It's almost like they tried to get the town going again at some point," said Jacker. He'd been eavesdropping and snuck up behind them with Aubrey to talk about what they were seeing.

Stephen cut around the side of the fire station and motioned for them to follow. He had two bags strapped to his back, filled with equipment that he'd gathered from the van. Paul and Jacker were similarly loaded, but the girls were only asked to carry the clothes and a few light bags.

"Does he know where he's going?" asked Alma about Stephen.

"Yeah," said Jacker. "He's been studying maps of Widowsfield. He talked about it in the van on the way here. I think he wants to check out Main Street first, and then head out to the elementary school that your cabin was near."

"He's going to get us busted," said Aubrey.

"Do you remember it always looking like this?" asked Alma. "When you came here with your friends the last time, were all the buildings boarded up or were they like this?"

"Like this," said Aubrey. "I think the company that bought the land did it."

"That's fucked up," said Paul. "This place gives me the creeps."

"Welcome to the club," said Alma.

Stephen led them behind the station and then stopped and retreated a few steps as he waited for the others to catch up. "This is Main Street," he said when they gathered around him.

"You sure this is a good idea?" asked Rachel.

"No," said Stephen, although he had a giddy demeanor that unsettled Alma. "Jacker, can you give me the green bag? There's a camera in there. I want to get some shots of Main Street."

"Why?" asked Alma. "What's so important about this spot?"

"Well, the rumor is that the emergency services in the area had a new computer system installed that recorded all of the conversations that happened in their station here. That's the station over there." He pointed across the street to a plain, brick building. A bank shared a parking lot with the emergency services building, and there was a digital clock on the sign near the road, but it didn't display any numbers now.

"So, what?" asked Paul. "Are you planning on breaking in there or something?"

Stephen looked confused by the question. "No, of course not. I just want to get some shots of it for the story.

219

The central command was outside of town, that's how people found out about the tapes."

"What tapes?" asked Jacker.

"The recordings of the calls that came into the center. Aren't you guys paying attention? They recorded everyone's 9-1-1 calls, and apparently they had some fucked up stuff on them."

"How do you know?" asked Paul. "Did you hear them?"

"No, the tapes all mysteriously disappeared," said Stephen as if he didn't believe the tapes vanished at all, but were acquired as part of a conspiracy to hide the truth. "Just like everyone in town."

"I hate this place," said Rachel. She crossed her arms as if she were cold even in the midday sun.

"Come on," said Stephen. "Don't wuss out on me now." He got his Canon digital video camera and started to get it ready to record. It wasn't the type of camera you'd see a tourist use, and was like a miniature version of something you might see on a movie set. It had a handle on the top that Alma assumed was to help it act as a steady cam and Stephen quickly got the machine up and running. Alma had forgotten that this used to be his profession, before he took on the mantle of a ghost hunter.

"Shit," said Stephen after a few minutes of filming.

"What is it?" asked Rachel.

Stephen closed up his camera and pointed back toward the fire station. "Go, go, go."

"What's wrong?" asked Rachel as they all rushed away from Main Street.

"Security truck coming this way," said Stephen.

They ran around the back of the used book store that they were beside and listened as the truck passed. It moved fast, and Alma saw the alley brighten with yellow, flashing light as the truck drove by.

"Okay," said Rachel. "We need to get somewhere safe. It's bad enough that we're here, but now we're sitting out here in the open, just waiting to get caught."

220

"I think you're right," said Jacker. "That truck was booking, man. They're looking for someone."

"Let's not get ahead of ourselves," said Stephen. "We don't know what's going on."

"Damn it, Stephen," said Rachel. "We're going to the cabin now. Alma, can you lead us there?"

"I think so," said Alma. "If you can get me to the elementary school, I think I can get us to the cabin. I remember the kids walking home from school. We watched them from the cabin."

"All right," said Stephen. "It's not far from here."

They went back to the field beside the fire station and Stephen led them past a small pond and through a children's park. He pointed up the hill to a building in the distance. "That's it."

"Are there people in there?" asked Aubrey.

Stephen squinted to try and see what the blonde bartender was apparently able to discern. He took his camera back out and used the zoom feature on it to get a better look.

"Fuck me," said Stephen. "She's right."

Everyone knelt lower in fear of being seen.

"What should we do?" asked Rachel.

Stephen continued to study the people in the school. "They're not moving. I can't see them real well; they're just shadows in the windows, but Aubrey's right. There're definitely people in there."

"And they're not moving?" asked Alma.

"No," said Stephen.

Alma looked at the camera's screen and saw the silhouettes that Aubrey had spotted. "That can't be people. They're just standing there."

"Well, let's not take a chance," said Rachel. "Let's go around the school and try to make it through the woods back there." She pointed to the wooded area that sat beside a soccer field. There was another building that looked like a school as well on the other side of the field.

221

They followed Stephen to the woods where they took a short break. Rachel took her shoes off and complained about not being told there would be hiking involved in this trip. Paul was silent, and barely spoke even as Alma wrapped her arms around his waist. She was thankful for the chance to stop walking for a bit. The cut on her foot was still bothering her from two nights ago. Jacker and Aubrey were investigating the area together while Stephen toyed with his camera.

"Holy shit," said Stephen. He was sitting on a stump with his camera in his lap. "Guys, guys, you need to see this."

"What's up?"

He flipped the viewer on the camera shut and looked up at Rachel, Alma, and Paul with wide, excited eyes. "You're not going to believe this shit. I can't even believe it myself. This is nuts."

"What?" asked Rachel.

"You guys ever hear of orbs before?"

"Yes," said Rachel.

"I know you've heard of them," said Stephen. "I was asking them." He pointed at Alma and Paul.

"No," said Paul.

"Orbs are something that appear on camera when ghosts are around," said Stephen. "They're little balls of light that zip around that some people think are actually entities."

"And sane people think they're just little bits of dust that the camera is picking up," said Rachel, ever the skeptic.

"Oh yeah," said Stephen as he opened his camera back up. "Look at this and tell me what you think."

They crowded around him to look at the viewfinder. At first, Alma thought there was a reflection on the screen, but then she saw the mass of light shifting, revealing thousands of tiny globes of light spinning in circles.

"Holy shit," said Paul as he backed away. "I'm starting to hate this fucking place, man."

"Wow," said Rachel as she leaned in closer. "You swear to God you didn't mess with this somehow? This is real?"

"I didn't do shit," said Stephen. "I swear! You guys were with me. This is the first time I've looked at it." He started to take the camera away to look at it himself, but Alma stopped him.

"Look in the background," she said and pointed at the screen.

"What?" asked Paul as he returned to see what Alma had pointed out.

"There's a man back there, by the building you were filming. And there's a time on the clock in front of that bank. I know there weren't any numbers displayed on there when you were filming."

"Where?" asked Stephen. "I don't see anything. All I see are these balls of light."

"Rewind the tape," said Alma. "There's a moment where the lights disperse a little and you can see through them to the building. There, there, stop," she said as Stephen rewound the recording. He played it in slow motion until Alma said, "Stop!"

A dark shape stood beside the bank's sign, a shade instead of a man, but clear enough to distinguish a head, body, and long, thin arms. The brick sign in front of the bank had a time on it that blended with the lights.

The time was 3:14.

Rachel yelped when she saw him and backed away with her hands over her mouth. "I want to go home." Her voice trembled. "Stephen, I want to go home. I don't want to stay here."

"Are you insane?" asked Stephen. He was overjoyed by the discovery of the spirit he'd recorded. "This is the greatest fucking thing that's ever happened to us." He couldn't stop smiling, even as Rachel was near tears. "You're out of your mind if you think I'm leaving now."

"You're going to get us killed," said Rachel. "We're getting into evil shit here, Stephen. Don't drag us into this."

He looked bewildered at his wife and then at Paul and Alma. "Are you nuts? This is one of the biggest discoveries ever."

"Yeah, and it's a discovery that some people are really serious about keeping secret," said Rachel. "Stephen, we need to get out of here. That's not normal. What you just showed us isn't fucking natural."

"Goddamn it, Rachel, I know that. That's the whole damn reason we're here. You're not going to back out of this now. No way."

"Maybe she's right," said Paul. "This is more than we bargained for, man. I don't know what it is you caught on tape, but it was staring right at us. What the hell was that, man?"

"I'm not leaving," said Alma. Her bravado shocked even herself, but she'd never been more certain of anything in her life. "I can't go, Paul. I understand if you want to run, but I'm not running anymore. Something happened here that ruined my life, and I'm going to find out what it was."

"Alma." Paul was going to try and reason with her, but Alma stopped him before he could get started.

"No, Paul. No. I'm not leaving. Not now."

"You two are insane," said Rachel. "You can go by yourselves. I'm done. How stupid would I have to be to stay here overnight after seeing that." She pointed at the camera. "Screw that."

"What's wrong?" asked Jacker as he returned with Aubrey.

The young girl's lipstick was smudged and Jacker was rubbing his lips clean.

"Stephen just caught a ghost on camera," said Paul.

"No shit?" asked Jacker. "Let me check it out."

"Hold on," said Stephen. He pointed out towards the fire station that they had been near moments earlier. "I just saw the security truck headed that way."

Alma looked back to see if she could see the truck. "I don't see it."

Stephen packed up his camera quickly. "I saw it headed over there, and there was more than one. This is our chance to head out to the cabin. Come on."

Alma was certain he was lying to try and get Rachel to go to the cabin.

"I told you," said Rachel. "I'm not going."

"Don't be stupid, babe," said Stephen. "This is our chance to get to the cabin where it's safe."

"It's not safe here! It's not safe anywhere in this fucking town," said Rachel. She was as terrified as she was angry.

"So what?" asked Stephen. "Are you just going to go walk right up to the security here?"

"I didn't see any trucks back there," said Rachel.

"Trust me," said Stephen. "I saw them. Now let's get to the cabin and if you're still set on going home we can figure it out there. Let's at least get out of the open."

"You're going to get us killed," said Rachel as she let Stephen lead her away.

Widowsfield
March 14th, 1996

Nancy staggered back inside of the Widowsfield County Emergency Services building. The fog had swept in too fast to be natural, and the crackling electricity zinged across the metal handle of the door.

"What the fuck is going on?" Nancy fell against the wall as she stared out the building's door. There were dogs barking, and the clock on the bank's sign seemed brighter than it should've been. As the fog rolled into the parking lot, the time continued to blaze through it, the light penetrating even the thick white cloud.

3:14

"It's different now," said Claire. The old woman stood up from her chair and took off her headset. "Nancy, get away from the door."

"What are you talking about?"

225

"Get away from the door!"

Claire reached out and took Nancy's arm to pull her back. The two women stared at the entrance for a minute, but nothing happened.

"What's the matter up there?" asked Darryl from his seat in the middle of the room.

"Shut up, Darryl," said Claire.

Nancy smirked, satisfied to hear the sweet old woman be nasty to Darryl.

"Nancy, this is all different," said Claire as she looked down at her seat. She rubbed her thigh and then her head.

"I think there was an explosion or something outside."

"Would you two get back on your damn phones," said Darryl. "The lines are lighting up. I need some help here."

Nancy glanced at her station and saw that every line was lit up red. "Oh shit, Claire. We need to get on the phones."

"No," said Claire. "Don't do it." The portly old woman grabbed Nancy's arm to prevent her from getting to her desk.

"Claire, what's the matter?"

"Do you hear that?"

"The dogs barking?" Nancy could hear dogs reacting to the strange fog outside, barking from far off.

"No," said Claire. "Not the children. Can you hear the chattering teeth?"

"You're starting to scare me," said Nancy.

"I think there's someone else in my head," said Claire. "Darling, I know that sounds crazy, but it's true."

"Maybe you need to sit down," said Nancy.

"No, absolutely not." Claire seemed suddenly frightened of her chair.

Nancy tried to get out of Claire's grip, but the old woman held fast. "I need to get some of these calls."

"Quiet," said Claire. "Don't move. He's here."

"Who?" asked Nancy.

"The one the children call The Skeleton Man. If he remembers us, he'll lead the children here. He's right outside."

"Claire, I don't know what's gotten into you, but there's…" Nancy looked outside where she had just been, confident that there was no one there hiding in the fog. She was wrong.

Standing outside the front door, seeming to hide from someone across the street, was a tall, dark figure. The fog shrouded him, but he was pressed against the glass, affording Nancy a view of his skeletal frame. He had long arms draped in a suit coat, and blood was dripping from the bone tips of his fingers. His face was a mask of sunken skin, pulled taut against a skull to reveal chattering teeth beneath. There were strips of wet flesh slapped against his skull and one of them slid down the side of his head. He had a hole where his nose once was, and his eye sockets were wide and black. Within the sockets sat two lidless eyes, smaller than the skull they dwelled in, bobbing in the blackness as they stared across the street.

Then he looked at Nancy.

The sound of his chattering teeth seemed to explode in her mind. She cried out and clasped her ears just as every pane of glass in the building exploded. The fog rushed in as The Skeleton Man turned his focus back on his victims. The children came to punish them, running on their bloodied paws and snapping their jaws. The adults would pay for what The Skeleton Man remembered.

CHAPTER 17 - Way Past Sanity

March 12th, 2012

Alma had no trouble finding the cabin. Despite how hard she tried to forget this place, Widowsfield was burned into her memory, and every street looked exactly as it did the night her father and she had fled.

"This is it." She stood on the walkway that led to the front door. She stared at the picture window where her brother and she used to sit and watch the children come home from school. They would walk down the thin road, past the cabin that was mostly shaded by the encroaching woods. Some of the children would wave at them, but most snickered and laughed at the two young faces that peered at them.

A sense of sorrow and loneliness swept through Alma.

"Let's get inside," said Stephen.

"Are you okay?" asked Rachel as she stood beside Alma.

"No," Alma stated matter-of-factly. "Not at all."

"You don't have to do this," said Rachel. "I want to leave too. I want to get the hell out of this town."

Alma broke her gaze at the cabin to look at her friend. She felt an intense sorrow for Rachel, though she didn't know why. "You should go." Alma didn't want Rachel to get hurt.

"Are you serious?" asked Rachel, excited. "Do you want to just go home?"

"No," said Alma. "I'm staying, but you should go. All of you should go."

Paul put his hand in Alma's. "I'm with you to the end, babe. Who else is going to protect you from the ghosts here?" He smiled and squeezed her hand.

"It's not locked," said Stephen as he opened the cabin's front door.

The gaping maw seemed to draw Alma's attention inexorably inside. She knew that the cabin wanted her back.

"Don't go," said Rachel.

"I have to. I've never been more certain of anything in my life."

"Why?" asked Rachel. "What do you think you're going to find in there?" She held Alma by the crook of her arm to stop her from going in.

"The truth," said Alma. "Something happened here sixteen years ago that I've blocked from my memory. It has something to do with the number 314, and the last time I was here I was able to remember my brother just by staring at the symbol for pi. I was too scared then to learn everything, but not anymore."

"This place is fucked," said Rachel. "The whole town is a nightmare. I don't know if the government has something to do with it, or if this is some portal to hell, and I don't care. I don't want to know. I just want to go home, and I want you to come with me."

"Guys, you have to see this," said Stephen from the entrance of the cabin. He had gone inside, and came back out to call them in. He waved at them, excitement lighting his features, like a mischievous child beckoning his siblings after discovering where their parents hid the presents.

"Don't go in," said Rachel.

Alma pried her friend's fingers from her arm. "I'm going. It's time for this to end. Whatever I've forgotten, I can handle it now."

The sun seemed to provide no heat, the wind held no sway, and the cabin dominated Alma's every sense. Even the sound of her friends' voices seemed lost as if in a cavern, far off and echoing. She walked to the threshold, and stepped through.

Her senses returned to normal once inside, although a moment of time seemed lost to her. Now everyone was inside, and Stephen was closing the door behind her. The cabin's door closed like the lid of a tomb, loud and with heft.

"Look at this shit," said Stephen as he walked to a couch in the living room where two mannequins had been set up.

The cabin was the same, eerily accurate. It was different from when Alma had come here with her mother, and had been reverted back to what it looked like on March 14th, 1996. It was as if someone had stolen Alma's memories to recreate the room exactly as it was.

The couch was brown and musty, with a pattern of waving lines that looked Native American. The area rug was green and plain, with a hole in it where a dog had eaten through while chewing on a bone.

That dog, the one with the missing eye and yellow teeth; the dog that belonged to the red-haired girl whose father owned the cabin.

Alma staggered and Paul caught her.

"What's wrong?" he asked as he steadied her.

"How crazy is this?" asked Stephen loudly as he knocked on the head of a mannequin that was sitting on the couch.

Alma stared at the child-sized mannequin. It was a boy in overalls and a red shirt with a pair of sneakers on that had been scuffed from playing in the dirt out back. There were two mannequins on the couch, one a boy and the other a girl.

Alma recognized the clothes that the girl mannequin wore. It was the same outfit she'd worn sixteen years earlier.

"This must've been what we saw at the school," said Stephen. "There must be mannequins like this all over town." He slapped the boy's head and the yellow mannequin slouched to the side.

"No," said Alma. "Don't hit it."

"Why?" asked Jacker as he set the gear he was carrying down. "What's wrong? Do you know what this is all about?" There was an edge of fright to his tone, as if he was struggling to maintain composure in the bizarre setting.

"That's my brother." She looked around at the familiar room. "Someone set up this place to look exactly like it did

230

when I was here with my father. Those mannequins are dressed in the clothes that my brother and I were wearing."

"I think we should go," said Aubrey. She had her arms crossed and was backing away, toward the front door. "This is fucked up."

"I agree," said Rachel. "Stephen, we need to leave."

"I can't believe you guys want to leave," said Stephen. He was exasperated, but his anger was unmistakable. "We've stumbled into one of the biggest paranormal stories of all time, and you guys want to just take off? You're insane."

"This reminds me of the towns they built while testing nuclear weapons," said Paul.

A yellow light pulsed outside.

"Get down!" Stephen knelt low and moved toward the kitchen.

The picture window's curtains were pulled back, revealing the street outside as a security truck came near. The group moved into the kitchen, which was to the right of the entrance, and ducked beneath the counters. The rotating yellow light on top of the truck illuminated the cabin with ghastly shadows for a moment, and then faded away.

Alma would've sworn the shadows cast by the mannequins were taller than they should've been. She was on her knees on the kitchen floor, exactly where the dog's crate used to be. It was also where her mother had written the symbol for pi on the ground and then circled it with lit candles. This would be where Alma would try it again, but this time she wouldn't be confused by the mathematic symbol. This time she would just write the numbers.

314

"Do you think they're looking for us?" asked Jacker.

"I don't know," said Paul. "But we're sure the hell not going to be able to get the van and my bike in here."

"There were never this many security guards before," said Aubrey. "When I used to sneak in here with my friends, there was never more than a few guards at the posts. Nothing like this."

231

"Did you ever come down here two days before March 14th?" asked Alma.

Everyone turned their attention to Alma as Aubrey answered, "No."

"Do you think the date has something to do with this?" asked Rachel of Alma.

Alma looked at all of their faces, stunned that they were surprised by this. "Of course it does. Don't you guys get it?"

"Get what?" asked Stephen.

"They're trying to recreate the event. Whatever happened on March 14th, 1996, they're trying to make it happen again. Or at least they tried, at some point. It looks like it must've been years ago, maybe when Cada E.I.B. first purchased the land. I don't know how they got it so perfect," said Alma as she stared at the back of the mannequins' heads while they sat silent on the couch. "But if the mannequins were in the school, then I bet they're set up like this in every house around here."

Rachel punched Stephen in the arm several times. The first seemed playful, but the next was with more force, and then by the third hit she started to slam both fists into him. "You dragged us into this, you bastard."

"Settle the fuck down, Rachel. Jesus Christ! Stop it." He grabbed her wrists and she struggled to get free.

"It's not his fault," said Alma. She looked around the cabin and felt a sudden chill. "Something wanted me back here. I think it's been trying to pull me back here for years."

"Well, it doesn't need me here," said Aubrey. "Sorry guys, but I'm getting the fuck out of this insane place." She stood up and headed for the door. "Jacker, it was good meeting you. If you ever get out of this place alive, give me a ring. Stephen, I'll call you later."

Aubrey opened the door and they all heard a distant, booming voice. Aubrey stopped in the threshold and looked back at them. "Do you hear that?"

The group went to the door. They were cautious to make sure no security trucks were nearby as they went outside. A grey wisp of cloud moved over the sun, and its shadow was cast over the cabin for a moment as the group listened to a man's voice in the distance.

"They must be playing some sort of message on a speaker or something," said Paul.

"Maybe on the security trucks," said Stephen. He then hushed the others as the voice grew louder.

"Come on," said Rachel as she pulled at Stephen's shirt. "Get back inside. The truck must be headed back this way if the sound is getting louder." Everyone else ran back into the cabin, but Stephen was intent on hearing the message. Rachel continued to pull at him.

"I can almost hear what they're saying," said Stephen. "Something about Hank? Hank Waxman, does that make any sense?" He relented and went back inside with Rachel. They closed the door and stayed low as a security truck rolled down the street, again illuminating the cabin with flashing yellow light.

The message was muffled, but they could make out some of it as the truck went by. "…if you leave now, we can forget that you were ever here. Hank Waxman, we will contact the police if necessary…"

"Well, at least they're not looking for us," said Stephen after the truck passed.

"Yes they are," said Jacker. He scratched his thick, wavy hair and grimaced before admitting, "My real name's Hank Waxman."

"Fuck me," said Rachel. "They must've found the van. Goddamn it." She stood up and started to pace.

"Calm down, babe," said Stephen.

"No, I won't calm down. We're fucked. We don't have a choice. We have to go out there and hope they just give us a slap on the wrist and let us go. That's the only option we've got now."

"I can't do that," said Jacker. "I can't risk them calling the police."

"Look," said Rachel as she tried to be reasonable. "We're just going to have to take that chance. If they do end up calling the cops, then we'll just get some minor trespassing charges. I know it sucks, but we don't have any other choice here."

"No," said Jacker. "You don't get it. I can't risk them calling the cops."

Rachel stopped pacing and stood stone still as she stared at the big man. "What are you saying?" She obviously already suspected Jacker's secret.

"I'm wanted for a few things back home."

"Oh for crying out loud," said Rachel. Her cheeks burned red as her anger swelled. "Do you see, Stephen? What did I say about background checks? Goddamn it." Her frustration boiled over and she balled up her fists, ready to hit something in anger.

"What did you do?" asked Stephen. "Was it that bad?"

"I don't really want to talk about it," said Jacker.

"Well, you'd better start fucking talking about it," said Rachel. She emphasized her curse as an expression of her anger. "What did you do?"

"I hit a guy," said Jacker in a near whisper, as if he were shrinking away from the conversation. Even his posture slouched as he leaned against the kitchen counter.

"You must've hit him pretty damn hard," said Rachel. "Am I right?"

Jacker nodded.

"Did you kill him?" she asked. "Are we traipsing around the country with a murderer?"

"I don't think so," said Jacker. "Last I heard he was in the hospital. He hadn't woken up yet."

"Oh, well, that's reassuring," said Rachel.

"Calm down." Stephen walked into the center of the group and held his arms out between Rachel and Jacker. "Let's just try and be rational for a second. Okay? Running out there now and begging for forgiveness is a stupid plan, especially if we're risking Jacker going to jail. Our best option is to just stay here and wait until after the 14th."

"What?" asked Aubrey. "That's the dumbest thing I've ever heard."

"She's right," said Rachel. "That's a stupid fucking plan, Stephen."

"Do you have a better one?" asked Stephen.

Paul stepped in and put his hands on Stephen's shoulders. The argument was getting out of hand, and Paul tried to calm everyone down. "Let's be smart, guys. If we wait here until nighttime, we can try to sneak out after that. Then, if we come back tomorrow we can go try to get the van. If they already got to it, then we can say we never went into Widowsfield. The van wasn't on their property, so they've got no right to keep it."

"What if they call the cops on me?" asked Jacker.

"You don't have to come with us. I can tell them that you let me borrow the van. Even if they call the cops, they can't prove you were here."

The group was quiet as they considered Paul's plan. Aubrey stood near the door, far from Jacker, and Stephen reached out to hold Rachel's hand. The tension had calmed, and everyone agreed that Paul's plan was the best option they had. Still though, the fractures in their group weren't mended, and everyone seemed ready to separate, even if it was just to opposite corners of the small cabin.

Alma held Paul's hands and stood on the tips of her toes to whisper to him. "I'm not leaving."

He was surprised, and scowled at her. "What do you mean?"

"I told you, I need this." She spoke in a whisper to avoid pulling anyone else into their conversation. "I want you all to leave, but I'm going to stay."

"I'm not leaving without you, Alma," said Paul.

"Yes you are."

"No, I'm not. You're coming with me. I know you want to stay here, and I've tried to be supportive of this whole

235

insane thing, but now it's gone too far. I don't know what's going on in this place, or why they've set it up to mimic the past, but I do know that if you stay here, you're going to get hurt. I'm not going to let that happen."

"If I leave, I'll never know the truth."

"Alma, you're being ridiculous. Listen to yourself. You don't even know that this is going to work. Do you really think if you just stay here until the 14th that you'll suddenly remember everything?"

"This place is trying to put us in order," said Alma. "It wants me to figure this out. I can feel it, Paul." She looked down at the kitchen floor. "I just have to try and calm down, and focus on the number. Maybe if I do it on the 14th, at 3:14…"

"Maybe what?" asked Paul.

"Maybe that's how I can complete the circle."

"Do you hear yourself?" asked Paul. "Do you hear how insane you sound?"

"Look around, Paul," she said. "We're way past sanity."

Widowsfield
March 14th, 1996

Raymond stood in front of his father to protect him from The Skeleton Man. The Salt and Pepper Diner had been enveloped in the fog, and a brick had been thrown through the front door, shattering the glass. This moment was similar to every other time it had occurred, but Raymond sensed a change. He hadn't been asked to kill his father yet, but The Skeleton Man would emerge from the fog to make a request soon. This was the way it always was, although sometimes the demon chose a different part of Raymond's father to covet. Would it be the eyes again? The tongue this time?

Raymond could never remember the past instances of this event until The Skeleton Man arrived, and then the memories would sneak in. During the scant minutes before

236

the clock struck 3:14, and before the fog rolled in, Raymond was always given a chance to enjoy a brief respite, where there was no violence. Every time the events of March 14th started over, Raymond would forget everything that The Skeleton Man had done, but a sense of dread had grown in him over the years. His desire to flee the town before 3:14 struck, although never successful, was a result of him slowly beginning to understand the nature of the demon that controlled him.

The fog seeped in like water and swirled at Raymond's feet.

The tall, thin silhouette of the man with the chattering teeth appeared in the threshold of the diner. "Raymond," said the demon. "I need your help." His voice was a series of echoes in Raymond's head, and though he spoke, the chattering never ceased.

"I don't want to hurt my Daddy anymore! I want you to leave us alone." Raymond held two kitchen knives, one in each hand, and was prepared to fight off the demon.

"I don't care what you want," said The Skeleton Man. "This time I don't want to play here. I need you to come with me." He reached out his bloodied, skeletal hand through the fog.

"Raymond," said Desmond as he lay on the floor. The fog thickened around the man's limbs and held him down. "Don't go with that thing!"

Raymond looked at his father, and then at Grace, who was behind the counter. The dogs were barking outside, and Raymond knew the mutated children would be here soon to murder whoever they could. This was a recurring nightmare that no one could wake up from.

"Raymond," said The Skeleton Man. "I want to take you to see your sister. I need your help hiding from her. I need time to find the one we lost."

"If I go, will this end?" Raymond's voice trembled.

"Let's find out," said The Skeleton Man.

237

The children swarmed outside, waiting for The Skeleton Man's permission to rush in and murder Raymond's father and the waitress. The creatures were already in the back of the restaurant, devouring the cook.

"Don't go," said Desmond as the fog started to choke him.

"I'm sorry, Daddy," said Raymond. "I have to try and help us die for good. It's the only way out." He took The Skeleton Man's hand and was pulled into the fog. The demonic children rushed into the restaurant, and Raymond heard his father screaming in pain as the creatures tore his flesh from his bones. He hoped it would be the last time he had to hear it happen.

CHAPTER 18 - Murder and Children

March 12th, 2012

"Alma," said Stephen from the stairs. He was ashen, and spoke quietly. The stairs in the cabin were beside the kitchen, and led to a hallway with three doors. There was a bathroom, a master bedroom, and a guest room on the second floor and Stephen had gone up to check out the rest of the house while the others waited downstairs.

"What?" asked Alma.

"I think you need to come up here."

Her stomach sank, an identical sensation to what she felt when coming over the hill and into the woods on the road before reaching Widowsfield. "Why? What did you find?"

"Just come up."

She didn't want to. The thought of ascending the stairs terrified her. She remembered how her father would scream at her whenever she dared go upstairs. Alma looked at the couch where her mannequin was sitting and remembered sleeping there instead of in the spare room on the second floor to avoid interrupting whatever her father was up to.

"Want me to go check it out for you?" Paul offered to go up in place of Alma.

"No," said Alma. The idea of Paul going up alone terrified Alma. She took his hand. "Just come with me."

They followed Stephen upstairs, and Aubrey came after them. When Alma turned to look at her, Aubrey said, "Hey, I want to know what I'm in for by staying here. Whatever's up there, I want to see it too."

"Me too," said Rachel as she came up behind Aubrey.

"Screw that," said Jacker from the kitchen. "You guys go ahead and check out whatever evil shit is up there. I'm staying right here. Fuck this place."

Stephen led them down the hall to the master bedroom. The door was closed and he paused in front of it, as if scared to open it. "I don't know what to make of this."

"What?" asked Aubrey. "Open the door. What's in there?"

"Alma, was there anyone else here besides you, your father, and your brother when everything happened?" Stephen still gripped the door's knob, but didn't open it.

"Yes," said Alma. "There was a girl named Terry. My dad was cheating on my mom with her. She's the one that owned the cabin."

Rachel put her hand on Alma's back and rubbed circles on her. "I'm sorry, Alma. I didn't know that."

"Are there mannequins of them in there?" asked Alma. "Are they in bed together?"

"Not exactly," said Stephen. He looked at the others and then at Alma. "You might want to go in there alone."

"No, it's okay," said Alma. "No more secrets. I don't care if everyone sees."

Stephen nodded and then opened the door. He stepped back to allow Alma the chance to walk in first.

She'd only seen the room a few times in her life, but the details were burned in her memory. This was where her father would disappear for days at a time with his girlfriend. They would appear occasionally, staggering down the stairs and to the kitchen for food, but most of their days were spent in this square prison. The chemical smell of their drugs would waft out from under the door, which was one of the reasons why Ben and Alma decided to sleep downstairs instead of in the spare bedroom. They would watch their movies, with the television turned up loud enough to drown out the sound of the bed creaking when their father and Terry were having sex.

The room was the same as it had been, with a disheveled queen bed in the center, the covers bunched up in the center. There was a dresser with a clock on it, and the time was stuck at 3:14 even though it was much later in the day. The sink was dripping in the attached bathroom.

There were two mannequins on the floor. One was hunched over the other, with his hands pressed inside the woman's chest. The mannequin on the floor was battered, bent at odd angles, and painted red. Its chest was cracked open and the male mannequin was reaching inside as if trying to pull the woman's heart out. His arms and chest were splotched with red paint.

"I need to get my camera," said Stephen as he went back down the stairs.

Alma felt dizzy as she stared at the depiction of murder, or cannibalism. She wasn't sure what she was looking at. Then the chemical smell of her father's drugs stung her nose, a ghost of a scent that seeped in through her frozen memories. She swatted at her nose and fell backward into Paul's arms. He held her and tried to pull her back, out of the room, as she flailed at the air.

"What's wrong?" Paul was frantic. "What's going on?"

"Get me out!" said Alma finally. "Get me away from here."

"Move!" Paul commanded the others to step aside as he carried Alma to the stairs. "We're leaving. Now."

"Wait," said Stephen as he held his camera at the bottom of the stairs. "You can't leave yet. We need to wait until dark."

"No," said Paul. "Screw it. I'm taking Alma home now."

"Wait," said Stephen as he stood in Paul's way.

Paul shoved his shoulder into Stephen. The cameraman fell backward and stumbled over the bottom step of the stairs. He fell and dropped his camera, which hit the floor hard. The viewfinder screen snapped off and skittered across the living room.

"You ass!" Stephen got back to his feet and was ready to charge at Paul.

"Stop it!" Rachel grabbed her husband and tried to pull him back.

241

Paul set Alma down and turned to face Stephen. "Come on then, little man. Let's do this."

Alma stepped between the two of them. "Stop it, both of you! I'm okay now. I'm fine. I don't want to leave."

"Yes you do, Alma," said Paul. "Whatever happened up there scared the shit out of you."

"I know, but I'm okay now. I'm fine as long as I'm down here."

"What about my camera?" asked Stephen, still incensed.

"You should know better than to get in my way," said Paul as he cracked his knuckles, still ready for a fight.

"Both of you stop it," said Alma. "We all need to settle down."

"Hate to interrupt," said Aubrey from the top of the stairs, "but did you guys look in the bathroom up here? The tub's painted red, like it was filled with blood."

"This place just keeps getting better and better," said Rachel. "Do you think they're turning this place into an amusement park? They could call it Fucked-Up-Disneyland and sell group rates." Her joke lightened the mood and she smiled as she went to pick up the pieces of Stephen's camera. "It's like Jurassic Park for ghosts."

Stephen took the camera pieces from his wife and groaned as he looked at them. "I can probably fix it."

"Sorry, man," said Paul. "This place just sets me on edge."

"The cabin is affecting us. I think we all just need to calm down," said Alma. "Maybe try to get some sleep. If you guys are going to try and sneak out of here in the middle of the night, maybe you should get some sleep first."

"I'm not going if you're not," said Paul.

"Yeah, I'm not going anywhere," said Stephen.

"Well," said Aubrey as she came down the stairs, "sorry to bust up the party, but I'm out of here as soon as the sun sets. Fuck this place."

"I'll go with you," said Jacker. "Then I can go get my van."

"You can't do that," said Paul. "Even if you make it out, what if they're watching the van? You'll get busted."

"That's the point," said Jacker. "I need to step up and face the music. I screwed up, and I can't run from it forever. You guys don't need to get dragged down with me. I'll go out there, get the van, and tell the security that I was the only one here. If they call the police, then I'll be the only one they charge with anything."

"I know a different way out," said Aubrey. "On the south side of town, near the school, there's a drainage pipe. I'm going through there. I'm not going back to the van to get caught. Stephen, if you think I owe you your money back, well whatever." She reached into her pocket to retrieve the money Stephen had given her.

"You paid her already?" asked Rachel.

Stephen was quick to stop Aubrey. "Don't worry about it. You got us here, so you earned the money." Then he glanced over at Jacker before looking back at Aubrey and adding, "Pretty much."

Aubrey looked at Jacker, and then at Stephen before saying, "Cool."

"I'll take you to the drain pipe," said Jacker. "And make sure you get out safe. Then I'll go get my van and take the heat off you guys."

"Wow, man," said Stephen. "Thanks."

"Come upstairs with me," said Aubrey. "Let's try to get some sleep in the spare bedroom before we head out."

The blonde bartender went back up the stairs as Jacker followed. He looked at Paul with a wide smile and a wink. Stephen patted Jacker on the back as he passed and said, "Go get her, big guy."

"I still owe you for this, buddy," said Jacker to Stephen.

"Not anymore," said Stephen. "If you're taking the fall for us, then we'll call it even."

Alma watched Jacker go up the stairs to sleep with Aubrey and she felt a sense of dread at the sight. A memory of her childhood was screaming in hateful terror. How many

243

times had she watched her father ascend those stairs, ready to cheat on Alma's mother? How many times had he forced Alma to promise never to talk about what happened in Widowsfield?

"I'll kill you and your brother if you ever say anything, Alma," he used to tell her. "I swear to God, I'll kill you both."

"Are they seriously going to go up there and screw?" asked Rachel. "In the middle of all this shit, they're going to have sex up there? Are they insane?"

Alma looked at the stairs as the hallway light shone down. "It's not their fault. This place is trying to manipulate us. It's putting emotions in us that were here sixteen years ago. It's trying to complete the circle."

Stephen focused on fixing his camera and ignored the debate.

Widowsfield
March 14th, 1996

"What did you see?" asked The Skeleton Man. He was hiding across the street, in front of a house where a little boy had just found his mother's body fused to the floor under his bed. The child's screams of terror were hard to ignore as Raymond stood in the yard.

Fog swirled around the demon, and the creature hid within it, staying a blur and lurking far enough behind the veil to shroud his features. His chattering teeth never ceased.

"I saw a little girl and boy," said Raymond. "I met them once before. Their father is one of my sister's friends. The boy was going up the stairs."

"No, no," said The Skeleton Man. "You're looking at the wrong moment. You have to look past that."

"I don't understand," said Raymond. "You asked me to look in there, and I did."

244

"Go back, look again," The Skeleton Man growled. "But this time forget what's always been there. Look at what's new."

"I don't understand," said Raymond.

The demon's rage was revealed by the crackling electricity in the fog around him. The green light snapped at the tree in the front yard, which caused the bark to sizzle. Usually the electricity only touched inanimate objects, and it seemed to have a violent reaction to striking something natural. "Fine. Come with me then. Just keep an eye out for your sister. I can't be near her. You have to keep her away. Do hear me? Keep her away."

They went back to the cabin, and the fog pressed up against the window. Raymond tried to peer in, but the electricity crackled around him and he flinched in fear of it.

"She's here," said The Skeleton Man. "I can feel her, but I can't find her. There're too many others. Who did she bring?"

Raymond looked in through the window again, but all he could see was a little girl crying in the kitchen. The boy was talking to her from the stairs as he carried a pot up with him.

"He's not here," said The Skeleton Man.

"Who?" asked Raymond.

"The one that burned us. The one your sister is waiting for."

Dogs ran through the fog behind them, growling and snapping their jaws as they fought with one another. Raymond was frightened of them, but knew he was safe as long as he was with The Skeleton Man. He wondered what was happening to the other children now that The Skeleton Man was fixated on the cabin. Surely they must be dead already.

He took The Skeleton Man's hand and felt the wetness of the demon's flesh sliding off the bone.

"I need to know them all," said The Skeleton Man. "I need to see if she's replaced me."

CHAPTER 19 - Brother's Parting

March 12th, 2012

Jacker was in an alley, though he didn't know how he'd arrived there. His skin was itching, as if bugs were crawling on it, and he scratched at his arms as he walked. There was a man beside a dumpster, smoking a cigarette. He was a young man, thin and fit, with shoulder length blonde hair. Jacker knew who he was.

"Kyle," said Jacker as he approached. "Kyle Beckner?"

"That's me," said the kid as he flicked ash off the end of his cigarette. He was wearing an apron with the logo of the grocery store on it. "What can I do for you?"

"You're the one that Debbie's been fucking," said Jacker.

The kid stiffened, fearful, and started to reach for the back door of the grocery store. Jacker slammed his hand against the door to keep it shut. "She's my girlfriend, you asshole."

"Look man," said the kid as he stepped back, "I didn't know she was with anyone."

"Bullshit," said Jacker. "I met you at the Christmas Party."

"Back off, pal. Maybe if you could keep her happy, she wouldn't go looking for stray." He flicked his cigarette at Jacker and it bounced off the big man's jacket.

Kyle's bravado was reliant on Jacker backing off. There was no question who would win this fight, but the kid assumed Jacker was too scared to do anything. He was wrong.

Jacker pushed Kyle off the stoop, and the kid fell into a pile of trash in the alley. He scrambled to stand up and threw a bottle at Jacker as he did. The bottle hit Jacker in the shoulder, but didn't faze him.

246

"You want to fight?" asked the kid as he started to hop around with his fists up. "I'm not scared of you."

"Big mistake." Jacker advanced, and Kyle threw a couple punches that connected, but delivered no sting. Jacker was too large, and too high, to feel any pain that this puny man could inflict.

Jacker grabbed the side of Kyle's head and slammed it into the brick wall on the other side of the alley. Kyle fell, dazed, as blood broke free from the side of his head, like oil seeping from dry earth. Jacker stared down at the beaten boy, and should've walked away.

"How'd that feel?" asked Jacker.

Kyle couldn't answer. He was on his knees, wavering as if drunk, and staring up as the blood gushed down his left cheek. The gash on his brow was already swelling, and it looked like a golf ball was trying to burst through the boy's skull.

The fight was over, and Jacker knew he should've walked away, but then he made the worst mistake of his life: He imagined this blonde haired teenager having sex with Debbie.

Jacker lifted Kyle up by the throat, and then slammed the boy's head against the wall again. More blood gushed forth, and Kyle's lip split open. Jacker hit the boy's head against the wall again, and again. This was the part where the boy's eyes were supposed to roll back in his head. He was supposed to start gagging on blood, and Jacker was supposed to drop him and run. That's the way this was supposed to happen, but everything had changed now. This wasn't a memory, but a nightmare.

Kyle looked at Jacker and smiled. A flash of green light illuminated the night sky as the teen started to laugh. "I see you now, Hank Waxman."

Jacker slammed the boy into the wall again and heard his skull split. Dark red blood sprayed out of the gaping wound on the side of Kyle's head, but the boy still laughed.

"I see you, Hank Waxman!"

Again, Jacker crushed the boy's skull against the wall, and again the boy laughed. There were specks of white bone in the pulp of flesh on the side of Kyle's head now, and Jacker sent the teen's skull into the wall to do even more damage.

"I see you, Hank Waxman!"

Kyle's voice was marred by the flaps of skin that drooped off the side of his head. Meat and bone, broken teeth and a swollen tongue, molars and blood, and two eyes still staring up at him.

"I see you, Hank Waxman!"

Jacker backed away.

"I see you, Hank Waxman!"

Kyle crawled toward him, his head broken and dripping, his brain pulsing beneath the gore. He reached out for him, but Jacker turned and ran.

"I see you, Hank Waxman!"

Jacker awoke, his head mopped with sweat, and struggled to breathe. He gasped and clutched his throat, then reached down to wake Aubrey. She was startled and turned to see what was wrong.

"We've got to go," said Jacker. "Now. Right now."

"Has the sun gone down?" she asked and looked over at the drawn shade.

"I don't care. We have to go, right now." Jacker got out of bed and started to put his clothes on.

Aubrey was nude, and pulled the cover over herself. "What's got you so spooked?"

"This place," said Jacker. "We've got to go. I'm going with or without you."

"Boy, you're a real love-them-and-leave-them type," said Aubrey in a frail attempt to make a joke.

"Look, babe," said Jacker as he tried to compose himself. He was sweating profusely, and wiped his brow off on his sleeve. "I'm not an idiot. I know Stephen paid you to sleep with me. So you can quit the charade."

"You knew?" asked Aubrey as she slipped her bra back on.

Jacker rolled his eyes as he searched the pockets of his jacket for a Valium. "Girls like you don't go for guys like me."

"That's not true," said Aubrey as she continued to scavenge for her clothes. "You look a lot like my fiancé."

Jacker cringed and scowled down at her. Aubrey was on her back on the bed, with her butt raised as she pulled her underwear on.

"You've got a fiance? Christ." He shook his head before popping a pill and swallowing it without anything to drink. "I'm going downstairs."

"Okay, for crying out loud. Give me a second to get my clothes on."

"Hurry up," said Jacker as he left the room.

He went downstairs and found the others. Paul and Alma were in the living room, while Stephen and Rachel were in the kitchen.

"Hey big guy," said Stephen. "Did you unwrap your present up there?"

"I'm leaving." Jacker wasn't interested in Stephen's banter. He grabbed his wallet and keys, which he'd left on the counter, and headed for the door.

"Jesus," said Rachel. "What happened."

Jacker stopped and looked at Alma. "You need to leave." Then he looked at the rest of them. "You all need to leave. Don't stay here. You don't want to be here when he comes for you."

"Who?" asked Paul.

"I don't know!" Jacker was still sweating and swiped his brow. He was panicked, and his heart thumped hard enough that he could feel it in his throat. The Valium had scratched its way down his throat, and he could still taste it as he tried to turn the water on in the sink to no avail.

Paul came over to him and pointed to the door. "Go outside with me. I want to talk to you."

"Be careful, guys," said Stephen. "The sun's not all the way down. Don't get caught."

Paul walked with Jacker out into the yard. Then he took his friend by the arm and spun him around in anger. "What have you been using?"

"What?" asked Jacker.

"You're high. What did you and that slut do up there?"

"I'm not high."

"Bullshit," said Paul. "I can fucking smell it. What was it? Meth? Were you two smoking meth up there?"

"Get the fuck off me." Jacker pushed Paul away. "I'm not high."

"Do you think I'm stupid? I can smell it. I smelled it ever since you went up there. I know you were cheating with her."

Jacker was confused and angry. "What? I'm not high." He took Paul's sobriety coin out of his pocket and threw it at his friend.

Paul caught the token and clasped his fist around it. "You're a cheater."

"I had some drinks with Stephen," said Jacker. "There. You happy? You caught me. I'm not as good as you. Okay? And I've been taking pain meds too. I'm an addict. Okay? I can't stop. I'd kill for a fucking drink right now."

"I'm not talking about drinking," said Paul. "You cheated on her."

"On who?" asked Jacker, abashed.

Paul stopped and his posture relaxed. "I don't know," he admitted as if worried by his own addled thoughts. He put his hand on his head and backed away as he repeated, "I don't know."

"It's this place, man," said Jacker. "I don't know what's going on in there, but it's not good. That place screws with your head. Do yourself a favor and get as far away from it as you can."

"I'm not leaving Alma," said Paul. "I have to protect her."

"Then you're going to have to figure out a way to get her away from here. You've got to. You're not ready for what's happening here. No one is."

The front door opened as Aubrey came out. "Everything okay?"

Jacker chuckled and shook his head. "No, not at all. Come on, we're leaving."

Paul grabbed Jacker's shoulder. "Come here, man." They embraced, and Paul placed his sobriety token back in Jacker's hand. "I'm sorry. I don't know what got into me. Be careful out there. I love you, man. I need you safe and sound, and sober."

"Thanks brother," said Jacker. "I'll be fine."

Aubrey took Jacker's hand as they headed up the hill, away from the cabin. Jacker saw Paul going back inside, and felt sorry for him. As much as he wanted Paul safe, he knew that his friend would never leave Alma. He'd worked too hard to get her back, and loved her too much to leave her here.

Aubrey and Jacker ran back toward the elementary school. Aubrey led the way, promising that she knew another way out of the cursed town.

They stayed quiet as they went, and reached the middle school quickly. They weren't worried about the figures in the building now that they knew someone had set up mannequins around town. They stayed close to the school to use it as cover as they snuck toward the park on the other side of the high school. A few security trucks passed, still blaring the warning to Hank Waxman about involving the police, and about how they knew he was a wanted man.

"This is it," said Aubrey as they reached the park. There was a small playground that was now dilapidated, the once colorful plastic slides weathered and dingy. Past the playground stretched a wide, grassy park.

"It's on the other side of the park," said Aubrey. "There's a ditch that runs up to the fence. We'll have to crawl through the drainage pipe, but then we'll be out. The

251

grass is pretty tall out there. If the security trucks come, we can just lay down to stay out of sight."

They stayed low as they ran across the playground and into the grassy park. They had to lay down once as a truck drove along the road near them, but it passed without incident and they quickened their pace through the field.

"This is it," said Aubrey as they got closer to the fence. "I can't believe we made it." She pulled Jacker down so that she could kiss his cheek. "Let's get out of this place."

Someone pumped a shotgun.

"Thought you might try to get out this way," said a man's voice. Three men rose up from the weeds near the ditch, each holding a gun.

"Oh fuck," said Aubrey as she put her hands in the air.

"Turn around and get on your knees," said the tallest of the three men. He had a grey beard and a barrel chest. His gruff voice sounded tortured by a lifetime of smoking.

"Fuck you," said Jacker. "Go ahead and call the cops. You can't threaten us."

"Son, I'm ten seconds away from shutting you up for good," said the guard. "You found your way onto private property, boy. By law, I can put a bullet in you. Hell, kid, that's my job. Now do as I say and get on your knees."

Jacker and Aubrey obeyed and the guards swiftly patted them down. After the men were convinced that the trespassers weren't armed, the older guard put a pistol to the back of Aubrey's head. The girl cringed and started to weep as she pleaded for her life.

"If you hurt her, I swear to God…"

"What?" asked the guard. "You'll try to fight me? Who do you think's going to win that little scuffle? Huh, Mr. Waxman?"

"So you know who I am? Big deal. Call the cops and get this over with," said Jacker.

"Not yet. First, I want to talk about your friends. Where are they?"

"It's just us," said Jacker. "We came alone."

252

"Now you're just pissing me off," said the guard. "We found your van, and the motorcycle. We know there're more of you here. We've got everyone's luggage. Unless you're trying to tell me you wear an awful lot of lady's underwear."

Jacker sneered back at the guard. "What can I say? I'm a freak."

"Aw screw it," said the guard as he put his pistol to the back of Jacker's head. "Say good night, fat ass."

"I'll tell you where they are," said Aubrey. "Just don't hurt him. Don't hurt any of us."

"Aubrey, shut up," said Jacker.

"No! This isn't worth dying over. Don't be crazy."

"All right," said the guard as he lowered his gun. "You should thank your little girlfriend. She just saved your life. Now get up. We're going to go get your friends."

Widowsfield
March 14th, 1996

"Why are they coming back?" asked The Skeleton Man.

"Who?" asked Raymond.

"The fat one and the whore. They're coming back."

Raymond looked down the road, in the direction that The Skeleton Man pointed, and saw nothing but fog. "I don't see anyone."

"We have to do something. We have to save my sister."

Raymond looked in through the window at the crying girl in the kitchen of the cabin. He suddenly understood who it was that he'd been watching. "That girl is your sister? Then, is the boy you?"

The Skeleton Man was crying, the tears seeping through the mess of blood and sagging flesh that decorated his skull – skin pulled from past victims that the demon had placed over his face to hide the bone.

"If they take her, I'll never be free."

"What are we supposed to do?"

"I have to find the one that loves her. He's here. I can feel how much he cares for her. He's the only one that can stop this." The Skeleton Man took Raymond's hand. "We're going to have to go inside. You're going to have to find your sister while I talk to the one that loves Alma. You have to keep your sister away from me."

The door of the cabin creaked as the fog pressed into it. Then the wood warped and the door blew backward as the children inside screamed. The Skeleton Man went in first, and then disappeared within the surging fog. Raymond ran in after, still unsure what he was supposed to do.

"Raymond?" asked Ben when he saw the boy enter. "What are you doing here?"

"Where's my sister?" asked Raymond.

Alma was sobbing as she pointed up the stairs. "She's up there, but you can't go up."

"What? Why?" asked Raymond.

Ben had on a pair of oven mitts and was holding a steaming pot of boiling water.

"What's going on down there?" asked a man's voice. Raymond recognized the hateful voice, but it had been a long time since he'd heard it.

A gaunt man, soaking wet with sweat, appeared on the stairs. His beady eyes caught sight of Raymond and the man froze.

"What are you doing here?"

"Run, Raymond!" Alma screamed.

Her father was too fast and Raymond collapsed onto the concrete as the man tackled him. Michael Harper had grabbed a knife off the kitchen counter and started to cut at Raymond with it. Raymond felt himself being turned, and then an intense pressure in his gut. The knife entering his stomach was a surprise, but no worse than the pain Raymond had experienced any of the other times he died. He felt his hands grow cold as Alma's father dragged his body back into the cabin.

"Shut up, Alma!" he screamed as he dragged Raymond inside.

That's when the altered past dissipated, and Raymond saw The Skeleton Man again. He was standing near another man, who was tall and had a shaved head. The Skeleton Man had his hands on the stranger's shoulders and was whispering in his ear. There was a tattoo of a snake on the side of the man's head, right beside where The Skeleton Man was whispering.

A woman's voice screamed from upstairs and Raymond shifted his head to look. He recognized his sister's pained cries. "Terry?" asked Raymond as he looked up the stairs. "Did he kill you too?"

"Keep her away from me," said The Skeleton Man.

The fog thickened, and the electricity zapped the walls. Raymond was living in two times at once, and saw both visions independently. He could see Alma as a child, and as an adult, and he knew that his sister was dying upstairs, while at the same time existing as a tortured soul, just like everyone else in the town. He looked up the stairs and saw Terry's mangled corpse begin to crawl down.

She was nude, and she was soaked with water and blood. Her innards slid down the wooden steps, slopping across each step as she descended on her belly. Her face was shredded, and her hair was falling out in clumps of gooey blood, revealing her white skull beneath. Her left eye was falling from its socket, and her face looked like it was melting. She wailed, and continued down the stairs, focused on The Skeleton Man.

"Terry!" Raymond was no longer trapped inside his body, but was a member of the mist, swirling and experiencing every emotion that existed in every mind among those gathered in the cabin. The fog was terrified of Terry, and avoided her as it swelled within the rest of the cabin.

Raymond looked down at his corpse and then at the children that cried as their father murdered another person.

He could see his sister's wailing spirit sliding down the stairs. "You have to stop, Terry."

"Murderer!" Her teeth were loose in her gums, as if someone had been trying to pry them free. "I'll slaughter them, all of them. I found them!"

Raymond had to force himself away from the rest of the fog, undeterred by their fear of his sister. A wisp of mist flung out of the fog like a tentacle from beneath the waves, and Raymond willed himself to reach out to Terry. The tentacle of mist wrapped around his sister to keep her from going down the stairs any further. He was able to hold her back, but her skin was sliding off her bones. He had to hook the mist through her rib cage to restrain her.

"I love you, Terry," said Raymond. "Dad and I loved you so much. It hurt us so bad to watch you do this to yourself. We never stopped loving you."

"Let me go!" Terry's bones cracked as she continued to try and crawl down the stairs.

"Stay with me, Terry."

"I hate them!"

"I love you."

"Hate…"

CHAPTER 20 - Ben's Secret

March 12th, 2012

Paul saw the security truck first and warned the others to get down. The yellow lights illuminated the living room, casting their eerie shadows throughout the cabin, but didn't pass this time. The truck had parked in front of the house.

"Oh shit," said Stephen. "They must've found Jacker and Aubrey."

A loud, gruff voice crackled to life outside, amplified by a loudspeaker on the security truck. "Alma, Paul, Stephen, and Rachel, please exit the house. We know you're in there. We don't want any trouble. If you come out, we'll escort you off the premises. No harm no foul. Okay?"

"Game's up," said Rachel. "We don't have a choice."

"I need to stay," said Alma. "I need to find out what happened to Ben."

"Alma, we don't have a choice," said Paul. "They caught us."

"No!" Alma pushed her way out of Paul's arms and ran to the kitchen. She pulled a steak knife out of a butcher's block. It was old and rusted, but she placed it against her palm and cut herself.

"Alma, stop it!" Paul tried to run to her, but she swiped the blade at him.

"No, you're not stopping me from doing this. No one is! I don't want to be protected from this." She fell to her knees as her palm gushed blood, and pressed her hand against the white tile. Alma used her blood to scrawl '314' on the floor and then sat back as she stared at it. "I don't care if it's too soon. I have to try."

"Holy shit," said Stephen. "What is she doing?"

"Alma, stop it," said Paul.

257

"Get away from me! Leave me alone." She stared down at the number and started to hum in an attempt to focus. She rocked back and forth on her knees as her hand bled in her lap.

Paul was going to try and stop her. He reached out, but then stopped. He caught sight of the number on the floor and his body froze. He felt a bone-chilling cold on both shoulders. Something had its hands on him, and he could feel the fingers wrap around his clavicles. Then the chattering began, a sound so distinctive that Paul could almost sense the teeth hitting one another.

"I'm going to show you," said the voice behind the chattering teeth.

The world around him was silenced, although he could see the chaos happening without him. He saw Alma on the floor, rocking as she stared at the number, and felt Stephen try to pull at his arm as he headed outside with Rachel. Paul turned to watch Stephen leave, and then saw the flash of gunfire.

Stephen fell dead as Rachel screamed, though Paul heard nothing but the chattering teeth as time slowed to a crawl. "I'm going to let you see the truth. You'll know why we have to protect Alma," said the voice behind the teeth.

Another gunshot shook the walls, and more blood spilled out across the floor. As the demon held him, Paul saw nothing but death. He watched his friends being murdered. Stephen and Rachel laid on the floor of the cabin, face up, and their clothes rapidly became soaked with blood from wounds that Paul couldn't see. Then he looked at Alma, and saw that she was staring back up at him. He wanted to reach out to her, but he was paralyzed by the demon whose teeth still chattered in his mind.

Then Alma's chest exploded as another gunshot reverberated through the home. She didn't recoil from the blast, and Paul watched her calmly look back down at the number on the floor as blood poured out of the gunshot wound on her chest. She continued to stare at the number, unfazed by the attack.

And then Paul's vision faded as he accepted The Skeleton Man's truth.

Widowsfield
March 14th, 1996

Ben got up to answer the door as his sister stayed on the couch. Terry's dog, the mangy, one-eyed creature that she insisted was a good dog but just hated kids, was in his cage in the kitchen. The dog barked and growled as someone knocked on the front door.

"Shush, Killer," said Ben as went to the door, but his command seemed to incite the dog rather than calm it.

"Hello?" he asked as he opened the door.

"Hello there little man," said the chubby stranger. He was older, with a buzzcut and beady eyes. His lower jaw jut forth and when he talked his lower teeth stuck out like a cartoon of a dumb dog. "My name's Desmond, and this is Raymond." He put his hand on the back of a boy that was standing slightly behind him.

"Hi," said Raymond, who looked remarkably similar to his father.

"I'm looking for my daughter, Terry. Is she here?"

"Who is it?" asked Ben's father as he descended the stairs. He saw Desmond at the door and exhaled as if disappointed. "Oh."

"Hello, Michael," said Desmond, his tone darker.

"What do you want?" asked Ben's father.

"I need to talk to Terry."

"Well, she's busy."

"I'm not trying to pester her, or you. If you two want to rot away in this place, I just don't have the energy to care anymore. I just need the keys to our cabin in Forsythe. I'm taking my boy out there for a fishing trip. We already paid the fees, but I'd rather not spend the money on a hotel if possible."

"Yeah, well, I think she's already planning on heading out there tomorrow," said Ben's father. He stayed on the stairs, and Desmond stayed outside. Ben was caught between the awkward standoff.

"Well, she's just going to have to change her plans."

Ben's father smelled his fingers, and then wiped them off on his already dirty t-shirt. "Maybe you're going to have to change yours." He put his hand on the wall, where the alcove from the stairs met the ceiling of the first floor. He tilted forward and then back again as he spoke. "We were going to take my kids fishing out there."

"No you weren't," said Desmond. "All you two ever do is sit in her room and smoke dope. Don't try to pretend like there's anything else going on here than that."

"You know, you've got a big mouth, old man."

"Raymond," said Desmond to his son, "go to the car. We're going to leave soon, just wait for me."

"No, Daddy," said Raymond. "Can we please just go? We can use the key in the rock, out by the river. We don't need Terry's key. Please, Daddy, I just want to go. Let's go see Grace and have some food. Okay? Can we please go?"

"Yeah, Daddy," said Ben's father with a mocking tone. "Go see Grace." He flipped Desmond off with both hands as he bit his lower lip.

"You're scum," said Desmond.

"Get the fuck off Terry's property," said Ben's father as he kept his middle fingers raised.

Desmond walked away, and Ben closed the door while Killer continued to bark. "Sorry about that, Daddy," said Ben.

"What did I tell you about answering the door?" asked his father.

"You never told us not to answer the door," said Alma from the couch. She put her hands over her mouth after daring to speak up. Their father glared down at them both, his eyes wide and his fists clenched.

"Do you guys want me to make you walk the dog?" he asked with a malicious grin.

"No," said Ben as he looked at the growling beast behind the bars. "He bites us."

"Then don't disobey me again," said their father. "And don't come upstairs. Terry and I are busy. Understand?"

"Yes," said Ben.

"Yes what?" asked their father.

"Yes, sir," said Alma and Ben simultaneously.

"You'd better understand," he said as he slowly went back up the stairs.

They waited for the bedroom door to close, and then sighed in relief.

"I hate him so much," said Alma.

Ben went back to the couch where they had a hoard of snacks and empty juice boxes. He hopped on the cushions and a mess of pretzel pieces flew into the air. "Don't say that," said Ben. "He's our Dad. You only get one Dad."

"Well, I wish we got a different one."

Ben reached across their mountain of wrappers and juice boxes to take his sister's hand. She was younger than him by two years, and suffered their father's rage more frequently than Ben. Over the years, he'd tried to protect Alma, but their father seemed intent upon scrutinizing the girl's every move. Nothing Alma ever did was good enough for their father, and Ben was always trying to convince the eight-year-old that she wasn't worthless like their father said.

"You'll always have me."

"Thanks, Ben."

Killer continued to growl as he spun in his cage, trying to get comfortable on the worn towel that he was given as a blanket. Ben looked cautiously over at the cage and muttered, "I wish we could get rid of that dog."

"We should just open the door and let him go," said Alma.

Ben chuckled and said, "Yeah right. Then he'd go infect everyone with rabies or something."

"What's rabies?" asked Alma.

Ben didn't know, but lied anyhow, "It's a disease that dogs get. It makes them real mean and they go around biting people and giving them rabies too. It's real bad. I think it's kind of like what causes werewolves. I'm pretty sure I read that somewhere."

"Do you think he's got rabies?" asked Alma as she dared to look over at Killer's cage.

Ben shrugged. "I dunno, but there's something wrong with him."

"Well, we can't let him out if he's a werewolf," said Alma as she pulled her knees up to her chest while sitting on the couch.

"Do you want to watch Toy Story again?" asked Ben, wanting to change the subject.

"Sure," said Alma, forlorn and distant.

"It'll only be forty five minutes until the school lets out," said Ben. "Aren't you happy about that?"

"I guess so," said Alma.

"I wonder if Jim and Laura are going to be holding hands," said Ben as he got the video tape out of the basket beside the television stand.

"You don't even know if that's their real names," said Alma.

Ben always knew when Alma was upset by the way she refused to play along with his games. Their annual vacation in Missouri was a boring exercise for them, spent watching the same movies over and over while their father stayed upstairs with the red-haired girl named Terry.

"What's bugging you, Alma?" asked Ben. "You're acting weird."

"I'm just sick of it," said Alma. "I hate him so much. I'm going to tell Mom that I don't want to come out here anymore."

Ben finished loading the VHS tape and returned to the couch. "No, Alma, you can't do that. You know what he'll do. You can't tell Mom."

"I don't even care anymore. I don't care if he does kill me."

"Don't say that." Ben pushed the garbage off the couch between them and scooted over to sit beside his sister. He put his arm around her and set her head on his shoulder. "If it weren't for you, I wouldn't be able to survive in our crazy family. We have to protect each other. I need you, little sis."

"I need you too," said Alma as she hugged Ben.

The movie started and they settled into their seat. They'd seen the movie far too many times already, but it was the only new movie in the basket this year. All of the others had been here the last time they were forced to camp on the couch for a week, and they'd watched all of them more times than they cared to remember.

Ben tried to keep Alma focused on the movie, but his sister became bored while watching it. She continued to stare out the window, as if hoping something interesting might happen outside. Alma was the first to notice the fog.

"Ben, look," she said and got off the couch.

She went to the window and climbed onto the loveseat that was pushed up against the wall beneath. Ben glanced out to see what she was looking at. A thick smoke was billowing forth from something down the street. It was a light grey cloud, but swelled as if made of foam or liquid. Then the cloud flashed with green light and the hair on Ben's arms stood straight up as if he'd been shocked. "Alma, get away from the window."

"What is that?" she asked, still perched on the loveseat in front of the window.

"I don't know, get away from there."

"Do you think it's a fire?" asked Alma as she continued to ignore her brother's command.

He grabbed the back of her dress and pulled her off the loveseat. The fog swept over the street and started to blot

263

out the sun, causing the cabin to grow dark. Green lightning flashed within the cloud, and it crackled along the frame of the cabin.

Soon the fog enveloped the house, blocking out all of the light except for what was coming from upstairs. Killer yapped furiously and spun in his tiny cage.

Ben gazed at the stairs, transfixed upon the light beaming down.

"I need to go tell Dad," said Ben.

"No!" Alma took her brother's arm with both of hers. "You know you can't. You can't go up there."

"I have to. I have to make sure he knows what's going on."

"He'll kill you, Ben. Please don't go up there."

He pulled out of her grip and went to the stairs. The green electricity continued to flash and illuminate the living room, casting wicked shadows on the walls. He reached the bottom of the stairs as Alma continued to plead with him to stop, but he knew that he had to tell their father what was happening. Ben raced up, choosing to face his fears without hesitation. The light in the upstairs hallway was still on, but it flickered as he made his way to the master bedroom door.

He knocked, but heard no response.

He tried again, and thought he heard someone in the room choking. Ben put his ear to the door, and was certain of what he heard. "Dad?" he asked and knocked again. The choking persisted, and no one answered him.

Ben pushed the door open.

Terry was on the floor, nude, and her hands were shaking as her head flopped back and forth. Her red hair was mopped with sweat and her eyes were aflame with red veins. She turned and stared at Ben and white foam formed on her lips as she tried to speak. The foam fell from her mouth and dripped to the floor as she reached out to him.

Ben's father appeared in the master bedroom's bathroom. He had a cup of water in his hand and stopped when he saw Ben. "What did I tell you?" He screamed and

264

dropped the cup of water. It bounced on the floor at his feet and water spilled out as the furious man charged through the room.

"What happened?" asked Ben, terrified.

"You little mother fucker, I told you not to come in here." Michael Harper grabbed his son by the arm and slapped the boy across the face. Then he slammed Ben's head into the door as he continued to curse at him.

Tears sprang to Ben's eyes as he screamed an apology. He could hear Alma crying at the bottom of the stairs, pleading with their father not to hurt Ben.

"Get in here, you little shit." He pulled Ben into the room. "Alma, shut up and stay down there."

"Daddy," said Alma. "There's smoke outside."

"I don't give a fuck if the Devil's at the door, girl. You shut up and watch your movie. If I hear one peep out of you, I swear to God I'll kill you." He slammed the door and then turned to Ben. "Well, kid, you did it now. You fucked up for real this time."

"What's wrong? What happened to Terry?"

"She's dying, that's what's wrong. The bitch OD'ed."

"Should we call an ambulance?"

"No," said his father. "No, that's not what we're going to do. You're going to help me get her up."

Terry started to convulse and her arms slapped against the floor as her head bounced. The white foam spewed from her mouth, followed by a putrid yellow fluid that splashed on her cheeks.

"Clean the shit out of her mouth," said Ben's father. "I'll get some more water for her."

"Daddy, she's naked."

He looked at Ben as if disgusted. "So what? You're the one that came in here when you weren't supposed to. It's time to grow the fuck up, Ben. Now scoop that shit out of her mouth."

Ben moved on his knees over to the shaking woman. Her breasts flopped around as she shook, and he was ashamed to look at her. The veins in her chest and neck were blue, engorged, and easily visible through her pale skin. He tried to put his hand on her head to hold her down and clean the foam out of her mouth, but the contact of his hand alerted her to his presence. She reached out and clawed at his head and shoulders in a desperate attempt to pull him down.

"Dad!" Ben screamed as the woman grasped at him. "Help!"

His father ran back in the room, but Terry's arms fell suddenly limp. They hit the floor and only had the strength to twitch. Ben fell backward and scooted away as he wiped foam and bile from his shirt.

"What did you do?" asked his father.

"Nothing. I tried to help, like you said, but she grabbed me."

His father bent down and placed his fingers on Terry's throat. "Jesus fucking Christ, Ben. You killed her."

"I didn't, Dad. I swear!"

"Well she's dead. She's dead, Ben. She's dead now!"

"I didn't do anything." Ben started to cry. "I was trying to help."

"Well, now we're fucked. You killed her."

"Dad," said Ben. "You have to believe me, I didn't do anything to her."

"Stop panicking," said his father. "We'll figure this out. I'm not going to let you go to jail. Okay, Ben? I'll protect you." He stood up tall and started to look around the room with his hand on his chin, as if surveying the scene in search of clues.

He snapped his fingers and pointed at Ben. "I've got a plan, but I'm going to need your help."

"Okay," said Ben. "What do you need?"

"Go downstairs and start boiling some pots of water. Then get all of the cleaners from under the sink. Don't ask questions, just do what I say." He bent down and put his arms under Terry as he started to drag her toward the bathroom.

"What are you going to do?"

He dropped Terry and her body thumped on the floor as he stood and glared at Ben. "What did I just say? No fucking questions. Go do as I say or they're going to put you in jail for this."

Ben wiped his tears away and ran back downstairs.

"What happened?" asked Alma, but Ben ignored her as he went to the kitchen. She followed and asked again, "Ben, what happened? Did you tell him about the smoke? Ben, talk to me."

"I can't, Alma." He got a pot out and started to fill it in the sink.

"The smoke is getting thicker, Ben. What are you going to do with that water? Ben, stop ignoring me. What happened upstairs?"

"Alma, shut up," said Ben, and the verbal assault stunned his sister. "You've got to just shut up and go watch your movie. Dad and I are doing adult things. Okay?"

"No, it's not okay. Why are you being mean to me?"

He put the first pot on the stove and turned the burner to high. Then he went to fill another. "I'm just trying to protect you."

"I'm going upstairs," said Alma in defiance.

"No!"

"Why not? You went up there, and Dad didn't kill you. I'm going up there too."

Ben grabbed his sister and threw her to the floor. "You do as you're told! Stay down here."

"Stop being mean to me," said Alma, and her voice cracked as she started to cry. Her tears broke Ben's heart, but he had to do everything he could to keep her downstairs.

"Do as you're told, Alma." Ben set the second pot on the stove and then started to gather the cleaning supplies. He went back upstairs with his arms full of various bottles for his father.

Ben found him in the bathroom. Michael had dragged Terry into the tub where she looked almost alive, her head drooped to the side as she sat against the porcelain. Ben's father took the bottles one by one. His eyes were bloodshot and his hands were shaking as he inspected the cleaners. He was biting his nails down too far and had caused a few of his fingers to bleed. Ben was terrified, but stayed stoic, hoping to impress his father.

"All right," said his father as he continued to chew his nails. "This is what we're going to do. This bitch is dead, and we're going to have to get rid of her body. I know we can do it. Okay?"

Ben saw Terry's eye twitch. "Dad, I don't think she's dead."

His father scowled and slammed his palm on the side of the tub. "Don't be an idiot. She's dead, dead, dead, and you killed her. You stupid fuck, I'm trying to help you. You want to go to jail for the rest of your life?"

"No, sir."

"Then do exactly as I say and don't contradict me again. Terry is dead. We have to figure out how to get rid of her body. Are you crying? Are you seriously crying?"

Ben shook his head, but the tears wouldn't stop.

"You're the one that did this. You're the one that came into the bedroom when you weren't supposed to. You're the one that thought he was an adult. Well, this is what adults have to deal with. Okay? You need to act like an adult now."

"I don't want to," said Ben pathetically. "I want to go watch my movie with Alma. I don't want to be an adult."

"Too late, Ben. It's too late for that. Now go downstairs and see if the water is boiling. Okay?"

"Yes, sir." Ben ran out of the bathroom.

His father yelled out to him, "Bring the water up once it starts to boil."

Ben ran to the kitchen and yelled at Alma to leave him alone as he cried. He got a pair of oven mitts and then stood by the stove, watching as the pots sat on the burners.

"Ben, please tell me what's going on up there."

Ben just shook his head and continued to cry. Killer spun in his cage and started to bark when a flash of green electricity illuminated the room.

Alma stood beside her brother and waited for the water to boil. She didn't say anything, but wanted to be supportive of her brother as he was obviously struggling with something terrible. Ben lifted the pot off the stove and walked past his sister. He was careful as he carried the pot up the stairs, but some of it still spilled over the edge.

His father was in the bathroom, and had filled the bottom of the tub with some hot water from the tap. Terry was now laying at the bottom of the tub, her hair waving in the water and her bloodshot eyes staring straight up. Her mouth was open and the white foam still bubbled between her red, chapped lips.

"Good job, kid. Set the pot on the toilet and get the bleach. That's the white jug over there with the blue cap. Yeah, that's the one. Go ahead and push down on the cap and turn it. There you go, you're doing good. Now bring it over here and pour it in the tub. We'll figure out how to do this. You and me, kid. We'll figure it out. We'll melt this bitch down to bones if we have to. Okay? Good, good. Just pour it in the water like that. You're doing great. You're a real adult now, a big boy. All adults have to do this kind of thing from time to time. There's no need to cry, just keep pouring. Yeah, all of it. The whole thing."

The bleach stung Ben's eyes and he had to turn away as his father continued to speak in a manic slur of words.

"Go ahead and get the purple stuff. The bottle with the yellow cap. Twist it off the same way you did the bleach and then pour it in too. That's a good boy. You're a pro. You're making me proud."

Ben's father stepped back and stood in the corner of the room. He continued to bite his nails as he watched his son pour the chemicals into the tub.

"Go ahead and pour all of the bottles in. Fuck it, just pour them all in there. One of them's got to do the trick. Is that everything that you could find downstairs? Yeah? Okay, well I guess it'll have to do. Pour the hot water in. Just do it. Don't even think about it, just pour it in."

Ben held the pot and leaned over the clawed tub. The smell of the chemical soup was sickening, and his eyes stung from it. Every time he breathed, the air seared his nose. He tipped the large pot and the boiling water started to pour in.

Terry screamed out as the water hit her skin. She wasn't dead, and the searing water awoke her from unconsciousness. She reached out and grabbed Ben's head in an attempt to find anything to hold onto. She pulled, and Ben felt his feet lift off the floor.

His face splashed down into the boiling soup of chemicals.

CHAPTER 21 - Alma's Lost Truth

March 14th, 1996

Alma was still in the kitchen, watching the water boil, when she heard Terry scream. Then Ben started to wail even louder and Alma refused to stay downstairs any longer. She took a steak knife out of the butcher's block on the counter and headed for the stairs.

The green electricity outside crackled again and she thought she heard her name, but wasn't sure who was speaking. When the light flashed, there was a tall shadow in the room with her, as if an adult were standing at her side. She spun and swiped through the air, but there was no one in the room with her other than the whimpering dog in the cage.

Alma went to the stairs and paused, terrified. Ben was crying out in pain, and Alma knew her father was killing him. If she didn't do something, her brother would die. She started to hum a tune, a trick her mother had taught her to help stay calm when bad things were happening. She took each step slowly and listened as Ben continued to cry out in pain.

She heard her father speak, "Hold the towel over your face, Ben."

"It hurts!" Ben cried out.

"Get back in the tub, bitch!" Her father hit something, and Alma heard water splash. Then she heard several wet thuds while Ben continued to cry, his voice now muffled by what Alma assumed was a towel.

She held the knife out in front of herself, ready to kill Michael to save Ben. If her father was hurting him, Alma was prepared to stop him any way she had to. She had to protect him, because they only had each other to depend on.

Alma walked down the hall and then pushed the door open. Ben was on the bed with a towel over his face, and

Alma could see her father in the bathroom, hunched over the tub. Ben was shaking as he held the towel.

"Ben?" asked Alma. "Are you okay?"

Ben dropped the towel and his lip snagged on the fabric. When the towel fell, a portion of his lower lip went with it. His face was scarlet red, and his eyebrows were missing. Blisters had formed on his cheeks and his eyes were wide and unblinking. His teeth were chattering as if his body couldn't stand the agony he was suffering. "Alma," he said and pointed to the door. "Get out!"

"Alma?" asked her father from the bathroom. He got up from the tub and walked back into the room. "What did I tell you about coming in here?"

Alma looked at him and held the knife out, still prepared to protect Ben no matter what. She saw Terry rise up from the tub behind her father. The woman's entire body was slathered in a putrid mess of blood and thick, syrupy liquid. Terry screamed in pain and pushed Alma's father out of the way as she rushed for the door. Michael tried to grab the nude woman, but when he gripped her arm a strip of flesh peeled off her. Alma closed her eyes and held the knife out.

Terry was blinded by the chemicals in the tub, and ran directly into Alma's outstretched blade. The force of Terry's lunge was enough to knock Alma back as the blade pressed into the nude woman's abdomen. Terry fell down on Alma and the stench of the chemical soup stole the young girl's breath away.

Terry was slick with the chemical sludge, and when Alma tried to push the woman away her hands slid through the muck. Terry sputtered and finally rolled off Alma as she clutched the blade in her stomach. She tried to get away, but Alma's father was already over her. He pulled the blade free, which caused Terry's body to lurch up before falling back down again.

"Die, you stupid bitch!" Alma's father stabbed the woman over and over just within the threshold of the room.

He wouldn't stop, and soon his fist was plunging into a large cavity in the woman's stomach.

When his madness subsided, Alma's father stood up, his hands dripping with blood and chunks of flesh, and panted as he stared down at his daughter. "What did I tell you about staying out of my room?"

There was a sucking noise from the hall. It sounded as if all the air in the cabin was being pulled away, then a boom shook the building as electric light flashed all around them. The fog swept in and enveloped them as shadows ran past. The creatures in the mist danced and spun, holding each other's hands as they went. The shadows were hunched over and sometimes howled as if canine. From within the mass of creatures came a tall figure, and Alma thought she saw the shadow of horns on the top of his head, but then realized that part of the man was connected to the walls by what looked like long strands of wire. He held his hand out to Ben, and Alma heard him whispering. The shadow then glanced at Alma, but ignored her as he led Ben away.

"I love you, Alma," said Ben. "I'll never stop loving you."

Paul was there in the fog, and he saw everything that Alma and Ben had endured. The Skeleton Man had revealed himself, and was whispering to Paul as the creatures danced around them.

"I met the Devil, and he ended my pain," said The Skeleton Man. "He gave me a chance to save Alma."

"How?" asked Paul. He couldn't see Ben, but could hear the man's chattering teeth.

"You should know that right now Alma is dying."

"What happened? Did someone shoot her?"

"The men that stayed in Widowsfield are murdering you both. Look at your chest."

Paul glanced down and saw three bullet holes, each oozing blood, in his chest. He put his finger in one and then glanced up at where he thought Ben's voice emanated from. "Why?"

"They went up the stairs," said Ben. "They opened a door that should've stayed shut, and now we're all paying the price. You had to be silenced, but they don't know the truth about our little town. Widowsfield will never be quiet. It's still alive, trapped in a place between Hell and Earth. But we can make it better, Paul. We can save Alma."

"How?" asked Paul. He looked down at Alma as she lay face up on the floor, partially covering the bloody numbers she'd scrawled on the tile. When he first looked down at her there was no blood on her chest, but then it suddenly began to pour out from under her until a pool formed and hid the rest of the number she was laying over. "Tell me what I need to do."

"The same that I did," said The Skeleton Man. "Sacrifice yourself to keep the truth hidden. Alma can't handle what she saw. No one could. She's fragile. She'll break if she remembers. You have to let her go."

"Okay, fine," said Paul. "I'll do whatever I have to."

He looked over at Stephen and Rachel's corpses, and saw that their wounds had disappeared. They looked like they were asleep, but then blood began to pool beneath them as well before the fog covered them, shielding Paul's friends from his view.

"Pay attention to what I say," said The Skeleton Man.

Paul's chest ached, and he glanced back down at the wound on his chest. The Skeleton Man's hand was pressed over his gun shots, and blood seeped out between his skeletal fingers.

"I just want to save Alma," said Paul. "I'll do whatever I have to for her."

"Will you?" asked Ben. "Do you love her as much as I did? Would you do anything to protect her?"

"I'll die for her, if that's what you're asking."

Ben laughed. "You're already dead, Paul. I'm asking for more than that."

274

"Then get to the point," said Paul as his patience waned. "What do I have to do?"

"You have to let her forget you." There was malice in Ben's voice when he explained the proposition. "Stay here with me, and let Alma go. She'll forget you ever lived, and that she ever loved you. She'll never know of your sacrifice, and will never lament your loss. That's the deal I was given, and I can offer you the same. Alma will never remember you, but she'll be safe. If you really love her, if you really want to protect her, then you'll do the same thing that I did."

"There's got to be another way," said Paul.

"There is," said Ben. "You're stuck here now, and if you want you can try and find a way out of Widowsfield. No one ever has, but you're welcome to try. If you refuse my offer, then you'll wake up in Widowsfield, moments before the event occurred that opened the doorway. Alma will be with you, but she'll remember what happened here when she was a child. All of her memories will come flooding back, just like they did of me the last time she was here. She'll remember what happened in that bedroom when her knife plunged into the whore's stomach. I don't think anyone could be expected to handle that realization, but it gets worse."

"What?" asked Paul. The demon seemed to be enjoying this more than a loving brother should. The Skeleton Man was a twisted creature, and Paul assumed there were more spirits than just Ben's that made up this demon.

"She used the number to remember, just before she was shot dead in the kitchen. She knows what happened, and she'll be forced to remember over and over again. Widowsfield lives perpetually within only a few minutes of time. The short window of time that the door was open now plays itself over and over again, and the tortured souls in the town are forced to live that moment for eternity. Now Alma and your friends will join us, and every time the moment starts again, they'll be flooded by the agonizing memory of what happened here."

The Skeleton Man materialized in the mist. He was tall, and his face was a mask of stripped flesh that covered a skull. He had eyeballs that were placed within a skull's sockets and his teeth chattered as he spoke, as if his voice wasn't emitted from his mouth, but telepathically. There was black wire sewed through the strips of skin on his face, and they bored through his jaw to tie his face together. It appeared as if the creature had tried to use the wire to stop his chattering teeth, but it hadn't worked.

"Make your choice," said The Skeleton Man as he held out his hand to Paul. "Join me, and let them forget you. Or torture her for eternity with the memory of what happened here."

Paul was given insight into what The Skeleton Man knew. There was too much to understand in such a short moment, but Paul knew that the boy had allowed his final few minutes to dictate what hell he wrought on the residents of Widowsfield that were trapped in the mist with him. Ben was a malevolent force whose pain and suffering in his last moments of life defined the existence of every soul left trapped in Widowsfield. He was their Devil, a mere child who learned of hatred and pain at the very moment that a doorway was unlocked.

Paul had no way of knowing if what the demon said was true, or if this was all a lie. But as he looked down at Alma, he had no other choice than to try and protect her. He would do anything for her, even if it meant saying goodbye to her forever.

A tear fell down his cheek as he focused on Alma's face. The Skeleton Man's teeth chattered incessantly beside his ear.

"Why are you doing this?" asked Paul.

"I'm the only one that can protect her, Paul," said The Skeleton Man. "She has to see that if we're going to get out alive."

"Why is this happening?"

"Evil has a home," said The Skeleton Man. "Its name is Widowsfield. Now make your choice."

* * *

Jacker was driving the van as they left Widowsfield.

Stephen was in the passenger seat and was toying with his camera. Rachel, Alma, and Aubrey were in the back, crunched together on the middle seat. The entire rear seat of the van was loaded with Stephen's equipment, which required the girls to all sit together, uncomfortably bunched up against one another.

"I can't wait to get home," said Rachel. "I'm going to sleep for, like, twelve hours straight."

Alma had her hands in her coat pocket and was rubbing her thumb against a small piece of soft fabric on her keychain. The sensation soothed her.

"I know the feeling," said Aubrey. "I am zonked."

Alma stared out the front window as they drove away. It was foggy out, and it looked like it was going to rain.

"Whoa," said Jacker as he pulled the van over to the side of the road. A car had pulled up behind them and then swerved into the other lane to pass them before jerking back over to their side of the two lane road. It sped ahead of them and disappeared into the fog. "What an asshole. I wonder where he was off to in such a hurry."

Alma stopped rubbing the fabric on her keys and pulled them out. She stared at the miniature teddy bear.

"I don't know," said Stephen. "And I don't care. I just want to go home."

"Same here," said Rachel. "I don't ever want to go back to that place."

"Widowsfield," said Alma as she stared at the teddy bear. She loved the bauble, and knew that it could soothe her when she was frightened. It was a source of happiness for her.

"Don't even say the name," said Aubrey. "I don't ever want to remember that place."

"Jacker," said Alma.

"What is it, beautiful?" asked Jacker as he started to pull the van back onto the road.

"Wait," said Alma.

Jacker and Stephen turned to look at her.

She stayed silent for a moment as she continued to stare at the teddy bear keychain. She couldn't remember where she got it.

"Guys," said Alma. "It's happening again."

"What is?" asked Aubrey

"Widowsfield. 314. It's the same as before. Do you remember going into town?" she asked. "We came all the way here, but I don't remember anything about the town. Do you?"

They all looked at each other, and finally Rachel spoke up. "I'm officially creeped out you guys. Alma's right. I can't remember anything."

"Neither can I," said Stephen. "Did we get footage for the show?"

Jacker pulled a purple coin out of his pocket and stared at it as the others spoke.

"We're going through the same thing that I did," said Alma. "Somehow or another we got tricked. The town turned us around. It stole something from us."

"Jacker," said Stephen. "Turn the van around. We're going back."

"What about the fence?" asked Aubrey.

Jacker turned the wheel and hit the gas. Gravel spit up behind them as they headed back to town. "Fuck the fence," he said as he sped up. "If there're no guards then I'll plow right through it."

"There's no fence," said Stephen. "Look, there's a sign right there."

There was a large, bright billboard on the side of the road that exclaimed, "Welcome to Widowsfield."

278

Jacker drove the van into town and turned left on Main Street. They pulled up to a stop light and looked around. The town wasn't abandoned like they'd been told it was. There were people on the sidewalk, cars on the road, and even a UPS truck parked in front of the Anderson Used Book Store.

"This isn't right," said Aubrey. "I've been here a ton of times. All of these buildings were boarded up before. I'm serious. None of this should be here." She watched a man with long hair walking on the sidewalk. He had a walkman clipped to his belt and was in the process of changing CDs.

"Look at the clock on the bank over there," said Jacker as he pointed at the credit union that shared a parking lot with the Widowsfield Emergency Services building.

3:13

"Guys," said Stephen. He looked ashen as he stared at the UPS truck outside of the book store. "This is Widowsfield, in 1996."

Alma saw the bank's clock change time.

3:14

AFTERWORD

Michael Harper followed the fence that surrounded Widowsfield until he found a sewer drain on the south side. He cursed under his breath as he got on his hands and knees to crawl through the slime. The pipe stank of mold and he held his breath as he made his way through. Once on the other side he climbed up a slight incline and found himself in a field with the middle school within sight.

He checked his pistol to make sure there was a bullet in the chamber. If his daughter and the reporter thought they were going to reveal what happened in Widowsfield, they'd have to go through him to do it.

It was one day until March 14th, and Michael knew just where his daughter would be staying. "Time to join your brother, Alma."

He would finish what he should've done sixteen years ago. Alma Harper had to die.

TO BE CONTINUED...

AUTHOR'S NOTE

And now you've officially been cursed! If you're anything like me, you'll start to see the number 314 everywhere.

The curse of 314 was something that started with one of my friends in high school. We worked at a fast food restaurant, and after tax several of the meals we served cost $3.14. All day long my friend would have to say to people, "That'll be $3.14." We all hated our job, and this monotonous repetition of a price started to haunt us. Before we knew it, the number 314 started to show up everywhere in our lives. It appears with such frequency that it has become a 20 year long joke between all of us.

That's the origin of the number, and how it became a theme for this book. However, there's a lot more to it than that. In this book, the characters just barely made a dent in the mystery that surrounds Widowsfield and what it was that caused the town to descend into such chaos. This book was focused on Ben and Alma, and what happened to them at the cabin at the exact moment that the 314 curse began. Ben was forced to stay, while Alma was saved. Ben's spirit was haunted by what he'd experienced, and the creatures in the mist used him to craft all of the horrors that were unleashed upon the populace time and time again afterward.

In the next book, the role of Cada E.I.B. will be revealed. Were they the ones that "opened the door" and caused the event to take place? Why did they purchase the land and then try to rebuild Widowsfield with mannequins? Those questions will be answered in the next book.

In each of my books I try to challenge myself to do something different. In 314, I played with the book's structure in an attempt to mimic the idea of the town being stuck in a constant recurring nightmare. There's a lot of talk of circles, or coils, in this book. The structure of the book itself is a sort of recurring spiral. It is split into three parts. In the first part, each chapter begins in 1996, and then switches to 2012. In part two, all of the chapters take place in 2012. In part three, each chapter begins in 2012, and then switches to 1996, opposite of what it was in the first part. I wanted to play with this idea of switching time frames in an attempt to make the reader feel like they were going in circles, as well as to push the idea that all of these events were happening simultaneously. I thought it was an interesting way to make the story-telling mirror the story itself.

I hope you enjoyed this book, and I also hope you've had a chance to read my other series, Deadlocked (the first one's free!) I love to discuss my books with readers and welcome you to join in the conversation. You can find me at arwisebooks.com, as well as on the AR Wise Fan Page on Facebook. I would definitely suggest liking the fan page, because I give away quite a few things to people there. Currently I am offering free signed covers of my books! Go 'Like' the page so you can find out how to get one! I can also be reached by email at aaron@arwisebooks.com.

Finally, if you enjoyed 314, please consider leaving a review on whichever site you downloaded it from. Customer reviews are incredibly important to independent writers like myself.

Chapter 1 - Dead Again

Imagine waking up in the middle of a maze. The walls are too high to climb and the floor is too tough to dig through. You have no idea how you got there, or which way is out. No one answers when you scream, and you're burdened by a sense of impending loss. You don't know what it is that you're afraid of losing, but the feeling is inescapable.

Of course, the thing you're losing is your sanity, which becomes more evident as you claw at the walls. Madness lingers in these long halls, and it's only a matter of time before they close in on you.

Now, do your best to imagine that the walls are made of memories. It's a maddening thing to consider, but that's the point. You're probably visualizing the walls as television screens, displaying your past, but that's wrong. There are no walls. Instead, you're walking consciously through a moment in time that has already passed, but is slightly different than it should be. You try to walk in the same direction that you did when the moment truly occurred, a slave to a recording, but it's impossible to recreate every step. These little deviations, whether it be turning left instead of right, or saying yes instead of no, are all that's needed to start you in the wrong direction. Then, before you know it, you become lost in your own mind.

The walls of your maze are made of your own past, but they're tricking you. As your sanity fades, so too does your realization that the walls are false. These aren't your memories, but that's not the sort of thing a rational mind could ever hope to understand. Memories belong to us. They're the only things we ever uniquely own. Thoughts and memories are what sanity clings to.

To get out, you have to be just a bit mad; you have to accept the maze. The only way to find the exit is to understand the walls, but once you do, you've already lost.

The Watcher in the Walls has won.

283

Lost in Widowsfield

Alma Harper couldn't speak.

She was in Jacker's van, seated between Aubrey and Rachel, terrified as the others stared in shock out the windows. It was a sunny, spring day in Widowsfield, and the people of the town were going about their business as if nothing was wrong. A UPS truck was parked outside of the corner book shop, and the driver was loading boxes onto a dolly at the rear. There was a long haired man switching discs on his Walkman as he passed the truck, and smiled at the driver as he went. Beside that building was a restaurant, called the Salt and Pepper Diner, and Alma could see a chubby man sitting in one of the booths beside the window with a young boy across from him. The child was staring at their van as they passed.

"What's going on?" asked Rachel.

"We're in 1996," said Stephen as he nervously pivoted in his seat. He looked back at them, and then out his window. "Look at the truck."

"What truck?" asked Rachel.

"The UPS one," said Stephen. "Remember how I told you a UPS driver disappeared at the same time as everyone else? And look at that car parked over there." He pointed at a green Ford truck parked on the side of the street, in front of the UPS truck. "See the license plate tag?"

In the center of the plate, between the numbers, was a green tag that had the numbers 96 on it. Jacker put the van in park, even though the light had turned green. "Holy shit," he said as he ran his hands through his hair. "Holy shit, holy shit…"

"This can't be," said Aubrey. She had her hands on the back of Jacker's headrest and stood, though she had to hunch over as she did. "You guys are pulling some sort of prank on me. Right?"

The car behind them honked, frustrated that the van was still stopped at the light. Jacker put the van back in drive and yelled, "This is no prank!" He turned into the parking lot of the credit union that was beside the Widowsfield Emergency Services Center. The bank's sign displayed the time, 3:14, and the green light flooded the van as they passed it.

"This place has been deserted for years," said Aubrey, her tone nearing panic. "This is insane."

"Hold up," said Jacker as he parked at the entrance of the Emergency Services building. He rolled down the window and leaned out to speak with a woman standing near the glass door of the center. "Excuse me, ma'am."

"Yes?" asked the woman after she took the last drag of her cigarette.

"This is a weird question," said Jacker. "But could you tell me what year it is?"

"Seriously?" asked the woman with a scowl. She dropped her cigarette to the pavement and stamped it out. Alma noticed that there was an ashtray several feet from the woman, apparently pushed away from the entrance to keep people from smoking near the door.

"I know it's a weird question," said Jacker.

"It sure is, pal." The woman stayed near the door, annoyed, puzzled, and slightly fretful of the big man in the van who was asking such an odd question.

Alma heard dogs barking and the noise caused her heart to beat faster. The sound was familiar, distinctive, yet she couldn't fathom why she felt that way.

"Please?" asked Jacker. "Just tell me what year it is."

"Or who the president is," shouted Stephen from the passenger seat.

"Get a life, weirdos," said the woman as she opened the door to the building to go back inside.

"Smooth," said Rachel. "Maybe she'll call the cops on us and we can ask them what year it is. I'm sure they'll be willing to listen to our story of how we time travelled here.

285

Maybe they'll ask about the flux capacitor you installed in the van."

"Just park in one of the spots," said Aubrey. "Let's get out and see if we can find a newspaper or something."

Jacker pulled the van into a parking spot as Stephen took out his cell phone. "Nothing," said Stephen as he showed the others his phone. "There's nothing on it. The damn thing won't work."

"Is it dead?" asked Rachel as she got her own phone.

"Yeah," said Stephen. "It won't turn on."

"Mine won't either," said Rachel. "What about the rest of you? Does anyone's phone work?"

Alma was going to look for her phone when a thunderous noise shook the van. Rachel and Aubrey screamed as Jacker cursed, but Alma covered her ears. While everyone else was shocked by the sound, she somehow knew it was coming. It would precede the fog.

"What was that?" asked Stephen.

A shadow blocked out the sun for a moment, as if a plane had flown low overhead. Then the dogs started barking again, this time closer.

"He's here," said Alma. "We have to run."

"Who's here?" asked Rachel.

"The one that controls the fog," said Alma, near tears.

"What fog?" asked Stephen.

"This fog?" asked Jacker as he pointed out the window.

Thick mist was rolling down the street, sweeping across the pavement as if made of liquid. Every shape caught within it seemed to disappear nearly completely, as if the fog was erasing everything in its path. Green electricity snapped within the cloud, carried across the features of the shapes that the fog had swallowed. Then they saw the silhouettes of creatures moving within the mist, short but fast, with canine heads. The top of the fog was draped with what looked like strands of black wire that twisted in and out of each other.

"Get us the fuck out of here!" Aubrey grabbed Jacker's shoulders and shook the big man.

286

"Yeah, yeah, okay," said Jacker as he put the van in reverse.

"No," said Alma. "We have to run! Just get out and run." She climbed over Rachel's lap and grasped the handle of the sliding door.

"What are you doing?" asked Rachel, unsure if she should restrain Alma or let her open the door.

"We had to run!" Alma was past desperation as she yanked at the handle.

"Had to?" asked Rachel.

"He's coming!" Alma was frantic as she pulled up the lock on the door so that she could open it. Jacker had already put the van in reverse and was screaming back at Alma to shut the door. His window was open and she could see the fog advancing when she looked back at him. It was sliding over the cars in the lot, the green electricity furiously zapping along the metal as it came closer to them.

"Close the door," said Jacker.

Alma paused and looked at him, dread and sorrow filling her as she saw the fog flow up to the side of the van. "Goodbye, Jacker," she said as the fog seeped in.

It came through his open window, tendrils creeping in like sentient roots digging for sustenance. They swarmed over him, wrapping coils around his neck and arms. He tried to scream, but the fog constricted until his voice was choked away from him. He struggled, but the force that collected him was too strong. It swept over his skin as the dogs barked outside, almost seeming to laugh at his pain.

Stephen, Rachel, and Aubrey screamed in terror as they watched the fog consume Jacker, but Alma looked away. She knew what it looked like to see a man's skin peeled off. Somehow, this all felt too familiar.

The mutated dogs swarmed the van, their ravaged hands scraping along the side. What had once been children had become a twisted mix of human and beast, nude and bearing large gashes across their pale skin. The children's hands had become shattered mounds of flesh and bone, as if they had been thrust into a grinder and smashed until useless. Their heads were not human, but canine, hairless and with wholly black eyes. Their teeth were too large for their mouths, sometimes tearing through the flesh of their own lips, seeming to grow larger as the creatures wailed.

Alma saw the fog seep out from under the van and had to leap a foot away to avoid it. Then she turned and yelled at the others to get out. The town had erupted into chaos as the fog descended, bringing the mutated children with it. One of the creatures appeared at the rear of their vehicle, its eyes locked on Alma, and it started to howl. Others had crawled over the hood, scrambling to climb using their shattered hands, hooking bits of twisted bone into the crevasses of the hood to pull themselves up. They all stared at Alma, intent as they swarmed, and each of them howled after a moment of watching her.

"Jacker!" Aubrey was screaming their dead friend's name.

Alma didn't need to look to know what was happening. The fog had dragged Jacker's head out of the window and the hideous monstrosities that swarmed the van were tearing his face apart as he squirmed in his seat. They didn't eat him, but clawed at his skin with their shattered hands while biting at his eyes. He couldn't scream, because the fog was choking him, but he could gyrate in his seat, fully conscious through the entire ordeal. That would happen until the fog decided to end his life. It would start by hooking into his skin, and then it would peel him apart, stripping his flesh away like the top layer of an onion.

"Get out!" Alma backed away, and then felt someone grab her shoulders. She turned and saw the woman that had been smoking outside moments earlier.

"Get inside!" The woman pulled Alma toward the door of the building as the fog swept over the van.

"My friends!" Alma cried out as the woman grasped her.

Rachel took Aubrey's hand and yanked the girl out of the van to follow Alma. The fog reached out from under the

288

vehicle in an attempt to catch them, but they were able to avoid it and make it to the door.

"Stephen!" Rachel yelled out to her husband who was still in the van trying to help Jacker. "Come on!"

His side of the van was already in the mist, and he had to crawl over the center console into the back seat. His face was splattered with blood, and he was terrified as he stumbled to get out the same door that the girls had exited. His foot fell into the fog below, and it swirled up his leg. "It's got me!"

"Stephen!" Rachel tried to run out to help, but Aubrey held her back.

The howling pack of demonic children cried out with nearly human voices. Their guttural noises sounded like laughter as they crept toward Stephen, but their attention was still on Alma.

"Leave him alone!" Rachel reached out to her husband as Alma and Aubrey restrained her.

Stephen struggled to free himself from the fog, but it inched up his body, toying with him as it constricted tighter each second. "Go, Rachel! Just go!"

"No." She was trembling and crying as she yelled out to him.

Alma was desperate to get into the building when she heard the chattering start. The Skeleton Man drew near, and he had seen her. The game was coming to an end now, and he would win if she didn't flee.

His chattering teeth echoed in her mind as he approached the building, hidden in the fog that surrounded them. It seemed as if the growing mist was avoiding the Emergency Services Center, forming a circle around it within which The Skeleton Man hid. His clicking teeth drummed in Alma's head, a piece of the nightmare that only she could experience.

"My children want to eat your friend," said The Skeleton Man, his voice reverberating in her mind like a thousand echoes.

289

"Who are you?" asked Alma.

"Who is who?" asked the woman at the door.

Alma let go of Rachel and clasped her hands over her ears to drown out the sounds that threatened to quiet the voice in her head. The chattering teeth got louder and she saw the man in the fog approaching from behind the van. His long arm wrapped around the corner of the van and he tapped on the side as the mist hid his features. He was tall and lanky, a corpse draped in clothes, and when the mist cleared enough to reveal any detail he shied away, drawing back as if unwilling to be seen.

"Who are you?" Alma screamed at the shade.

The air above them swirled, as if the eye of a storm had descended upon the building, trapping everything around it in a maelstrom of fog and lightning. Time seemed to flow differently for the others, and Alma was trapped in a world that The Skeleton Man controlled. She felt linked to him, blessed by his attention, and damned by it all at once. He laughed at her, and she tried to move forward but discovered that her body was caught in the same slowed movements as the world around her. Only The Skeleton Man seemed unfazed, and he tapped his fingers on the side of the van with the same cadence as he had when time flowed normally for all of them. His chattering teeth never slowed, and his laughter wavered in her mind as if affected by the beat of her own heart; swooshing in and out like waves on a beach.

"I will guide you, Alma Harper," said the demonic voice. "I have waited so long to have you with me. Together, you and I will help Ben get free."

Alma tried to speak, but felt the muscles in her throat react slowly to her wishes. What she had planned to say was lost by her inability to speak, so she stared at The Skeleton Man and tried to communicate with her thoughts instead.

'Leave my friends alone.'

The demon didn't respond. He just continued to linger in the fog, tapping on the side of the van as his minions took slow steps toward Stephen. Alma could see the muscles of the children tense as their feet propelled them with each step, but they didn't move any faster than the swirling mist, or Rachel's grasping hands. All of them were caught in the flow of time, a trap that The Skeleton Man was free of.

"You have to help me save Ben," said The Skeleton Man. "Ignore the liars, and save your brother."

A woman's shrill cry drowned out the demon's voice. It was a sound unfettered by the restraint of the slowed flow of time, resounding at the same bone-chilling depth that The Skeleton Man's chattering teeth did. He tensed, his fingers settling on the side of the van, and Alma saw that he was frightened.

"She's found us," said The Skeleton Man. "I have to leave." He looked directly at her and Alma saw his skeletal face revealed as a flash of green electricity skipped across his arm. "Alma, run!" Then he retreated and the mist seemed to swallow him as time returned to normal.

"Stephen!" Rachel screamed to her husband as the demonic children overtook him. They leapt through the mist and it moved to accommodate them, happy to hold onto their victim until the creatures got to him.

"Run!" said Stephen as the demons started to bite into him. The dog-like creatures clamped their jaws on his exposed flesh and then shook their heads back and forth, tearing the skin like a starved hound. Blood cascaded down his body, but he couldn't fight them off as the tendrils of fog held him still.

"Christ!" said the woman that had been smoking at the front door. "What's going on?"

"Nancy," said another woman from inside the building. "Get in here!"

Aubrey tried to hold Rachel, but the strawberry blonde reporter was too devoted to her husband. She writhed free and ran into the mass of undulating flesh that had swarmed over Stephen. She gripped one of the children by the neck and threw it aside, but then they turned on her.

The mist engulfed her, as if pulling her in for an embrace, and dragged her closer to Stephen. She slapped into her husband's wet body, the blood splashing away from her as she did, and then her cries were silenced as the demons tore her to pieces.

"Rachel!" Alma was horrified to see her friends die, but knew there was nothing that could be done to save them. Only fear of pain convinced her to even fight for her own life. She was cursed with a sense of inevitability to this entire nightmare, as if she already knew they were doomed.

"Someone call 9-1-1," said Aubrey as she grabbed Alma and pulled her into the building.

"We are 9-1-1," said the woman that had been smoking outside when they arrived.

"Then fucking do something!" Aubrey pulled the door shut once they were all in.

There was a large, older woman in the building. Her blue eyes were wide as she stared out the window. She didn't look away as she screamed at another person in the building with them. "Darryl, did you get anyone?"

"I can't get through," said a man's voice from somewhere within the maze of fabric dividers that housed each desk of the call center. "The station's lines are all busy."

"That's just fucking great," said Aubrey. "What are you supposed to do when even the 9-1-1 operators can't get through to the police?"

"It's okay, darling," said the older woman, although her quaking tone revealed the falseness of her calm. "We're linked to their system. They know we need them. They know we need help. I'm sure they'll be here any minute."

"No they won't," said Aubrey. "Because this is happening all over. Because this is 1996, isn't it? Isn't it?"

"Yes!" The smoker screamed out at Aubrey, her nerves frayed. "Why do you people keep asking what year it is?"

"Because everyone in this fucking cursed town dies today." Aubrey's face turned red as she screamed. "Every single one of you!"

292

"What are you talking about?" asked the older woman.

Alma saw a man rise up from between the fabric dividers in the call center. He had a headset on and his mouth was agape. He was overweight, with no discernible chin if not for the way he trimmed his beard, and his neck was jiggling as if he were trying to speak. "Help," he finally managed to say. Then he seemed to shrink a foot and jerked forward. His face shook as if he was in pain, and then he lifted his hands to reveal that they were covered in blood. He said again, "Help," but his voice was weaker than before.

"Darryl?" asked the older woman as she started to head toward the man's desk.

"Claire, don't," said her coworker.

Claire reached the aisle where Darryl's desk was and then let out a high pitched cry as she stared at him. The rest of them rushed to see what had frightened her and were stopped in their tracks. The middle-aged man had sunk partially into his own desk, his belly fused to the table and keyboard, like some sort of grotesque magic trick.

"Help," he said again as he dug his fingers into his stomach in an attempt to free himself. He tugged at his skin, but it ripped away from the top of the desk and blood seeped out. It looked as if he had grown into the inanimate object and only his flesh could move, but every time it did he was ripping himself to apart.

That's when they saw a woman's arm reach out from the desk and grasp Darryl's shirt. She clawed at him, like a drowning victim reaching out to be saved, and with every tug she pulled his body further into the desk. He choked as she pulled at him, and then vomited blood. The gore spewed from his mouth, at first just liquid, but then fleshy strips began to fly out. His face smashed into the top of his computer monitor as if he was suffering a seizure, and more of the strands of flesh slipped away from between his open lips. He gripped the sides of his cubicle and tried to pull himself up as his head continued to shake. They heard his bones breaking, but he continued to pull as his body separated.

The woman's hands tugged at him until her face was revealed within the desk itself. Her eyes bulged and were only white, with no pupil or iris in either of them. Her skin was badly burned, and her cheekbone was revealed as if her skin had melted away. The specter's teeth were mostly gone, and the ones left were loose and bleeding as her mouth gaped open. It looked as if someone had been trying to pry her teeth out.

Aubrey gasped and covered her mouth.

The specter's formerly milky eyes rotated, revealing two irises that had been rolled back in her head. She focused on Alma, and then jerked on Darryl's body to pull herself further out of the furniture.

Flesh dripped from her face as if made of a slimy, crimson liquid. Her mouth gaped, and then snapped shut on her bulbous, purple tongue. The creature screamed, "Alma Harper!"

"Holy fuck!" Aubrey fell back against the wall in fright.

"Look what you did!" The specter dragged herself out of the table as if emerging from a secret door. She pushed against Darryl's writhing body until she was able to fall to the floor. Her body splashed, covered with red and white ooze, and then she coughed up a mixture of foam and bile that hung in strands from her lips. "Look what you did!" Her words were accented by the wet flapping of her shredded, bleeding lips.

The creature was on her belly on the floor, ten feet from Alma. She clawed at the floor and dragged herself forward while screaming Alma's name. Every inch she moved tore away bits of her flesh that were left behind on the Berber carpet like a snail's trail.

"Let's go, Alma!" Aubrey and the other two women had already fled, but Aubrey returned to pull Alma away. "What the hell are you standing there for?"

"Look what you did!" The woman on the floor screamed out again.

Alma turned to look back at Aubrey, lost for words, and then looked back down at the creature on the floor. To her horror, the specter was gone. Her trail of slime and gore was still there, as was Darryl's writhing body, but the woman had vanished.

"Come on," said Aubrey. "There's a back entrance. We have to run!"

Alma nodded, the shock of what she'd seen still silencing her. The demon that had appeared and killed Darryl had known who Alma was, and for some reason Alma knew that she would. Alma was scared of the woman, but not because of what she'd just seen, but rather that she felt as if she'd been frightened of her for years. It was like a recurring nightmare had finally come true.

Aubrey led Alma to the back door that the other two employees had escaped through. The fog lurched around the corner of the building, and snuck over the roof, but it didn't descend over them. Aubrey staggered as she saw the fold of mist lurking over the exit. She was aware of how it had captured Stephen minutes earlier.

"Should we just run?" asked Aubrey as she stared at the lingering mist.

"I don't…" Alma was interrupted by the screaming specter that had killed Darryl.

"Alma! Look what you've done!" The ghost materialized in the wall behind them, her face at eye level, pushing through the white paint and causing blood to slide down across the surface. One of her teeth fell to the floor as she oozed through the wall. Her eyes were rolled back in her head, and her fingers protruded from the wall, clawing as if she was desperate to pull herself free.

Aubrey screamed and took Alma's hand as they ran out of the building. There was a small patio out of the back door and a sidewalk that led around the building to the parking lot where Jacker, Stephen, and Rachel had died. To the side of the walkway, away from the building, was a ditch that led up to a black wire fence, past which was another, similar office building. Aubrey pulled Alma along as she tried to escape.

"Come on, Alma!" Aubrey jerked at Alma's arm to try and snap the girl out of her docility.

"We're already dead," said Alma.

"We will be if you don't move your ass." Aubrey tried to go left, toward the street, but Alma held her back. "Come on!"

"Don't go that way," said Alma and she pointed toward the rear of the building. "We need to try and go that way."

"Why?" asked Aubrey.

Alma couldn't explain herself, and just said, "Because we die that way." She pointed at the street as if waiting to be proved right.

"What are you talking about?" asked Aubrey. "Okay, fuck it. I don't care. Let's just get out of here."

Aubrey and Alma ran along the side of the building as the fog stayed above them, looming over the lip of the roof as if ready to descend, but kept at bay. Alma glanced back and saw that the white fog was sliding off the roof beside the exit, willing to cover their tracks as Aubrey guided them forward. Then the electricity popped within the cloud and coincided with an explosion somewhere on the street, now hidden by the mist.

Alma didn't need to see the accident to know what happened. A truck had plowed into the cars parked on the side of the road, and that's where Aubrey died once, pinned between the vehicles. Alma could see her pained expression as if a poignant memory had been revealed. She was reminded of how thoughts of her brother, Ben, had returned to her in the kitchen of the cabin when her mother had scrawled the symbol for pi on the floor.

Alma could hear the scrambling, bony hands of the children as they crawled across the roof of the Emergency Services building. The fog hid them as they scurried toward

Aubrey, but they were revealed as menacing shadows when the green electricity sparked.

"Come on," said Aubrey as she saw that Alma had slowed down. The fog rushed around the building and toward the young girl. The Skeleton Man's hand came around the corner just as Alma was about to scream in warning. His fingers tapped, one by one, on the brick before he appeared. He spied on them like a devious child sneaking into his parent's bedroom at night, his chattering teeth ever present in Alma's head.

"How should we bleed her?" asked The Skeleton Man. His demonic horde scurried across the roof and Alma heard their steps slow down. The fog swirled at a lethargic pace, and Aubrey's movements became caught in the mire of The Skeleton Man's hold on time. The blonde bartender tried to scream, and perhaps in a different sliver of reality she could be heard, but Alma's mind was trapped by the will of the demon that lingered in the fog.

"Should we be quick about it?" asked The Skeleton Man.

He stepped away from the wall, revealing his skull face, the bones held together by the fog itself as the green cloud slipped in and out of his features. A single eyeball sat within his left socket, lazily rolling in the bottom until the fog carried it up to focus on Alma. His jaw was wrapped in what appeared to be a strip of human flesh, stitched with wire that tied it to his cheekbone. His teeth chattered, and when he spoke his jaw didn't move to accommodate the words, as if this demon wasn't actually the one that Alma was hearing.

Alma wanted to scream, but her every movement was caught in the web of time; only her thoughts were free of the prison.

"Does she have pretty eyes? Do you like them?" asked The Skeleton Man. He reached up to his own, lonely, wobbling eye and plucked it out. He let it drop into the mist, and it hung there as if suspended in thick liquid, only slowly descending to the pavement.

"Alma, should we steal her eyes?" The Skeleton Man moved to stand behind Aubrey. "They're such pretty eyes, don't you think?"

The Skeleton Man grasped one of the hounds at his side. He took the child by the snout and then lifted the creature up as the mist swirled around it. He held the lower half of the monster's jaw and ripped it apart. The fog pushed into the creature's mouth and seemed to help mutilate the hound, tearing it apart until The Skeleton Man was left holding just the upper jaw, the teeth now dripping with fresh blood. The Skeleton Man plucked out one of the canines and tossed it into the mist where it floated away like the eyeball had moments earlier. He examined the mangled snout, with only one long canine still protruding from it like a jagged barb.

Alma was forced to watch as The Skeleton Man used the fleshy tool on Aubrey. He wrapped his arm around her neck and then stuck the only remaining canine of the upper jaw against her left tear duct. Then he pressed the tooth in, causing Aubrey's eye to bulge from its socket. He scooped the eyeball out, and Aubrey's slow expression of pain and horror was torture to witness. Her eye protruded from her head as The Skeleton Man wormed the tip of the jaw into the socket.

"There we go," said the demon as Aubrey's eye flopped down into the curvature of the hound's severed upper palate. It was still connected by the white optic nerve like a ball on a string. The Skeleton Man reached up and gripped the eyeball before jerking it out of Aubrey's skull. When the white strand was pulled forth, a blob of pink matter came with it before snapping free.

"I love her eyes," said The Skeleton Man as he put the eyeball into his own socket. It twirled as the fog positioned it, floating in the empty socket as the optic nerve spun behind it. "Don't you?" he asked as he looked at Alma. "Let's get the other one."

"Look what you've done!" The tortured spirit screamed as her face sprung from the side of the building. She was unfettered by the slow progression of time, just like The Skeleton Man, and reached out in a desperate attempt to grasp the demon in the mist.

The fog receded, seemingly frightened by the woman in the wall, and The Skeleton Man fell apart as it went. The eyeball that he'd stolen from Aubrey fell to the pavement along with the jawbone that he'd ripped away from the hound. The Skeleton Man crumpled as the woman in the wall grasped at his form. She tore at his cloak and pulled it to her, revealing nothing but fog and bones within.

Aubrey cried out in pain and covered her eye as her movements returned to normal. The woman in the wall was attracted to Aubrey's screams and grasped at her once The Skeleton Man had disappeared. She gripped Aubrey's leg and dragged the girl down, causing her legs to sink into the cement walkway.

Aubrey struggled, but the woman continued to drag her down, just as she had done to Darryl at his desk. The spirit disappeared beneath the ground, and only her arms sprouted forth, fingers digging into Aubrey as the young woman cried out. Alma moved forward, intent on helping, but the spirit pulled Aubrey down until the bartender was waist deep in the cement, as if she'd succumbed to quicksand in the middle of the town.

"Take my hand," said Alma as she reached out for Aubrey.

"No!" The spirit lunged from the walkway, lashing out at Alma. "She's mine now. I'll use her to watch you."

Alma fell back as the spirit pulled Aubrey further down. The young bartender was lowered to her waist, trapped within the cement, and succumbed as the woman pulled her even further. Aubrey tried to speak, but blood came from her mouth instead of words, spilling out onto the walkway like vomit, and chunks of meat and flesh were mixed in the puddle. A strip of pink flesh hung from her lips, still attached to some part of her innards, and her mouth continued to open and close as if she was trying to tell Alma something.

The woman below pulled Aubrey even further down, sinking the girl to her chest as Alma backed away in terror.

"I'm so sorry," said Alma as she watched Aubrey's head bob. Gore flowed from the girl's mouth, adding to the pool of blood and flesh on the sidewalk. Then the spirit's hand rose to grasp Aubrey's face, and her finger sunk into the bartender's empty eye socket before tugging her below. The pool of blood rippled where Aubrey had been.

"Oh God," said Alma as she tried to stand up. She knew she should run, but she was nearly too weak to move. The pool of blood seemed to slither across the pavement, running in thin streams towards her like a squid's tendrils.

"Ma'am," said a young boy's voice.

Alma screamed out in terror and clasped her hand over her heart as she looked back toward Main Street where a group of children had gathered. There were at least twenty of them, wearing thin coats and backpacks over their shoulders. She'd never seen them before, yet they were still familiar. They were all boys, some older and taller than others, but all of them were elementary age.

"What are you?" Alma screamed her question. She was still seated, and crawled backward, away from the mob of school children. Her hand slapped into the pool of Aubrey's blood, which initiated another cry of horror from her. "What do you want with me?"

"We're alone here now, but we don't have much time," said the boy at the front of the group. He was chubby, with blue eyes and a buzzcut. There were red speckles on his cheeks, and he held a knife in his right hand that was dripping blood.

"Don't have time for what?" Alma was frantic as she cowered from the children.

An alarm roared over the town, and the children were startled by it. It sounded like a tornado warning, but with a lower tone and far more ominous. Each time the alarm sounded, it seemed to grow louder until it was shaking the ground, causing Aubrey's blood to splash.

"You have to go where the witch was." The boy tried to scream over the alarm.

"What?" asked Alma, unsure that she heard him correctly.

"Go where the witch was! Where the girls are headed."

"Who's the witch?" asked Alma, but the boy couldn't hear her anymore. The alarm was so loud now that it hurt their ears. The children winced and covered the sides of their heads. Alma did the same, but kept yelling out her question until the pain from the alarm was impossible to overcome. She closed her eyes and fell to the ground where Aubrey's blood wet her cheek.

Then it was over, and Alma felt her stomach lurch, just like it did when she descended the hill on her way into Widowsfield.

* * *

Jacker was driving the van as they left Widowsfield.

Stephen was in the passenger seat and was toying with his camera. Rachel, Alma, and Aubrey were in the back, crunched together on the middle seat. The entire rear seat of the van was loaded with Stephen's equipment, which required the girls to all sit together.

"I can't wait to get home," said Rachel. "I'm going to sleep for, like, twelve hours straight."

Alma had her hands in her coat pocket and was rubbing her thumb against a small piece of soft fabric on her keychain. The sensation soothed her.

"My eye won't stop watering," said Aubrey. "And I've got the worst stomach ache."

"Stop the van!" Alma's sudden outburst scared everyone in the vehicle. She leapt from her seat between Aubrey and Rachel and grabbed at Jacker's shoulder as she pleaded again, "Stop the van!"

Jacker hit the brakes and the van skid to a stop on the road leaving Widowsfield. It was foggy out, and there was a heaviness to the air that hinted of rain. Alma felt lost for breath as the others asked what was wrong.

A car honked from behind them, and then swerved to go around. The car's tires squealed as it passed on the wet road and Alma caught a glimpse of the driver.

It was her father.

314 Book 2 is now available on most ebook sites.